T0392283

SEEKING OUR HUMANITY

OTHER BOOKS
Presented by Claudia Helt

The Answer in Action
2020

The Answer Illuminated
2019

The Answer
2018

The Time When Time No Longer Matters
...Continues...
2018

The Time When Time No Longer Matters
2016

The Book of Ages
2016

Messages From Within:
A Time for Hope
2011

Messages From The Light:
Inspirational Guidance for
Light Workers, Healers, and Spiritual Seekers
2008

SEEKING OUR HUMANITY

CLAUDIA HELT

BALBOA.PRESS
A DIVISION OF HAY HOUSE

Balboa Press books may be ordered through booksellers or by contacting:

Balboa Press
A Division of Hay House
1663 Liberty Drive
Bloomington, IN 47403
www.balboapress.com
1 (877) 407-4847

Because of the dynamic nature of the Internet, any web addresses or links contained in this book may have changed since publication and may no longer be valid. The views expressed in this work are solely those of the author and do not necessarily reflect the views of the publisher, and the publisher hereby disclaims any responsibility for them.

The author of this book does not dispense medical advice or prescribe the use of any technique as a form of treatment for physical, emotional, or medical problems without the advice of a physician, either directly or indirectly. The intent of the author is only to offer information of a general nature to help you in your quest for emotional and spiritual well-being. In the event you use any of the information in this book for yourself, which is your constitutional right, the author and the publisher assume no responsibility for your actions.

Any people depicted in stock imagery provided by Getty Images are models, and such images are being used for illustrative purposes only. Certain stock imagery © Getty Images.

Print information available on the last page.

ISBN: 978-1-9822-4543-6 (sc)
ISBN: 978-1-9822-4544-3 (e)

Balboa Press rev. date: 03/31/2020

Acknowledgement

Dear Reader, we are so grateful for your participation in this reading experience. Often one is attracted to a book for reasons that are initially obscure, and yet, he or she knows without knowing exactly how it is known that the book that rests in his or her hands is indeed one that must be attended. *Seeking Our Humanity* is such a book. Please ponder the title of this small book and allow your heart to embrace the message that this title brings. These three words inspire numerous thoughts and may take the mind in many different directions; however, it is your heart that will be your guide as you read the story that awaits you.

Through this fictional tale, many truths will be revealed about the evolution of humankind. Hopefully, these truths will clarify the misunderstandings of the past while also shedding light upon the necessity for immediate changes in advancing forward. One of the purposes of this book is to inspire the peoples of Earth to open their hearts to new possibilities.

Seeking Our Humanity has been a project long in the making and it is fair to say that it remains a work in progress. Your participation, Dear Reader, is an essential element for the completion of this effort of good will. Hopefully, you and all the readers of this text will actively pursue the opportunity of seeking your own humanity. Just imagine what might happen if humankind decided to do so. Humankind's true potential is yet to be reached; however, in seeking and finding our humanity, a greater understanding of our unlimited potential is possible.

As said before Dear Reader, your participation is greatly appreciated. To understand the potential of one's own humanity, one must be fully and actively involved in its creation. If you choose to follow a path of compassionate, loving co-existence with all other Beings in existence, what might your life be like? Ponder this please. What might it be like to live peaceably with all others who surround you? And what if all others choose to do the same in their various locations around this beautiful planet? Such remarkable thoughts to contemplate...such wonderful possibilities to create! What might transpire if you and all the other readers of *Seeking Our Humanity* decided to pursue a way of being that was founded in the acceptance and mutual respect of all other Beings? By seeking our individual humanity and by allowing our hearts to be our guides, we may truly discover who we really are.

INTRODUCTION

Breathe deeply, Dear Reader! The breath you inhale now will lead you to a place of readiness, for the words that you are about to read are actually messages from your past that were specifically prepared for you, so that this vitally important information could be delivered to you at precisely the time when it was most needed. Although you may not be aware at this point in time of the need for such an oddly announced message, the truth must be delivered nonetheless. Dear Reader, the time is now!

In days ahead, Dear Reader, changes will be necessary. For too long, humankind has unfortunately advanced in a direction that is not in alignment with your destiny. You are indeed much more capable than your current circumstances indicate. No disrespect is meant; however, the truth must be spoken. You are so much more than you presently appear to be. For reasons yet to be discussed, you have forgotten who you really are, and because of this, your evolutionary process has moved in a direction that was not intended to be. Your capabilities are far more advanced than your course has taken you. Having said this, please accept the truth of your circumstances, and also, please hear with certainty the truth of your true potential.

You are more than you appear to be and the time has come for appropriate measures to be taken so that your full potential will be actualized. As said, changes will be necessary, and for some who are not inclined to do so, the consequences will be challenging. However, those who recognize and accept the opportunities provided by change will enjoy the abundance of life that has always been intended and available. The path taken thus far has not resulted in peaceful relationships among the peoples of this planet. Nor has it fostered good will within the human species or with the countless numbers of other species existing upon this remarkable Life Being called Earth. Change is inevitable, and it is inevitable for everyone.

The lack of peaceful co-existence upon the Earth has resulted in a most precarious situation. Her vibrancy is in great decline. Evidence of her ill health in indisputable and no more need be said of this. The truth is known and denying the truth or lying about it will not change the reality of the Earth's crisis. No one will be spared the aftermath of her continuing decline; therefore, the obvious will be repeated. Change is inevitable.

Dear Reader, speaking the truth is not pleasant when the truth is associated with great tragedy; and still, the truth must be stated so the reality of possibilities are understood. There is reason for hope! Humankind has the ability to right their wrongdoings. Although time is of the essence, there is still time for humankind to revitalize the Earth's life force, enabling her to return to good health. This is a truth that must be accepted; for, in accepting this truth, you also accept responsibility for taking immediate action on her behalf.

By deliberately and earnestly pursuing our humanity, humankind can initiate the necessary changes that will bring about peace on Earth. With the elimination of our hostile, destructive energy, the Earth's health will quickly improve. Our efforts on her behalf must continue as long as we inhabit her. We cannot return to old ways of disrespect and misbehavior towards her or towards one another. Our changes must be sincere and they must be permanent. Fortunately, we have the ability within us to do this. Dear Reader, please take the necessary steps to learn more about the changes that must be made on behalf of our civilization and the planet Earth.

You are invited now to take one step forward in changing the future of humankind. Please open your heart to the story that awaits you, and remember what was stated earlier. This book and the messages within it were prepared for you long ago. Keep this in your mind and your heart as you participate in this reading experience. The time is now!

1

*

A passage from
Beyond The Day of Tomorrow
A Seeker's Guide
(Chapter One)

"We begin this journey by offering a reminder. The reminder consists of the most significant gift of the Universal Source of Oneness. The gift is free will.

In all ways and for all times the gift of free will has permeated the depths of being. Without free will there would be no journey, for the desire to know all there is to know comes from the freedom to wonder about all there is to know. This wonderment sparks the curious nature within the existing being, propelling the being forward on the never-ending search; the ongoing adventure to seek, to find, to know all there is to know.

This search, the adventure to know all there is to know, evolves into the 'journey' that provides endless opportunities for exploration, all of which are guided by our free will to choose, and thus, through the gift of free will, we choose our adventures and we create our journeys."

*

*Q*uestions, questions, questions? Will they never stop? Day in and day out, the questions invade my mind. Am I asking these questions or are they the questions of another that I am somehow eavesdropping upon. How that could possibly be, I do not know, but these questions intrude upon my mind as if they were entitled to do so. The repetitive nature of these incessant questions is confounding. I do not believe I am consciously asking these questions, and still, I hear them within myself as if they are of my own making. "Goodness, this is ridiculous! If I am not hearing the questions, I am ruminating about them! Enough, I say! I have a life to live. Leave me

1

alone." The melodic tone of an often-misplaced cellphone made its presence known from an adjoining room. A welcomed distraction from the antics of my mind, the hunt for the elusive device began. Here and there, under this stack of papers and then the next, the search progressed. More often than not in these situations the unknown caller would give up long before my task was completed, but not this time. This time, my quest was successful.

"Is that you?" My words directed towards the technological marvel were loudly spoken before the phone actually reached my ear.

"Of course, it's me, Silly You!" My friend responded with similar volume. "Who else would be calling you at this time of day?" The familiar voice, immediately recognized, brought a smile to my face.

"No one, of course! Only you would dare risk calling at this hour! And I am so glad you did! Obviously, you're back in town. Tell me everything!"

"Your place or mine?" Knowing my dear friend, Barbara, as I did, and also knowing that she had just returned from three weeks of travel, I assumed she might not be ready for a visitor.

"You decide what's best for you. I'm happy to come to your place, and I'm equally happy for you to come here. The coffee is brewing, as we speak, and if memory serves me there are numerous possibilities for breakfast just waiting to be popped into the oven. What's your preference?" Her sigh of relief steered me in the direction of the kitchen.

"I'll see you in a few minutes!" Quick goodbyes were offered as I turned on the oven and readied the breakfast table for Barb's arrival.

*

A passage from
Beyond The Day of Tomorrow
A Seeker's Guide
(Chapter One)

*"While **A Seeker's Guide** may more aptly serve the seeker who prefers to be actively involved in the formation of their journey, it is also a resource for those who await the journey to unfold before them. How one chooses to approach their journey reflects individual free will, and one approach is not deemed better than another, but*

*recognition that one is indeed participating in a journey
is of extreme usefulness."*

*

The knock at the door came more quickly than expected. Although this should not have surprised me, it did anyway. Lost in my personal curiosity and excitement about Barb's trip, my own sense of time escaped me. Compound that with the reality that my dear friend was one who typically moved at lightning speed, it made sense that her arrival seemed faster than anticipated. Even though we live only a couple of blocks away from one another, she is able to traverse the distance in half the time it takes me to get to her house. I am convinced she has a short cut, but she assures me that is not so. She claims that her long legs give her an advantage, and of course this is true; however, I am still certain there is a secret short cut yet to be discovered.

As I approached the door, I paused briefly to take a deep breath. My excitement about seeing Barb again was so heightened that it was difficult to contain myself. *Calm down! Don't bombard her with questions. She's had an adventure. Give her time to share her story.*

"Let me in! I'm here!" Barb's announcement pulled me away from my unspoken self-talk. I immediately unlatched the lock and came face to face with my friend of many years.

"Hello, You! It is so good to see you! Has it only been three weeks?" We hugged each other for what seemed a very long time, but probably wasn't, before we both stepped back at the same time and stared at each other.

"We need to talk!" The words spoken simultaneously made us both roll our eyes and shake our heads. "Hmmm!" Again, we spoke in unison. This pattern that often occurs between Barb and me never fails to amaze us.

"I need to talk!" Barb asserted. The plea underlying her declaration was obvious. I was eager to provide a listening ear.

"And I want to hear everything!" came my reply. I grabbed her arm in mine and led her towards the kitchen. "You look great, Barb! I'm assuming that you had a life changing experience and that your story is going to blow my mind." Grasping my arm tightly, she nodded her head enthusiastically.

"You've summarized my experience succinctly. It was life changing!

3

And you will be very proud of me. I kept a record of my experiences everyday. Thank goodness, you advised me to do so. The time was so rich that even with my daily entries, I fear some events may have slipped my mind. So much was happening at once! It was like living in a kaleidoscope of different realities with one transpiring within another. I was never really sure where I was in these various realities even though I felt certain, almost, that I was within each one as they whirled about me. I know this sounds odd, maybe even crazy, but these experiences were real. Unfortunately, I just don't know how to accurately articulate what happened. So as you might imagine, my friend, I really need to process these unusual events with you. Hopefully, you are up for hearing each and every detail." Again, there was a tone in Barb's voice that made me wonder. My curiosity, which often is difficult to manage, was struggling to behave itself. I reminded myself that Barb's need to discuss her recent experiences was more important than my curiosity's need to be sated. *Calm yourself, old girl; just be a good friend!*

"The coffee is ready and my morning is open, so let's just settle in and thoroughly work our way through the events of the last three weeks. I'm getting a sense that your adventure was much more than you had anticipated." Barb closed her eyes, inhaled deeply, and sat quietly for a minute before she returned to face me.

"I am so grateful you're available," she reached over and placed her hand on mine. "And more importantly, I am grateful for our friendship. I cannot imagine having this conversation with anyone but you. Thank you, thank you, thank you!"

*

A passage from
Beyond The Day of Tomorrow
A Seeker's Guide
(Chapter One)

"The level of involvement in participation, again, is an element of free will. How actively or passively one chooses to engage in participation may or may not influence the outcome, but it may perhaps influence the perception of the experience. How often have we experienced an event

*from a perspective of surprise rather than expectancy,
based upon our degree of participation in that event?"*

*

"Oh, Barb, the feeling is mutual! I cannot tell you how excited I was to receive your call this morning. And I'm embarrassed to admit how much you've been missed these past few weeks. At one point during your absence I sank into a ridiculous state of despair thinking you might not return from your trip." The fear of having my dear friend move away engulfed me once again. "Oh, goodness! Please tell me you are not planning to move away to some distant land, where I will rarely ever see you." Recognizing that my selfishness was running away with me, I attempted to silence myself. "No! No! No! Forgive me for that outburst, Barb, and please disregard what I just said." Realizing that I was much more concerned about the idea of Barb relocating than I had thought, I took a deep breath and stated the obvious, "The possibility of your leaving has been on my mind, but that's not why we are here now. So, let's please not be distracted by my foolishness! I want to focus on you! And I want to hear every minute detail of your journey." A look of mutual fondness exchanged between us. Barb and I refer to each other as Sisters of Choice, a descriptor chosen long ago that honors our relationship. Over the years, as the bond between us grew deeper, the title became a term of endearment.

"Oh, Sister, I appreciate the sentiment. And I must admit that the urge to pick up the phone and call you was ever-present. But every time I started to do so, your words of wisdom came to the forefront of my mind. 'Just be with whatever unfolds,' you said as I was leaving for my trip. It was stellar advice, Sister. And strangely as it may sound, there were times when it seemed as if you were there with me whispering the message in my ear. I guess that was just wishful thinking. The point is, Dear Sister of Mine, I missed you as much as you missed me." Barb paused for a moment and looked about the kitchen. I imagined she was reminiscing about all the long talks we had shared at this table, but as is often true with my Sister of Choice, her mind was focused upon more relevant matters.

"I'm assuming the oven is on for a reason," she declared pointedly, "but I'm not smelling any delicious aromas. Perhaps, we should remedy this issue before we delve into our conversation."

"You're right!" I jumped up from the chair and produced two options from which to choose. "Apple cinnamon or classic blueberry?"

"Both!" she responded quickly. I agreed wholeheartedly with her strategy. We needed sustenance before engaging with Barb's life changing experience. I prepared a small bowl of sliced fruit and she poured us each a cup of coffee while the muffins warmed in the oven. Within minutes, the desired aromas filled the room and we could not resist our need to sneak a peek.

"They look perfect!" Our words emerged simultaneously from our respective mouths. "Grab the plates," we each directed the other. "Will this never end?" The question asked in unison resulted in a round of giggling. My side ached from the impromptu episode, reminding me of countless times when we had shared similar outbursts of laughter. I was so glad that Barbara was home.

We eventually managed to settle down enough to decorate our breakfast plates with the colorful bits of fruit and a quarter section from each muffin. With coffee cups in hand, we toasted our friendship. "I'm so glad to be home," Barbara softly whispered. I wondered if her comment was in response to my earlier unspoken thought, but it didn't matter. These coincidences are so frequent that I usually just take them for granted. Sometimes, I note the so-called coincidences, but other times, I just let them slide. Today is a day to do the latter. Barb has a lot on her mind, and in her heart, and the time has come for us to have a heart-to-heart. Over the years, we have come to call these intimate experiences 'Conversations from the Heart.' It is an appropriate title, one that holds significant meaning for us.

*

A passage from
Beyond The Day of Tomorrow
A Seeker's Guide
(Chapter One)

"The unfolding of a journey is not unlike the birth of a child. In the beginning, there is willingness to co-create and there is intention to participate. Then there is expectancy, during which one prepares in various ways to ready oneself for the arrival of the new unfolding.

Unknown is it to the expectant seeker precisely what the new unfolding will bring, but as best able, the seeker anticipates the new arrival and awaits the unfolding birth, and then the process begins again. One unfolding births another unfolding, evolving one from another, with or without recognition by the involved participant. The ongoing nature of this process provides infinite opportunities for a seeker to explore every aspect of every curiosity for endless time.

This occurs! Whether it is in your awareness or not, it occurs. How aware you wish to be is your choice. You are a recipient of free will. Remember? You are free to participate and you are free to choose how actively you wish to participate, or perhaps it is better stated that you are free to 'consciously' participate, because you are participating whether you are conscious of that participation or not.

Since participation is a given, why not choose to be aware of the participation? All it requires is free will, which is also a given. So if participation is a given and free will is a given, what do you have to lose? Except conscious awareness."

*

"Well, Dear Friend, are you sufficiently nourished to begin our Conversation from the Heart?" Her reaction indicated no hesitation. She carefully placed her cup at the edge of the placemat, leaned back from the table, folded her hands in her lap, and stared deeply into my eyes.

"Are you, Dear Friend, ready to listen with the ears of your heart?" Tears welled up in my eyes as I struggled for the right words, but before I could articulate any reassurances, she reassured me. "You've always been here for me. Always! I actually remember the first time when you introduced that phrase into my life. I was very upset at the time and you quietly said to me that you would be honored to hear my story. I was so ashamed and afraid to reveal my deepest heartache to anyone, but you offered to listen to me *with the ears of your heart*, and those words melted my fears away. The memory of that incident still touches me deeply. I have no doubts that you are wholeheartedly present, and I am grateful once again for your friendship."

"We're very fortunate, aren't we? Your absence has reminded us of the precious nature of our relationship. I am so glad your home. A-n-d," my exaggerated pronunciation of the three-letter word indicated a manipulation in the making. "Barbara, dear, my curiosity is reaching a level of desperation. Please tell me EVERYTHING!"

As my friend often did before embarking upon an important topic, she took a long deep breath. "My experience began in the taxi on the way to the airport. My treks to and from the airport are usually uneventful. Typically, I sit quietly drifting about in the confines of my mind while the driver silently meanders along the route to the airport. We arrive, I provide the appropriate compensation for the trip, and we wish each other a good day. It's a very simple, disconnected interaction with another fellow human being that is forgettable. That was not the case the morning I departed on my adventure. In truth, the drive to the airport was the first chapter of my journey." Barb paused briefly before continuing. "Yes," she acknowledged more to herself than to me, "the drive to the airport was definitely an experience in itself. The driver, who was very formal and professional, introduced himself immediately as he placed my luggage into the trunk of his vehicle. I was quite taken not only by his behavior, but also by his multi-syllabic name, which I'm afraid I cannot pronounce. It's regrettable, because his name was musical and merits being spoken correctly. He was very gracious about my limited abilities and reassured me that he had met very few people who were able to enunciate his name. He proceeded to tell me that in his native language his name meant friend and he invited me to call him Friend instead. Well, I was deeply taken by this gesture, and in turn introduced myself and told him that I would be honored to call him Friend. My response seemed to please him. He thanked me, and then reached out to shake my hand, and in the most gentle and caring way he stated that he would be honored to call me Friend as well. It was odd, Sister, because it felt as if time stood still as two Old Friends met again for the first time." My thoughts concurred with Barbara's interpretation and my curiosity wanted answers to dozens of internal questions. I chose to remain silent.

"He eventually motioned me toward the back door of his beautifully polished black sedan, but then in mid-motion seemed to change his mind, and instead suggested that I might be more comfortable in the front seat. I suppose my body language indicated a moment of indecision because he paused respectfully before saying the most curious thing. 'When beginning a journey, madam, one must seek a position of openhearted anticipation.'

Bemused, I yielded to his suggestion and situated myself in the front passenger seat. As he fastened his seat belt and motored the car out of the driveway, I pondered his statement. How did he know I was on a journey? Besides the fact that he was driving me to an airport, how did he know I was embarking up a journey rather than a business trip or a self-indulgent vacation? He used the word journey in the context of my newly developing understanding of the word. This new friend was not referring to a trip per se; his intention was much more focused. As if responding to my thoughts, he said quote-quote, 'you are one who has the aura of a Seeker. Your heart aches for answers to age-old questions. Who am I? Why am I? How am I? You seek the meaning of life. Your aura reveals your inner quest.'

Do you believe that, Sister? I hadn't even gotten to the end of the block, when this incredible experience unfolded around me. That was no coincidence!" Nodding my head in agreement, I urged her to continue. She did not hesitate.

"Well, as you might imagine, my mind was reeling. Finally, I was able to articulate my surprise. 'How do you know this? We just met, and yet you apparently know more about me than I know about myself. Who are you?' He didn't respond immediately. His manner was pensive. In fact, I remember thinking that he was carefully selecting his words, but now in this moment, I think he knew exactly what needed to be said. He was just waiting for the right moment. And when the time came, he said, 'I am your Friend. And I know these things because these truths reside within you. They are in your heart waiting for you to acknowledge them.' He paused from the conversation while traffic demanded his attention. Once the road had cleared again, he continued. 'Our paths have crossed for a reason, madam. You have reminded me of my own journey, and I have had the honor of acknowledging yours. We are both Seekers, and friends of ancient beginnings, who have had the pleasure and the blessing of reuniting for a brief moment in this present experience. I am most grateful to see you again, Old Friend.' Tears welled up in my eyes, Sister, because I knew he was speaking the truth.

When we arrived at the airport, I stalled for a moment thinking there was more that needed to be said, but nothing emerged from my overloaded mind, nor did my Old Friend offer any more words of wisdom. He unfastened his seatbelt, gracefully exited the car, and proceeded to fulfill his duties as a professional driver. My luggage was properly placed on the sidewalk with its handle perfectly situated for my immediate use and my coat was retrieved from the backseat and carefully placed over my left arm. We both started to reach out to shake hands and then we hugged instead, as only Old Friends are given to do. 'I pray your journey will be filled with blessings, my Friend.' His sincerity touched my heart and I was overwhelmed with feelings that seemed inappropriate for the occasion, and yet, they were authentic. I thanked him for his honesty and his kindness. And then the urge to stroke his cheek overcame me, and when I did, tears streamed down his face. In that moment, I knew with all that I am that his words had spoken the truth. We were indeed, Dear Old Friends. And then he said, 'Till we meet again, I will hold you in my heart.' And I heard myself say, 'Forevermore!'" Barb fell silent. I assumed she was reliving the story in her mind and hoped that she was not having any doubts about this remarkable experience. It deserved full and openhearted acceptance.

"Do you believe this actually happened?" Her question did not surprise me. Even though I knew she had no doubts about the reality of her experience, I also knew how important it was to receive validation from a trusted friend or family member when such an incidence occurs. It can be difficult to remain solid and unwavering when one experiences such an unbelievable event.

"Yes, Barb, I believe your experience was real and I am both delighted and grateful that you shared it with me. You know how I am. I love stories like this. I don't doubt the experience, nor do I doubt you. You, my dear friend, would never make up a story like this. It simply isn't in you."

"No, it isn't. But it really is a bizarre experience. There aren't many people with whom I would feel comfortable sharing this story. In fact, you're probably the only one. So, thank you for believing me." Barb paused, started to speak again, and then paused again.

"What's on your mind, friend? Just put it out on the table. You began this conversation by saying you really needed to process your experiences. So, let's do it! One experience at a time."

"Well, actually my question is more about you than the experience I just shared. How is it that you can be so unconditionally open to this story? Do you not have any doubts? Why are you so confident that my story is real? Sorry to bombard you with questions, but I'm curious how you deal with stories like mine. I know I'm not the only person that shares unusual experiences with you and I just want to know how you deal with this on a day-to-day basis? Am I being intrusive?"

"Goodness no! You're not being intrusive at all. I'm just trying to sort through your questions and wondering if I should address them now or if I should encourage you to continue your story. I don't want to interfere with your momentum."

"Actually, I think it would be very helpful. These are questions I've often wondered about and I would like to hear more about your journey as it relates to trusting the unusual. If you're okay with that." Similarly to my friend, I also had the habit of taking a deep breath before embarking upon an important topic. It readied me for the challenge.

"First of all, I will speak the obvious that you have momentarily forgotten due to the emotional intensity of the story you just shared. I believe your story, dear friend, because I completely and totally trust you! Why wouldn't I? We share years of history. As I said before, you would never make up a story like this. Why would you? Why would anybody do that? Let's face it! One does not get bonus points for making up these kinds of tales. So in regards to your story, my answer is yes, I am unconditionally open to your story because I trust you.

And regarding your questions about doubts...the answer is also yes! I have many doubts about the unbelievable, because that's just the way people are. It's humankind's nature to want proof...to demand proof...as if life cannot exist without it. I suspect this is related to our fears of the unknown and/or our fears of not having control over every aspect of our lives. I think it's sad actually. In our incessant need to have proof about everything, I'm afraid we have slammed the door on many possibilities. We seem unwilling to give the unbelievable the benefit of a doubt, which is most unfortunate, since it is through our doubting behavior that we learn more about the unusual and unbelievable unknowns. It's true that our doubts sometimes confuse us. They get in the way and dissuade us from what we actually know. But more often then not, I believe our doubts help us to clarify our understanding of a particular situation so that we can discern what we really know. This process enables us to feel more confident about what we believe and what we are willing to accept.

Through the various ups and downs of my own development, I have had to confront my doubting behavior, and in so doing, I learned to accept my doubts as an asset. As a result of this self-examination, I stopped doubting my doubts. I think it is fair to say that I am now better at trusting myself when it comes to working with my doubting mind." As I completed that last sentence, a moment of doubt surfaced from within me, and my doubting mind, ever vigilant, was ready and available to evaluate my articulation of humankind's doubting ways. I could not refrain from chuckling at myself. I acknowledged to Barb what was transpiring and we agreed to have compassion for the tenacity of our doubts. This simple act quieted my mind, and in the next moment I realized there was more to be said.

"Let me share one more thought with you about believing the unbelievable. There are times when we encounter something or someone that is so remarkably unique and confounding that it seems too amazing to be true; and yet, we know from deeply within that we have experienced a truth unfolding before us. We willingly choose to believe this unbelievable truth because we know that we must. To deny it would be a betrayal of self and of the truth that revealed itself to us. I believe your encounter with the cab driver was such an experience. And because you had the courage to share your experience with me, I have had the privilege of encountering the unbelievable as well. Thank you, Barb. Your story is a gift that will live within the chambers of my heart forevermore." Her nod of agreement was barely noticeable, but her sigh accentuating the response affirmed for me that my assumption was correct. I quietly rose from the table and placed the remains of our breakfast muffins in the microwave to warm. The mere fifteen seconds provided ample time to grab the coffee pot and refresh our cups. We sat in silence each sipping and munching away while lost in our own thoughts.

"That was a lovely response to my story, Sister. Very helpful! You've given me much to think about. Thank you for listening and for being so supportive." She patted my knee that was intruding upon her space and announced that I was the best sister ever. Before I could decline the Best Sister Award, she stopped me with the wave of her finger and declared, "Just say thank you!" So, I did.

"Thank you for the compliment, but more importantly, thank you for sharing your story, Barb. I honestly believe that we are intended to share our unusual stories. You truly gave me a gift this morning. Hearing about your experience brightens my day. It gives me something to ponder, and that pleases me. Because of your willingness to share your story, I am more in this moment than I was before. Please think about that. There is a reason for us to share these experiences. It opens people's hearts and makes them more receptive to and aware of the incredible world in which they exist. I believe delightful events, such as yours with the cab driver, happen all the time, but most folks are so busy that they simply don't notice it. What a loss that is! You've done me a great favor, my friend." Barb was also a very good listener. I knew she was taking every word in and that she would continue to mull over our conversation, integrating what was right for her and releasing what was not. Barb was very dedicated to pursuing her journey and allowing time for contemplation was a regular part of her discipline.

"You've made similar comments about this before, Sister, but this time your logic is really sinking in. I agree with you. Sharing these stories is important. I suspect there are many, many stories waiting to be told and I wonder what would happen if everyone simply accepted responsibility for doing so. How might that change the way we live our lives? Begs one to wonder, doesn't it?"

*

A passage from
Beyond The Day of Tomorrow
A Seeker's Guide
(Chapter Two)

"Conscious awareness! To be consciously aware of all we have learned over ages of experiences and to be able to access that awareness at any give time. Would that not be an eventful experience worth pursuing? To consciously know everything that one has known, not only in this present experience, but also in prior experiences as well, and to have full awareness of this knowingness at all times. Does this sound like folly? Does it stretch your imagination? Or perhaps you find it delightfully intriguing? If your intrigued light just flickered, then stand up and be counted with the many other adventurers who are also intrigued and mystified by this idea of eternal life. This is what we are speaking of, you know. Yes, Eternal Life! This elusive journey everyone is talking about is not just about this life experience."

*

"Well, dear friend, does this mean you are ready to continue processing your adventures?" I raised my eyebrows as high as possible in hopes that the gesture might entice her to take the lead...and it worked! She quickly acknowledged that there was much more to tell, but also expressed her concern about the length of time we had already consumed with the first chapter of her story. Reassurances were given as was my own fascination and excitement about her experiences. "I'm intrigued! And eager to hear more! If you have the energy to continue, I have the energy to listen."

"Great! Then let's continue! So...as you might imagine, I was flying high after my uplifting experience with the wonderful cab driver. My mind was still in a whirl when I entered through the oversized automatic doors into the airport terminal. And then, I found myself in the midst of utter chaos. The queues twisted back and forth in an effort to afford some type of order to the excessively dense crowds, but the endeavor was not successful. My anxiety skyrocketed to match the energy of the masses. Fears of missing my flight surfaced, as was true for everyone else standing in the mile long line, but then I chose another path. I decided this was all part of my journey and whatever was intended to happen would happen regardless of how I chose to approach the situation. So I chose to handle it from a place of peace and serenity. And guess what? It worked! I lost track of time as I proceeded forth from a contemplative state, and in no time at all, I was checked in, processed through the security gates, and then found myself leisurely strolling down the concourse towards my departure gate. I arrived with time to spare and enjoyed a few moments of silence before the boarding procedure began. The flight itself was uneventful. My plan of reading and journaling during the flight did not come to pass; I was fast asleep before the plane even lifted." Barb paused briefly and I took advantage of the moment to commend her approach.

"Well done, Sister! You completely altered that chaotic state of energy you entered into and turned it around for yourself. Simply stated, you chose not to participate in the anxious commotion. Good work!" We exchanged a high five to herald her success. Part of me was surprised that her flight was so uneventful. I anticipated she would experience another life changing event with the passenger sitting next to her, but one can only manage so much of this type of exhilaration before fatigue sets in. Apparently, the ride to the airport was enough excitement for her, and the rest period she enjoyed while on the plane was most likely provided for a reason.

"In retrospect," she continued, "I am so grateful that I had a chance to sleep on the plane, because I definitely needed the rest to manage everything that happened once I landed." Once again, I wondered if her response was related to my unspoken thoughts, but as before, it didn't matter. There was no purpose in distracting from the moment. Barb was on the brink of sharing another one of her experiences. I took a deep breath as she indulged in hers. My curiosity was running away with itself. Her next comment alleviated any doubts I had about her responding to my unspoken thoughts.

"Still yourself, my friend. I'm trying to figure out how to talk about the next incident that happened." Her mood changed to one of frustration and disbelief. I watched the change wash across her face. It was fascinating to witness. "And I'm realizing that my mind is trying to convince me that my stories are not worthy of being repeated. Why does the mind do that? I sometimes believe that my mind has a mind of its own, and its preferences are not necessarily in alignment with mine. Does that sound crazy?" Before I could answer, she responded to her own question. "Well, I'm not crazy! Even if I don't know how to articulate what I'm trying to say."

"Bravissima! Thanks for standing up for yourself! No, you are absolutely not crazy, and yes, the mind can sometimes make us feel as if we are. Barb, I'm not sure where those negative notions come from, but the fact that you are aware of the antics of your mind gives you an advantage. And by the way, I thought you expressed yourself really well. In fact, you nailed it! I too believe that my mind often behaves without my lead. It creates its own thoughts and has its own opinions while I stand by observing it in astonishment...and amusement. And this does cause you to question your sanity. I'm so delighted you boldly denounced your mind's deception.

Of course, your experiences are worthy of being shared, and I wish to hear about them now!" My friend accepted the sincerity of my support without question. She returned to her story with renewed confidence.

"Well, there's not much to report about until I finally arrived at the destination that I had secured over the Internet. It was much more than I had expected. The apartment itself was comfortable and provided everything that was needed, but the view was more than I could ever had wished for. You know how much I love large bodies of water. Well, Sister, the ocean was awe-inspiring. I just stood there on the balcony for what seemed an eternity looking at the robust waves produced by

Mother Nature's powerful sea merging beautifully with the expansive sandy beach that appeared to be miles in length. Far in the distance was a lighthouse partially hidden by a thin stretch of wispy clouds that demanded further investigation. And the sea birds were abundant. Some were soaring above proudly exhibiting their aerobatic skills while others were racing along the water's edge in search of tasty morsels brought up by the surging tide. I was entranced and grateful...overwhelmingly grateful. Why me, I wondered. Why should I be so privileged? The question daunted me. Why was I so privileged, so fortunate, to be in this incredible location for three weeks? The answer remains a mystery." Barb's thoughts went inward. I could tell that she was still mulling over the question of privilege. I sat quietly until she was ready to return to our discussion.

"Eventually I forced myself away from the balcony, which felt like a hardship in the moment, but it seemed important to attend housekeeping responsibilities. Although a walk on the beach was much more appealing, I chose to take care of the chores first. I found the view from the small living room equally alluring as the balcony view, so taking care of the practical matters that needed to be addressed was not a burden. My clothes were quickly unpacked, which is atypical for me. Usually, when traveling, I just live out of my suitcase, but for a trip this long, it made sense to make this charming place my home. The idea pleased me. I marveled at myself as I went about nestling into the small studio apartment attempting to make it into my own sacred space. The laptop and all its necessities were located in a suitable place, as were the tools of my journey. The Tibetan bell, which always accompanies me, was carefully placed on the selected end table. Also situated on this chosen table was The Journal, commonly referred to as the Keeper of All Things Notable. The Favorite Pen used only for entries in The Journal was perfectly placed on the diagonal of the precious book's surface. And of course, two tea candles were strategically placed to complete the setting. With all these special tasks attended, I was ready to face the next task. Groceries demanded my attention!" My friend laughed out loud and joked about herself. "Can you imagine these silly antics? I confess that it is all true! I really painstakingly placed the beloved pen upon The Journal as if it was a ceremonial event." She chuckled at herself again. "I guess I was trying to create a setting that would facilitate an exceptional experience. Who knows? Anyway, the setting and the ritual gave me hope that something special might happen."

"I appreciate your humor and also the underlying motivation for creating a setting worthy of an exceptional event. I know these rituals well, and after all these years, I still participate in them with anticipation. Hope burns eternal."

"Do you really?" she asked inquisitively. It seemed to surprise her that she was not alone in her fascination with ritualistic preparations. I assured her that she was not and admitted to several decades of similar activities. "I find that very comforting to hear. Do you think it actually helps? I mean, do you think these preparations facilitate opportunities for special experiences?" For a brief moment I wondered if this topic was a distraction, but I suspected Barb's questions were far more important than she realized, so it seemed wise to address them.

"I cannot speak for everyone, my friend, but I personally believe these rituals are very helpful. They quiet my mind and prepare me to be available for whatever might unfold. I also believe it enables me to be more consciously present. One must be available consciously if you expect to benefit from a quote-quote special experience. As we both know, exceptional opportunities surround us at all times, but too frequently we are so distracted by our personal matters that we fail to notice. So yes, I do think these simple acts of gracious hospitality are extremely important. They are an invitation, a beckoning if you will, for an engagement with another being with similar intentions and hopes. I must admit that I truly enjoy these acts of kindness. It makes me feel that I am welcoming Old Friends into my present life. Perhaps, this sounds a bit fanciful, but whether it is or not, the ceremonial activity brings me great pleasure, and that in itself makes it helpful. A-n-d," I enunciated the elongated version of the three-letter word to emphasize another thought that deserved articulation. "Because I am one who believes in the appearances of unusual experiences, I feel a strong sense of responsibility for creating a setting that is comfortable for my guests. I wish to honor them for the efforts they have contributed to the occasion. Sometimes, many times in the past, my excitement took over and I forgot to acknowledge the efforts made by my visitor or visitors, which left me feeling remiss afterwards. I felt as if I was receiving all of the benefits from the encounter while he, she, or they were doing all the work. Preparing my space for them makes me feel good. I want them to know how much I appreciate their presence. Yes," I repeated more to myself and to my future potential guests, "I want them to know how grateful I am for every encounter we share." My eyes met Barbara's. Tears moistened her cheeks, evidence that she understood the gratitude of which I spoke. My hand reached out to comfort her while words continued to formulate within me. Trusting this process, I shared the words with my friend.

"It is the overwhelming sense of privilege that is felt during these precious occasions, Barb, that propels me forward. The 'aha' moment! The 'why me' wonderment when you doubt your worthiness while still begging for more! Even now, a part of me is deliberating over the interaction that you and I are sharing. I feel the longing stirring within me again, wondering when the next opportunity of privilege will unfold. Will it be my own experience? Or will it be as it is now when I am blessed to bear witness to your experience? Either way will be a privilege beyond my imagination. You have honored me, dear Sister, by sharing your story with me, and I am so, so grateful. And now, in thinking about our discussion regarding rituals and preparation, I realize more preparation could have and should have been done for you." Barb shook her head in disagreement and was about to contradict me, when the mighty index finger of my left hand gave notice to be obeyed. "Dear one, I'm not being hard on myself. I'm simply recognizing that our conversation is an exceptional experience that deserves more attention. I suppose making coffee and treats is a way of demonstrating hospitality, but something more ceremonial could have been done. See, my friend, you have awakened me to expand my menu of gracious activities. Though this may seem silly, it isn't. Courtesy and respect should be a given, regardless of the setting or the event. Every interaction should be regarded as an exceptional experience, because in essence, every one is. I realize in my endeavor to gain greater understanding about what I perceive as the 'exceptional' experience, I have become less appreciative of and attentive to what is misperceived as an ordinary experience. Hmm! My friend, your visit this morning has been anything but ordinary. And I know there remains much more to process. So I will make a quick mental note about my revelation regarding how I evaluate certain experiences. It appears that I've been judging one set of experiences as more important than others. This deserves careful study in the immediate future." My thoughts continued to flow, but I knew it was time to return to the purpose of this gathering.

"Thank you, I am learning so much from your story and your presence. See! The value of sharing our stories is incalculable. Oh, goodness! I've gone on and on! Are you able to return to your topic? Please do so; hopefully you haven't lost your momentum."

"Not at all," she reassured me. "Our conversation is fascinating and I too am grateful for the fullness of it all. Sharing my story is helping me to learn more about my experience, and as we discuss it, your commentary helps me tremendously. I've said this to you before, but it deserves repeating. Our conversations, each one of them, feel like a year's work in graduate school. Actually, that doesn't come close to describing the amount of growth that I experience through our talks. Thank you, dear friend, for having time for me. And if you want to take it up a notch by lighting candles, playing peaceful meditation music, and burning incense, that works for me as well. Just don't forget the delicious treats, okay?" Barbara's humor was ever-present, and always appropriately delivered. She had perfect timing. And she was the perfect guest! Not only did she accept responsibility for refilling our water glasses, but she also took care of us by announcing that we had reached our limit of caffeine. "No more coffee! We're high enough from this conversation as it is." In typical form, Barb took a long deep breath and I followed in like manner. She closed her eyes and minutes passed. In support, I closed mine as well. The silence continued without our notice, and then as often is the case, we opened our eyes simultaneously.

"I'm grateful for our friendship," she whispered and I nodded in agreement. I put my hands in prayerful position and gently bowed to her hoping she would receive the gesture as an invitation to continue. Her response was immediate.

"Well, Sister, as you probably already know, my desire for another unusual experience was granted before day's end. The last task, the trip to the grocery store, was completed quickly and efficiently, because the call to walk the beach was literally reverberating throughout my entire body. Perhaps I was just imagining that, but then again, maybe not. I simply knew without knowing how I knew it that a visit to the ocean's edge was necessary. So, in less than thirty minutes, groceries were bought, stored away, and I was out the door." Another deep breath was taken.

"In mere minutes, dear Sister, I found myself on the beach. There I stood captivated by the indescribable beauty of Mother Earth. She is a magnificent Being! Her ocean and all its glory, played before me, while forested mountains rising up into the clouds held my back. And to the left and right of my position, miles and miles of awe-inspiring sandy seashore dotted with large boulders and varying sizes of smaller rock masses stretched beyond sight. My eyes looked in every direction, trying to capture every sight for storage in the memory file of my mind's library. I remember thinking that such beauty must not be forgotten, but at the same time, there was no compulsion to take photos. At some level, there was clarity that technology should not be involved in this experience.

As I viewed each scene in every direction over and over again, an unexpected realization came over me. I was alone; no one else but me was occupying this expansive space. I wondered how that could be. It didn't seem real. And yet it was! My selfishness could not be contained. I was extremely pleased with my good fortune.

My enchantment with the seascape lasted for an unknown amount of time until an incoming wave slapped me in the shins, swiftly bringing me back into the present. Clearly the frothy, bone-chilling water swirling about my feet had served its purpose. Back in my body, I was finally able to do what I felt called to do. I took the first step and began walking the beach. For no reason whatsoever, I chose to go north first. It was marvelous. Oh, Sister, please excuse my limited descriptive abilities, but the beauty of Mother Nature truly is beyond words. And for reasons I do not know, my love affair with seacoasts is particularly inexplicable. Suffice it to say, I felt as if I had returned home. The sand beneath my feet made me joyously happy and the music of the ocean opened my heart in ways not known before. I felt..." she paused, seeking a word that might adequately explain her sense of self, but to no avail. Eventually she said, "I felt eternal." Barb paused again, perhaps waiting for a response from me or for more insight from within. Regardless of the purpose of the pause, I simply gave her space to be. Whatever was intended would come to her. That was a truth that could be trusted.

"Yes," she confirmed to herself. "I felt eternal. It was as if I was in touch with the past, the present, and the future, all at the same time. I knew without reservation that there was more and I know this because I had experienced more...more than just this lifetime. My awareness of these lifetimes was vague then and remains vague now, but they existed. I am certain that I existed in these other lifetimes. Some occurred long, long ago, while others were more recent, but I don't think it even matters when or where these lifetimes were lived or who I was in any of them. What matters is that they transpired. Because I know these other lifetimes existed, I know that life is eternal, and that matters. At least it matters to me!

Sister, while I walked along the beach, I felt in Oneness with the ocean, with the Earth, and with the Universe. I felt as if I was indistinguishable from Existence. I was existent within Existence and She was existent within me. We were One and we were Many, all united in Existence, yet individually existing within our own existences. Oh, geez, this is difficult to articulate."

"Barbara, please do not worry about expressing yourself perfectly. You are doing a beautiful job, and I am intrigued. What you are sharing with me is breathtaking, so please do not stop yourself. I am so grateful that you are sharing this experience with me. You had a unique experience, and now I am having my own unique experience because of your willingness to share this remarkable moment of insight. I am so grateful. Take a deep breath, friend, and continue when you are ready." Barb did as I asked. She did take a deep breath and then several more while she took in my words of support and comfort. She understood the importance of our exchange and was determined to continue.

"Whew! Thanks, friend. I heard everything you said, and I know how important this conversation is. And I know you understand that I just want to do justice to this experience. The truth is I'm not sure I will ever really be able to describe the depth of awareness that was felt in that precious moment. I hope more clarity comes to me. I would love this to happen and my heart remains open to that, but I honestly don't know if it matters. Must we recall every feature of an insight for the insight to be beneficial? Must we have absolute clarity about an insightful event for the insight to be trusted? I don't know the answers to these questions any more than I know if it is important that we precisely remember everything about a previous life for us to believe in eternal life. I don't know any more than I have shared with you other than I had an incredible experience that will never be forgotten.

Oh, goodness, there is more to share." Delight washed over Barb's face. "It surfaces from the recesses of my mind. Sister, when I walked the beach, my feet merged with Mother Earth. I could sense the passion that she carries for all her inhabitants...the love that she has for every being that resides upon and within her. What a remarkable Being she is!

When you walk along the ocean, you feel the pulse of the Mother and you experience the oneness that exists between you. It is breathtaking! As her heart beats, your heart aligns itself with hers. I suspect this is the way it is intended to be. Perhaps, if we humans could align ourselves with her, we might find ourselves in a much better situation than we now face. I wonder if that is true. Wouldn't it be interesting to know the answer to that? Do you know?" Barb's mind worked at lightning speed. She could manage numerous tasks simultaneously and live into her creative side at the same time.

"Before we leap into this discussion, let's keeping walking the beach for a while longer. Okay? Tell me more about being alone on that massive piece of landscape."

"You're right, of course! But make a note regarding humankind's alignment with the Earth, because I think it is important to explore. A-n-d, I also think you know more than you're telling me. So mark this down on our To Be Discussed list." I theatrically followed her orders and made the notation as ordered.

"Back to the beach!" she announced excitedly. Once Barb returned to the topic, her demeanor changed. You could see a misty look in her eyes and a sense of wonderment that enveloped her. She truly was at the beach again. "Oh, Sister, even now, I can feel the ocean's breezes, smell her smells, and I can hear her call for me to return home." She was lost to her thoughts for a moment and then returned. "My walk lasted for over three hours. Most of that time was just an ordinary walk in an exceptional location, but it was more than just ordinary. There was a sense of peace and well being that came over me that frankly is an enviable way to be. I was at peace with the world. Oh, don't get me wrong. My mind attempted to play tricks with me, but the temptations for self-agitation were not successful. I simply didn't bite. Thoughts came to mind that would typically get under my skin, but as I said, it didn't happen on this walk. The peaceful state that I found myself in was much stronger than I've ever experienced before. And it did not succumb to any tactics of distraction. I can't really explain why this was, but I assume it had to do with my affinity for the Earth, or perhaps, my alignment with her. Or both!"

"Yes," words of agreement surged from within me. "I suspect your strong connection with oceanic waters facilitates this type of union for you, Barb. Once again, it appears we are witnessing a situation where the reasons underlying a reality do not necessarily matter, but the truth of the reality does matter and this should be acknowledged and honored. The ocean, for whatever reasons, is extremely important to your development, your spiritual advancement, and I strongly encourage you to embrace this."

"I agree! Being near the ocean awakens my need to know *more*," replied Barb with a twinkle in her eyes. "And this in turn opens my heart to being aware and accepting of the *more* that is going on around me. It seems to be a wonderful cycle that fuels itself. Hopefully, one can develop this curiosity and passion in any setting because traveling can be expensive, but I understand that visiting preferred places can spark the excitement within you. I would love to feel that solid sense of peace wherever I am. That's a goal for me. But if it is necessary, I will go wherever I must to reignite and/or maintain that incredible sense of well being.

"Your commitment is impressive, Barb. The sense of urgency in your voice inspires me. This is another advantage of sharing our stories. Because you willingly shared your wonderful experiences with me, I also feel ignited. Your faithfulness to your call makes me want to kick-start my own journey."

"Sister, you live your journey!" Barb emphatically announced. "It's because of you that I am now involved in this new way of being. At least it's new to me. Lest you forget, it was your stories that inspired me to seek within. And look what happened. One story was shared and another story began. I am so grateful to you!" Her expression of gratitude touched my heart and I felt the same towards her. There was reason for our mutual appreciation of one another.

"And then another story, your story, was shared that has ignited me and which will undoubtedly result in more stories. The process has come full circle, as they are intended to do, and validates the importance of these exchanges. We all need inspiration, regardless of the age or stage of our journey. Whether we are seasoned Seekers or Initiates of the process, we always need fresh energy to renew us and keep us moving forward. This is so rich! We are very lucky to have our relationship. Not everyone is so fortunate."

"No, and that really makes me sad, because you're right, Sister. Our relationship enhances these experiences. We energize each other. I cannot imagine doing this alone."

"Nor can I! Please forgive me for repeating myself, Barb, but the importance of sharing our stories is, in my mind, incalculable. I don't think we have yet seen the power of these exchanges. Not only do we learn more about our existence and our roles in existence by listening to other people's stories, but we also create new relationships that are founded in curiosity, hopefulness, and goodness. The stories that you and I have shared, and the many others that I have heard from individuals similar to us, are uplifting. They broaden my scope of awareness and they spark my desire to know more. And that's just a few of the advantages that immediately come to mind. As more people become involved in this sharing process, more will understand that there really is much more going on around us than we presently know, and people will feel that their unusual experiences are validated. Bottom line, when one person has an unusual experience, it can be unnerving, but when many people have similar unusual experiences, it's a phenomenon that demands openhearted consideration." We both nodded in agreement and then Barb took the lead again.

"Isn't it interesting that people want to know more about who they are and why, but when they start gaining more information about these unknowns, they are fearful of sharing their own quote-quote unusual experiences. I personally understand this because you do feel odd when you've had such an experience. You are both over the top excited and at the same time in doubt about the event. I remember thinking that no one would understand what had happened and there definitely was fear about being judged and/or possibly diagnosed. Truth is, some of these fears are rational and you do need to be careful when making the decision to share your story."

"Yes, you're right, Barb, however, another truth also exists. A lot of folks truly are open to unusual experiences and these people are eager to hear about them and most of them have their own stories to share. So this is how I would summarize our thoughts regarding the initial phase of sharing stories about unusual experiences. While in the beginning phase, one must choose wisely before sharing his or her story; but another factor in this important decision-making process is this. One must take the risk.

In my humble opinion, these unusual experiences are happening in increasing numbers. Of course, I have no data to prove this, but that will not keep me from speaking out. Again, I believe these incidents are more prevalent now, and I believe that increase is happening for a reason. Of course, it is true that we have more information about these experiences now because of the Internet. Information spreads around the globe in an instant, and perhaps, that is why it seems there is an increase, but I don't think it matters whether there really is an increase in numbers or if the perspective is related to technology bringing the information before us. The point is there seem to be more conversations about *unusual experiences* now than in the past. And again, let me repeat myself. I believe this is happening for a reason."

*

A passage from
Beyond The Day of Tomorrow
A Seeker's Guide
(Chapter Two)

"Picture this, please. You are watching, addictively and hopelessly, the longest mini-series in the history of humankind and each episode represents another life experience. So, in Episode 1, you're a wealthy overseer with servants at your beck and call...an interesting perspective, when you're the overseer. But guess what? In Episode 2, guess who gets to play the servant? Different perspective, right? And what is the purpose of the mini-series? In TV Land, perhaps there is no other purpose than monetary gains or from the viewers' perspective, a test of endurance. But what about real life? What about the ongoing, never-ending serial called eternal life? What would be the purpose of this fanciful, yet fascinating concept and how would we go about answering this thought provoking question?

If this concept of eternal life causes you to ponder and to wonder about its efficacy and its viability, then your curious nature has been touched and the first phase of the journey has begun."

*

"It's interesting, my friend, that you have reached a point in your life where you are choosing to challenge some old norms." Barb witnessed her friend's eyebrows raising in a curious way, which led her to believe that her Sister of Choice was somewhat taken aback by her comment. "Let me elaborate on that," she reacted quickly. "You are a person who revels in evidence, and you prefer to have statistics to back you up, but now, I see you boldly declaring that there is more in the world that demands attention and consideration than only those things that are considered proven facts. It seems you have once again made a choice to take a risk. And I want to thank you for doing so!"

"Thank you, Barb. I guess you're right. I am taking a new approach and yes, it is probably a bit risky, but what's the worst that could happen? Someone might disagree with me. And they might demand evidence and belittle me for my lack of it, but so what. It is unwise to pretend that these unusual events are not happening. They are happening, and they are happening for a reason. I will not pretend that this is not occurring. And I will not remain silent about it." My friend stared at me. It was obvious that she wanted to say something. Although I was curious to know what was going on in her mind, my intuition led me to refrain from rushing her.

"Thank you for giving me a moment to collect my thoughts," Barb's reaction once again made me believe that she was responding to my thoughts. "Well of course, I am!" she giggled. "You've taught me well, dear friend, and sometimes, I am actually successful in connecting with your thoughts. I hope my behavior is not intrusive. It is odd when it happens, and also exciting, but I do not wish to trespass upon another's private thoughts." I reassured her that she had not violated my space.

"Not at all, Barbara! I assumed my assumptions were correct, but having them verified is so satisfying. Your existential communication skills have improved greatly. I am so proud of you!" My friend beamed with appreciation. Her reaction was a good reminder for me. Words of approval should be expressed, not thought.

"Actually Sister, I was having similar thoughts regarding your decision to speak out about these wonderful unusual events that you are privileged to witness or hear about from others. I am proud of you. And I'm grateful for all your assistance over the years. It has been so comfortable to have these delightful conversations. Because of your patience and guidance, I do feel as if I've really grown. My world is much bigger now than it was before, and it's because of you. I feel very fortunate, my friend, and I agree with you that these stories must be shared. You spoke so confidently just now that I'm inspired to do the same. Although I do not have the years of experience that you have, my recent experiences embolden me. Like you, I believe these are important stories that should be shared. So what do we do now?"

"Hmm! That's a good question and I do have some ideas, but we have strayed from our path. So, let's turn our focus to you again, and we will spend some time later discussing what we might do to get these remarkable stories out into the public eye. Tell me more about your adventures?"

"Well, there is more to tell, but I'm wearing down." Barb chuckled at herself, and was a bit embarrassed about admitting her fatigue. "I'm both exhilarated and exhausted at the same time. Is that possible?"

"Indeed it is, Barb! And it makes sense. You've just relived each of the precious events as you shared them with me. I am so grateful. You've made my day, but let's continue our discussion another time." Barb looked relieved but she still wanted to know more about my thoughts regarding bringing these stories out into the open. "I still have the energy to discuss your ideas about gifting stories of this nature to the world. Curiosity is driving me!"

"Well, as said, I do have some ideas, but I suspect you do as well, so let me make a suggestion. Why don't we each spend some time thinking about this opportunity and then regroup, share our ideas, and formulate a plan? Truth is, my ideas are still flitting about in my mind; I need to sit with them so that they will crystallize into something more than they are now."

"Sister, that's a great idea! Will forty-eight hours be enough time for you?" Nodding my head in agreement, I reached over to confirm with the sisterly high-five gesture.

"My dear Sister, my dear friend, I am so grateful that you shared your experiences with me today. They are precious and will keep me energized for days. What a gift you are! Thank you for being in my life!" We exchanged hugs. Barb whispered similar sentiments in my ear, and then we set a time and date for our next gathering. I watched her progress down the street until she was out of sight, and praised the Universe for bringing us together. How dear our relationship was! What a blessing!

*

A passage from
Beyond The Day of Tomorrow
A Seeker's Guide
(Chapter Three)

"The purpose of each seeker is to seek. What, you may wonder, are we intended to seek? And with that question, you commence the search. Each day begin with the conscious thought, 'What am I to seek?' This thought-provoking question may create timeless thinking and endless suppositions, which can be helpful or impeding to your journey. Carefully watch your deliberation process. If it feels useful and pushes you forward, then continue, but if it feels sluggish and tedious, consider it a sign that your process needs adjusting. Do not misjudge this as a negative, but view it clearly as the positive gathering of information that it indeed represents. Each time we gain enough data allowing us to eliminate an option, we have learned valuable information about our searches, our journeys, and ourselves."

*

2

As Barbara walked back to her house, she expressed her gratitude for her dear friend. Their relationship had grown over time from teacher/ student to friends, to Sisters of Choice. *Why am I so lucky,* she thought? *Why am I so blessed to have this remarkable woman in my life? Whatever the reason, I am so grateful. Whoever is in charge of orchestrating friendships...thank you very much! You do good work!*

"*So do you, dear friend!*" Barbara turned around to see who had spoken to her, but no one was near. She turned in a circle trying to catch view of anyone who may have been the source of the communication. She was confused, but didn't know what to do about it, so she continued her walk.

Who was that? I'm certain someone spoke to me. This doesn't make sense. Barbara stopped suddenly. "No, this doesn't make sense," she declared loudly, "But it's happening for a reason!" Again she turned around to see if anyone was in sight, but the sidewalk was empty. "If you're here, I cannot see you, but if you really are here, I would like to hear more from you." Her heartbeat was racing so fast she could hear it thumping in her ears. *Be patient!* She quickly rejected her words of advice. *Ridiculous! How could one be patient in this situation?* "Well, are you going to speak to me or not? I cannot wait all day!" She remained still for a few seconds, which seemed more like an hour. *Be patient!* The words of guidance rushed through her mind again. Silence persisted and she began to wonder if she had imagined the experience. She waited a few more seconds, just to prove to herself that she truly was a person of patience. Her attempt fell far short of thirty seconds before she headed towards her house again. Before closing her door, Barbara took another brief look down the street to satisfy her curiosity. What she saw was not the least bit satisfying. On the contrary, it was just an empty street. Shaking her head in frustration, she locked the front door and marched through the house to her favorite room. This was her Sacred Space. She kicked off her shoes, curled up in the favorite chair that looked out over a favorite view. "I'm so glad to be home." Anyone listening could hear the truth in the statement that Barb just announced to the empty room. "My adventures were exceptional. The time was well spent and I am very grateful for every minute of the trip. And I am so, so happy to be sitting here in this beloved space." Barbara sighed heavily, closed her eyes, and sat still in the peaceful silence.

"This is an extremely pleasant setting. You are most fortunate." Barbara's eyes popped open. Convinced that she had heard the voice again, she quickly glanced about the room. No one was in view. Once again, she appeared to be alone, and yet, she knew the voice just heard was the same voice heard on the walk home.

"I am not imagining this!" she boldly declared to the empty room. "I heard you. I know that you are here. Please identify yourself. And make yourself visible if you can. I prefer to see the person that I am speaking to." Having just been reminded how impatient she really was, Barbara continued her pattern by hoping that a response would be immediate. Her wish was accommodated.

"Presently, I am unable to produce a visible form. I apologize for this momentary shortcoming. It can be disconcerting for some individuals, but I believe you are one who will quickly adapt to the unusual nature of my present situation. My dear friend, you are correct in your assessment of my presence. I am here!"

"Please excuse me while I catch my breath." Barbara did just that! Inhaling deeply several times helped stabilize her emotions. Thoughts were racing through her head while she remained at a loss for words.

"Not to worry, Old Friend. Patience is one of my skill sets and I am happy to wait while you adapt to this unusual situation. Do you mind if I sit in the chair opposite to you? Perhaps, knowing my position in the room will facilitate your adjustment to my presence."

The question was simple and brilliant. It brought Barbara back into the present. "Oh, yes, please do make yourself at home." She pointed to the worn, comfy chair as she welcomed him to sit down. "As you probably know there are oodles of questions zooming about in my mind. You are really here, aren't you?" Without waiting for an answer, she asked another question. "I'm not going crazy, am I?"

"Ah! Easy questions! Yes, I am most definitely here, and no, you are not crazy. My friend, you are having another unusual experience, which you will be able to share with your Sister of Choice. And soon, many others will be hearing about your experiences, as will you be hearing theirs."

Barbara stared at the empty chair. Again, questions zipped about, but this time she was able to capture a few of them. "How do you know about my Sister of Choice? Were you at her place earlier when we were discussing my recent trip? You seem to be in the know. How come you've not made your presence known before?"

"I have been observing for quite some time, and because of this, I am aware of many matters in which you and your beloved friend are associated. Until now, observing and assisting from afar was satisfactory. Unfortunately, changes are on the horizon, therefore it is essential that we develop a more frequent means of connection and communication. As you experience now, we are communicating easily; however, it is necessary that all involved are highly skilled in this type of exchange. Practice will facilitate rapid advancement in our communication capabilities.

Each of you, dear friend, is here for a reason. Clarity of this is necessary. This means that you and the Sister of Choice have much work to do. I hope you will quickly remember who you really are. It is my pleasure to be working with you two once again."

"Goodness! Do you realize how many more questions just surfaced? Have you visited my friend as well? Do the two of you already have an established relationship? And what work are you talking about? Do you realize that I have a job?" A deep breath was taken before she attempted to speak again.

"My friend, you have always been one of many questions. Such a delight it is to be in your presence once again. I know that you prefer quick responses to your questions, but this time the answers will not come quickly. I came to deliver a message. The task has been done; the seed has been planted. Now, my friend, I invite you to ponder about what has transpired. Journal about this encounter please, and then, we will meet again."

"Before you leave, I have one more question to pose, please. You refer to me as friend, yet I do not recall who you are. So, who are you?"

"You have known me by many different names in many different places, and always, regardless of the time or the location, we have assisted one another in our work and play. We are most definitely Dear Old Friends.

Countless times have we addressed tasks of mutual interest and always we have called each other Friend. I hope and prefer that this will be true in our present engagement. I wish to call you Friend, my Old Friend, and hope that you will choose to call me Friend as well. I am most delighted and grateful to be in your presence again."

Barbara was overwhelmed by the gentle presence of this invisible individual. His words resonated within her. Even though she had no memories of the times they shared, she knew he spoke the truth about their relationship. Her heart was filled with tenderness and her inquisitive mind with curiosity. "Well," she spoke softly, "since our relationship is of long standing, you must know me very well. So you readily understand that I have many questions," she paused, looked out the window and chuckled at herself, "but this is not the time for my curious nature to take charge." I am deeply touched by your desire to call me Friend, and I will be honored to call you the same." She heard a quiet sigh come from the empty chair.

"I'm glad that you have come, Friend, and I look forward to working with you again. I assume we will be having more encounters soon."

"Yes, we will, my Friend. I too look forward to the adventures that are ahead of us. Your acceptance of my presence is most comforting. And now, I must take my leave of you. I wish you well, Old Friend, and hope the rest of your day brings you joy."

Barbara sat quietly wondering if her invisible friend had actually left. *How does one know? The guy is invisible! How do I know if he's here or not?* "Excuse me, Friend? Are you still here?"

No reply came. She waited. Practicing patience, she waited a bit longer. And then, she again stared at the vacant chair and asked, "Hey! Are you here?" No response was forthcoming.

"Okay! So, I've just had another unordinary experience. What do I do with this? I could call Sister and get some advice from her, but I've already taken up a lot of her time today. And who knows? Maybe the invisible guy is over at her place right now?" Barbara thoughts turned inward. *What would Sister say about this experience? She would probably encourage me to journal about it.* "That's a good plan, Sister! You're the best!" And with that said, she grabbed her journal and her wonderful Tibetan bell from their respective places of honor and began her ritual. The journal, accompanied by its special pen, was gently placed upon her lap. The bell was perfectly situated on the corner of the nearby lamp table. She took a deep breath, settled comfortably into her favorite chair, and then, reached over to ring the cherished bell. The melodious sound echoed throughout the room. Time passed by as she allowed her thoughts to materialize upon the pages of her journal.

*

A passage from
Beyond The Day of Tomorrow
A Seeker's Guide
(Chapter Three)

"At this time it is important to discuss another concept, which is essential to the seeking process. This concept is another reminder to all who have forgotten this along the path. The concept, critical to one's wellness, is the truth about failure. It does not exist! There is no such thing as failure.

Remember this one, please, for the idea of failure in all its various forms plagues this planet. We are too short or too tall, too fat or too thin, too black or too white, too religious or too not, too this or too that, etc., etc., etc. The point of all these comparisons is related to judgment, which purports failure. From the moment we are born, judgments regarding us are birthed. We are measured, weighed, poked and prodded to evaluate our vitals in comparison to other newborns. Perhaps we were the perfect baby, or more likely we were not, and then we grew up to be the perfect toddler, or more likely not, and then we started kinder care and immediately became a comparative subject with every other child present. From the moment of our arrival, we are judged, compared, and evaluated along every step of our path towards maturity. So, is there any wonder why we are a people ruled by and obsessed with the idea of failure?

Then, at some point along the way, you begin hearing about this journey that everyone is talking about and writing about, and you begin realizing that people have been exploring this journey phenomenon for ages, and now, you're just hearing about it. So you're already behind...there's no way you'll ever catch up, and even if you decide to pursue this journey, which guru do you listen to? There are oodles of them out there, each saying something, but darn if you know what they are talking about, but each one is very convincing, and if you're going to do this, you want to do it right and you want to do it fast, and you want to do it now, so you better make the right choice now, or else...you've failed!

And here we are. This life long process of instilling the belief in failure unfortunately also permeates our process of self-discovery at the most intimate level. Our journey within to find the true meaning of who we are, how we are, and why we are is contaminated by this concept of failure."

*

Being in my Sacred Space brought me great pleasure. No matter what time of day I entered into this special place, it seemed to welcome me as if I had arrived at just the right time. And today, I felt particularly certain that I had. Don't know why, but I felt expectant. Of what, I did not know, but it was an interesting feeling. I wondered what might happen during this visit to my Sacred Space.

Room preparations were quickly completed as they always were. The curtains were drawn and blinds were raised so that the sun could stream through the windows brightening the room as only the sun can do, while also casting the most fascinating shadows in unexpected places. The Tibetan bell was properly situated on its designated spot. The journal and the favorite fountain pen, recently filled of course, were at my disposal. The vanilla scented candle was ready to participate and my recently purchased swivel chair, still an item of great satisfaction, called to me. I settled in! Positioning the journal on my lap, I enjoyed a deep breath, closed my eyes, and immediately relaxed. The new chair was so comfortable! *Thank you for this new chair! It is a treasure! And thank you for this morning's adventure with Barb. How sweet it was being in her presence. She is a dear person...with great potential!*

"*And so are you!*" The voice, though unexpected, didn't startle me. I was accustomed to such visits and always welcomed whoever the passerby might be. My eyes instantly opened to see if there was a visible form accompanying the voice, and as is often the case with these visitors, there was not. This too, I was accustomed to.

"Welcome, my friend, please make yourself at home!" Pointing to the adjacent chair, I imagined in mind's eye that my guest had followed my invitation and sat down across from me. So I automatically directed my conversation to what I believed was an occupied space. "Have you travelled far?"

"Thank you for your hospitality. I am, as you imagined, directly across from you, and I am most grateful to be in your presence once again. In regard to your question, My Dear Old Friend, my travel was far, yet instantaneous, so the event was uneventful. As you know so well, travel from this perspective is, shall we say, easily managed.

You look well, my Friend!"

His compliment made me chuckle. "I am glad to hear that and wish I could say the same for you, but you have me at a disadvantage. So tell me. Are you well?" My guest enjoyed the humor and proclaimed his good health.

"Complicated health issues are of no concern for me when I am in this amorphous state. I am happy to report that all is well with me. However, my Dear Friend, I am here for reasons that involve complicated issues. I come to ask for your assistance."

"You know that I am always happy to serve. I assume we have worked together in the past. And that another situation now demands our attention."

"Your assumption is correct. A critical situation that demands immediate attention is unfolding upon the planet Earth. My words do not surprise you; however, many upon the planet still refuse to accept the truth of what is happening. Old Friend, the Earth's health is declining at an exceptionally rapid pace. She cannot continue without the assistance of those who reside upon her. Some nations and individuals are addressing her issues while others who deny the reality of her situation counteract the positive actions that are in motion. The inhumanity demonstrated astounds all members of the Existential Community. Greed and selfishness lead these misguided individuals towards a point of no return. Their foolishness affects every other life being on the planet including the Earth herself. As you know, my Dear Old Friend, it is the negative energy of the misguided individuals that is the heart of the Earth's crisis. Their cruel, insensitive ways sicken the Earth, and unless their manners change, she will fall into dormancy. She can no longer sustain herself without the positive energy that once existed among and within the peoples of this planet. Their ill will is destroying her vitality.

For millennia, humans have treated one another shamefully. They slaughter their own kind with the same disrespect and disregard as they do other life beings with whom they co-exist upon this incredible Life Being Earth. Their behavior creates a toxic energy so destructive that they infect everyone around them, and the one that incurs the greatest impact from this negativity is the Earth. She feels every insult, every injury, and every outrageous act that humans perpetrate against one another. She is the primary recipient of the negative energy of every action of unkindness that they manifest. The negative energy of the peoples of Earth is the primary toxic pollution that sickens the planet. This factor must be dealt with if the planet is to survive her declining spiral. This factor is one that is not being addressed by anyone at this time, and yet, it is the most important issue that humankind must face. For the sake of their continuance, this reality must be faced now.

My Friend, I know my words are difficult to hear, but you are one who understands the truth of this message. You are one who must speak the truth truthfully and you must do so quickly. The continuance of the human species depends upon their willingness to heal their ill will. If they refuse to participate in their own healing process, then their future will be limited. All in the Universe pray that the peoples of the Earth will choose to change their misguided ways.

Great goodness remains in the hearts of many, and because of this, there is reason for hope. But those who are in touch with the ways of goodness must step forward. They must take the lead. No longer can the energy of the misguided be the way of the peoples of Earth." The voice stopped and a faint sigh was heard. Invisibility complicates a conversation. One does not have the visual cues that we are so accustomed to. I did not know if my visitor was finished or merely taking a necessary pause before continuing. I chose to be patient.

"Thank you, my Friend, for your patience. As you can tell, we must commence our work with haste. Others around the globe are also receiving similar messages this day. You are not alone in this cumbersome project, but your attention to detail will facilitate a quick completion to the task before us. I also visited your Sister of Choice earlier. She will be a valuable assistant in this project. She is one of strength and humor. Admirable qualities!

There is much to do, my Friend. I am most grateful for your assistance. It was good to see you again."

"It is good to be in your presence as well. Although memories fail me, I sense the closeness of our connection and I look forward to working with you again. Before you leave, do you have any suggestions on how I might best prepare for our next meeting? I assume you will provide guidance."

"Indeed! The first step is to connect with the Sister of Choice. Please strategize who you might wish to join your efforts. A team will be needed. Please ponder this and create a list of possibilities. Let us meet again before invitations are extended. May I call on you tomorrow?"

"Of course," I replied.

*

A passage from
Beyond The Day of Tomorrow
A Seeker's Guide
(Chapter Three)

"My Dear Old Friends, let me again remind you. Failure does not exist! It is a concept born of the ego, not of Oneness, for in Oneness all experiences gained are honored equally. What may be judged from a human perspective as an experience with positive or negative qualities is in Oneness merely regarded as another opportunity for gaining more knowingness, which is always valued and cherished even if the acquiring experience was one of difficulty. Our realization and acceptance of all experiences as equally valuable lessens our susceptibility to self and other judgments.

The journey before you offers many mysteries and many opportunities for expansion, but the challenge most often addressed will be the one to persevere. It is not how you meet a challenge or why you choose to meet a particular challenge that is important. That you choose to continue is the significant factor.

Movement is the optimal function. The belief in failure stagnates the seeker and paralyzes movement. To practice failure offers no purpose other than to accentuate its failings."

*

3

The absence of his presence was stunningly felt. One moment we were engaged in conversation and then we were not. *Will I ever truly be at ease with the comings and goings of these wonderful visitors? Will I really ever accept that we are Dear Old Friends? What a lovely title! Dear Old Friends! It warms the hearts and fosters connection. Oh, Dear Friends, please do not listen to the ramblings of my mind. I am so grateful to be part of these unusual episodes, and still, they make me wonder. At times, as you well know, my mind drifts to doubts. Perhaps, in my own weird way this is my path to affirmation about my belief in these experiences. With all that I am, I know these encounters are real and that the interactions shared are genuine. I know this! I trust this! And I so enjoy participating in these precious experiences; each one has been a privilege!*

"Well perhaps, I should give Barbara a call. I imagine she is beside herself at this point." The peculiar saying made me smile. "Wonder who originated that saying? And what was his or her initial intention when it was said?" Not surprisingly, my phone started vibrating in my vest pocket. I laughed out loud while trying to dislodge the device, which clearly didn't want to come out from its hiding place.

"Hey You! Have you had an interesting encounter this afternoon?" My friend could not contain herself. Completely understandable under the circumstances.

"Yes! And I assume you have as well, so what should we do? Your place or mine?" Barb was an action-oriented type of person, and as a result, a very highly productive individual. Her energy demanded attention, which gave me an idea.

"Barb, knowing you as I do, I feel certain you have already done this, but let me ask anyway. Have you recorded your experience in your journal yet?" She responded immediately as if she was intuiting my thoughts.

"I have! But there are so many unknowns whirling around in my mind, and I suspect you have more information about what's going on than I do at this point, so I would love to share our stories if possible.

Are you up for that?" Needing to deliberate for a moment raised the impatience trigger for my friend.

"Please forgive me, Barb, but I actually haven't had a chance to journal yet and I need to jot down a few notes. It will only take a few minutes. Can you burn some energy off by walking around the block a couple of extra times? I too would like to discuss what has happened, but I need just a few minutes to conclude my thoughts." Barbara understood and respected by request. She suggested that we delay getting together for an hour, but was happily relieved when she heard that was not necessary. "Give me fifteen minutes. I'll see you then!"

*

A passage from
Beyond The Day of Tomorrow
A Seeker's Guide
(Chapter Four)

"As discussed earlier, it is time for all to remember that the Gift of Free Will is a primary factor in the unfolding of our journeys. It is true that we are all here for a reason. You know this. You feel it deep within you, and at times it speaks so loudly to you that it feels as if you ache from its presence. This ache is your signal, Old Friend. Embrace it! Invite it to share its knowingness with you, for this ache is like an Old Friend, and this Old Friend is here to remind you of something you have always known, but has slipped your memory."

*

"Welcome! It's good to see you again!" We hugged as if we hadn't seen each other for years rather than a couple of hours. "Shall we convene in the kitchen again?" We both agreed that a cup of tea was needed.

"Sister, have you had enough time with your journaling?" She was relieved when I gave her a thumb's up. "Thank goodness! I so want to talk with you about what happened, but first you must share your experience with me. I insist!" Her command, accompanied with humorous facial expressions and body posturing, made me laughed.

"Oh my! You are such a rascal!" Barb gathered the cups and saucers

40

as I managed the kettle. "Please sit down, dear, and tell me why you want me to go first. I'm glad to do so, but why are you so insistent." Her reaction differed from her usual quick fashion; she appeared to be processing some internal struggle.

"Well, the truth is, I'm somewhat embarrassed about taking more of your time today. I know you are capable of setting limits, but I also know how giving you are. And I just don't want to take advantage of your time. After all, you do have a life."

"Yep, I do! And I appreciate your efforts to honor that, but it seems that our lives have just become much more intertwined than before. So, please trust me to manage my affairs, and I will trust you to honor yours. You know that you are always welcome here, but if something or someone else is demanding my attention, I promise you that I will inform you of this. And I expect the same from you. Agreed?" Our high five gesture confirmed we were on the same page.

"Ordinarily, Barb, I would accept your invitation to take the lead; however, in this situation, your story must be related first. Trust me on this, please." And she did! As she shared her story, I was captivated. Her experience was curious, rich, and left her with many questions, some of which I could answer, but most were beyond my scope of awareness. The manner in which she managed the situation was impressive, as was the manner of the visitor. It was fascinating to see how he orchestrated tasks.

"Dear friend, you've had another remarkable experience! Thank you for sharing your story, and may I also say that you handled yourself very well. I think you are becoming a pro at dealing with unusual events."

"Thank you, that's reassuring to hear. As you might imagine, Sister, I felt totally incompetent in the moment. It was very confusing engaging with an invisible being. There are no visible cues to work with, as you well know. I never imagined it would be so odd, but it was. Hopefully, my next experience will be less intimidating." She paused briefly and then reengaged. "Actually, I enjoyed the whole experience immensely, but next time, it would be great if I were more at ease. He seemed so comfortable with me. I would like to show him the same courtesy." Another brief moment of silence followed this statement of kindness and then she added, "This is a day that will never be forgotten. I am so grateful to be alive. And I cannot wait to see what happens next."

*

A passage from
Beyond The Day of Tomorrow
A Seeker's Guide
(Chapter Four)

"Deep within is an awareness that we are here for a reason, but sometimes our outward lives become so busy, so hectic that the inward life is lost in the pandemonium we call living.

What does it mean, 'We are here for a reason?' What is this ache supposed to tell me? And why is this so elusive anyway? If I'm here for a reason, just bottom-line it for me. Send me an email! Enough of this 'I'm here for a reason' already. Sound familiar? If you are like me, you have said similar phrases repeatedly, but in the heat of the moment, they were a bit more flowery! This journey stuff can be incredibly frustrating, and I can assure you that in the privacy of my own mind, I do not call it stuff.

One minute, you think you've got it, the next minute, you're clueless, and the next minute, you're feeling the ache all over again. No matter how hard you try to find it or how hard you try to ignore it, it exists. The ache, the awareness of the ache, and the uncomfortable not knowing what the ache means, exists. You cannot deny it. As much as you would like to and as much as you have tried, you cannot deny the ache. No more than you could deny an Old Friend in need, can you deny this ache, because this ache is indeed an Old Friend. An Old Friend, here to remind you as long ago agreed that there was a reason for which you came and there was a purpose to this coming. And as all who come can attest, once you arrive, you forget the purpose and the reason for coming.

Thus, the purpose of the ache! The reason for the ache is to serve as a reminder. It is not meant to be the answer to your reason for being here, but merely a reminder that you are here for a reason and that it is time to begin your search for the reason why you are here. And thus, the purpose of the ache is served by motivating you to take action and to begin your journey. As an Old Friend would do, the Old Friend Ache nudges you forward to pursue your destiny and to find answers to your questions of why you are here, and once you begin this journey of self-discovery, the Gift of Free Will begins to function."

*

"So, tell me Sister," my friend directed the conversation towards me, "when did our invisible friend visit you? Before or after me?"

"After," came my reply. "I know this because he mentioned his time with you. He was most grateful that you readily opened to his presence. Isn't it wonderful to meet someone with whom you have had many lifetimes? I find it absolutely fascinating, and selfishly wish that all that was known before could instantaneously be remembered. What a trip that would be!" My imagination became energized, and was eager to pursue infinite options, but fortunately, I was able to still its excursions.

"It seems we have been asked to join forces on an urgent project. This project concerns the Earth's declining health, which has undoubtedly taken a rapid downward swing. The situation is critical. What he explained to me, and which was amazingly articulated, is the reality that humankind is ultimately the reason for the Earth's decline, and if she is to continue as we now know her, we must change our ways. We, meaning all of us, are the cause of her poor health, and we must accept responsibility for correcting this terrible situation. Obviously, he said more, but that was the most succinct summary I could come up with." I was in need of deep breath, and so was my friend. The act symbolized for me that we were committing ourselves to the task ahead. Barb released a loud sigh before speaking.

"Oh my gosh! Did he tell you what we are supposed to do? This is an unbelievably huge task! Where do we begin? And exactly what are we to do? " She was poised on the end of her chair. Barb wanted answers. I shared her sense of urgency. We both took deep breaths together again.

"Well, let me also share the positive news that he relayed. We are not alone in this project!

He said that people all across the globe were also being informed of the truth about the Earth's crisis. And he also said that humankind basically are people of goodness and that we are capable of making the necessary changes. So that's good!" Barb nodded in agreement and asked if the visitor provided any specific instructions.

"Yes, he did. He said that we were going to need a team and

encouraged us to give this some thought. He would like for us to create a list of folks that might be interested in this project. And he also said that the three of us should convene tomorrow. Hopefully, we will both be able to come up with some names before then." My friend looked puzzled.

"How can we devise a list when we don't really know what the project is? It's difficult to come up with names for a project that still remains unknown. Did he give you any more information?" I wondered how much our visitor shared with Barb. My thoughts were abruptly interrupted by my wonderful intuitive friend.

"Sister, it seems obvious that you received more information about this project than I did. So, bring me up to speed, okay?"

"Perhaps, I did, Barb. As you well know, the information I just shared was not news to either of us. We talk about the Earth's decline all the time, and often express our concerns about people's lack of interest. Unfortunately, it just doesn't seem that people are tracking the seriousness of her situation. Our Friend did indeed provide more specific details about the Earth's condition that are not being discussed. At least I'm not aware of this. He told me that the primary cause of the Earth's ill health is the ill will of humans. Our negativity is so toxic that we are killing her. Let me try to quote one of his statements because it was stunning. He said that the Earth feels every insult, every injury, and every outrageous act that humankind perpetrates. Can you imagine this? No wonder she is so ill! This is heartbreaking!" My emotions surfaced. Barb and I both took more deep breaths as tears trickled down our cheeks. I knew we were taking the first step into our upcoming project.

"And he also said that the Earth will fall into dormancy if we don't change our ways. All the actions that are already being addressed around the globe will not correct the damage that has been done and continues to be done by humankind. The actions being taken are absolutely necessary and must continue to expand, but the negative energy that we personally produce every day is the main reason for her decline. We've got to take responsibility for this! Each and every one of us must address our ill will and we must change. This is definitely going to be an interesting project, and as I speak of this, various ideas are entering my mind." A smile came to my face, as if an 'aha' moment had occurred.

"Barb, numerous names are coming to mind! We have mutual friends who will be very interested in helping. And I'm sure more names will

44

come to us when we give more thought to this. I'm getting very excited about this opportunity."

*

A passage from
Beyond The Day of Tomorrow
A Seeker's Guide
(Chapter Five)

"As with every question asked, answers abound. So many options are available that it is mind-boggling to discern which answer is the appropriate answer for any given question. And then the realization hits you.

With all these options and all the possibilities available, there is a strong probability that there may be more than one answer to the question.

At that moment, you know more than you knew before. Until that point of awakening, you were convinced there was only one answer to your reason for being and now, in a flash of intuitive brilliance, you realize there is much more to all this than just one answer, and in this fleeting moment of awareness, you are at rest."

*

4

"Hello, dear friend! Have I called too early?" My thoughts rationalized my actions. *Of course, Barb would be up. We're both early risers; just one of the many similarities that we share.* Much to my surprise, I found myself in an embarrassing situation. The voice on the other end of the line was definitely not one that was ready to face the day.

"Oh Sister, I must admit you caught me sleeping in this morning. Too many thoughts running through this mind of mine! I'm not even sure when I finally fell asleep. But not to worry, it sounds like you are up and about! And I think you have a plan! So out with it! Tell me everything!" Barb's resilience was amazing. She moved from drowsy headed to peak alertness in seconds. I apologized for the early call, but she was already beyond that phase and encouraged me to continue. "I can tell you've got something cooking. So let's talk about it. I'm headed for the kitchen now for my daily caffeine fix."

"You're amazing! And accurate as always! But before I launch into my spiel, update me please. You must realize that in all the years we've known each other, I've never known you to sleep in. Was your evening okay?" I suspected the happenings from yesterday kept my friend up most of the night. It was a full day that naturally would invite a great deal of rumination. My own excitement was difficult to quiet and required numerous attempts before I finally fell asleep.

"My excitement was high as well," her response to my unspoken thoughts didn't surprise me. Her skills were rapidly expanding. "Until it wasn't!" This response definitely got my attention.

"Please tell me more, Barb."

"Oh dear," her words accompanied a loud and long sigh. "I'm ashamed to share this with you, Sister, but it is necessary. This project is exciting—fascinating actually. And I want to participate! But as I wondered about it, my minded started speculating about what might be necessary, which led me down paths of doubts and insecurities, and as a result, I found myself reluctant to invite anyone into our confidence. The process unfolded smoothly and quickly, as the mind is so capable of managing. One moment there was excitement and in the next moment, I found myself doubting me and underestimating my friends. Truth is, my friend, at that point I didn't trust my friends to be able to handle this. How crazy is that? You and I are blessed with the most wonderful group of friends. I know this and I am so grateful for these incredible relationships that have developed over the years. We have a Family of Friends!" I nodded in agreement.

"Yes, we really are most fortunate. So what happened between the initial moment of openness and the next moment when you found yourself shutting down?" Her answer was immediate and adamant.

"It was fear!" The words expelled from her mouth. The phone, magnifying her heavy breathing, made me realize the level of shame that she was experiencing. I wanted to reassure my friend, but believed it would interrupt her rhythm, so I reluctantly remained silent. "The ridiculous notions that came up were just that...ridiculous! I wish I had a videotape of what my mind so rapidly created. Nonsense!" She said loudly. "Pure nonsense! And this led me back to what our visitor shared with you. Ill will! Humankind's ill will is the major factor in the Earth's decline. Sister, what I experienced last night was my own ill will. In a matter of seconds, I went from excitement to despair because of the ridiculous scenarios that were produced by my fear. I was afraid of being judged by others and then found myself judging others for judging me. I feared our friends would discount the information we were provided and ridicule us for believing it. And it was worse than that. I feared we would lose people's respect. First, I feared this. Then I got angry about it. And then I fell into a deep slump.

I'm not sure how long this absurd scenario actually took, but the replays went on for what seemed an endless about of time. I would quiet myself and think it was under control and then another rerun would rush through my mind. The repetition itself was self-abusive, and its tenacity was astonishing. This episode of mindless ill will truly wore me out.

At one point, I realized the importance of this experience. I witnessed first hand what people do in the confines of their minds without even realizing it is happening. Perhaps this statement is incorrect, but I don't believe it is. I am not the only person that does it. And I know this happens a lot of times without my awareness, but it has a negative effect nonetheless. When I think of all the negative energy that I generated last night, it makes me understand the fullness of what our friend related to you. This is just one example of what he was talking about, but can you imagine the other offenses that he intends us to correct. We are a civilization of anger, hatred, and violence. It flourishes! And it feeds upon itself! That was the other thing that was so obvious last night, Sister. Even though I didn't want to participate in this ludicrous process, my mind did. It was captivated by the negative energy and each time the tale repeated itself, the mind was satisfied. This is a cycle that must be addressed.

So that's what happened, Sister! I'm ashamed to admit this, but it is true. And at the same time, I am extremely grateful for the information gained. What I learned last night about my mind and about myself is life changing. This is important information that needs to be talked about." A deep sigh came through the phone.

"Dear, dear friend, I am honored that you shared this with me and deeply grateful. What a powerful piece of work you achieved last night. And if you don't mind, Barb, I'm going to use your experience as a teaching tool for a moment. First, let me say that I understand your feelings of shame and embarrassment about sharing this story. I have had similar reactions to my own mind games and the word you used is on the mark. They are tenacious! And you are also correct about their abundance. I truly believe this happens with everyone. For some it may be more frequent than others, but the mind does have a mind of its own, and that mind will do what it wants to do unless someone takes it to task. I think the biggest factor, which you already noted, is the reality that few people are aware of the complexity of their thoughts. And they certainly don't know about the energetic impact these thoughts have on self and others.

But look what has happened here! Because we received new information yesterday from our friend about the ill will of humankind and its effect upon the planet, you were able to bear witness to the process in motion during your ruminations last night. And you did a phenomenal job, Barb. I am so grateful to you and for your willingness to talk about this. Because you did, I have been able to clarify my thoughts about this elusive process. When we talk about similar experiences with our friends and others, they too will have greater understanding about the nonsense the mind can create and the dreadful effects it can generate.

Barb, you just added another dimension to the work that we must address."

*

A passage from
Beyond The Day of Tomorrow
A Seeker's Guide
(Chapter Five)

"Then, just as quickly as you experienced the awakening and the calming awareness that there are many reasons for your being, you abruptly return to the ache of not knowing your reason for being here.

This process of unknowing, followed by an awakening, resulting in an awareness, which then quickly returns to a state of unknowing is the ongoing process of the journey. Know it as such and begin to embrace its cyclical nature, for it is as it is. How you choose to accept this evolving process is, of course, your choice because remember, you possess the Gift of Free Will. Choose the process as tedious and monotonous and it will be so, or choose the process to be alluring, mysterious, and exciting, and this will be so. Your choice! Choose wisely, Old Friend."

*

"Sister, you have the most remarkable way of turning every situation into a positive experience. And I always reap the benefit of this skill you are gifted with. Thank you for sharing that perspective as well as your own experience with these tedious encounters. It is comforting to know that I am not alone in this cycle of diminishment. Whew! The benefit of the lesson, as I said before, was life changing, but that was a class that I would prefer not to take again.

So, now that you are thoroughly updated with my affairs, it's your turn. Tell me everything." Barbara's experience was not easy to let go of, because it brought up so many similar but different experiences of my own. Even now, those past experiences tantalize the mind that has a mind of its own, and that part of me would gladly jump in and relive any old episode that was readily available. I witnessed the process, made a mental note of it, and chose to refrain from traveling that misguided path again. I acknowledged to my friend what was just internally experienced and told her of my decision.

"This is a very old habit which will demand our attention, but our conversation just now will keep us alert to the tenacity of this behavior. We will need to be vigilant, Barb. But we are capable of creating new habits. That's very good news!" She agreed and made mention of the smile adorning my face.

"How do you know that I'm smiling? Are you now enjoying existential sight?" We both laughed and she encouraged me to continue. The fact that she did not answer my question left me wondering.

"Okay, dear one, my evening was different from yours. I think my mind wanted to go in a similar direction as yours, but for whatever reason, I was able to resist. Instead, I forced myself to think about opportunities of self-discovery regarding this topic of humankind's ill will. And it was much more tantalizing than a trip down into despair. I know that path all too well, and thank goodness, I was able to escape it last night. Don't get me wrong, Barb, fears did arise, but I was able to sidestep them.

I think the appearance of our friend was so compelling that the commitment he requested overrode any other options. The truth he spoke resonated within me and the hopefulness expressed gave me hope as well. So thankfully, I was able to maintain focus. The more I thought about my own ill will and how it plays out and how it must be affecting the Earth, the more determined I became to learn everything about this, so that I can change my ways, and hopefully help others to reconsider their own behaviors.

One of the things that became abundantly clear is this is not a solo project. As he said, we need a team. People need support while doing their own work, and then, those who feel called to do so will also need help to bring this message forward to the public. This is not a project for the few; it is an essential movement that demands massive participation. People must make changes. And so must nations and governments. We are talking about changing the personal and interpersonal dynamics of a civilization." The magnitude of this project humbled me, and as always a deep breath was necessary. *Thank goodness for that meditation class that I took years ago. The positive effect of a deep breath never ceases to amaze me.* I could hear my friend joining in the process. We were becoming more and more in sync.

"So these thoughts led me down the trail of sharing these new adventures with others. And I thought about how naturally the process has unfolded between you and me. What a remarkable gift this has been! No coincidence that we were invited to do this together. So, the simpatico relationship that we share guided me to other relationships that have similar intimacy. And then the faces just started popping up in my mind. The Andersons are a couple that we have both known and loved for years. I would love to talk with them about this topic. I think it would be fascinating, and I also think they would be on board with this commitment.

Then Sally and Dave Moore came to mind. You know how deeply involved they are in environmental issues. I think this ill will issue will be very intriguing to them. As I thought of these two couples, I realized how comfortable it would be to discuss the issues with them. We have shared wonderful intimate conversations over the years. I would feel totally safe being vulnerable with them.

Other faces appeared before me as well, which brought up the subject of how many team members we need to start with. I'm still uncertain about this and would like to hear your perspective about that." Barb's silence surprised me. I wondered if our phone conversation had overreached its welcome. The hour was still early and I had awakened her from a sound sleep.

"Oh, don't worry about me, Sister, I'm fine. I'm just mulling over your thoughts, and realizing how lucky I am to be your Sister of Choice. You are a remarkable woman. And please don't roll your eyes at me." My friend giggled quietly knowing full well that she had caught me in action.

"Actually, you are really impressive. Your success at outwitting the mind leaves me very hopeful. It truly is manageable, isn't it?" A victorious affirmation came through the phone, which brought another smile to my face. It wasn't difficult imagining Barb's antics. High fives, thumbs up, and her always appreciated happy dance! She was a character—and a dear, dear friend.

"Sister, the Andersons and the Moores will be wonderful additions to the team. I was also thinking about Mark and Faye Goodman as possibilities. We've all been hanging out together for a very long time and we have enjoyed many heartfelt conversations. Including discussions about the misinformation about climate change. The Earth's situation is a concern for all of us, so it just makes sense that we put these folks on the invitation list. And for me, eight seems like a good number to start with. Because of our comfort level with one another, we may be able to expand our numbers quickly, but perhaps, our visitor will have more insights about that." Barbara appeared to be finished, so I jumped in again.

"You know, I just realized that telephone conversations are very similar to engaging with our invisible friend. No facial cues! One must presume what the other person is thinking, and then, hope that your assumptions are correct." We both agreed that we preferred face-to-face interactions.

"So, are we in agreement regarding the initial invitation list?" Barb inquired. I indicated that the Goodmans were also on my list and agreed that eight was a suitable size group. "Is there more that we should think about before our meeting with our friend today?"

"Yes, I think there is, and probably the most significant factor deals with our own commitment to the project. Barb, I believe at some point we will be very involved with other folks. This is going to be a public matter. So, for me this means I must have clarity about my own commitment. This isn't just another activity to participate in; this is a lifetime commitment to being a caregiver for another Life Being. I'm absolutely certain that I feel called to do this, but as yet, I don't feel certain how I wish to articulate this to others.

My mind tends to drift in the direction of administrative aspects of the project. This is important as well and we will need to face this soon, but until we have more information, I think working on details is premature. I certainly have fantasies about what maybe coming, but that's all they are at this point. Just fantasies! This is one of those times when I need to trust myself. My administrative and organizational skills are keen, and I can cool my jets now, knowing full well that those instincts will kick in rapidly when the necessary information is available. What I anticipate at this time is that we will be distributors of information. We will educate as best we can those who are willing to listen. I imagine there will be written communication, maybe even a book or more, and there will probably be workshops with lots of interactions among the participants. Those are some of my thoughts, but I believe we will discover more ideas and gain greater clarity about what we need to do when we actually initiate our own group. We will learn from one another and this will prepare us to meet the public."

"Sister, it sounds as if we will be doing outreach work. I'm comfortable with that. And it makes sense. How else will people create the personal changes that are called for unless they are informed? This sounds right to me. Do you have any idea when we will be meeting today?" Barb's energy was percolating. I could tell she was reaching action mode.

"When can you come by? I have time between one and three o'clock. Will that work for you?" We agreed upon 1:30 pm. The time nicely suited both of our schedules. And then we parted company, each with our own tasks to address.

*

A passage from
Beyond The Day of Tomorrow
A Seeker's Guide
(Chapter Six)

"This process, called the journey, is indeed mysterious in nature, but is it not the mystery of the unknown, which calls to us from deep within the ache?

What many regard as frustrating, unsettling, and elusive is actually what piques our curiosity and provides interest in continuing the pursuit. Without mystery, we would become bored, without curiosity, there would be no driving force, without the calling, we would not recognize the ache as the Dear Old Friend beckoning to us to remember that we are here for a reason."

*

5

The knock at the front door came just at the right time. My paperwork was done and I was ready for another visit with my dear friend. Walking to the front door brought a smile to my face, which happened frequently when I was with Barbara. She was such a dear friend. Bright, intelligent, inquisitive, gifted with remarkable skills, and one of the most fun loving people I've ever known. One never knew what Barb might be up to at any given time. She so often surprised me with her playful tricks that I was always on guard for the next unexpected, eye-opening event to occur. As I approached the door the thought occurred to me that she might be up to something at this very moment, but I dismissed the idea. *Surely, she would not do this today. We were about to meet an invisible friend to discuss an extremely important project. Surely she would not act out at a moment like this.* I was wrong. There stood my friend, at least I thought it was my friend, hidden beneath a white sheet. As I stood there with my mouth open, the individual turned around presumably to face me. Pinned to the center of this shapeless form was a small, subtle sign that one could barely read. Leaning in closer for a better view, the words became legible. "I can see you! Can you see me?" And it was signed, The Invisible Visitor.

"You rascal! Get in here right this minute. Did you walk over here in that ghost suit?" My attempt to sound firm fell flat. Laughter burst out of me. "You are such a nut! Are you going to wear that for our guest?" As my friend removed her so-called costume, we both laughed until our sides ached. She was such a delight.

"Great fun you bring to our meeting!" declared a voice from out of nowhere.

"Oh gosh!" gasped Barb. Her face turned several shades of red. It was apparent that my fun loving friend was not ready to communicate, so I took the lead.

"Thank you for coming, Old Friend. As you can see, my Sister of Choice is one who loves to play pranks. She is delightful, is she not?" My words were sincere. I admired Barbara's lust for life and the joy that she brought to every situation. She is indeed a delight to be around.

"I am most grateful to meet with both of you again, and pleased that the meeting begins in lightheartedness, for I fear the content of our meeting will be laden with difficult information to hear. I trust you are able to handle this discussion." Barb and I both acknowledged that we were ready to discuss the specifics of the project that was proposed the day before.

"My friends, shall we relocate to my Sacred Space? It is more comfortable than standing here by the front door. I led the way. Not knowing where our invisible guest was, it was easier to simply take the lead. A third chair was situated across from the other two that were permanently located in their present positions. I took my usual place and invited Barb to take the one to my right and invited our friend to take the remaining chair. "Does this suit everyone? Are you both comfortable?" My friend nodded her head and reassured me that she was fine.

"This is a most suitable space for us to join together. Thank you for hosting our gathering. My friends, may I take the lead?" We both indicated that we hoped he would do so. And he did.

"Please join me, my Dear Old Friends, for a moment of silence for our Beloved Friend Earth. Breathe deeply please, and allow your heart to open to hers. Let the Mother know that you are here on her behalf. In silence be!" Time was lost as we sat in the silence. I thought hours had passed, but presumed my perception was distorted. I wondered if Barb's impression was similar to mine, but it really didn't matter. What was, simply was, and the amount of time that was expended was irrelevant. In due course, my thoughts stopped invading my silence and I fell silent. I simply was. Where I was, I did not know, nor did it matter. I simply was.

With each breath that I took, I felt another's breath beside me until eventually the breath beside me was within me, and I was One with the breath of the other. We breathed together. We existed together. We were One with the Other... and yet, there was more. And we were One with the More as well. I was. We were. And we all were One. Greater peace have I never experienced. Time escaped me, as I existed in the existence of Oneness.

"Dear Friends, please take another deep breath before you return to the present." And this we did. And then, Barb and I opened our eyes and found our invisible friend had acquired a form. He bowed and looked

lovingly upon both of us. *"How delightful it is to be seen! I am so grateful for this opportunity to be with you."*

*

A passage from
Beyond The Day of Tomorrow
A Seeker's Guide
(Chapter Seven)

"Now, perhaps it is time for another gentle reminder. Long ago, we all decided to participate in this journey called life. If this surprises you, perhaps you are not intended to continue reading A Seeker's Guide, but I suspect if you are reading this type of book, then this notion is of no surprise to you at all.

However, let me affirm you. If you are not resonating with this book, trust that reaction within you and know that for a purposeful reason A Seeker's Guide is not your path at this moment. Accept this as your Truth and honor that Truth.

As with all momentary guides we must learn to discern when we are to embrace them and when we are to release them. A Seeker's Guide is just that...a momentary guide, which you can choose to access or not.

For those of you, who choose to remain on this path a while longer, let us continue. Indeed it is true, long ago we all made decisions to become involved in this serial episodic journey called life. What we forgot along the way was that it is never-ending and that in fact, life is eternal. Well, my Friends, that was a rather significant factor to forget, for without that detail, our perspective of the process is hampered.

Is it any wonder why we take life so seriously when we function from the perspective that in a mere few years it will all be over? Is it any wonder why we get so frantic about our calling and our ache, when we believe we are here for a reason and we only have a brief finite time to figure it all out, as well as, accomplish whatever it is we are meant to achieve?

Is it any wonder we are all so confused? Well, perhaps it is time to remember our reminder. We all chose to participate in life, and we all knew that life is eternal. My Dear Old Friends, remember this and accept it as Truth, for it makes the journey so much more pleasant."

*

Barbara was unable to contain herself. "You're here! In the flesh! Well, not in the flesh, but we can see you. You can see him, can't you Sister? This isn't a trick, is it? I really am seeing you, right?" Our guest burst into laughter and I could not help but join him.

"*Yes, you are truly seeing me,*" he laughed again, "*and I am most pleased to be seen. Thank you for witnessing my appearance, my dear friends. It is such a gift to be seen.*" I understood Barb's reaction to our visitor's visual presence and shared her delight. Even though this was not my first time to witness such an event, this occurrence was as powerful and as mesmerizing as the first. I wondered what it must be like to be invisible, to be unseen. And I realized that I had never put myself in the place of those who cannot be seen. The glee demonstrated by our mysterious friend gave me a glimpse of what being invisible must be like. I felt for him. And I also felt for all those visible beings on our planet that are also not seen, not noticed. My thoughts took me to many places. *What must it be like to exist, but not be seen? Plants and wildlife that are taken for granted! Sea creatures that are rarely noticed except on our dinner plates! Insects that are crushed beneath our feet without concern or remorse! And what of our own kind? Those who are marginalized in all the insidious ways in which it is done, and ultimately treated as if they do not exist! What of those invisible ones?*

"*My dear friend, your heart bleeds for the unseen. I am grateful that you mourn this most unfortunate circumstance, for it is most unpleasant to live as if you do not exist. Sadly, most who offend in this way are completely unaware of their offense. Their lack of awareness for others with whom they co-exist is one of the significant problems occurring on this beautiful planet. Suffice it to say, all life beings prefer to be noticed and respected.*"

"Thank you for coming, my friend, and also for expending the energy necessary to be visible. I understand this is not an easy feat. So thank you again for the effort made. It is a pleasure to be in your company and to have the privilege of seeing you.

"You traveled far in your quiet time, my friend. Do you wish to speak of this?" The invitation took me back to the meditation just experienced, which now seemed ages ago.

"Goodness, thank you for bringing that back to mind." Our friend actually put my mind in a whirl. Only a few minutes had passed since his arrival, and yet, so much had already happened. *How can this be?* "My friend, it seems that time has been altered since you appeared. I am aware that you have been here for a very brief time, but my experience has already been expansive. Can you explain this to me?"

"Yes, please do!" added Barbara. "I am having a similar experience and would love to learn more about this if possible." It was comforting to hear that Barb was having her own experiences. One prefers not to be alone in these unusual experiences. Our friend just smiled. He appeared to be thinking or possibly listening to another. My curiosity was running away with itself.

"Indeed, time is known for its elusiveness. It comes and goes in the most delightful ways. And those who live in time find its ways most curious and mysterious. There is a phrase often used by people of your realm that expresses the confusion as well as it can be done. 'Time stood still.' It is true that time does appear to stand still at times for those who live in the existence of time; however, those who do not live in the existence of time do not experience it in that manner. For these, time is irrelevant. It simply does not exist." Barbara and I sat still, not unlike the time when we both felt we had lost time. His discourse was exceptional, but left one wondering. Barb spoke first.

"Okay! I wish I could say that I understood what was just said. But I can't. I'm still confused." She turned to me for reassurance, but I was as confused as she was.

"Old Friend, your understanding of the concept of time undoubtedly is far beyond us at this point in time, but I appreciate what was said, even if it was as mysterious as time itself. And perhaps that is your point. Time is mysterious."

"Yes, my friends, time is mysterious. Since time entered into existence, it has delighted all in existence with its comings and goings. It is accurate to say that sometimes time is more confusing than other times. But do not despair, for you are not alone in your confusion about time."

"Well, that's comforting," sighed my fun loving friend. She sat quietly for a very brief moment before her energy could no longer be contained. "Since time is so complicated, maybe it's just best that we move onto another topic. We have gathered here for a reason. So shall we focus on the topic now and can we begin with specifics? Exactly what does this project entail? We need more information before we can move forward." I tried to hide the smile that so wanted to express itself. My dear friend was a true taskmaster and I suspected our Old Friend was as well. I looked forward to working with both of them.

"Your energy is most exhilarating! We are definitely gathered here for a reason. I assume our mutual friend has apprised you of the mission we are undertaking. To speak bluntly, the Earth is in crisis and action must be taken. The negative energy created by humankind can no longer be endured. She cannot continue to combat the incessant negativity produced every minute of every day. Her health is severely compromised and time is quickly reaching a point of no return.

There is only one solution to this tragic situation. All of humankind must change their ways." My mind immediately responded to this discourse with a list of alternatives that it believed were possibilities for handling this situation. Yes, buts, and many maybes filled my head. I wondered if Barb was having a similar reaction.

"Yes, I am," she replied, "and we must reel our minds in." She turned to face our visitor. "My Friend, I am so grateful you are here. We need you! My heart resonates with your words and I am deeply saddened. What you speak is the truth. I truly believe you and I trust you are here to help us. Thank goodness, because we need your help. When you said there is only one solution to the problem, my mind immediate reacted to that supposition. And," she continued as she looked my way, "my Sister had a reaction as well. I think we, meaning humans, are just made this way. Perhaps, it is better to say that we have evolved to believe that we have an answer for everything and that our answer is better than any others. I suspect that you and Your Kind have been attempting to assist the Earth for a very long time. And every time you make a step forward, we do something to counteract your actions and you find yourselves back on square one again.

Our reaction to climate change is evidence of our resolve to remain in ignorance. Scientific data is ignored and devalued. Advances made by those who are fighting for change are scoffed at and interfered with by foolish, greedy adversaries who are selfishly committed to their own pocketbooks. Young people who are begging adults to take action are openly mocked and shamed rather than applauded for their courage and commitment to the planet. We are in serious trouble here and we need all the help we can get. Please tell us more. Tell us how we can help."

*

A passage from
Beyond The Day of Tomorrow
A Seeker's Guide
(Chapter Eight)

"If you choose to accept this reminder as one of your Truths, then your outlook for the road ahead becomes much more relaxed and forgiving. No need will there be to hurry or to worry about all of life's concerns, for the experience at the moment will simply be the experience you are meant to be experiencing at any given point in time. This awareness, this acceptance allows one to fully embrace the present experience rather than worrying about a future experience yet to be encountered. So often, in our quest to find our answers, we look forever forward, thus overlooking that which lies before us. How will we ever find our answers if we are unwilling to experience the experience, which is unfolding directly ahead?

In the world of psychotherapy, therapists frequently remind their clients to be in the present. Expand that notion to eternal life and you can better grasp the significance of being present in the moment. If you wish to live life to the fullest, you must be present for the life experience. That which you seek lies before you each moment of each day. If you focus only on tomorrow, then what of today? What lessons will you miss? What answers will be overlooked if before the day of tomorrow, you choose not to be present?"

*

"I am most grateful for your trust, Old Friend. And you are correct, we have been attempting to assist the Earth for a very long time. Our progress has not reached the goals that were desired and necessary. For reasons most complex, humankind's fears have grown disproportionately

as opposed to their need for peace of mind. Typically, as a civilization matures so too does their understanding of the significance of peaceable ways. This unfortunately has not been the case for most of the human residents of the Earth. With increased fear has come increased violence, leading to more fear, more distrust, and more violence. The cycle of disruption has gained in its velocity creating more devastation than is imaginable. The hearts of all in existence are in despair over this unbelievable tragedy." A deep breath was heard from our Friend. His eyes closed as if in mourning and Barbara and I immediately joined him. Time passed in its mysterious way, which was more easily accepted this time than before. At some point, a voice was heard from within me. '*Wellness to the Earth.*' Uncertain if the words were a prayer or a greeting, I simply repeated the phrase as if it were my own. It was comforting. Where the words came from was not known. Did I overhear the words of our Friend or were they of Barb's creation, or did they come from another? I did not know, but it didn't matter. I simply knew the words were significant. *Wellness to the Earth!* A greeting, a prayer, a mantra, an intention! *All of the above,* I thought to myself. Our Friend eventually opened his eyes and ours opened at the same time. His appearance was grace personified. He placed his hands to his heart in a prayerful manner and bowed to us.

"*Wellness to the Earth, my friends! May she flourish for all eternity!*"

"Wellness to the Earth!" We replied simultaneously.

"You honor us with your presence," added Barbara.

"*As do you me,*" he whispered. A deep breath was taken before he spoke again. "*My friends, we have much to do, but I prefer that you take the lead for a moment. Will you please inform me of the list of names that you have prepared?*" Glances were exchanged between Barb and me. She indicated that I should go first.

"We have agreed upon three couples that we believe are perfect for this project. They are people that we have both known for a very long time. The advantage of their presence is multifaceted. We've worked well together on other projects in the past. We have similar beliefs and concerns about the Earth's situation, and most of all, we enjoy each other's company. Our relationships are founded in trust and respect. Hopefully, they will be interested and available. Would you share your perspective, Barb?"

"Yes, I too am very excited about getting these folks on board. By the way their names are Sally and Dave Moore, Mark and Faye Goodman, and Jim and Annie Anderson. We have other folks who also are good candidates and who are, shall we say, on the short list, but we thought a smaller group might be an advantage in the initial phase of this project. We would like your opinion on that. Because we have a heart connection with these couples, we feel that progress can be made quickly. Since time seems to be relevant when it comes to saving the Earth, we thought this might be an expeditious way to approach the project." Barb paused briefly before another idea came up for her. "I'm curious about many things, of course, but particularly about these invitations. I'm assuming if these folks meet your approval that we should invite them over for a meeting. Is my assumption correct or are you planning on approaching them as you did the two of us? The reason I'm asking is because..." Hesitancy was not Barb's style, but for some reason she appeared reluctant to continue. She looked to me for guidance, which was difficult to give since I didn't know what the issue was.

"Your concern for your friends is mine as well." Our delightful guest inserted. *"I believe it is in their best interest to meet with you first. An appearance from me may be unsettling for them. I wish our introduction to be a positive experience not a frightful one."*

"Perhaps, you could make use of my ghost costume," teased my mischievous friend. Barb's playfulness tickled our guest. The three of us laughed together as if we were old friends, which of course, we were.

"As you know, my friends, I am aware of the individuals on your list and we are most pleased with your choices." Neither of us missed the obvious, but Barb was the first to respond.

"We? We who?" The interrogation was about to begin, but I intervened. Evidently, our friend was not alone.

"You are accompanied, my friend!"

"Yes, I am accompanied by many who also are involved in this matter of extreme importance. As discussed previously, this is not a solo affair. All are needed to rescue the Earth from her unfortunate circumstances."

Barb immediately piped up. "Will we meet them as well? Will they be joining us in our meetings?" Her curiosity was unlimited as were her questions, but our guest was ready to return to the topic of the day.

"My friends, we need not concern ourselves with that matter at this time; however, we will have more time to discuss my companions at another time. At this point I must ask you to quiet your minds for I need your undivided

attention. *Open your hearts to what is next to come for it is news that none will wish to hear."* Deep breaths were taken about the room. And in that moment I was certain that we were not alone. The breaths heard were more than just three. They encircled the room. I took another deep breath feeling more secure about our mission. We definitely were not alone.

*

A passage from
Beyond The Day of Tomorrow
A Seeker's Guide
(Chapter Nine)

"As in times past, we must again pursue that which remains elusive to us. Just out of our reach, it appears to be, just hovering there before us, almost recognizable, but not quite, almost understandable, but not quite. Perhaps each life experience is just as frustrating as this present one, and then you wonder why would one continue to do this over and over again, if it is this frustrating each time we experience it?

Well, maybe it isn't. Maybe, sometimes it is actually easy or at least less frustrating. The point is, we don't know, but in typical human fashion, we tend to believe the worst and expect the worst, and then if the worst doesn't happen, we are relieved...an interesting way of approaching life. Do you really think if all these life experiences were so awful that we would continue to participate? Something very important very powerful must be happening or we would not continue to persevere."

*

"My friend, it is with great sadness that I am the bearer of such difficult news, but it is a task that must be done, and it is my duty to do so. Times ahead will be extremely unsettling for the peoples of Earth. None will escape the ramifications of the changes within and upon the Earth's surface. She is in extreme discomfort because she is transforming as a result of the injuries she has incurred. Her transformation will inevitably create hardships around the globe.

I ask you to breathe deeply now and try to still your fears. The truth must be spoken, and at the same time, one must have faith. The Life Being Earth is a Beloved Friend to all those who inhabit the Greater Existence. She is not alone! Her condition has been carefully monitored for millennia, but the necessary changes that were required to alter her declining health have not come to pass. Her situation worsens and the source of the problem remains oblivious to her needs.

My friends, we come forward to beg you for help. There remains time to save the Beloved Earth. With your cooperation and the assistance of many others who are prepared to aid her, she can recover from this dreadful state of ill health. There is reason for hope! We hope you feel more secure knowing that you are not alone in managing this crisis situation. We hope you will allow us to participate in the rescue mission for our Dear Old Friend. We hope you will trust our appeal and that you will open your hearts to our assistance.

We are hopeful because of You! Because the peoples of Earth have the ability within them to save the Earth, we remain hopeful. Because you are founded in goodness and kindness, we remain hopeful. Because you have the power to change your ways on behalf of the Earth, we remain hopeful.

Our mission is to assist you in changing your ways and also by reminding you of a skill long ago forgotten. By changing your negative energy to positive energy, everyone will benefit. Everyone! Family, friends, and the passersby that cross your path on the street! Everyone will benefit from your healthy energy, and as a result, they will be inspired to change their energies as well. This can be done; it is a choice. Those who are willing to change immediately must step forward. All that is required is openheartedness and willingness. If you are one who is willing to change now, please step forward. The Earth needs your positive energy and you need hers. Without her vibrant energy, humankind will cease to exist. This is not intended, but it will happen if the peoples of Earth refuse to change their negative behaviors.

My friends, you and many others who have recently been approached are the ones who have stepped forward first. Because of your willingness to participate, we are hopeful. And we are grateful to be of assistance."

*

A passage from
Beyond The Day of Tomorrow
A Seeker's Guide
(Chapter Nine)

"Think about this for a moment. Look around you. Perhaps you know someone who is experiencing a really difficult lifetime, or maybe you need only look in the mirror for your example. Ask yourself, why is this person here? What is their purpose? Why did this person choose to participate in this life experience? What did this person want to learn?

Remember, we all began with an insatiable desire to know all there is to know and we were all given free will with which to pursue that desire. So, no matter how mystified you are in the moment about a particular life experience, remember, there was a reason that individual chose to come, and that brings us back to the purpose of A ***Seeker's Guide***. *You are here for a reason. And it is you who must choose to participate in this journey called life and discover your reason for coming.*

As with all mysteries, one must investigate the clues to produce viable deductions. So too with this mystery called life. There are clues, you know, but you must be open-minded and curious if you are going to find them. At times the clues will abound and your movement will proceed at rapid speed, but then in an instant you will find yourself at a standstill. During the bursts of accelerated growth, you will most likely feel energized and excitement will exude from you. These are the moments we all long for and when experiencing these waves of knowing, we are in 'joy' of our journey.

As much as we do not want to accept it, we simply cannot experience these huge leaps of awareness for extended periods of times. We must have periods of rest allowing for the assimilation of all the new awareness and understandings that have been gained. These rest periods are unfortunately perceived by most as abrupt standstills. This indeed is an erroneous perception and a disservice to the journey and the seeker.

Too often when experiencing this downtime, the seeker falls into discouragement and/or frustration which leads to various judgments about self and the journey. It is at this time of the journey that we are most vulnerable. The critical nature that has been instilled in us since birth quickly begins to take action, working in opposite, but equally destructive ways. First, there is a tendency to glorify the periods of bursting awakenings and second, the tendency is to condemn the periods of restful rejuvenation. In truth, both these periods are of equal importance to the cycle of evolution and both must be honored with extreme gratitude. Without one, the other could not be, and without the other, the one would hold no meaning.

It goes without saying that the times of enlightenment are the times most invigorating. We are giddy with the awareness of new understandings and we are exhilarated by the growth we are experiencing within.

This, my Friends, is natural. It is to be expected, anticipated, and experienced fully, for this too is part of the journey, and it is also natural after the birth of new awakenings that the seeker must rest from the birthing process.

This is the period of recuperation and rejuvenation while all that has been learned is assimilated. This time is extremely important to the evolving process and should be treated with gentle care. It is indeed unfortunate that during this period, we often misunderstand its purpose judging it as a waste of time. What is meant to be a period of healing and transformation, we treat with critical assessment and disdain.

My Dear Old Friends, you must review this with accurate discernment and please allow this to serve as another gentle reminder. Resting is not stagnation; it is the pause before movement."

*

The message delivered by our guest was humbling. Knowing that others in existence cared so deeply about the Earth and her inhabitants brought tears to my eyes. *How could these beings outside of our range of awareness be so attached to us? What was the connection? Whatever the reason, it was extremely reassuring that we are not alone.* I wondered if the people of Earth were up for this challenge. Clearly our reactions to climate change were evidence that many care very little about anyone but themselves. *But I must remember all the people who are actively pursuing methods of improving the Earth's situation. There really are positive actions being taken, but these stories do not attract the attention of news providers. Shh! Mind of mine, be still! Focus on the positive not the negative.*

"Dear Friend, that was a critically important message to deliver. It must have been very stressful to present that information. But you did it well! And I am grateful that you were willing to do so. What you are doing for us, we will have to do for others. You're a very good role model, my Friend. Thank you, again!" Much more begged to be said, but I chose not to. *Not at this time,* I thought.

Barb waited to see if I was finished before expressing her own thoughts. She too needed to articulate her appreciation to our friend for his commitment to the Earth and to us. And there was another matter that she wished to explore as well. "I could just say ditto to everything Sister just said, but that would not feel right. I really am grateful Friend for everything you are doing for us. It saddens me that people do not know what is going on behind the scenes. I'm astounded to know that so many other beings from unknown places are standing by to assist us. This is amazing! And I wonder how folks will react to this when the news about you and your companions comes forward. Have you and your Friends discussed this? Are you concerned about how you will be received? And are you also concerned whether or not people will give your messages any credence if they are confused about your origins?" Before any more questions were offered, our gentle Friend replied.

"Yes. We have concerns about all of your questions and many more, and still, actions must be taken. We cannot remain silent for fear of your reactions. We mean no harm to anyone and we regret having to bring such dreadful news to the peoples of Earth, but we cannot and will not stand idly by as the Earth's health continues to decline. Her wellness affects everyone in existence. She is a Beloved Friend and we are devoted to her well being."

*

A passage from
Beyond The Day of Tomorrow
A Seeker's Guide
(Chapter Ten)

"To continue our journey we must be in clear understanding of the difference between rest and stagnation. Rest is of wellness and a necessary component to our evolving process. Stagnation is not of wellness. It is the symptom of infection resulting from critical assessments and unkindly regard by self and others. It is this contamination of our spirit, which disrupts our journeys and impedes our progress."

*

"My Friend, may I ask a question?" Our guest had been so patient with us that I hesitated to ask another question, but his statement about the Earth's health affecting everyone else in existence puzzled me.

"Please do so, my Friend. It is through your questions that you will be prepared for what lies ahead."

"Do you already know what I'm about to ask?" Suspecting he was highly intuitive and capable of hearing my thoughts, I was simply curious about his own particular skills and limitations, if he had any.

"My limitations are abundant, Old Friend, but this does not keep me from living a productive life. And yes, I have overheard your thoughts, but your friend has not. Although her skills are developing nicely, at this point in time, she is distracted by her own thoughts. Barb admitted that she was off creating another list of questions. However, the interaction between her Sister of Choice and their guest had captured her attention.

"Then I will ask the question aloud. I am puzzled by your earlier comment regarding the effects of the Earth's health on other members of existence. Can you provide more information about that?" A look of satisfaction crossed Barbara's face. It seems my question was one already on her list.

Our companion sighed. My thoughts jumped on this small, but effective gesture. *I wonder if his energy is waning. Should I address this with him?*

"Old Friend, I am fine! While I appreciate your concern for me, it is not necessary. The sigh that you just witnessed denotes nothing negative,

but in truth was the release of a desired expectation fulfilled. We had hoped this question would be addressed during this meeting, and now, it has come to the forefront.

My Friend, you have not yet fully discussed your travels during the meditation we began with. You mentioned your confusion with time, but there was another event that was not discussed. Shall we do so now?"

"That adventure seems like a life time ago." A few minutes were needed to recapture that fascinating experience, but once the memory returned, I felt the sense of bliss once again. "Oh yes," a sigh not unlike the one just heard from our friend came from within me. "What a remarkable experience that was. Thank you for bringing it back to mind. Barb, I wish you had been with me. You would have enjoyed the experience as much as I did. Basically, I felt as if I was adrift in space and realized that I was not alone. At first I felt as if someone was breathing right next to me, and then, I felt this same breathing companion within me. Then, there was a realization that the breather was within me and I was within the breather, and still there was more around us. And I knew that we were all One. It was remarkable. Please forgive me for not giving this experience its due, because it truly was extraordinary. The sense of Oneness was so much more than I can explain. This probably sounds crazy but I truly felt as if I was One with All in existence. Wow! Thank you, dear friend for reminding me about that experience. But I am curious, why have you done so?"

"Because it is relevant to your question. The sense of Oneness is real and I am so glad that you enjoyed that experience. Many seek this magnificent blending, but few have found that which they seek; but you did today without realizing it was on your agenda. I am most happy for you.

And now I will, with your permission, access your experience as a teaching moment. The sense of Oneness that engulfed you is the Essence of All in Existence. The Earth is a dynamic member of this union of energies. She resides within All in Existence and All reside with her. Without her energy, the sense of loss would be heartbreaking. None can imagine existence without her vibrant presence. The concept of her loss is incomprehensible." Our Friend fell silent, as did we. He closed his eyes; we followed his lead. And then, he began to speak again.

My friends, I beg your forgiveness. This topic is difficult for me to broach. When one is deeply loved by many, the loss of that Life Being affects everyone within the circle of that individual. What was is no longer. The absence of this individual cannot be denied. Because the energy of the departed was interlaced with all those within his/or her circle of existence, the void that remains is indescribable. One grasps for the energy that was taken and aches to bring the energy back into its previous place, but this cannot be, because the energy that once was is now a transformed energy that may or may not be recognized.

Perhaps, you can understand this relative to the loss of one who was dear to you. One moment he or she was there and the next moment he or she was absent. We long for the absence to be filled again, yet that which was is no longer. This is the reality of the life process. Having said that in such a matter of fact way, let me also state that this reality is not easily accepted. Adapting to this new way of being, to the absence of one that is dear to you, requires time.

Because the Life Being Earth is a being of ancient beginnings, she is greatly loved by more than one can imagine. Her circle of reach is also beyond the scope of imagination. Suffice it to say, she is very, very loved and she will be deeply missed because her energy has merged with so many other energies that she is essentially connected to everyone in existence. The effect of her absence upon existence is without comparison. No one wishes to think about this. Just as those on the planet do not want to believe that her health crisis is real, nor do those who exist elsewhere. And yet, we must! Just as the peoples of Earth must address this issue, so too must we!

We are all One with this remarkable planet and we must come to her rescue. There is no other choice. Those who think this situation can be ignored are foolish. Everyone will feel the consequences of her decline, and it will not be pleasant. The truth is difficult to hear!" Our companion fell silent again.

"Old friend, please continue. We wish to share this experience with you. Please do not worry about us. Barb and I are here, and we want to help."

"Your support is most welcome. I find your gesture of kindness uplifting. You have offered your assistance to me as I wish to offer mine to you. Dear friends, I am not alone. Both of you are aware of this, but unfortunately, not everyone shares this awareness. This lack of understanding is of concern for those of us who have volunteered to be of assistance. Many of us have enjoyed numerous life experiences on this planet. We are the

family members, friends, and associates of those who still reside on the Earth. We are collectively referred to as Those Who Came Before. It is a lovely term of endearment that is fitting, and it also is a way of informing the peoples of Earth that those who have previously departed still remain. We hope this news will bring relief and satisfaction to everyone. They, your forebears, are here and eager to help their descendants. In essence we are speaking of eternal life. The validation of this long debated reality is just one of the ramifications anticipated as a result of the Earth's decline. We are hopeful that this ramification is one that will be reassuring.

My friends, another topic of importance relates to this. It may come as a surprise to some of the residents of Earth, but it must be addressed nonetheless. The statement utilized to apprise individuals that they are not alone actually encompasses much more than some may presently understand. Existence is occupied by many more beings than the good people of Earth are aware. This may be difficult for some to hear, but the truth is truth whether one is aware of it or not. Your introduction to these other inhabitants would have occurred naturally as your evolutionary advancement progressed forward; however, as a result of this crisis situation, the opportunity to meet your neighbors is coming much more rapidly than expected. We hope it will be comforting to know that friends, throughout the galaxies, are amassing to be of assistance to the peoples of Earth." Our Friend paused in anticipation of our reactions. Barb did not hesitate. Her enthusiasm could not be contained.

"Awesome! This is incredible!" Rising to the edge of her chair, she leaned forward and stared into the eyes of our remarkable guest. "That took a lot of courage! And I am so grateful, so very grateful that you shared this information with us. You had no idea how we were going to react to your news, but you spoke the truth anyway. As you spoke, my Friend, I wondered what it must be like to be you. You are obviously in a rather vulnerable position. Most of the time, you're invisible, which I suppose is an asset in many ways, but it also makes you a suspicious character. Compound that with the fact that you are bringing forward information that many folks may take issue with. This is huge responsibility! And you just did it! More importantly, you presented this extraordinary information with grace and dignity.

And then, at some point, I realized that we," she motioned to me, "will be delivering the same message to others in the very near future. That made me gulp, but then, I knew, I simply knew that we could do it, because you showed us how. You are a wonderful teacher and role model, and I am so grateful to be part of this. Please hear me when I say that I heard every word that you said and I was very comforted. You validated what I've always believed about eternal life. And it gives me hope.

Now, in regards to neighbors from outer space! I am so there! For me, this is a dream come true. I am such a believer! And the idea that these beings desire to help us is humbling and fantastic. I never understood why sci-fi movies portrayed beings from other locations as aliens with menacing intentions." Barb paused as she reviewed her last sentence. "Unfortunately, that's exactly what we do here on Earth as well. We are so accustomed to creating 'us and them' scenarios among ourselves that we naturally apply that same mentality to imagined intergalactic interactions. No wonder you and your companions have reservations about connecting with us." She mused about this a bit longer before adding, "But you have to! It's necessary! And we will have to take the same risks that you just took. Thank you again, for doing so." My friend turned to me and quietly said, "I just had another life-changing event!"

"Your reaction is most reassuring. I am honored by your kind words and empowered to continue. Although we all hoped and believed for such a reception, I am deeply relieved. My associates are having similar responses. It is for us, as you just said, a dream come true. We know our words may cause unrest for some, but your reaction gives us great hope.

And what of you, dear friend?" Our visible invisible friend turned his attention to me. *"How do you feel about the message just provided?"*

Tears filled my eyes as emotions rose to the surface. "My heart is full, my Old Friend." Several elongated breaths were necessary before continuing. My companions held the space for my restorative self-care and even my inpatient friend waited patiently for me. This came as no surprise. Another deep breath boosted my energy, and I was able to repeat myself. "My heart is full, my Old Friend, because I now understand the true meaning of Dear Old Friend. We are friends of long standing, are we not? I wish the memories of those times past would return to me, but it truly doesn't matter. You remember for both of us! Knowing this fills my heart with joy. Even without the memories I know with all that I am that we are truly Dear Old Friends. I am so grateful to be in your presence again. We are sharing another life of service. I understand that now, and again, I must repeat myself.

Gratitude abounds! The three of us have come together for a reason, and in this life experience, you are the one who holds the memories. You are our Guide! How fortunate we are!" Another breath engulfed me as revelation reached every cell of my body. Everything was happening for a reason. We were in the right place at the right time and we were living into our reason for being.

"Oh, I pray that others will have similar reactions."

"As you well know, Old Friend, some will and some will not. Thus, our work is to empower those who respond positively while also holding the space for those who do not. We cannot work with only one group, for all are needed in this expansive project of rescue. Those like you who responded enthusiastically will propel our mission forward. Those who struggle with this news will require additional loving care. We will not turn our backs on anyone. All the peoples of Earth are the Children of Those Who Came Before, and each and every one of you is deeply loved and cherished. This truth must be understood. All in Existence are essential to the well being of all others in Existence. The Children of Earth need our assistance, as does the Earth herself, and assistance will continue to be provided." Barb waited patiently before interjecting a thought into the conversation.

"My Friend, your willingness to speak so openly about the relationship between our people and Those Who Came Before is so helpful. When we first began our discussions about assisting the Earth and the peoples of Earth, I wondered why you and others, such as yourself, would be so dedicated to us. Obviously, ideas popped into my mind about this, but you have succinctly clarified the reason for this devoted commitment. We are Family! This I can understand. I'm still trying to grasp the full extent of the concept of Oneness, but I am not giving up on it. It's complex, and probably simple at the same time. Let's just say that I have a ways to go yet, but my heart is open and with time my confusion will diminish.

As I said before, you are a good teacher. An excellent Guide, as Sister referred to you. If the rest of your companions are as capable as you, we're in good shape. I just hope we, meaning all the people of Earth, will stand up for her the way you have."

*

A passage from
Beyond The Day of Tomorrow
A Seeker's Guide
(Chapter Ten)

"Perhaps this contamination was a factor that an evolving individual wished to experience and this is a possibility, which must be considered. If it is to be known, then the question of the acquiring seeker must again be asked. What am I to learn from this?

Difficult as it may be to comprehend why an individual would select to experience a lifetime of hardships and indignities, we must accept that this is an option sometimes purposefully chosen. Our challenge and our responsibility are to honor that difficult and courageous choice. Know that each of you has made such a choice and each of you knew before you made the choice that it would be one of extreme difficulty and you chose to do it anyway.

My Friends, is this not a lesson in itself? To know that an individual, in full awareness, accepted the life of hardship is evidence that the benefits gained outweigh the difficulty of the experience.

As you ponder this possibility, know that your present life experience will influence your perspective. Much easier it is to accept this notion when your circumstance is such that you are not actively involved in a difficult situation. However, if you find yourself embroiled in an abusive relationship or a terminal illness, or some other variety of hardships, then this concept will be extremely difficult to accept. But if you find yourself, as many will, feeling defensive about your circumstance, then please calm yourself quickly and remember, do not have judgment about one's journeys. Not yours, or anyone else's. To do so actively engages the contamination factor once again.

Our human side judges harshly and critically; our spiritual side courageously accepts criticism and harshness as a lesson to be explored, from which knowingness is gained.

If you find yourself living a life of hardship, remember you have free will. You may freely choose to accept this circumstance, and if you do, also accept the honor and courage of this decision, or you may choose to accept that you have learned all that was desired from this circumstance and now you freely choose to change your circumstance. Either choice is of honor and is yours to make, but do make it, so that stagnation does not occur."

*

Barb's enthusiasm about alien assistance tickled me. Truth is, the science fiction genre played a large role in her spiritual journey and her vision of the Universe. She often spoke of various movies and the profound influence each one had upon her. She wondered if some of the authors had been inspired by divine guidance. Although Barb readily acknowledged that many recent sci-fi movies were made strictly for financial gains there were others that she found captivating. They spoke a truth to her that was undeniable. Once she asked me if I thought these movies were being produced for a reason. My response was lacking and I often felt guilty about that. For whatever reason that old guilt surfaced as she spoke about her joy regarding the possibility that she might actually have an opportunity to work collaboratively with them. "My Friend, may we speak more about the other inhabitants that are standing by to provide assistance?" His barely noticeable nod was the cue to continue.

"I'm curious about this, as you can imagine. Who wouldn't be? Intergalactic beings, eternal life, purpose of life! These are huge questions! Questions of the ages! These topics will definitely attract attention, and as already stated, some will have positive reactions to these possibilities, and some will not. I assume you and your companions have given this a great deal of consideration. Is there any more information that you might share with us? I'm feeling a bit ill equipped in this area. Which is not to say that I'm not interested, because I am! Like my friend here, I have dreamed about having contact with other beings since I was a small child. It just never made sense to me that we were the only ones in existence. As a child, I wanted playmates! As an adult, I want answers and relationships. Please excuse my bad manners, but I really want more information. Will we actually meet these other beings? Will they look like us or do we need to be prepared to meet individuals very unlike us? If the latter is true, we need to prepare our citizenry about this. We are not people who adapt well to differences! Our history reflects the atrocities that have been committed around the globe because of perceived differences.

My friend, we must be prepared if we are to be effective. What more can you tell us?"

*

A passage from
Beyond The Day of Tomorrow
A Seeker's Guide
(Chapter Eleven)

"In this existence of free will and abundance of choices, is it any wonder that we would choose to come and come again? For with each coming, there would be a new opportunity and a new adventure to experience, resulting in new awareness and greater understanding. Thus in each lifetime we would gain more of that which we all so desire to know.

With each life lived, we would come closer to knowing all there is to know, and it is this desire which propels us ever forward in the pursuit of All That Is, for to know all there is to know is to know All That Is.

*

"Old Friend, your sense of responsibility expresses itself. You desire to be of service and you wish to be qualified to do so. This is not a demonstration of bad manners, but an indication of your commitment. You have waited for a very long time to fulfill the duties of this lifetime, and you will be prepared, my Friend. Do not fear; you will be informed and you will inform others. All will be prepared for the transitions that are coming. For the sake of all involved, it is necessary.

My Friends, let us speak more about the life beings that surround you. You live in an existence filled with existences and each one is equal to all others. Our neighbors come in many different sizes and shapes, and each form is equally appreciated and loved by All in existence. Differences are embraced and cherished by your neighbors and they will accept you as equals as well. Your neighbors reside throughout the galaxies that your peoples already know about, and they also reside in other galaxies and dimensions of existence that are yet to be discovered by your scientists. There is no cause for discomfort about this lack of awareness; it simply is the reality of your evolutionary development. Because existence has always been, there are those so ancient that they remain unknown to those of us who are on the other end of the age continuum. We ponder about their existence, and long to meet those of ancient times, but we accept what is. When the time is as it is intended to be, our knowledge of All That Is will advance forward. This is true for all in existence.

Many of your neighbors, who are amassing on your behalf, will travel great distances to be of assistance. Others have already arrived. As said before, you will not be alone during this time of great transformation. The crisis will clarify for the peoples of Earth their misunderstandings about differences. It is most unfortunate that greater understanding about differences was not learned earlier. Our project would be so much easier if you trusted one another." Reality sank in. Of course, humankind's distrust of each other would be a critical factor in this unthinkable rescue mission. My mood shifted, but before it dipped too far, Barb intervened.

"Sister, trust in us! Our friendship gives us strength. We must not forget the potential of a positive experience. One leads to another and to another. We can create change by effectively offering positive energy and interactions to those we encounter. And let's not forget the incredible acts of kindness and generosity that transpire now when crises occur around the globe. There is goodness in humankind! We are more than we appear to be. We cannot lose sight of that!"

"Well done, dear Friend! You stopped the downward spiral of optimism and hope. Please notice what just happened because you will need to facilitate this in the work that you do. In the blink of an eye, one's mood can shift and the positive energy that was surging forward can take a turn and diminish in an instant. You, dear Friend, felt the energy shift in your Sister of Choice, and you skillfully intervened. Well done!"

"Thank you, Barb! Our Friend here is right. You handled this situation beautifully. This truly was a great teaching moment. I anticipate that we will need to be very vigilant when we are engaging with other folks about theses issues. The realization that my energy slip directly affected the Earth is shocking. Look how quickly this can happen! We really have a lot to learn if we're going to create change.

You know I really have to think about this, because this small incident was an eye opener. I've foolishly been focusing upon large offenses like wars, nuclear discharges, and violence that erupt in city streets. Of course, these acts are outrageous, but it is the smaller acts of negativity that must be faced as well. Barb, we need to observe our behaviors for the next few days to get a clear picture of how many times during the day we say or do something that creates negative energy. I know that I'm guilty of doing various things during the day that cause harm, but I need to obtain a sense of how much negativity I'm really generating. Are you on board with this, Barb?" The thumbs up gesture answered my question.

*

A passage from
Beyond The Day of Tomorrow
A Seeker's Guide
(Chapter Twelve)

"When the time comes for all to decide that which is their choice, each must go within to find the answer to that decision. As with all questions, there are many answers, but the deciding voice, which knows the answer to all questions resides within.

*My Friends, you know this. This is not news to you or you would not be reading **A Seeker's Guide**. Each one of you has at some point known, yet not known how you knew, that the answer to your most important question lies deep within you.*

The ache that burned loudly and the longing, which called to you, were your reminders that you are here for a reason, and in the quiet of the moment, you knew from whence the ache came and from whence the calling called.

Old language or new, old lifetime or present experience, at some point, at some time you knew the answer to your yearning. You knew who you really are, and why you really came and how it all came to be. You knew this before and you will know it again.

Accept this as Truth, Old Friend, for it is. What you have once known, you will always know, and what you will come to know will be known thereafter. Yes, this is a gentle reminder."

*

"My Friends, our first meeting has gone exceptionally well. Your participation is deeply appreciated by All who have observed us during this time. There is reason for hope, my Friends. You work well together and the ones who you intend to enlist will also be people of good faith. We are most optimistic. The next step must be initiated. Please make contact with your friends and call another meeting. The conversations from the heart must begin.

I bid you farewell now. Gratitude abounds!"

And with that said, our guest, our Dear Old Friend, vanished before our eyes.

*

A passage from
Beyond The Day of Tomorrow
A Seeker's Guide
(Chapter Thirteen)

"At times it will seem that this journey is all consuming. Some will say you must rise early. Others will encourage you to sit in meditation for endless amounts of time. Still others will say go the mountains or some place in nature that speaks to you, while other others will urge you to visit ancient ruins. All this well meaning and sometimes, useful advice is given with great intentions, and my Friends, I invite you to listen with a grateful ear to all these words of wisdom from the experienced seekers. But as you listen, remember your journey is uniquely yours. The paths of others may indeed offer you guidance and there may be times when the advice is exactly what you need to push you forward. However, as with all well intended guidance, the offerings from fellow seekers must be reviewed with discernment.

If we all rise early, meditate long hours, and travel all over the planet searching for our answers, how on

Earth are we going to support ourselves? Let's face reality, people! Few of us are independently wealthy and most of us have families, who depend upon us, and then there's the job thing!

Living life is a full time occupation, and now, somehow, someway, we're supposed to do this journey too. Sounds impossible, doesn't it? Well, do not despair. Living life is part of the journey. In fact, living life is the journey. Yes, this is another gentle reminder. Living life is the journey.

It is regrettable that in our enthusiasm of discussing and sharing ideas about the journey that the journey has taken on an identity of its own. We now talk about the journey as if it were a separate experience, which we must devote our lives to, but in truth, the journey is our life. How we choose to devote time to this life will bring meaningfulness to this life."

*

6

"Welcome! Please come in...it is so good to see you again!" Our guests, our dear friends, were gathering. This was not new for us; we often visited as a group. This began years ago when we realized how comfortable we were with one another. We truly enjoyed one another's company. Barb and I were so happy and relieved when everyone was available for the first date offered. That is not always the case for our friends, because we are all busy living our lives. While we share many similar interests and activities, we each have our own preferences, and sometimes our individuality makes gathering a hassle. But there were no negotiations necessary for this meeting. I wondered if we had unknown assistants helping us. The thought pleased me, and whether it was accurate or not, I enjoyed the possibility.

Everyone gathered in the living room, which is the norm for us. Each person has his or her own favorite sitting place and within a few minutes we were happily situated. There was a bit of small talk that followed, which is also the norm when friends come together. What wasn't the norm for this get-together was the fact that there actually was an agenda, which had not been announced when the invitations were extended. As the group reunited, sharing news about recent events and bringing each other up-to-date on personal matters, my mind questioned if we had made an error. *Maybe we should have been upfront with everyone before setting this date.* My mind took off in an undesired direction, but fortunately, my eyes were drawn to Barbara who captured my stare and then subtly took a deep breath. I followed her lead and did the same, and within an instant, the doubts dissipated.

"Okay, you two! What's going on?" Faye Goodman inquired. "You're up to something, so just fill us in, and let's get this meeting rolling." Her husband Mark just shook his head and giggled. He was accustomed to his wife's straightforward style and also acutely aware of her intuitive abilities. She knew when Barb called that something was up, and of course, she was delighted! It was not unusual for Faye to grasp things before the rest of her friends did. Her comments evoked curiosity among the group. Her friends looked as if they were at a tennis match. First all heads turned toward Faye, and then in sequence, they all turned to their host.

Annie Anderson was the first to speak up. "My goodness," she asserted. "I didn't know we were here for a reason. Please enlighten us!" Barb was stunned by Annie's choice of words. We didn't dare look at each other. But our thoughts did merge. *Can you believe that?* Our internal questions were thought simultaneously.

"Well yes, we, Barb and I, have invited all of you here tonight for a reason, because something is up, and we need to talk about it with you."

"And," added Barb, "we thought it would be more efficient to do it together as a group rather than separately, so here we are." Her smile was radiant and it made people even more curious.

"Look, you two, I'm sorry to have put you on the spot." Faye, fearing she had acted too quickly, attempted to the shift the process that she had initiated. "Please excuse my manners, or lack thereof. Just take your time and let us know if there is anything we can do to help."

"Thank you, Faye! I guess you did surprise us a bit. That intuitive streak in you keeps getting better and better."

"You have no idea!" Mark casually affirmed. Faye's husband, a quiet man who was very proud of his wife, rarely brought attention to her so-called unusual abilities. In fact, no one outside of this Family of Friends knew about her skills, or his. The couple assumed most people would not be accepting of their abilities so they chose to be quiet about it. Sally Moore, sitting next to Faye, was a friend of hers since grade school. She wished the Goodmans would be more open about their talents. Although she understood why they were apprehensive, she believed more people than not would be very interested in and understanding of their circumstances. Sally openly acknowledged her envy of their telepathic abilities. She wondered if Faye actually knew about the unspoken topic, but chose not to pursue that.

"I just want to say that I'm delighted to be here. It's been way too long since our last gathering and whatever it is that you two want to talk about, I'm up for it. For some reason, I feel the need to know that you are both okay. You're both well, aren't you?" Sally's concern sparked another layer of curiosity that required addressing immediately.

"Absolutely!" I affirmed. "We are both fine. In fact, Barb is just recently back from a trip and has some exciting adventures to share with you at some point, but it's best to save that for right now. We do not mean to be creating a sense of mystery here, so let me get focused. Friends, Barb and I have had a very unusual experience, and of course, we want to discuss the matter with all of you." My brief introduction naturally heightened everyone's interest.

"So, tell us!" The words of encouragement came from Jim Anderson, Annie's husband. He loved listening to stories about unusual experiences. As did all the members of this Family, which is why we enlisted them to the yet to be revealed project.

"Thank goodness you are here!" I exclaimed with great relief.

"Amen!" muttered Barbara.

"Well friend, where do we begin?" My question directed attention towards Barb. Since she received the first visitation, it seemed appropriate that she should take the lead.

*

A passage from
Beyond The Day of Tomorrow
A Seeker's Guide
(Chapter Thirteen)

"The journey of life is an experience we are all experiencing whether we are conscious of it or not. As we become more conscious of this experience, our choices and our decisions regarding the experience become more relevant, for now our awareness is heightened and our knowingness is more known.

When we accept that the journey and living life are the same experience then we must again ask our questions: Who am I? How am I? Why am I? Living life is indeed all consuming, but how we choose to participate influences the flavor and the enjoyment of the experience. As with all good meals, we choose how we wish to indulge ourselves. Some prefer the entrée, while others relish the desserts. The meal, as is life, is a cornucopia of choices.

You decide how you will experience the meal by the choices you make. If you choose to overindulge in one choice, you may experience consequences, or if you choose to deprive yourself of another choice, there may be other ramifications, but if you choose to consume the meal in a more balanced way, the meal is more fully enjoyed and experienced.

So too with life! Our plates are filled, usually running over, with responsibilities and self or other imposed obligations. These distractions, relevant or not, can consume us and cause frustration and irritation. Consider these as the signals they are meant to be. Too often we fall into despair and hopelessness resulting in an inability to recognize the signals. Frustration and irritation are our guides, letting us know that we are out of balance. Welcome the guides and accept their information.

Before movement can occur, first we must recognize the reason for the lack of movement. Once done, movement continues. When we recognize the importance of balance, we can then determine how to achieve balance, and when balance becomes a focus, the journey of life is less consuming."

*

"My friends, I cannot tell you what a blessing it is to have you in my life, and I know my Sister of Choice feels the same way. I'm actually not sure how to begin this story," Barb chuckled at herself and then made eye contact with me. My response was an internal one. *At the beginning!* She smiled and nodded. "Of course, the story has a beginning, a middle, and an end. I should do the obvious." She took her deep, elongated breath and our friends did the same. It was a lovely demonstration of support. These good people had no idea what was coming, and it didn't matter. They knew Barbara was in an awkward moment and they just held the space for her. How fortunate we all were. I wondered how life would be without these wonderful friends. It was unimaginable.

"So, dear friends," stated Barbara, "I will begin at the beginning. Once upon a time, I went on a trip, and had some very interesting experiences. Upon my return, the very first thing I did was to come by here to visit my Sister. We talked for a very long time, and as always, she shared many words of wisdom, and as a result, I felt better about myself and with my life. Then as I was walking home from here, I had another very unusual experience. A voice from out of nowhere spoke to me. I looked about, but no one was to be seen so I continued home. Obviously, I remained mildly rattled for a bit, so I decided to settle myself with a meditation. And as I readied myself for said meditation, the voice spoke to me again. This time, the voice without a form wanted conversation. I found it rather difficult to talk to an invisible being, when you have no idea where the individual is. To assist me, he announced that he would take the chair across from me so that it might be easier for me to focus. It worked! I was surprised how quickly one can adapt to talking to an empty chair." Again, she laughed at herself before continuing with her story.

"So, now, my friends, the plot thickens. The invisible voice told me that I was here for a reason. Hmm, was my response to that comment! And then, he said that we were Old Friends who had worked on many projects in other lifetimes and that he was excited about working together again. He made the loveliest comment about how we had called each other Friend many times before and hoped that we would again in this life experience. It was a sweet moment that solidified our relationship. I cannot explain it, but his tenderness actualized my belief in what transpired. I had many questions as you might imagine, including doubting my sanity, but his gentle manner triggered a sense of acceptance that is unexplainable. I simply believed him. And I still do. He encouraged me to journal about our encounter. Oh, another point of the story was that he indicated that Sister and I were both here for a reason and that we would be working together on some project that was yet to be explained. I inferred from this information that he would be visiting her as well.

So that concludes the first chapter of this story, and I will just add that there is more to come." The room remained silent for another second or two before the questions began flying. Excitement was evident, as was acceptance. Sister took charge!

"My dear friends, what marvelous people you are! Do you know how wonderful you are? Please forgive me, but I observed you during Barb's story and your behavior was exactly as I expected. Your support of her was so kind and generous. It was sweet beauty in action." My comments momentarily quieted the rush of questions. Barb quickly affirmed my observations and took a brief moment to express her gratitude.

"What Sister just said is the norm for this group. Even though I was nervous about how to begin telling the story, I was not afraid of sharing it with all of you. I have such trust in our relationships. I just knew you would stand by me. So thank you for listening and for taking care of me."

"That's just who we are!" Faye announced with certainty. "Or better said, this is who we've become. And aren't we fortunate? We've been having heart to heart conversations for so long that it is just the norm for us. And I'm very grateful for our relationships, and I appreciate your acknowledgement of our way of being. We mustn't take this for granted, Dear Ones. What we have here is very precious."

"Well said!" responded Dave Moore in his typical gentlemanly manner. "I sometimes wonder about our group. In fact, I think it would be interesting some day to reminisce about how we all came together. Some day, but not now! We've enjoyed each other's company for so long that we really do take this for granted. We simply expect that love and support will be provided. And I wonder about that. How many people don't have this? How many people live in fear of relationships rather than finding comfort and solace in them?" A sign of worriment passed over his lips. "We need to work on this," he said more to himself than to the rest of his companions. "Too many folks are suffering. It's just not right." Dave looked up and realized his friends had fallen silent. "Oh my," he declared. "Please forgive me, I didn't me to bring the group down. I'm afraid my conscience took over."

"You didn't bring us down, Dave. You spoke the truth and the truth gave us pause." Jim's response was as sincere as Dave's comments. They were both men who were able to speak their feelings. "I have similar concerns, Dave, and wonder what we can do about it. So far, I haven't figured out an answer to this dilemma. Just thinking about it makes me feel helpless...and hopeless. And then my mind saves me by distracting to other more hopeful thoughts. At some point, I would like our group to talk more about this. I think there is more potential for ideas if we all put our heads together." Barb and I quietly listened and marveled. Without even knowing it, the group was moving in the intended direction.

Annie was sitting on the edge of her chair again when she announced her excitement. "I just love our group! Even when we seem to go off track, we still manage to have important commentary that is relevant to the original topic. We are a lovely group!" Annie's energy was dynamic. Her positive energy uplifted everyone around her. "Wouldn't it be wonderful if we came up with an idea to be of service to others? We are so blessed in our relationships. It would be nice to share this heartfelt connection with others." Nods of agreement circled the room.

"So, when are we going to hear about Chapter Two of this story?" Annie's question returned us to the topic of the evening. The next chapter of our story was mine to share and even though I was prepared to do so, the feelings of awkwardness that Barb had experienced earlier were now mine to manage.

"My friends," I declared forthrightly and followed with a deep breath. "I trust you completely, and still, my words are racing through my head. Give me just a moment to quiet this antsy mind of mine." As I breathed deeply in an attempt to settle myself, my friends did the same. Some closed their eyes to afford me privacy, while offers focused their opened eyes downward. *Such grace! Such kindness!* "Dear Ones," my eyes reached out to my friends, "we are here for a reason. Dave, I agree with you, it would be very interesting to remember how we all came together. At the time, whenever that was, I remember wondering why we were all pulled towards one another. Now, even more I marvel at the reality that we were brought together for a reason. We've shared good times... and we've helped each other through our respective life heartbreaks. Thank goodness, you were here! I am a better person because you are in my life." A tear trickled down my cheek as I embraced my friends through inadequate words. I wished I were more skilled at articulating my feelings, but one is who one is. I perceived my words as ineptly shared, but I knew these wonderful people felt the kinship that was intended.

"Well, my dear friends, I think the door is opening up for us to gain clarity about why we were brought together." My statement aroused interest. Eyebrows were raised, deep breaths were subtly taken, and everyone remained silent in anticipation. "So, in attempting to follow my friend's tale, let me begin in like manner." A smile crossed my face as I began, "Once upon a time, I was resting in my Sacred Space, and a voice was heard. Our Friend had just called upon Barb and was then visiting me. He was, as she already described, both invisible and delightful. Without knowing how or why, I immediately felt at home with him. It was very comfortable to be in his presence. Needless to say, this fine fellow, this Friend of Old, had come for a reason." Another pause was necessary. "And friends, his mission of purpose is important!"

"I'm not exactly sure how to summarize his visit. Although our time together was relatively brief, during that time he described a reality that everyone must face."

*

A passage from
Beyond The Day of Tomorrow
A Seeker's Guide
(Chapter Fourteen)

"As all of you have experienced, there are some lessons we seem to learn over and over again, and each time we encounter the lesson, it appears new to us until we reach the aha part of the lesson, at which point we slap ourselves on the forehead and chastise ourselves for being in the same place again. If this sounds familiar to you, and I am certain it does, then welcome to the journey of life.

How often this repetitive learning occurs and how often we participate in it without conscious awareness! Perhaps, conscious awareness is the point of this repetition.

As seekers of all there is to know, the point of the seeking is to actually be aware of all there is to know. When we are experiencing the journey in an unconscious way, then the lesson being learned is about unconsciousness, which is also an important lesson, but it is not the desired lesson. To live life in an unconscious state certainly accentuates living life in awareness, but regaining consciousness seems to be a difficult task and maintaining consciousness is an even greater challenge.

This condition of fluctuating between consciousness and unconsciousness may influence our need for repeated lessons. Rarely are the lessons offered difficult to comprehend, but if we are not fully focused on the lesson when given, then the lesson is not entirely learned, thus creating the need for another lesson.

Now before we continue, I want to make certain that you haven't gone off on some critical assessment journey. If you have, STOP IT! Come back and focus or you're going to miss this lesson and have to repeat it.

Personally, I do not believe that the repetition of lessons is a sign of failure or any other negative assessment. It's simply part of the evolving process. The more we engage in life, the more actively aware we are of life, and the more aware we are of our circumstances, the more we are living our journey.

Active participation and involvement influence our learning process, thus influencing our journey, but what does this mean...active participation and involvement? Have we returned to our earlier discussion of rising early and meditating long hours? The answer is yes...and no.

Yes, to actively participate, one must be willing to commit to involvement in the journey, but no, it does not mean you must rise at a particular time or you should meditate for an allotted period. Nor does it mean that there is a right way of being actively involved.

Each seeker must find their own unique way of participating and once found, the commitment of involvement must be addressed with discipline, but please understand what is being proposed. The way you participate will be of your own choosing and it will be uniquely suited to you. How much you involve yourself will also be of your choosing and whatever method of discipline you ascribe to will also be of your choice.

Remember, Dear Old Friend, you possess free will, and self-determination is yours to master."

*

"Sweet Friend, please tell us more, and don't worry about reporting the conversation perfectly. Just give us the gist of it and then we can fill in the blanks as we mull over it. And by the way, you are one of the most articulate people I know. So, just let go of the inept issues." Sally's appeal and kind words touched my heart. *She wants to hear more!* Were those my words or Barb's or someone else's? I truly didn't know the answer, and it didn't matter.

"Thank you Sal! That means a lot to me, and you're right, I just need to do this. So, fasten your seatbelts! Our friend presented us with a truth that is difficult to hear. I suspect none of you will be surprised to hear that our planet is in big trouble. We all know this! Even with all the misinformation that is being propagandized, one cannot be oblivious to the changes that are occurring around us. His message included more startling news than this, as if anything could be more startling than the fact that the Earth is declining. Well, according to our Friend, she is declining more rapidly than we know and we, meaning humankind, are reaching a point of no return. Evidently, the planet's continued failing health will cause her to fall into dormancy. This will become necessary if immediate changes do not occur. For our sakes, she has continued functioning, while depleting her own life forces and by putting her own well being in jeopardy. She cannot continue to do this nor can she allow our immaturity to silence her. The Earth has other responsibilities and commitments that she must uphold. So, if we do not change for her sake, then she will be forced to enter into a state of dormancy. The ramifications of this are unthinkable. Humankind and the other residents of Earth will not survive this period of suspended activity. As she lies dormant, her vital energy resources will be rejuvenated, and she will become a vibrant life being again, but this process will take millennia and during her restorative period, she will be uninhabitable." I paused for myself, for my friends, and for the others who were present. I knew we were not alone. The magnitude of this information was silencing. Time passed without our notice. Eventually, Barb softly brought us back to the present.

"My friends, I apologize for interrupting this moment of extreme grief, but we must push forward. We are here for a reason and we have work to address." Her words were gentle and beautifully stated, and her timing was perfect. One needed only a glance around the room to know that she intervened well.

"Ah, thank you Barb, and you're right we must complete this story so that we can move on." So I did, as was my way. I began with the necessary deep breath that braved the path for me. "My friends, excuse me, but it is possible that the 2nd and 3rd chapters of our story have merged together. Briefly, I will say that Barb and I met again the next day, and again were visited by the same invisible friend, who this time was visible to both of us. That's the sequence of our connection with him, even though the story is melding together.

So the additional news that he presented to us was as shocking as the information about the Earth's rapidly declining health. He specified the primary cause for her illness and it is difficult to hear, but the reality of it makes sense. Of course, there will be people who refuse to accept this, but I believe each of you will hear the truth in this message. With great sorrow, he informed us that the greatest factor contributing to the Earth's health is the negative energy generated by humankind. And he said that no matter what we do pragmatically, our negative energy overrides the efforts being pursued on her behalf at this time. He applauded the progress that is being made, and expressed gratitude to all who are participating in these efforts, but he adamantly declared that these efforts are not enough. The ill will that humans perpetrate on one another sickens her. Every offense we commit against self or another depletes her energy. Every act of unkindness causes her extreme hardship. Just imagine this, my friends, and as you do, remember we are a civilization of over seven billion people. How has she survived our ill will this long?"

*

A passage from
Beyond The Day of Tomorrow
A Seeker's Guide
(Chapter Fifteen)

"Question? Are you beginning to feel frustrated with all these 'free will and it's your choice' scenarios? I suspect you are, and for this, I do apologize, but Old Friend, a point is trying to be made.

*A **Seeker's Guide** is a reminder that each path taken is the right path at any particular time and any particular place. Each choice chosen is the right choice. Each decision made is the right decision. Each action taken is the right action, and each time you choose to decide upon an action, you must ask, what am I to learn from this? For each time, a lesson will be learned, pushing you ever forward in the quest to know all there is to know."*

*

"And how are we to help?" asked Faye. I turned toward Barb and invited her to address Faye's question.

"We don't have all the specifics about that at this time, but the first step was to invite all of you to this meeting to apprise you of what we know thus far. The Earth is definitely declining at a much faster pace than anticipated, and the negative energy created by humankind is the primary factor for her ill health. Turning this terrible scenario around means that we, the peoples of Earth, must change our ways.

From what was said, we are not the only people being approached. Undoubtedly others around the globe are also being contacted. And somehow, in some way, those of us who are on board with this project need to educate the public about this situation. Our participation is needed.

We were also informed that we are not alone in this project. And please think expansively when you hear this. Our gentle friend informed us that we have friends throughout existence. Some of these friends are our departed forebears who now reside in other locations than we do." Barb glanced around the room to check on everyone. "Yes, I did say departed forebears! Our friend verified that eternal life is real and that our loved ones continue to exist. Naturally, they are very concerned about the Earth and about us, so they are ready to help us.

Then he also brought up the matter of other Life Beings that populate existence who also are aware of the Earth's dilemma. Evidently, they too consider us to be family and they are also preparing to assist us. Naturally, this will be another complex issue that requires attention.

I think this brings you up to date!" Barb turned the lead over to me with a wave and a nod. "Your turn!" she declared as if handing over the baton.

"My friends, as you can see, the last couple of days have been full, and now we are here soliciting your assistance with this sizable project. Personally, I'm still reeling from all of this information, but even in my bewilderment, I know this is something that I must participate in. Dear Ones, you must be filled with questions. I know my list is long. So, shall we settle in and have one of our wonderful conversations from the heart?"

*

A passage from
Beyond The Day of Tomorrow
A Seeker's Guide
(Chapter Sixteen)

"Since the beginning, all have been of curious nature and each has desired to know how their existence came to be. From that beginning so very long ago, the seeking process began.

From the first sound heard in the Universe came the evolution of consciousness, for when the sound was heard, wonderment occurred because the sound heard had never been heard before, and when wonderment occurred, the desire to know all there was to know about the sound evolved. Who created the sound? How was the sound created? Why was the sound created?

Since that time, all creations have yearned to know all there is to know of their Creator."

*

"I'm in!" declared Annie Anderson. "And so is Jim!" Turning to her husband of many years, she sought affirmation. "You are in, aren't you Jim? Oh goodness, am I putting you on the spot, Dear?" Before he could answer, she responded to her own question. "Surely not! This is such a marvelous opportunity to be of service. We've been looking for a way to help others, Dear. And this is it!" Jim burst out laughing.

"Isn't she a wonder?" Jim turned to his friends and laughingly added, "Doesn't she remind you of the energizer bunny? That's my lovely lady!" Enjoying the banter of this amusing couple, their friends joined in with the laughter. "Now, Dear Love of My Life, will you allow me to have the floor for a moment?" Annie, chuckling at herself, nodded in agreement.

"I'm intrigued! And of course, many questions are running through this old mind of mine, but this project, as it is being called, is important. No one is talking about this aspect of the Earth's problems. Nor is anyone talking about the damage our negative energy is doing to one another. We've grown so accustomed to our hostilities that we act as if it is normal behavior. We see violence everywhere. News media, television, movies, the Internet! Violence dominates in our society, and it seems to be growing more prevalent every day. I'm very worried about this and I know all of you are as well. It is sickening, but it never occurred to me that it was sickening the Earth as well. My goodness. This is so sad. Why didn't we realize that our horrible actions would affect her? This is just unbelievable! But I get it now, and I believe what you two were told is the truth. So yes, Dear! I am definitely in!" Annie was beaming, but she remained silent.

"Your words were well spoken, Jim," praised Mark Goodman. "And I agree with you. Like you, I don't remember anyone approaching the Earth's health crisis from this perspective. And it's a shame this hasn't come up before because it makes so much sense. Toxic energy infects everything! And here she is. This beautiful planet is the recipient of every misdeed, every unkindness, every act of meanness. What have we done? How could we be so careless in our actions? Folks, my heart is aching. I am so saddened by this news." Mark paused for a moment because he needed to. His emotions were fully present. We all shared his sorrow. Eventually he concluded with a tone of hopefulness. "But I am also uplifted by the idea that there is something we can do to help. This gives me hope! I'm definitely onboard with this project. I want to assist the Earth in whatever way is possible. Before I close, I just want to thank you two for bringing this information to us. I know it must have been challenging for you to do this, and I want you know how grateful I am that you took the risk. This is transformative work! So thank you from the bottom of my heart." Tears were shared among the friends and more compliments were offered to Barb and her Sister of Choice. The affirmations felt good and so did the commitments that were coming forward.

*

A passage from
Beyond The Day of Tomorrow
A Seeker's Guide
(Chapter Seventeen)

"As the seeker's curiosity peaks with each new knowing, more the seeker wishes to seek, for it is this driving need to know all there is to know which propels the seeker ever forward.

Well, now you may be thinking to yourself that you're not particularly curious and you're not aware of any driving force, and you really aren't that interested in this journey stuff anyway. If that were really true, then why would you be spending money on a book such as this? It was a present, you say. Then why are you reading it? Just to be nice, you say. Old Friend, we're in the seventeenth chapter, why are you still reading?

The point is that you are reading A Seeker's Guide and even if you are unaware as to why you are doing this, you are doing it for a reason. Inside you, deep within, knowingness resides. At times you may experience awareness of this knowingness, but then in an instant it vanishes. As quickly as it appears, it disappears leaving you once again in unknowingness, yet knowing there is more that you are to know.

The awareness that there is more is known by everyone, but it is not experienced by everyone at all times. This awareness is fleeting and functions on an unscheduled timetable, coming and going at unannounced times. Predictably, yet unpredictably, the new knowing continues to come and when briefly captured into awareness, the moment is affirming, for once again the seeker has experienced that which the seeker seeks. Just for an instant, the fulfilling experience is enjoyed and then in another instant, the experience is gone, but not forgotten.

What was momentarily known and instantaneously lost is not remembered, but the experience of the knowing is remembered, and it is remembered deeply within."

*

Faye patiently waited for her friends to quiet themselves after her husband's moving response to the call to assist the Earth. She was very proud of him and not at all surprised. His concern about the Earth was life long. Even when he was a small child, he understood that life, all life, should be respected and held in high regard. While his father played a role in Mark's approach to life, he openly acknowledged that his son was born with this instinct. He was a child that was abundantly curious, who wanted to know everything about everything; and most of his curiosity was focused upon nature and all her grandeur. He was an amazing child who grew up to be an amazing man. His name exemplified his character. Mark Goodman was a good man. She looked lovingly towards this wonderful man who was the love of her life. *Why me? Why was I so lucky to be the one he chose as his life mate?*

"Because you were made for each other!" announced Barbara, whose bluntness even surprised herself. Everyone turned towards her in puzzlement and then Faye playfully pointed in Barb's direction and responded.

"She's showing off again! Here I am minding my own business, just have a private conversation with myself, and look what happens! She accesses that super powerful hearing of hers and provides me with answers to my unspoken questions." Recognizing what Faye was referring to, everyone laughed at her joviality. Barb turned several shades of red and apologized for her actions.

"Good grief! I am so sorry. Sometimes, I just don't realize when I'm hearing something that hasn't been spoken aloud. It just all seems the same to me. I really am sorry, Faye, but my response was accurate. You and Mark belong together." Barb raised her eyebrows and pointed at both of them. "You two truly are intended to be together. It's obvious! And I am so glad because it just wonderful being in your company. You are role models for all of us."

"Goodness, Dear. What was the question you were pondering over?" Mark inquired.

"Oh, I was just wondering why I was so lucky to be your spouse, Dear. And then, this goofball interrupted my thoughts." Mark turned to Barbara and boldly declared that he had married Faye because she was the hottest chick on the block. This brought about another round of laughter.

"And she was and remains the love of my life," he tenderly added. "I knew the minute I laid eyes on her that she was the one for me. And it was the same for you, wasn't it Faye?" She nodded immediately.

"Oh yes, I knew he was the one, but it didn't occur to me that he was having the same response. Aren't we a pair?" She leaned over to give her love a kiss. They were indeed a special couple.

"And what about you, Dear? Are you interested in this project?" Mark knew the answer, but he wanted Faye to have an opportunity to express her thoughts with the group. She knew that he was opening the way for her.

"I'm very interested in participating and eager to hear more about it from our invisible assistant. He sounds like a remarkable fellow. The thought of having a Guide intrigues me. And it's comforting, because we are going to need guidance to finesse this work. This information is a slap in the face with reality, and we will meet up with some challenging experiences, but we are up for it. The eight of us work well together. You know, I must admit, the idea that we can actually effect change is exhilarating. I'm tired of feeling helpless and hopeless. We can improve ourselves! This news about our negative energy is fascinating and inspirational. I guess one can look at this as an insult. That would be a poor choice, but one could choose to do that. On the other hand one can look at it as a blessing. We've been given a gift of awareness. We've been apprised of our shortcomings, and now, we can take action. We can do something about our ill will! We are capable of changing and I want to be a better person. And I want to help others to improve themselves as well. Just imagine the possibilities, Friends! This truly is transformative work. We can change our ways and change the energy of the planet. We can bring her back to full health again." Faye paused briefly and her friends watched an insight cross her face. "My word," she asserted. "If we release our ill will, the Earth will be healed, and so will we!" Faye's inspirational speech ignited her friends and also gave them much to think about.

*

A passage from
Beyond The Day of Tomorrow
A Seeker's Guide
(Chapter Seventeen)

"From the depths of our knowing burns the ache to remember all that we have known and the desire to know all there is to know. For some, this ache and desire is more keenly known than for others, but even those who claim no such awareness possess the same ache, the same desire, the same curiosity as do all others, for it is not the clarity of the acquiring seeker which determines the

seeking nature, but it is the seeking nature which brings clarity to the seeking seeker.

Awareness of the seeking process develops with time, but it is not dependent upon time. Each seeker evolves uniquely in a way and time particularly suited to that seeker. How and when the development occurs does not merit applause or critical assessment. It is as it is.

In typical human fashion, we tend to applaud faster as better, and we view any mode less than fast as less than. This erroneous manner of interpretation is damaging and contaminating to the novice seeker. As each seeker grows in awareness, the seeking process evolves proportionately, but the evolutionary pace is irrelevant, for each seeker begins anew each life experience. In the evolving process of self-discovery we are continuously beginners and more than beginners simultaneously. We come, we begin, we mature, and we begin again. Forever novices and forever evolving. Where we are on our evolutionary journey is of no matter to our essence, but where we are going is of importance.

Perhaps as we continue our process of growing and evolving, it would be wise to remember the insignificant factor of status to the journey. Who appears to be a beginner may in truth be one of ancient ways, and who appears to be of elder status may indeed be a youthful journeyman. As such, what one sees is not necessarily what one is, and the point of this is to remind each of you to honor the other's journey as if it were your own. Regard no one higher than another, for all are equally valued and cherished. This reminder is reminiscent of the Golden Rule, which is equally applicable to the journey process. Honor each seeker's journey as you do your own. Do unto others, as you would have them do unto you.

There are no rules or restrictions that one must follow when pursuing the journey; however, there are courtesies that one might choose to practice. Think harshly of no one. Act ungraciously towards no one. Hold no malice in your heart and do no harm to anyone. If all would choose to practice these kindnesses, perhaps the journeys would be more pleasant and less tedious."

*

"Faye, as always, you have given me pause. And as usual, I am grateful!" Sally's expression of gratitude spoke the truth for her friends as well. "Needless to say, this has been an eventful evening. Perhaps, this has been our all-time best gathering, which is quite a compliment, since we have enjoyed some great times together. Never did I imagine when Barb called to invite us over that we would be in for this kind of evening. Wow!

My heart is full with anticipation and hopefulness. And I feel young! The thought of being able to assist the Earth is riveting. What an honor this is! She's done so much for us, while our neglect of her is shameful. How could we not notice what was happening to her? How could we think that we were not harming her? Our greed blinded us to the reality of her situation. All we cared about was progress without any concern of the consequences that our so-called progress was bringing. We didn't even notice our own degrading behaviors. Along with our progress came progressively more aggressive behavior. As she deteriorated because of our ill will, we fell deeper and deeper into a milieu of violence and cruelty. How did this happen without our notice?

I'm afraid that question will haunt me for years to come, but in the meantime, I want to be of service. I want to help turn things around for humankind and for the Earth. For the first time, I feel like there is something I can do beyond recycling, composting, and turning the lights off in rooms not being used. Please don't misunderstand. I know these actions are important, but I want to do more. We are not people of means that can invest money in projects of sustainability, but that doesn't mean we don't want to help. And this project is available to everyone. We can effectively assist the Earth by improving ourselves. There's no excuse for not participating in this improvement project. It costs nothing. We can practice being better people wherever we are. At work, at home, at play! It doesn't matter where we are, we can clean up our behavior. This transformation project can be worked on no matter where we are at any given time.

This is an incredible opportunity. And yes! I most definitely want to participate in this project. We can do this, my friends!" The circle of friends was sparked again by another uplifting commitment to the Earth. As I watched our friends, my heart raced. *These are people of goodness! And there are more good people all across the planet!* Being in my friends' company made me realize the potential of humankind.

"My friends, I am so grateful for what is happening here this evening. One can lose sight of the goodness that exists among us because of the sensationalism of acts of ill will. We are bombarded with bad news, but rarely do we see or hear about events of good will. And this is a shame! We need to be reminded that goodness still exists. That's what I'm experiencing this evening being in your company. I am witnessing goodness unfold around me and it fills my heart with joy and optimism. Many of you have utilized the words helplessness and hopelessness in expressing your feelings, and unfortunately our world is burdened by these feelings. How can we not be?" I looked about the room and saw good people coming together to share a heartbreaking reality, and I also saw hopefulness.

"We have shared our sorrows and we have transformed them into positive intentions. This has been a remarkable evening and it gives me great hope. I really feel optimistic about the future and about our ability to create change within ourselves, with each other, and with all those folks that we may encounter in the upcoming days, weeks, and years to come."

"I want to tag onto your observations, Sister. I too think this meeting has been astonishing. Here we are, a group of old friends, who have come together to discuss a potential project that is on the horizon, and with no specific details of this project, we are already putting our energy into it. This is noteworthy! Not only are we surprising ourselves with our own exuberance about said project, but also, I think we may be witnessing how others might react to this opportunity as well. Remember, we are not the only ones that are being approached. Just imagine the possibilities, my friends. Our responses to this call to action have been positive and immediate. Multiply that by all the other invitations that have been presented." Barb's curiosity soared. "I wonder how many other folks have been solicited. I would love to know the answer to that question. Oh, excuse this mind of mine! The point of my ramblings is this: we've gathered for the first time to discuss a possible project and look what has happened. We've already made great progress! Good for us!" Smiles came to everyone's faces. Progress had indeed been made and the evening was still young. Dave Moore's comments were still to come.

"Well, hasn't this been an eventful evening?" Dave's gentle smile was a calming factor. "Like the rest of you, I had no idea that we were going to have such an exciting experience." Turning to both Barb and me, he expressed his gratitude. "I just want to thank the two of you for hosting tonight and also for sharing this incredible news with us. I'm still a bit confused about all that's happening, but so far, everything looks and sounds good to me. Of course, the unknown specifics are tweaking with my restless mind, but I can handle that. I've grown accustomed to the challenges of a mind that has a mind of its own." Once again he showered the room with his gentle smile.

"My curiosity about the invisible fellow is running high. Have to admit that I would like to know a lot more about him, but I doubt that he carries credentials or a resume with him. Bottom line for me is your trust in him. Obviously, he's made a positive impression on both of you or we wouldn't be here now. Please don't misunderstand me. I'm not questioning his sincerity about this project, but I'm just curious. How did he get involved with the project? How long has he been participating? How much longer does he plan to be involved in this work?"

"I have been involved with the project for a very long time and my commitment to the project is never-ending." The voice came from outside the circle and grabbed everyone's attention. Heads turned and excitement rose. Everyone was hopeful that the invisible being would appear.

"Dear Friend, thank you for joining us. Let us bring in another chair." Before I could rise from my own chair, Barb was up and bringing one in from the other room. Everyone scooted about so that space was made for the visitor. With the chair placed, anticipation rose. We all remained silent, not knowing if our guest had seated himself. Only a few seconds had passed but we were all antsy, so I attempted to ease the situation. "My Friend, we are most pleased that you are here. I assume you have been monitoring our conversation."

"Yes, it has been most enjoyable to be in your company. What a lovely evening you have experienced." His voice seemed to move from one side of the room to the other, but I was not certain of my perceptions.

"Have you joined our circle, Old Friend?"

"Yes, I have. Thank you for making room for me within this network of energy. You are people of good energy and it is refreshing to be in your company. I have come without form so that each of you can experience my presence without the luxury of sight. Although this can be unsettling at first, I wish for you to feel my presence even when you cannot see me. I am here. And for convenience's sake, it is hospitable to have a place upon which you can focus your attention." He paused for a moment and

I sensed that my friends were cautious about speaking. Without visual cues, it is complicated to know when one can respectfully speak.

"My friends, may I ask you to enjoy a deep breath?" Everyone responded immediately. *"Now if you will, please just be in the company of your dear friends."* His invitation changed the mood. The anxiety stirred by his presence shifted as everyone positioned themselves more comfortably into their chairs. So, quickly, they adjusted to his presence. *"How wonderful it is to have such good companions. Old Friends are you! The energy within your circle is a most delightful place to be. I am most grateful to be in your presence. Please envision me sitting in the chair that was so graciously provided. Know that I am here and please accept me as one of your own."* Gentle sighs were released around the room. With so few words and so little time, connection was made. Our new Old Friend had established himself within the group. He invited us to take several more deep breaths and then welcomed us back to the present. Such intense relaxation had been attained during the brief meditative induction that a few moments were required to return. Sounds of movement became apparent and eyes slowly opened. Much to everyone's surprise, the empty chair was now occupied by One with form. Gasps were heard and welcome comments were made. Our guest smiled lovingly and bowed his head in response.

"So, now my Friends, you can experience my visual form. The energy that is emitted by your circle enables me to materialize. It is a complicated process that demands a great deal of energy, which is why we do so limitedly. What I desire is that you realize that I was here before you were able to see me and I am here now while you can see me. I am real! And I am not alone. Many have enjoyed the camaraderie of your friendships this evening. We hope that our presence is not perceived as poor manners. We did not wish to interrupt the fine work that was achieved this evening; however, we admit that we selfishly did want to observe your interactions. You work well together my Friends, and we are most pleased that you are willing to participate in our project, which of course, is your project as well. We are all here to save the Life Being Earth. And we have been addressing this issue for a very long time. Our progress has fluctuated. Sometimes great movement has occurred while other times have been most disappointing. Recent years have seen a rapid increase in her decline as well as a decrease in humankind's concern.

Suffice it say, we have much work to do and it must be done quickly."

"How can we be of assistance?" asked Dave.

"Ah! You are on board, Mr. Moore?"

"Yes, I am! I still have many questions to ask, of course, but that can wait. I definitely want to help in any way possible. And please call me Dave. My name is Dave."

"The name of your father suits you, Dave. He is a wonderful man, as are you. And he is highly regarded in his new location just as he was in your time with him. He sends his love." The room fell silent. Dave had not anticipated this response. Sally leaned over and placed her hand on his knee, as he tried to compose himself.

Dave's response was softly spoken. "You know my Dad?" he asked. He could do no more than a whisper.

"Yes, my Friend, I know him well and have for many lifetimes. Like you, he is one of service. We have worked on many projects together, and now, we do the same. Our shared commitment to Earth is resolute." The amiable guest, the Dear Old Friend, changed his focus to the group. He was aware that Dave needed time to incorporate the information just received.

"My Friends, you are not alone! This message is one that must be remembered, for the comfort it brings is restorative. On this planet you are surrounded by beings of all kinds and each being is equal to all others. You are equal and you are same, and yet, you are different. And you are abundant! Never are you alone on this beautiful planet. And there is much, much more for you to understand about the concept of never being alone. Those who are here on this planet depart from here when it is their time, but they do not cease to exist. The form that was utilized in any particular lifetime does waste away, but the essence continues to exist forevermore."

*

A passage from
Beyond The Day of Tomorrow
A Seeker's Guide
(Chapter Eighteen)

"As in all life experiences, this lifetime involves the awakening of old memories. Each new awakening is experienced as an aha and then quickly moves into a

hmm. Is that not true for you, Old Friend? You proceed through your daily activities and from out of nowhere comes an aha moment, and in that moment you are thrilled with the new awareness. The range of feelings is quite expansive. You are delighted, you are grateful, you are amused, you are confused, you are filled with a sense of connection and closeness and you are filled with a sense of loss. And you are mystified.

As you bathe in this pool of emotions, you wonder where these aha moments originate. Surely, nowhere is not an appropriate answer. During these times of contemplation and introspection, the hmm is birthed. For as quickly as the aha moment appears and disappears, so too does the awakening experience, and in that instant of transition from appearance to disappearance, enlightenment occurs.

The nowhere is the darkness that holds all our forgotten memories and the flicker of awareness is the enlightening of the darkness. Brief, but momentous are these fleeting occasions of reminiscence."

*

"My friends, your mood is serious. Do my words surprise you?" Our guest seemed confused. Certain that he had just delivered positive and hopeful information, he was confused by the silence that engulfed the room. Eventually the one referred to as Sister replied.

"Old Friend, once again you have brought remarkable news to us, and even though this news is positive, it gives one pause. Excuse me, I can only speak for myself. It gives me pause. While I wholeheartedly believe in eternal life, having you speak of it in such a matter of fact way is both validating and stunning. I am stunned to hear it announced with such absolute certainty. So I was excited about your confirmation! But then my mind immediately went to another place, which is yet another eye-opener. It occurred to me that my end of life scenario may coincide with the Earth's ending scenario, and that was not a possibility I wanted to think about. So I'm reeling from that unsolicited possible preview of the future. However, now that I'm speaking about this, my attitude is changing. I want to help the Earth as much as I can before it's my time to depart. My generation made this mess and we need to clean it up.

So forgive me for that downward spiral; I understand why you would identify my mood as serious. It was, briefly, but I'm beyond that now. I'm determined to effect change."

"Thank you for clarifying your situation, Old Friend. And for your rapid turnaround! Let us hope that others on the planet will gain similar resolve as quickly as you just demonstrated. Acceptance of responsibility is necessary. Present attitudes are not in alignment with the reality of your circumstances. What has transpired upon the Earth is not of natural causes. Her decline is directly related to the incomprehensible actions of humankind. What is profoundly sad is the continued denial of this truth. Do those who disregard the obvious honestly believe that they can survive the consequences of a planet transitioning into dormancy? Can they be so foolish? Wealth will afford no one with special privileges. Those who think they can escape the ramifications of the Earth's decline will not find themselves welcomed in other sectors of the universe. The cruelty acted out on this planet will remain on this planet. The situation that has arisen because of abusive disregard of this magnificent life being must be resolved on this planet by those who perpetrated the ill deeds."

Once again, the mood turned serious. The guest remained silent as his companions mulled over his remarks. Barb's patience was running thin, but she didn't know what to say. She was impressed by her Sister's statement of resolve; she wished that she shared her determination. Finally, she blurted out the question that was on the tip of her tongue.

"What do you mean when you say we will not be welcomed in other parts of the universe? Previously, you told us that many from all parts of existence were rallying about the Earth to provide us assistance with this problem. That was so comforting to hear, but now, it sounds as if you are saying something very different. Can you please elaborate on this?"

"Both statements are true and one is predicated upon the other. The peoples of Earth must change their ways or the Life Being who provides them residence will not be able to sustain her vibrancy. This is a truth that your scientists have known about for quite some time, but their opinions are ignored and discredited by those who are not qualified to make such assessments. Unfortunately, too many do not wish to hear the truth, so they foolishly follow the lead of those who are misguided.

Let me speak truthfully, dear friends, efforts are being made on behalf of the Earth, and those who are already participating in changing their ways are the ones to follow. They take the lead while the foolish ones mock their progress. The Earth needs assistance now. She cannot continue much longer. The answer lies within each resident of this planet. Each one of you has the ability to help, but you must choose to make this a priority. You must choose to change your ways of harmful influence. You must make decisions that take others into consideration. You must care about others as much as you care about yourself. And you must sacrifice your luxuries for the sake of others' survival. Attitudes of greed and superiority cannot be your guide. These changes must be made.

Many are here to assist you in these transitions; however, you must address the issues of your individual and collective transformation. No one can do this for you. We stand ready to aid you, but if you choose to continue upon your present course of ill will, you will suffer the consequences of your poor judgment.

You are blessed with an ability of healing powers and you must choose to access and utilize this ability on the behalf of the Earth and all your other fellow beings. This gift is not special to you alone. All in existence are endowed with this ability. By choosing to pursue your healing abilities, you will heal the infliction of ill will that dominates your civilization.

My friends, many are here to assist you, but you must accept responsibility for the problems that you have created and you must take action to correct the harm that you have perpetrated. For the sake of the Earth, for the sake of your own kind, please take appropriate steps to rectify what you have done. We are here, Old Friends. You are not alone. Please do what must be done."

*

A passage from
Beyond The Day of Tomorrow
A Seeker's Guide
(Chapter Nineteen)

"Does this challenge you, my Friend? Could it be that the way to enlightenment moves not only forward, but also gathers momentum from the past? Observe your next aha experience. Notice for yourself how initially the new awareness feels refreshingly new and then instantaneously, it seems as if you have known this new awareness for all times. Old Friend, you have!

*What was forgotten was remembered, and now
perhaps it is time to remember the earlier reminder.
What you have known before, you will always know, and
what you will come to know you will know thereafter."*

*

"Sir," asserted Faye. "You refer to us as Old Friends, so I will call you the same if that meets with your approval."

"Always you have done so in the past, my dear Friend, and it will please me greatly if you do so again in this life experience."

"Thank you," she continued. "I'm grateful for your willingness to speak bluntly with us. Admittedly, it is difficult to hear these truths, but denial serves no one, and I personally don't want to be someone who goes around ignoring the truth because I'm too afraid to face it. That's not going to get us anywhere.

Old Friend, I'm assuming that you and your companions have a plan or you wouldn't be contacting us. So what is it? We're all on board with this project. We want to face the truth of our irresponsible actions and we want to change our ways. So let's get started!" Faye's insistent call for action tickled her friends. Her husband simply smiled and shook his head.

"Old Friend, you need to know that this lovely lady is a take action kind of gal. Always has been; always will be! And I think she is speaking for all of us," Mark glanced about the room for confirmation. "Just tell us how to proceed."

"Gratitude abounds," whispered the guest from where they did not know. *"I am most grateful for your willingness to proceed. So, there is a request I must make of you before our next meeting. Consider this to be our second step towards saving the Earth. The first was your attendance of this meeting. The next is an analysis of your personal characteristics. I ask that you review your behaviors from various aspects of this life experience and try to determine your assets and your problem areas. In other words, what are your positive traits and what are the traits that you believe require improvements or adjustments. Once you have determined what you would like to change about yourself, then think about the ways that you can approach this challenge. My friends, this is not a simple task. It is one that requires time and careful consideration. You may find writing*

about your experiences will facilitate your growth and possibly hasten it, but the particulars of your self-discovery process are yours to discern.

The point of this task is evident. One must review one's behaviors before you can know what you must change for the betterment of self and those around you. As you ponder this, please take the Earth into consideration throughout your exploration process. Remember your behavior profoundly affects her. So attempt to accurately assess the impact that your behavior is having upon this beautiful Life Being.

My Friends, before we end this gathering, may we agree to meet again in forty-eight hours?" The circle of friends agreed immediately to his suggestion. *"Thank you for your quick attention to this lesson in self-knowledge.*

Before I leave, may I ask for a moment more of your time? Please join me in a brief meditation with the Beloved Earth. Breathe deeply, my friends. And take yourselves to the place of silence that you so ably know how to do. Be in that space. Wherever you are, allow your heart to open to the idea of merging your energy with the Earth. Take another deep breath and accept the opportunity to share your energy with this remarkable Life Being. Breathe deeply again, and simply be in the Sacred Space that you have entered.

Old Friends, you are one who holds within you the energy of the Beginning, the Present, and the Future. This energy is the Essence of the initial energy that created existence. This initial energy still exists to this day and you are the possessor of this original Essence of existence. Ponder this truth, Old Friends. Within you, the Essence of All That Was, All That Is, and All That Will Ever Be exists. You are all this and more. The Essence within you is the Essence within all and this Essence was and remains able to create and to heal all others in existence. This energy is all-powerful and can be used to enliven and empower those who are in need. Breathe this awareness in, Dear Friend, and simply be with this newfound information. As unbelievable as it seems, it is simply the truth.

As you rest with this information, remember that all others possess this gift as well, including the dear Friends who join you in this circle. For a moment, let us merge our energy together. Each of you, please imagine a small particle of your True Essence exiting from your heart and moving into the center of this room. Picture this in your mind please. Nine particles of energy emerging from each of us and joining together in the core of our meeting space! Now, take another deep breath and imagine enhancing your particle of energy and then visualize our combined energies growing bigger and more powerful. And now, let us envision the energy rising from the roof of this house and let it move above the trees to the empty park two blocks away. Visualize the energy moving to that location. Let the energy hover there as we request permission to share this energy with the Earth. With her permission, we offer our energy, our Essence of Life, to her so that it can provide her with sustenance. Envision this transfusion of energy from us to her. And feel her gratitude.

Now return yourself back to your present location and relax back into your own body. And be in gratitude for this sacred exchange of energy that you just participated in. Be in peace, my Friends." Time passed, as is its way, until the Old Friend took his leave from us.

"My dear friends, I am most grateful for your assistance to the Earth. And I look forward to our next meeting. Until then, I bid you adieu."

*

A passage from
Beyond The Day of Tomorrow
A Seeker's Guide
(Chapter Twenty)

"In the days ahead, your journey will take you many places to explore and investigate. Along the way, remember to be gentle with yourself. The journey is ongoing, the experiences are never-ending and the purpose is to grow in knowingness. As you gain more awareness of knowingness, you will also gain acceptance of your circumstances and of others. Often in our busy and somewhat chaotic lives we become so involved in the acquisition of possessions that we overlook the abundance already possessed. Our perspectives and our definitions of abundance vary from experience to experience, but our abundance within remains a constant.

As we struggle to remember our lost memories, our amnesic state also impairs the awareness of eternal abundance, which is of our possession. Because we do not remember this gift or how to access its bounties, we move through our experiences ever seeking that which we already possess.

111

Along the way, we will experience the confusion of existence in many different bodies. These shells, which are temporarily ours to enjoy, are also our responsibilities to attend and care for. This burden falls upon the inhabitant of the shell. Each life experience we choose a shell in which to experience the next phase of our journey. This shell, another gift of initiation, requires attention and deserves respect. As the shell offers the inhabitant endless opportunities for adventures of seeking, the inhabitant in return must offer dedication of care and consideration to the wellness of the shell.

As such, Old Friend, be very gentle with yourself and the shell will serve you well."

*

Barb's eyes popped open the instant she heard their visitor's voice. Her desire to see him disappear again was embarrassing, but not enough so to still her curiosity. Much to her surprise he was already formless. As he said goodbye, her heart ached even though she knew he would soon be in their company again. *What a remarkable experience!* Her thought did not go unheard.

"Indeed, it was!" affirmed Faye, as her friends looked on curiously. "Oh, don't mind me," she laughed. "I'm just responding to Barb's thoughts about tonight's experience. What a hoot! My goodness, haven't we had a good time?" Everyone reacted positively to Faye's remarks. Her husband Mark noted that her comment was the understatement of the year.

"Old girl, that was the best time we've had in a long time, maybe ever! We just had a very unusual experience that felt absolutely normal. Obviously, his appearing and disappearing takes some getting used to, but other than that, it was an evening with good company and great conversation. We've definitely got some work ahead of us. I'm up for that!"

"It was breathtaking!" signed Annie. "I am just so grateful. This truly is an opportunity of a lifetime for us. I don't know why we are so lucky to be a part of this, but I really am happy that we are. Thank you, thank you, thank, you!" Her eyes turned upward as she repeated her expression of gratitude. "I'm up for this too, Mark. In fact, it's timely!

I've been longing for something more in my life lately. Which is not to say that I am unhappy with our lives," she added as she placed her hand on her husband's knee. "Actually, I feel Jim and I are blessed, and I can't imagine being any happier, but this work brings new meaning into our lives. This is very important work, and I want to be a part of this project." Jim nodded in agreement as he listened to Annie. His internal smile was even bigger than the outward one that was gracing the room. He couldn't help himself. His emotions just came flowing from his mouth.

"I love this woman! And I love listening to her. She lives life so beautifully; I am truly the luckiest man in the world." His friends applauded Jim's praises for his spouse of many years. His shyness took over for a moment, but he rose above it. "It's no news to any of you how I feel about her, but sometimes, it just needs to be said. And I'm with her in this project! The notion that we can actually do something to help the Earth enlivens me too. I'm tired of feeling helpless. I want to do more. And I want to learn more about everything and 'everyone' that our new Old Friend talked about tonight. Life has quickly become very exciting." Barb watched on with enthusiasm. She wondered how other people in other groups were reacting to the news this Old Friend was bringing forward. She hoped they were as excited as the friends in our group.

"Well, needless to say the Andersons are a hard act to follow, but I share their sentiments," stated Dave. "I feel empowered to take action, which hasn't been the case lately. Every time I watch the news and hear another story denying climate issues, I just go into a slump. But tonight changed that for me. Wish I had known about this possibility a long time ago. I'm feeling very optimistic now. And I know Sally is also." His wife was indeed revved up. Her mind was already on task.

"I am optimistic! This project is so important. It places Earth's care in the hands of the people rather than governments and industries that have their own selfish agendas. We can effect change; I truly believe that! But time is the crucial issue. We must act with haste! And having said that, we might turn our focus to the assignment that we were given. Let's share some ideas and then get started on our individual work." Sally's initiative inspired us all.

*

A passage from
Beyond The Day of Tomorrow
A Seeker's Guide
(Chapter Twenty-One)

"How often have you heard yourself complain about your present circumstances? Our human inclination is to admire that which we do not have and to disdain that which we possess. Invariably, we want what we don't have and we're dissatisfied with what we do have, and then to add insult to injury, someone else has what we want.

This disgruntled way of experiencing abundance offers few rewards, yet it is practiced by many who struggle with the concept of acceptance. Unfortunately, when one is unaware of the gift of abundance, the concept of abundance is difficult to accept. This lack of awareness fosters dissatisfaction, and breeds discontent.

In belief that one is lacking, one finds fault with those perceived as having, and thereby, envy and jealousy are created. Proliferation of these deceptions of truth further removes us from the awareness of our own abundance. So focused are we on what we perceive is missing that we are unable to see what is present, and in this state of misperceived deprivation, we live life as if we were barren of abundance. From this misunderstanding many suffer, but of this misunderstanding, few know it as such. No further from the truth could this be."

*

I started to take the lead, but instead led with a question. "Sally, dear friend, do you have any thoughts about how we might proceed?"

Without hesitation, she proposed a noteworthy suggestion. "Yes, I've been thinking about this in-between being attentive to everything that's been going on during this event. What a joy this as been!" She briefly lingered with the energy of the evening and then returned to focus. "It occurred to me that it might be in our best interest to focus on our assets first. Trust me, this is a good strategy. If we address our negative aspects first, we may fall victim to our own frustrations and disappointments with ourselves. This will not serve us well.

So, I strongly recommend that we each make a list of our positive qualities. And oh, by the way, actually write this down, either on paper or on your computer, so that you actually get these positive aspects out of your head and recorded somewhere. We need to have easy access to these positive attributes so that we can refresh our memory once we move into the second part of the assignment. I also encourage you to elaborate upon your positive tendencies. Bring your good points forward. This is an important part of our self-discovery processes. We need to be as honest about the good side as we are about the negative. This is no time to be humble, my friends. Get to know the positive aspects of your true self because that good energy is going to help you look at the other side of you that requires some improvement.

Now, let me throw out a couple of pointers regarding the other side of the continuum, friends. Just remember, you are not alone. We all have traits that we need to look at and it may be difficult to do that, but just remember it's for the Earth and you also reap the benefits from doing this work. And also, please remember to take care of yourself while you're reviewing your not-so-great characteristics. Address what you can and then take a breather. Actually, if you're able, try to make your list without any judgment and then, come and deal with one item at a time, taking breaks whenever you need to. The last thing we need to do is to wear ourselves out while addressing this exercise. We will not change all our habits overnight. And we cannot tear ourselves apart while dealing with issues that are painful. If we approach our individual challenges in this manner, we will not have the energy to help the Earth. Improvements come in increments, my friends! Please remember this.

I suspect we will need to take care of each other as well during this project. We're all good people and we are also people who need to improve our ways for our sakes and for the sake of the Earth. But we are also people, just ordinary people, who will need a helping hand while facing our negative attitudes and behavior. I certainly know that I will need assistance, so I'm asking for it now. If any of you sees me sinking, please jump in and rescue me. And I offer to do the same for you." Sally paused to take a deep breath, and everyone joined her.

"Goodness, Sal, you really have been thinking about this. What a remarkable set of ideas. Thank you so much!" My admiration of Sally, which was already very high, just took another leap. Dave, smiling proudly, acknowledged that his beloved was a powerhouse.

"No doubt!" exclaimed Faye. "Great suggestions, girl!"

*

A passage from
Beyond The Day of Tomorrow
A Seeker's Guide
(Chapter Twenty-Two)

"As we begin the journey towards increased understanding, let us first remember our initial reminder. Our paths may cross many times and repeatedly we will meet Old Friends in new circumstances and perhaps new relationships, and in these meetings, often one or the other will sense a relationship of distant standing. We have all heard ourselves or others say words such as, 'Geez, I feel like I've known you forever' or 'Wow, we just clicked the minute we met each other.' Or perhaps this one sounds familiar, 'We're soul mates.'

Does this have a familiar ring to it? On one or more occasions have you not experienced this or known someone who shared a similar tale with you? These chance meetings are not serendipitous at all. In truth, we plan our comings quite extensively before we return and these designs are managed with care and the cooperation of other Old Friends and cherished seekers.

With each plan devised, there is a purpose to that design. The designing seeker with a desire to acquire a particular lesson or lessons strategically creates a Master Plan with the hopes that the plan will actualize upon returning to a new life experience. In devising this plan, others volunteer to cooperate in the unfolding of the desired plan by participating in ways that might facilitate the desired lesson.

Many who volunteer for the privilege of participation do so with no other purpose than service, for it is considered the highest honor to serve another in their quest for increased knowingness. This act of generosity, while offered selflessly, does not go unrewarded, for each participant gains benefits from experiencing a life of service. As a design unfolds, not only does the designer of the plan gain the incredible gifts of opportunities from the unfolding experiences, but the volunteers in service do as well. In this way, all who participate benefit from the participation and all participants participate for a reason. Thus, a gentle reminder is provided for our initial reminder. We are all here for a reason; i.e., 'You are here for a reason.'"

*

"My friends, does anyone else have any thoughts about our assignment?" My question seemed to fall upon blank stares and a few shoulder shrugs. I wondered if Sally had any other ideas racing about in her mind, but she too remained quiet.

"Well, I have an idea to bring up," I said with a bit of reluctance, "but it seems rather important."

"Please do so, dear," urged Faye. "We must look at all aspects of our behaviors, even if it is unpleasant."

"Yes, you're right, of course. There is another factor that we must face, I'm afraid. And it may be complicated, but hopefully, you will agree that we need to pursue this level of clarity about ourselves." I felt myself tightening up, which was a clear indicator that this idea was one that caused me some concern. It was obvious to me that I needed to fess up about my reluctance to talk about this. "Okay, friends, truth is I'm nervous about suggesting this, which is all the more reason for me to do so. I don't want to admit this, but I am rather certain that some of you, perhaps all of you, know more about my quirks than I know about myself. I'm sure that I am blind to many of my traits that I just don't want to face. And," a deep breath was taken and noticed by my friends, "I need to know the truth about myself, so I'm asking all of you to be honest with me at our next meeting. Please note that I'm saying next time not now, because I'm too tired to face the truth now. I also ask that you tell me the truth with loving kindness, which I know you will, but please be gentle with me. Whew!" More deep breaths were consumed. "Okay, so you can see that I'm feeling fragile about this. I'll just thank you in advance because you are all wonderful friends and I know you will help me through this."

"Well, that was courage personified," declared Annie. "Thank you, dear one, for being so vulnerable with us. I doubt that you realize it, but you've done us all a huge favor. I for one was thinking about this, but didn't have the guts to bring it up, so thank you for taking the risk.

And you are right about this! We all have blind spots. Personally, I'm not sure I would be willing to do this anywhere else except with you guys. I trust all of you and I'm still nervous about it, but I'm asking for feedback from all of you as well. This needs to happen folks. I offer all of you a listening ear and a promise that I will hold you in my heart as you do your work. And I need the same from you."

"Okay, everyone! We've just witnessed another brave soul open her heart to us. Let's have a show of hands, please. Are we all willing to make this part of our assignment?" All hands went up in response to Faye questions. "Great! This is a really important aspect of our work. We need to practice with one another. Sharing feedback in a gentle, loving way isn't always easily done, nor is it always easily received. So, we can bear our souls to one another and practice tender-heartedness at the same time. This will prepare us for future activities when we are reaching out to other folks." Faye turned in my direction to impress upon me that this last important step in our assignment was a result of my speaking up about a sensitive matter.

"Thank you, Faye. I do see how the group benefitted. We are so fortunate. Our friendships have sustained us for years and now it's the foundation for work that was unexpected. I'm so glad we are all in this together." Similar comments circled the room before we all agreed to bring the gathering to an end. Goodbyes and warm hugs were exchanged as folks headed to the door. Barb was the last to leave.

"Incredible evening!" she said while exiting the door. "See you tomorrow!" I watched her until she reached the end of the block and moved out of sight. *What a remarkable night!*

*

A passage from
Beyond The Day of Tomorrow
A Seeker's Guide
(Chapter Twenty-Two)

*"The system is one of simple, yet complex beauty. We
all serve and we are all served. At times our service may*

be completely selfless, other times, it may be conjointly self-serving, and there will be other times when the Grand Design is of our own creation and the primary focus of service. In this way, all serve and all benefit. All are given opportunities to be of service and all are given opportunities to be the recipient of service. This mutually collaborative sharing of experiences through joint participation offers all involved endless opportunities to acquire more knowingness. Through individual and shared experiences, all gain from the preplanned designs. When the seeker plans the next desired lesson in anticipation of another coming, unknown it is to the seeker exactly how the plan will unfold.

As with all plans many factors may influence the unfolding process, which may in turn complicate and/ or complement the desired experience, but this too offers continuous opportunities for new experiences and the unknown aspect of the unfolding happenings provides mystery and intrigue for the seeking seeker and all involved.

In sweet simplicity, all participate and all benefit. In complex ways of unforeseen anticipation, the ones involved experience consequences of great diversity, all of which contribute to the desired goal of attaining new awareness and more knowingness.

As the new coming begins to unfold in delightful and unpredictable ways, the seeking seeker and all the participating seekers begin journeys anew, for with each participation in a new life experience, each involved must discover their reason for involvement and their purpose for participation.

When the coming experience comes, those involved will know from deep within that they have come for a reason, but the memory of that reason for each participant will be elusive. Yet each will know and each will feel compelled to seek the purpose of their being, the reason for their existence, and from this knowing deep within, each who comes knows what all know. You are here for a reason."

*

7

"**G**ood evening, my Old Friend, may I have a moment with you?" The voice of our new Old Friend came from the corner of my Sacred Space. Once again, I wondered who he was and how we had met, etc., etc. But I knew it didn't matter.

"My friend, did we deplete all of your energy this evening?" My question referred to his invisibility. I assumed that he had expended too much of his reserves during our long gathering.

"Not at all, my friend, but I am waning. The meeting was exceptional! We are all most grateful and delightfully surprised by the immediate acceptance shown by your friends. They are good people, who will take the word forward with grace and dignity. This gathering has exceeded our expectations. Thank you for your assistance."

"You are very welcome, but my contributions were few. As you have seen, these are ordinary people who care very deeply about the Earth and who are willing to change on her behalf. I do not believe that the outrageous media coverage reveals the truth amount humanity. I believe more of us than not are sincerely worried about the planet, but we have been burdened by the madness of the few who usurp the energy from the Earth, as well as from those of us who are committed to her. These people prey on fears and rely upon lies to manipulate whatever offenses they strive to create. Don't lose faith in us, my Dear Friend. Now that we have a plan, we can and will take charge of our negative behaviors that worsen the problem, and our positive energy will override the ill will that is presently operating.

We will need your assistance, my Friend, but we are fast learners and there are more advocates for the Earth than the media presents. Too many of us have been stunned into helplessness, but you have given us hope. And as the word spreads that there is a way to help her without the aid of those who are of a different mind, our numbers will rise. We now have a means to work on her behalf from our own determination and commitments. I am so grateful to you. Thank you for helping the Earth."

"She is a Beloved Life Being that is cherished by all in existence.

None of us can imagine life without her presence. We are committed to her well being. My Friend, much more will we ask of you and your friends. We are most pleased at your willingness to immediately engage with the task of reviewing your behaviors. This is a challenging task from which you will greatly benefit. Even those who are founded in goodness need to review themselves on a regular basis. Eventually, each of you will feel renewed from the experience. Although this task is essential for the next step, I offer you a gentle reminder. Humans are obsessed with perfection. Their obsession lies in their misunderstanding of the concept. All in existence are works of perfection, but perfection is ever changing. We grow, we expand, we acclimate to our new being, and then, we begin the process again. I urge you to encourage your friends that your assignment is founded in this development process. We do not seek perfection from every participant at the same time. Instead, we seek movement that facilitates more movement as the task of healing the Earth advances at the same time. Your companions are people of good standing and they will approach this exercise with fervor, and again, our gratitude abounds, but we ask that this task is the beginning of an ongoing process because that is in alignment with the existential evolutionary process.

One never reaches perfection, as humans perceive it. One is always a work in progress. So, what is needed at this time is improvement in wholehearted acceptance of all in existence. Let this be your guide. The notion that one is better than another is inconceivable among your neighbors in Existence. This misunderstanding causes great problems among the peoples of Earth and it demands a choice to think and act differently. The inequality that exists on this planet saddens all. Lack of concern for others who are perceived as different has greatly contributed to the Earth's declining health. The fact that many humans do not even regard her as a Life Being is significant evidence of the problem that must be addressed.

My Friend, the issues are surmountable and we believe this group will advance through the issues quickly. Again, I express gratitude for your assistance. If you require my assistance, remember that I am but a breath away. In peace be, dear Friend!"

"Thank you, my Friend, and please stop by any time. Sleep well, Old Friend."

*

A passage from
Beyond The Day of Tomorrow
A Seeker's Guide
(Chapter Twenty-Three)

"As in many circumstances when options are presented to us, we are faced with the dilemma of making decisions. For some, the effort of deciding is one of extreme difficulty, and often those who suffer from the fear of making decisions will choose to avoid circumstances rather than engage in the decision-making process. This process of fearing that which is a gift, is one worthy of exploration. The gift of free will offers everyone the privilege and the freedom to discern likes and dislikes. Preferences can be established and more awareness gained by practicing discernment through the utilization of the gift of free will.

Each experience of choosing provides additional information for the seeker to process. While one decision may bring dissatisfaction or discontent, another decision may bring the opposite. Regardless of the information gained, whether it is perceived positively or negatively, the new awareness acquired from the choosing process is of importance to the seeker's self-discovery.

Unfortunately, the practice of judgment is intricately involved in the decision-making process for many seekers. Whether self-imposed or other influenced, many are stifled and sometimes paralyzed by this pervasive procedure. When in fear of retribution by one's own critical mind or by another's unkindness, one has a tendency to avoid such a circumstance, and it is this fear of harsh assessment that inhibits one's ability to make decisions and to enjoy the gift of free will. This punitive approach to exploring and investigating one's life experience creates painful and debilitating consequences. Certainly one has the free will to choose this approach and learn the lessons of this path, but once learned, one does not need to continue this method of acquiring information.

How often have you derided yourself or been shamed by another for a particular decision made? Most of us have participated numerous times in such events, either as a recipient or as an offender. How did you feel about that situation? Did you enjoy being abused by yourself or chided by another? And how did it feel to put someone else down?

Think about this, please...from all angles. Study this through an example of your own choosing and realize the destructive nature of this process. No wonder some of us are terrified to make decisions. No wonder we try to avoid such situations; and how incredibly unfortunate it is that what was meant to be a gift and a mechanism for self-discovery, instead evolved in a manner that inhibits growth rather than fosters it.

For those who suffer from this misunderstanding of the gift of free will, remember you are still in the possession of free will. How you choose to proceed from this point is your choice; however, clinging to the old misunderstanding as Truth does not serve you."

*

8

"**B**eloved Friend, I am so grateful for everything that you are doing on our behalf. Your generosity amazes me. We have treated you so unkindly, so disrespectfully, and our misbehaviors continue. I am truly sorry. Recently, I learned how profoundly destructive our behavior is, and it is embarrassing for me to acknowledge that I was not aware of this. I am so deeply sorry. But the lesson has been learned and I promise you that my manners will improve. Now that I am aware that my behaviors, including my silent, private emotions, have tremendous negative impact upon you, I will monitor my actions and I will improve. You deserve so much better from me. I wish to make amends, if you will allow me. I cannot change what has been done in the past, but I can change how I proceed. I promise to carry you in my thoughts, words, and deeds everyday. I promise to rectify any misdeeds that I commit towards you, others, and myself the minute I recognize that an offense has occurred. I promise to hold you in my prayers and send you positive energy every day and this I will continue to do until it is my time to assist you from another plane. Mother Earth, I ask your permission to hold you in my heart. Please grant me permission to assist you as best as I am able." My prayer seemed too little, too late. Tears rushed down my cheeks. Remorse for my acts of ignorance and my insensitive disregard for our beautiful planet flooded through me. Finally, I was truly aware of the negative energy that I had perpetrated against her throughout my entire life. It was unbearable to think that I had been so oblivious to her needs.

"I am so, so sorry. Please allow me to assist you now and in the days to come. Please allow me to infuse you with some of the positive energy that naturally resides within me. I so wish to share this essential life energy with you." I fell silent. More tears were shed. My heart was filled with sadness.

*

A passage from
Beyond The Day of Tomorrow
A Seeker's Guide
(Chapter Twenty-Four)

"*Old Friend, now is the time to bring judgment into closer scrutiny. Judgment serves no purpose. It is the embodiment of unkindness. How can such assessment, whether self-inflicted or other imposed serve to enhance or inspire motivation?*

Search your memory. Certainly each of you has an experience related to judgment, which can serve as an example for self-exploration. Before the judgment occurred, what were you feeling? How were you feeling? When the judgmental event invaded your awareness then, what and how were you feeling?

Use your example to do a self-study and study the event thoroughly. Learn all you can learn from the experience. For those of you who benefit from writing, you may choose to use this approach to enhance your study, but if writing is not your style, then choose your preferred approach that typically serves you best during your introspective journeys.

I urge you to review the circumstance as it occurred and attempt to remember as accurately as possible the impact of the judging occurrence. Again, remember what and how the situation made you feel when it occurred, and now, how does it make you feel reliving the event in this remembering phase of your self-study?

Carefully watch the process as it unfolds. Each of you will have your own unique way of responding, processing, and reacting to the offending judgment. What you learn from this exploration of your process will provide you with new or renewed awareness of how you function in a world plagued with judgmental actions.

After you have explored your example of being the recipient of judgment, then you must open-mindedly and truthfully examine an example in which you are the offender of judgment. Be very honest with yourself. We are all capable of and inclined towards judgmental behavior.

However, most of us are truly unaware of this unhealthy trait in ourselves. We quickly are able to recognize it in others, but not so in ourselves.

One reason, which contributes to this imbalance of recognizing in others vs. recognition in self, relates to the concept of intention. Few of us accept the idea that he or she is a person who would intentionally harm another. Nor, are we aware when we actually do harm another. This self-portrait of being a good person and also being unaware of our impact greatly contributes to the proliferation of judgmental actions.

Another significant contributing factor, which we discussed earlier, is the inclination many have towards presuming the worst in another. While we think the best of ourselves (I am a good person and don't have a judging bone in my body!), we presume the worst of others (That person deliberately said that to hurt me!).

Well, what is it? Are we all good guys or are we all bad guys? Doesn't it make sense to presume that we are some of each, and so is the other person.

Without doubt there are some individuals who function from a very mean, misguided place, but those are the minority. Most of us function from innocence and unawareness. We voice cruelties and behave ungraciously without awareness of the powerful impact of our words and actions because rarely are our intentions meant to be so destructive. Dear Friends, we are responsible for our impact, and we are obligated to gain awareness of our impact so that it is positive not negative.

No longer can we claim unawareness as a reason or as an excuse for our words or our behavior. We are responsible for our impact no matter what our intentions are. Now, if you are presently reliving your example of being offended and feeling self-righteous towards the offender for not accepting responsibility for their impact on you, realize you are in judgment.

Before you begin teaching others about their responsibilities, I urge you to practice what you have just learned and then begin teaching by example."

*

What do I do now? Tears continued to stream down my face. *How do I know if the Earth has heard my request? And if she did, what is her response? How will I know?* Heartbroken, confused, and impatient were words that accurately described my mood. I wondered if I simply took action if the deed would be helpful or intrusive, or maybe even harmful. I truly didn't know what to do. The Earth has been disrespected for so long, I was afraid this might be one more action taken without regard for her best interest. I was torn. My inclination was, of course, to attempt the energy infusion, and then, I thought better of it. *My impatience is taking the lead. I'm so busy thinking about what I want to do that I'm not paying attention. Perhaps, she's already responded.* "I've done it again, Old Friend! I put my needs and wants above yours. My attention has been occupied by my own selfishness. Once again I must apologize. Let me try again. Mother Earth, I would be honored to offer you the essential life energy that naturally resides within me. May I do so now?" My Sacred Space grew silent, and in the depths of the silence I heard the sweet sounds of oceanic waters. The rhythm of the waves seemed to call to me, and with each breath that I took an alignment with the pulse of the Earth seemed to transpire. I felt in unison with this magnificent Life Being. Her embrace erased my doubts and I knew, without knowing how I really knew, that she welcomed the energy infusion. And I complied. I envisioned the positive energy residing within me passing through my body and spreading throughout her beautiful oceanic waters. In my mind's eyes, the Earth's fluids sparkled with delight. The moment was one I will never forget. We eventually separated; she retreated back to her realm and I to mine, but the Oneness that was felt when we merged together still remains within me. And as I drifted to sleep, once again the song of the ocean was heard, and from deep within the rhythmic melody, gratitude was expressed.

Morning arrived too soon the next day. Still lost in my interaction with the Earth, I remained in bed far beyond my usual hour. Fortunately, my early rising friend did not. When the phone rang, I knew it was Barb. "Good morning, You!" I hoped my voice sounded alert and cheerful, but figured that was wishful thinking.

"Good morning, You!" she replied. "Are you up for a walk?" Her enthusiasm challenged me. *Should I fess up and tell her that I'm still in bed or should I push myself into this exercise invitation.* Before a decision was made, my friend offered another suggestion. "Ah! Why don't I swing by the bakery and pick up a couple of goodies and then join you at your place? Would thirty minutes work for you?" I tried to hide my sigh of relief but knew it was a wasted effort.

"Actually twenty minutes will be fine, dear. I'm out of bed now. That was the first giant step of the day. Everything else will be easy at this point." She giggled in response, and then declared she would select some delectable treat en route to my place.

*

A passage from
Beyond The Day of Tomorrow
A Seeker's Guide
(Chapter Twenty-Five)

"To fully appreciate newly gained knowingness, often we must experience repeated lessons to capture the true meaning of the awareness.

Through various scenarios, we experience the lesson, each time learning more than we had known before. The repetition and the variety offer more opportunity for comprehensive study, practice, and acceptance.

In a scenario involving judgment one may understand the concepts of presuming the worst and intentionality, but in the initial stages of experiencing this lesson, understanding these concepts does not protect one from the impact of the judging offense.

It is with time and practice that one moves beyond merely understanding the concepts to a level of acceptance of the concepts.

Acceptance entails understanding without judgment."

*

Moving towards the front door, I expected to find my friend energized and boisterous, which was typical for her. When I opened the door, she was in tears. "Oh my goodness! What is going on? Get in here right this minute and tell me everything." She immediately stated that she was fine and that there was no need for worry.

"And do not roll your eyes at me!"

"I already have!" Grabbing her hand, I led us towards the kitchen. "Let's pump ourselves up with caffeine." Once there, we each addressed our tasks. I poured the coffee as she plated the most delicious looking almond croissants that I've ever seen. We both just stared at them as she lovingly placed the plates in their appropriated spots.

"They're huge!" she noted.

"Thank goodness! I'm starving!" My ravenous response surprised Barb. But she seemed to be in agreement.

"Yay! Let's eat a few bites of this before we start gabbing." Powdered sugar dusted our faces and we didn't even care. We were both so hungry that manners didn't matter. We finally took a breath after consuming at least half of the exceptionally big treats. "Geez! That was delicious!" Barb announced.

"Yes it was! Good choice, girl friend! So are you ready to talk?" My question was meant to be an invitation and Barb received it as such. She nodded her head and then took a moment to dust off her powdered sugar mask. I took advantage of the moment to do the same.

"Better?" she asked. I gave her the thumbs up gesture and she took a glance at me and did the same. "Well, I must admit, my mood has shifted since we had something to eat, but the tears were about the Earth. As I walked over from the bakery, there was a crew of workmen taking down a huge beech tree. I couldn't believe it! It's that old, old tree on the corner lot at Spring and Elm Streets."

"No!" The news was shattering. "That tree is over two hundred years old! Why would they do that?" My emotions were strong. "We've got to do something! We must stop this!"

"It's too late, Sister! I feel the same way, but it is too late!" Barb and I sat together with tears streaming down our faces. Once again, the Earth was experiencing another profound trauma and we sat there feeling helpless. And then, my tears stopped.

"We must address her pain! Help me, Barb. Let's send some healing energy to her immediately to alleviate some of her distress." We both moved into our meditative posture. "Join me, please, Barb. Let us both take the necessary deep breaths to reach our respective states of intentions. We know the Earth is in incredible pain now, so let's focus our intentions upon assisting her. She is in need! Let's just assume that she will gratefully receive our assistance.

Remember what our Old Friend told us last night, Barb. Within every existence within existence, the essential energy of life resides. This energy resides in us too, so let's share a particle of our true essence with the Earth now. Breathe in now and ignite your powerful energy on behalf of this recent injury. Feel the powerful surge of energy within and trust what you are experiencing. When you are ready, send a particle of your empowered energy to the intended location. We do this for the highest good of the Earth. We ask that the energy be used to ease her pain. And we express our sorrow for what has happened.

Now, we must retreat from that location and return to this place." I reached out to grab Barb's hand and we held tightly to one another. We both attended our individual prayers before returning to the present moment. Once done, we sat quietly staring into empty space. Eventually, deep breaths were taken and Barb broke the silence.

"That was nicely done, Sister. I hope it helped." Still silent, I nodded my head in agreement. "How do we know?" she asked. "How do we know if this energy transfusion really helps?"

"Barb, we must have faith! And we must resist the doubts that are nagging at you right now. Let me offer a gentle reminder to you. You just returned from an adventure, which ignited your spiritual journey. Remember that experience! Every bit of it! And remember the exhilaration you felt when you shared it with me. You were on Cloud Nine, Barb, and filled with joy and anticipation. Those moments happened for a reason, and one of the side effects of these experiences is that they sustain our hopes until the next experience comes along. You've had your share of incredible experience in the last few weeks. Utilize all that positive energy to help you through this very disappointing and tragic incident." Barb nodded her head in agreement, took a deep breath and stared deeply into my eyes.

"I agree with what you said, but I want to know if you believe we assisted the Earth." Her question was reasonable, but how does one answer a question when no proof is available.

"I believe when a mother loses a child that the pain is excruciating and words are of little solace. However, I also believe that good intentions and prayer have a positive effect upon that woman even if it doesn't seem apparent at the time.

Our actions just now will not bring the beech tree back to us, nor will our efforts instantaneously relieve Mother Earth's pain, but I truly believe that she felt our presence and was grateful for our companionship and our good will in that moment of great despair. And I also believe that the memory of our support will aid her for far longer than we imagine. Barb, we need to help each other whether we get to witness the final impact of our good or not. So today, we assisted the Earth and we will never know the end result of our help. Nevertheless, I'm so glad we did this. And now in this moment, we're also helping one another, as we talk about our experience of the death of that magnificent beech tree. What is transpiring here is good, and we really need to be cognizant of our emotions and our frailties during difficult times so that we can avoid and withstand our bouts with doubts. I'm very grateful we were able to stand together through this trying event.

Also, Barb, we must express our gratitude to the beech tree. What great pleasure she brought to us over all these years. Every time I walked by her, a smile crossed my face. She was awesome and she graced everyone who ever encountered her. What a blessing she was!"

"Yes, she was," declared Barb as she repositioned herself in the chair. "And so are you, dear Sister. I'm aware my question was unanswerable and still, you answered it beautifully, and I am deeply comforted by your words. Thank you for standing strong for both of us. This has been a remarkable experience." After a brief pause, Barb raised another very important topic.

"Sister, can we finished these delicious croissants now?" With that question asked, we proceeded to dust ourselves with more powdered sugar.

*

A passage from
Beyond The Day of Tomorrow
A Seeker's Guide
(Chapter Twenty-Six)

"Acceptance of another's faults without holding judgments of those faults is a task most difficult. How often have you requested either mindfully or verbally that someone just accept you as you are, and how many times have you been able to offer judgment-free acceptance to another?

Be truthful now. Thinking judgmentally is equally as judgmental, as speaking judgmentally. Perhaps you think that silence does no harm. Rethink that please. Not only does silence have impact, but you also are responsible for the impact of your silence on you and the other person.

If you really believe silence causes no harm, remember an example of a time when your partner, friend, or someone treated you with silence. Remember how it felt, and remember how your mind engaged in excessive thinking about the purpose of the silent treatment and the intentions of the silent offender.

As you are remembering this example, notice the impact this memory is presently having on you emotionally and physically. Where are you feeling your emotions in your body and what feelings are you experiencing? Do you still believe silence has no impact?

One of our most difficult challenges and the lesson most repeated involves the concept of acceptance. That with which we are all naturally birthed is that which we most seek. Through each life experience and endless lifetimes, all seek the acceptance of those participating in the experience. Different names, different faces, different roles, but always the intent is the same. Always we seek acceptance, for the acceptance fills the void of not remembering from whence we came.

In gaining acceptance from others also, we come closer to remembering the acceptance that we were birthed with and that has been ours since the beginning, for in experiencing acceptance from another such as oneself, we remember more of who we really are and from whence we really came."

*

"Barb, when you called this morning, something else was on your mind. Shall we discuss that now?" Still enjoying the last of her croissant, she indicated that it was not necessary.

"Nope!" she asserted. "Even though I wasn't in the state that you found me in upon my arrival, I was having doubts about last night. Can you believe that? Isn't that ridiculous? After that exceptional experience that we all shared, I woke up this morning questioning this and that and creating chaos when none was necessary. I knew my thoughts were founded in the unrest of my mind, but for some reason, I just couldn't shake it.

Anyway, our conversation regarding the beech tree has really quieted my doubts. The way you spoke of our assisting the tree was really beautifully done, Sister. That image of a mother losing a child will be helpful for a long time. So thank you! I feel much better now.

What about you? You aren't one that typically sleeps in? What's going on with you?" It took me a moment to remember my circumstance.

"Well, truth is, I had a bout with my doubts last night. I was overcome with my lack of consideration for the Earth. All of my life, I've really taken her for granted. When I realized how irresponsible I've been, the reality just made me plummet. I desperately wanted to make amends, and particularly, I wanted to send her another infusion of energy. So, I made a request to do so and then I didn't know if it was okay to proceed or not. I didn't hear a response from her, so I felt stymied. I didn't trust myself, and my impatience got the better of me. Eventually, I realized that it was time to go within. Actually, thinking back on that now, I doubt that it was really my realization. I suspect someone helped me with that. Anyway, I finally quieted my mind and then an incredible experience happened. It was sweet and wonderful and amazing. And when it was all said and done, I felt good about myself again.

And now, it's essential that I record my memories of what happened last night before I lose them. Again, this is one of those situations where we need to make a record so that we have that positive energy to sustain us in the future. Because of what happened last night, I was capable of walking us through your crisis and also facilitating the energy session for the Earth regarding the loss of the beech tree. So in essence, I feel confident about our work and our intentions and I truly believe we should trust what is going on within us and around us. Life is rich, Barbara! And it is such a privilege to participate in this remarkable life experience."

9

*

A passage from
Beyond The Day of Tomorrow
A Seeker's Guide
(Chapter Twenty-Seven)

*"As awareness of judgmental tendencies increases,
the possibility for change will also profoundly increase.
When one seeker gains knowingness of the concept of
judgment, progress is made, but when the masses gain
such knowingness, the potential for evolutionary change
is feasible. For such an event to actualize, willingness to
change and to embrace new ideas without judgment of
the ideas or their presenters will be necessary.*

*Ask yourself, can you be this involved? Can you be
open to change and be willing to consider new concepts?
Are you able to embrace another's idea without judgment?
These are legitimate questions and they are questions of
great importance. Just thinking about the idea of giving
up our old ways and accepting new approaches stirs up
a conglomerate of feelings. The process is instantaneous.*

*Imagine change, for just a moment, and now access
your feelings. Which feelings were aroused for you? Where
in your body did you experience these feelings? Perhaps
you were filled with excitement and enthusiasm at the
prospect of change, while another part of you may have
reacted with anxiety and fear.*

*Your reactions will be uniquely yours and certainly
what you experience will be influenced by previous
experiences. All the reactions experienced by all the
readers of* **A Seeker's Guide** *are reactions that are
appropriate.*

*This must be remembered by everyone! In anticipation
of adjusting to change and gaining acceptance of change,*

the potential for judgment regarding another's reaction to change will be prevalent and pervasive.

Understandably, attempts to change the mood of a judgmental nature will create a reaction of another judging nature. Difficult it will be for the seekers to adapt, and more difficult it will be for the seekers to foster change in others.

This will be the challenge, and the process begins within. Before challenging another to accept responsibility for his or her judgmental ways, first one must accept the challenge oneself and master the art of holding no one in judgment.

It serves no purpose to pass judgment onto another when one's own example is one of judgment. Each will pursue the mastery of a judgment free existence in their own time and their own way. This pursuit can come now or at a later time, but remember Old Friend you are free to choose. If you choose to delay, ask why. Perhaps your reasons are clear and purposeful, and if so guided, must be honored, but if you respond with uncertainty, ask again, why do you delay?

Old Friend, if your answer does not compel you to remain the same, then open your heart to change. The time for change is now. No longer can we continue in an existence filled with harsh insensitivities and cruel unkindness.

We are gifted with free will. Choose wisely, Old Friend."

*

"Good morning, Sunshine! Are you awake, dear?" Faye's early morning enthusiasm was well known in the Goodman house. Her need to greet the sun every morning was the first act of kindness that she performed each day. "Mark, dear, the sun is about to peek over the horizon. I'm headed for the outer room; please join me if you like." And with that said, Faye rushed out of the bedroom. His head still under the covers, Mark just smiled. *That's my girl!* He rested a minute longer before jumping out of the bed, putting on his slippers and robe, and rushing to the back deck that provided another living space for them. Faye's creativity was evident here. It truly was the favorite area of their home. Plants of many different varieties were beautifully situated in just the right places so that they enhanced the deck and also enjoyed the nourishing amount of sunlight that was needed for their particular species. The outer room, as they lovingly called it, occupied much of their time. Long conversations were had at the table where most meals were shared between themselves and with friends. It was the gathering place of their comfortable home. "Oh, wonderful, Mark, you are just in time. Look, here it comes!" With arms wrapped around each other, they greeted the sun as the sun greeted them. "Oh, how lovely it is to see its beauty again."

"Yes, dear, it is indeed. It's looking rather rambunctious today, don't you think?" His remark caused Faye to take another look. A grand smile spread across her face.

"You're absolutely right, Mark. Master Sun is looking very robust today. I hope the Master has a wonderful day. You know it must be frustrating at times when the clouds usurp its view. Bad manners!" she declared.

"Not necessarily!" retorted Mark. "The clouds and the Sun surely have an arrangement whereby each has ample time to view the sights and to attend the tasks that each is responsible for. I don't think we need to worry about this, dear. I believe it is an arrangement of long standing." They laughed at themselves as they enjoyed the remarkable sunrise event.

"Thank you for indulging this passion of mine, My Love. It is such a blessing to begin the day in this manner. I wish everyone would do so. Perhaps, then we might have greater respect for the grandeur of this marvelous planet." They stood closely together as they continued to revel in the beauty of the rising sun. "Ah!" The sigh was barely noticeable and both Faye and Mark thought the other had expressed their awe of the moment. Little did they realize that the expression of wonder came from another, who was also enjoying the beauty of the Earth from the opposite perspective!

"Well, dear, my growling stomach demands attention. If you would like to linger a while longer, please do so, but I must attend my hunger pangs." Faye indicated that her morning engagement felt complete. She blew the Master a kiss and confirmed their date for the next morning.

Back in the kitchen, the real magic began. The two prepared breakfast as if it were a choreographed performance. Coffee was brewed, the tiny breakfast table was lovingly set, and the day old apple crunch muffins were perfectly warmed in the toaster oven. "How blessed we are!" Faye whispered.

"Yes, we are Love, and you are the greatest blessing of all. Thank you for loving me!" Her husband was a dear man, who was able to express his feelings easily...at least in the privacy of their own abode. Like many men, he was less inclined to emote in public, but at home, he made his feelings known.

"We are fortunate, Mark. Our relationship seems to keep growing in positive and delightful ways. It's working for me!" she announced cheerfully. "And I'm glad it's working for you as well." Her husband chuckled and agreed that their marriage of forty plus years was successful thus far.

"And speaking of our delightful and positive growth," he added, "how do you feel about our new adventure?" His question focused their table talk. Caught in the middle of a bite of muffin, Faye gestured her first response with a quick thumbs up. After she swallowed her bite of muffin and followed it with a sip of coffee, she was ready to articulate her thoughts.

"Mark, I am so excited. I feel as if we have been chosen to participate in this project. I do not mean that we are special, but we certainly were in the right place at the right time, and I'm very grateful that we were. This adventure, as you referred to it, feels like an extremely important opportunity for us to effect change. And that really feels good to me." Faye's body reacted with excitement, shivering from her shoulders down to her toes. Her eyes were twinkling with joy. "How about you Mark? How are you feeling about this new development in our lives?"

"Similarly to you," he replied. "It took me a while to fall asleep last night because I couldn't let go of our assignment. I must admit my To Do List was long. Faye, I have a lot of work to do. You know, you just fall into routines that seem to be okay until you really look at yourself, and then suddenly, you realize that you are falling short in lots of ways. I started feeling low about myself and then just had to stop ruminating about all of my flaws."

"Mark, dear, remember what our Old Friend and Sally both encouraged us to do. Start with the positive aspects first! Dear One, you have so many wonderful qualities and behaviors. You really are a very special person, unique in your own way, and deeply grounded in goodness and kindness. My dear sensitive husband, when we start reviewing our negative components, trust me! My To Do List will be far longer than yours."

"Never!" he insisted. "You're the rock in this household and amongst our friends. You're a role model for all of us, Faye, and that's just a truth you're going to have to deal with!" Mark stared at his beloved until she quietly thanked him for the compliment. And then she added another remark that was on the mark.

"Okay, so I see what's happening here. We think the worst of ourselves in this particular situation, but we see the best in our loved ones, and we need to trust the observations made by our loved ones, because we may be too hard on ourselves during this self-discovery process."

*

A passage from
Beyond The Day of Tomorrow
A Seeker's Guide
(Chapter Twenty-Eight)

"It is how we choose, which involves the decision-making process, and for this reason it is essential that all must gain comfort with the Gift of Free Will and the abundance it brings.

Abundance, my Dear Friend, includes all that is available, and all that is available is available to all who choose to access what is available. The Gift of Free Will is far more expansive than most know. It is with this gift that all can choose all that is desired, and from the choosing of all that is desired, abundance abounds.

What is abundance for one may not seem bountiful for another, and what serves another as bounty, may provide no such satisfaction for the other. As is beauty, abundance is in the eyes of the beholder."

*

"So, Dear One, I suggest we spend some time after breakfast reviewing our positive attributes. Let's begin there, Mark, so we can avoid the pitfalls of disappointment and discouragement that you encountered last night." They each agreed to tackle this project, which would then be discussed over lunch. After the breakfast table was cleared, they each went off to their favorite zones in the house.

*

"Dave, do you have any work that must be addressed today? What's on your agenda, dear?" Sally's questions had an ulterior motive and her husband knew it, which is why he had risen very early this morning to attend his commitments.

"I've already taken care of things, dear. Sent the article off to the editor early this morning with the corrections she had encouraged. And of course, she was right as usual. So the article is looking good and my day is free until you tell me what your plan is." They both laughed together. Dave knew his wife well, and she was glad that he did. It made life so much easier.

Sally put her hand on her husband's knee and announced that it was time for a heart-to-heart. "David, something very important is transpiring about us that we must discuss." When Sally used his proper name, he knew immediately that a major conversation was about to take place, and in this instance, he agreed with her initiative.

"Where would you like to do this, dear?" It was not uncommon for the Moore family to take to the woods when important issues arose, and Dave expected this would be his wife's preference this morning; however, she surprised him.

"I would of course prefer to go for a long walk, which always works well for us, but for some unknown reason, I feel we should remain at home. Shall we adjourn to the sun porch?" Both agreed the porch would be a lovely place to discuss the previous evening's meeting.

Relocating to the favorite space in their home was always a good idea for the Moores. The sun porch was a peaceful setting delightfully furnished with white wicker furniture and accompanied by many happy plants including a plethora of spider plants, all of which were lovingly provided by the gorgeous and prolific mother plant. Received as a birthday present several years before, this plant truly is the gift that keeps on giving. Their sunroom is an indoor garden, which graciously invites guests to enter into serene, harmonious conversation. Dave was the first to acknowledge their sanctuary.

"Sally, you did such a good job with this room. Thank you for creating this space and for suggesting that we meet here." She accepted his compliments and nodded her approval of the setting.

"We are so blessed, Dave! Finding this house was a magical experience in itself, and little did we know then, that this room would become the epicenter of our lives. I love it here and of course, I love it even more when we are together." They both basked in the sunlight for a moment before engaging in discussions. Actually, each was blending into the energy of the space. Their methods of doing so were different, but the results of their efforts were the same. They became One with the space and with the world at large.

"So, dear, tell me about your reactions to the gathering last night."

Dave's eyes opened widely as he released a huge sigh. "Actually Sal, I found it illuminating. Our guest certainly validated our belief that there is more going on in the universe than most people believe. I made some suppositions, dear, which of course cannot be verified, at least I don't think they can. But who knows, if we have the opportunity to spend more time with this fellow, we may find out a lot more information about the *more* we both want to know about." His wife wholeheartedly agreed and encouraged him to speak more about his suppositions.

"Well, the first question that immediately came to mind was who is this guy? And where does he come from? And why is he here? Etc. We certainly found out about his reason for being here quickly. He's on a mission and his sincerity is compelling. I found him very believable Sal. And his cause certainly seems to have our best interest in mind...and heart. His love for the Earth was obvious. Every time he referred to her as Life Being, tears welled up in my eyes. His compassion and concern are evident in everything he says. So, bottom line for me is I believe him. He spoke our language, Sally. But his knowledge of the Earth's condition is far greater than ours. In fact as he spoke about the urgency of her situation, I had to manage my anger. We've been lied to about the seriousness of her decline. So, what I took away from the gathering is this. I want to be a part of this project! We've both wanted to do more and now we can. We must!" Dave looked at his dear wife and saw a sparkling tear clinging to corner of her eye. He wasn't surprised, nor was he worried. Sally could handle heartfelt conversations. "How about you, dear heart? What were your reactions?"

"Very similar! Lots of questions, intense excitement, and a very strong sense that the oddity of it all was real! As strange as it seems to me, everyone seemed to trust what was transpiring last night. It was an instantaneous reaction by all of us. I'm not sure why that surprises me so much, because we are all very open to unusual occurrences, but this was more than our usual unusual stories. This was big! First we were listening to and engaging with an invisible voice. And then, we were talking to a faintly visible form as if it were normal to do so. What an adventure we had. I loved every minute of it and I want to know more! And I want to have more interactions with this fellow. And I want to know everything he knows about 'the more' that you and I are seeking to know! Dave, this is exhilarating!" Her husband began to laugh and Sally joined in the reverie.

"Once again," declared Dave, "the Moores want to know more about everything! Will we ever be satisfied?"

"No!" the couple responded simultaneously. Again, laughter overcame them. The sun streaming through the porch windows seemed to enjoy the frivolities, as did the children of the mother spider plant.

"So, dear, shall we begin our assignment?" Sally's request met with a bold response.

"I've already begun! But there is much more to do, so yes, let's work on ourselves!" The Moores, with the understanding that they would return to the porch in two hours, each retreated to their private working areas and delved into their innermost beings.

*

A passage from
Beyond The Day of Tomorrow
A Seeker's Guide
(Chapter Twenty-Eight)

"What Dear Friend do you perceive as abundance? Give this some good thought...and then think of it again. Perhaps you may wish to discuss the idea of abundance with a friend or loved one and gain more information from the exchange.

This is another exercise in self-study. Much awareness of ourselves, as well as others, can be gained through the exploration of such ideas and our perceptions of these ideas.

Typically when asked about abundance, people respond to the question with remarks such as winning the lottery or Publisher's Clearinghouse. This is the usual light-hearted and immediate response. However, when given more time, the responses to this inquiry grow in the most interesting and delightful ways.

Abundance is: Good health, Good friends, Community, Family, Freedom, Career Satisfaction, Nice Car, Flexibility, Vacations, Financial Freedom, Beautiful House, Art Supplies, and MORE.

These are just a few that came to mind from previous discussions. What I find delightful is the variety of responses. What I find interesting is the constraint that most feel when thinking of abundance. Just pondering the idea of abundance arouses self-imposed or other perceived judgment.

Is it wrong to want abundance and if we do want abundance, how much are we allowed to want? Is there a certain amount that is acceptable? Beyond that point, does it become wrong? And what is acceptable to want? If we want abundance of good friends, health and family, are we within the lines of acceptability. If, on the other hand, we want money and things, are we finding ourselves in the range of unacceptable?

Isn't this interesting? We are again discussing the concepts of free will, judgment, and acceptance, but remember we really were discussing abundance...how did we return to these topics again? Pervasive, isn't it?

Dear Friend, let me reiterate. We are all born with the Gift of Free Will and this gift was purposeful. From this Gift, all are recipients of all that is available, and all possess this Gift so that each can access all that is available, when it is desired or needed. All can freely choose all the abundance and the abundance is free to all. No rules, no restrictions, no judgments apply to abundance.

All That Is, is All That Is, for All That Is."

*

"Annie, can you come down for breakfast in a few minutes?" The voice from the attic studio was faint, but Jim Anderson interpreted the response as a yes. Today was his day to manage the breakfast scene, and he was taking it very seriously. The coffee was brewing, the quiche was nearly ready, and the table was set just the way his beloved liked it. "Well done!" he said proudly.

It was opportunistic that today was his day to take care of breakfast, because Annie was one who sorted through conundrums by creating various pieces of art. She was always working on some project in her attic, but when there were important matters to discern, she also relied upon her journal. He suspected this was a journal morning, but wouldn't be sure until she came down the stairs. If her hair was in a mess and paint covered her fingers, then she definitely was engaged with the easel, but if she came down looking clean and proper, then the journal had been her companion. Jim didn't really know what to expect this morning. All he knew was that his dear sweet wife was gone before five o'clock when he briefly awoke to an owl's hooting.

As he pulled the quiche from the oven, he heard the attic door open and close. It was hard to miss because it squeaked rather loudly. "Good morning, dear!" Annie's voice preceded her. "The aromas are tantalizing!" When she entered the kitchen, they hugged a long hug, as was their way. The Andersons always began and ended the day with a hug to last the ages. *Just in case*, Annie would say. *Just in case!*

"Wonderful to see you dear, as always," announced Jim. "How early did you decamp this morning?"

"Oh, I'm not sure. Hope I didn't disturb you on the way out of the bedroom."

"No, not at all. Didn't know you had gone until around five," he replied. "You know me! I still sleep like a teenager. Late to bed and late to rise." This really was not Jim's usual manner, but he did like to think that he slept late every day. Somehow, this illusion made him feel more rested throughout the day. "So what's going on in the Upper Room?"

Annie checked out her hands and proudly revealed the remaining paint spots on fingers. "Still working on that abstract piece. The one with the bright colors! It's moving in the right direction, I think. One never knows with an abstract. That's why I love them so much. They are a mystery right to the very end." She smiled her mischievous smile and then added the rest of her truth. "Actually, most of my time was spent with the journal. Of course, you already know that." She stopped suddenly in reaction to all the wonderful aromas. "Wow!" she declared. "You've created a feast! Oh my, gosh! Let's eat!" Their focus shifted from the attic to the breakfast table, and within minutes they were staring at the most beautiful quiche ever known to humankind. "This is a masterpiece!" pronounced Annie. Reaching into her deep painter's pocket, she pulled out her phone and captured the moment with a superb photo of the multi-inch high slice of quiche. Her inclination was to dig in, but she stopped herself. Grasping Jim's hand, she looked deeply into his eyes, "I love you so much! And I'm so grateful for our relationship. Thank you, for all you've done this morning. This is a wonderful way to begin the day." Jim reciprocated with similar but different affirmations.

"Thank you for being the love of my life! I'm almost certain this is the best lifetime I've ever experienced." They both chuckled about that comment, but Jim reassured Annie that he was certain that no other lifetime could top this one.

"Thank you, dear! I think this one is the best, myself." She chuckled again and then remarked that she hoped they were not jinxing future lifetimes. That comment gave both of them pause and then they simultaneously announced that they were both open to even better lifetimes.

*

A passage from
Beyond The Day of Tomorrow
A Seeker's Guide
(Chapter Twenty-Nine)

"As we continue to expand our awareness related to the gains and the losses of living in judgment and the powerful impact this process has on all involved, we move forward in our own evolution. Until one experiences the impact of judgment and its negative influence from various perspectives, one does not truly comprehend the magnitude of destructiveness encompassed by this concept.

Infectious and pervasive, judgment breeds rampantly, passing from one unknowing recipient to another. The disease-like quality to this psychologically based conceptual pattern demonstrates itself in a variety of forms ranging from insidious unawareness to intentional acts of unkindness. As a recipient of judgment, one experiences the pain of the unkindness whether the act was one of intention or based in unawareness. Both have impact and each causes extreme wounds leading to the contamination of another innocent who will invariably spread the disease to another through some variation of the unkind act.

This behavior and its infectious pattern have become the plague of this planet and it populace. Spreading to all cultures and touching all lands, the disease of anger, hatred, and violence birthed from judgment. Before the plague can be treated and cured, first there must be an awareness and recognition that it indeed exists. To cure one of a disease, before one acknowledges the illness exists, is a task most difficult. So easy is it for us to recognize sickness in a friend or loved one, but less so for ourselves. Perhaps the fear of being ill inhibits our ability to accept it in ourselves.

The illness of which we speak is far more complex than a physical ailment, for we are so resistant to accepting the idea of psychological frailty, and in fact, we are quite judgmental about it in others. Knowing this as part of the human resolve, is it any wonder why this plague runs so wide and so virulently?

How will we each accept that within us lies this infection and that each of us is a carrier for this disease? How can we face this? Why did it happen? Who allowed this to happen? My Dear Friends, there is no one to blame. There is no one to lay responsibility upon. It is as it is."

*

"So, were you processing your thoughts about last night's gathering?" asked Jim.

"Yes, I was. It was fascinating, Jim. I'm so grateful we were part of that experience. Why are we so lucky? Don't you feel lucky?" Before he could answer her questions, she was off and running with another aspect of the evening.

"Didn't you think it was amazing that we were all talking to an invisible being, as if it were a normal thing to do? I mean, really? What a hoot!" Annie chuckled at herself and acknowledged she was emoting excessively. "Please excuse me, dear, but I found the entire event one of the most interesting experiences I've ever had. What about you? What was it like for you?" Jim didn't respond immediately even though he had been thinking about the experience off and on throughout the night and also since awakening this morning.

"The experience was memorable indeed. I believe everything that happened, and still, it is difficult to wrap your mind around this. Annie, who was that invisible fellow? Is he someone who once lived on Earth? Or is he from another area of the Universe? Or is he an Angel? I guess it doesn't matter, because his commitment to the Earth seems very sincere, but I would like to know where he comes from. I know curiosity killed the cat, but this CAT," Jim pointed to himself, "is very, very curious." Annie giggled at his antics and followed up with a significant question.

"If you find out he is someone other than a departed loved one of someone on Earth would that alter your perspective of what happened last night? Would someone who previously lived on this planet have more credibility that someone from quote-quote outer space?" Jim looked stunned and confused.

"Wow! Those questions never even occurred to me, but they certainly are provocative. Where did this come from Annie?" His wife sat quietly, which was unusual for her, as she wondered the same thing about the questions that seemed to flow through her. "Jim, I'm not sure, but they appear to be very important questions that we need to explore, and I think we should also share these questions with the others in our group." Both were silent as they pondered the questions.

"Would it make a difference?" Jim wondered aloud. "This truly gives one pause. As someone who eagerly wants to meet beings from beyond and from outer space, I don't think it would alter my perspective. I feel open to meeting anyone, and I would like to have greater understanding about our fellow family members, as he referred to those from other locations. It's comforting to know that individuals we've never met before regard us as family. I hope that I will be equally openhearted."

"Well said, dear! I too want to know more about this visitor, but I also want to know more about everything and it seems to me, he is one that can expand our awareness of the universe very quickly. I too was deeply touched by the level of earnestness that he exhibited when talking about the Earth. His love for her is sincere. And his willingness to speak the truth about our behavior towards her leads me to believe that he has had many lives on this planet. I had a sense of deep regret for previous behaviors and a resolution to make amends for what was done in those other lifetimes. Again, I'm guessing, which stirs up the desire to know everything.

Jim, I want to spend time working on the assignment today. It's a little daunting to review one's negative attributes, but like he said, it's necessary. Even if the Earth were not in crisis, this would be an extremely important action to take. If we don't look at ourselves and make the necessary adjustments, then how will we stay on track? This just seems smart to me. In fact, I think it should be an annual event." Annie paused again, but her mind was still occupied with the day's assignment. "What about you, dear? Are you going to tackle the assignment?"

"Yes, I am! As soon as I tidy up the kitchen, I will take on the challenge!"

"Let's do it together, dear. Then we can both get started sooner."

*

A passage from
Beyond The Day of Tomorrow
A Seeker's Guide
(Chapter Thirty)

"It is indeed a difficult thought to ponder, for none wish to believe they suffer from judgment nor does anyone wish to believe they are capable of passing judgment on to another. 'Goodness, that just isn't who I am. I'm a good person!' And you are! Do not lose sight of this throughout our discussion. In this beginning phase of awareness, it is critical to remain judgment free of self and others as you explore more deeply your personal understanding of the concept of judgment.

Perhaps it is easier to recognize the persistent nature of judgment through examples of long-term cultural conflicts, which are evident on our planet. How you perceive such an example will greatly depend upon your involvement and your awareness of the particular situation. If you are a party to one of the feuding factions, your perception of the opposing faction will certainly be different from your view of the faction of which you are a participant. So too for a member from the other faction,

148

while another individual, free from party loyalty, will have yet another perception.

Rarely will anyone view the situation with open-minded compassion, but instead the typical response will include critical assessment and harsh reaction. Someone must be blamed, who will in turn blame another, but none will wish to acknowledge self-involvement. None will wish to accept responsibility for one's own actions. Always, someone other than self is at fault.

Cultural prejudices, racial prejudices, gender prejudices, just to name a few blatant examples, abound planetary wide. You designate a region and with certainty know that some type of judgmental prejudice flourishes in that locale.

This disease knows no boundaries; it is not isolated to a particular country or land, for it has spread across the mighty oceans and contaminated every continent and all peoples. Unimaginable as it seems, the disease promulgated in judgment touches all, and all must accept responsibility for its manifestations and its cure.

This illness, so powerful and negatively influencing exists without a fever, yet when it fevers the results can be and usually are tragic. History provides horrifying examples of the disease at its worst. Global wars and regional conflicts epitomize the disease in its feverish state and still we choose to ignore, deny, and distract from the evidence history provides.

Historical facts demonstrate the epidemic proportions and the longevity of this infectious plague, yet it continues to grow untreated and unattended.

Until the masses recognize the actions of judgment from a perspective of wellness, the tragic effects of the disease will continue."

*

10

My Sacred Space was dimly lit as I nestled into my favorite chair. For a brief moment I wondered if the other chair felt slighted. *Goodness, this has never occurred to me.* Leaning over towards the matching chair, I gently stroked her and committed to giving her more attention in the future. *Have I always been this oblivious to my surroundings?* For a moment, I tried to brush this notion aside. I ridiculed myself for ignoring a piece of furniture. *It's a chair for goodness sake! This is not a life being that demands my attention!* And then, I wondered about my rationale. Then, I questioned the entire conversation and decided to address the puzzling exchange at another time. *Odd interaction! Is this happening for a reason? Maybe this is one of those coincidences that I don't believe in. Hmm! Or maybe, it's just a distraction from the assignment that I need to address.* This was not how I expected my day to begin.

"Okay, dear mind of mine, I need your cooperation. I know that you are aware of the tasks that must be faced today and I need you to work with me, not against me." Of course, the mind that has a mind of its own did not reply to my appeal. It rarely did! I turned my attention to the first task of the day, which for me was the most important. A pathetic attempt was made to assume a graceful yoga sitting position, which once, years ago, was within my means to do. It was a brief moment of wishful thinking. Sitting on crossed legs was not an option this morning. So with feet flat on the floor, I began my breathing exercises. During this time of quieting my body and sinking further within, the rhythm of my breath welcomed my expressions of gratitude. *Dear Ones, I am so grateful for everything that is happening around me. I am alive with your energy and the insights that you are bringing forward. Gratitude abounds! I so hope you can feel the sincerity within me. I am stunned by the amount of information coming forward and also grateful for the companionship of dear friends during this moment of expansion. Please help me to see, hear, and feel everything that I am intended to receive. Allow me to be your humble assistant, please. Help me to be a servant of All That Is for All That Is, and if I miss one of your messages, which probably happens more frequently than I am aware, please nudge me. Get my attention, so that I may serve, as you desire me to do. Thank you, my Dear Friends, for everything you do for everyone. In peace be!* With gratitude expressed and appeals made, I drifted into silence.

*

A passage from
Beyond The Day of Tomorrow
A Seeker's Guide
(Chapter Thirty-One)

"Perhaps now it is time to look more closely at this disease, identified as judgment, as it resides within.

Take a deep breath...fear not, for together we can approach this with kindness and an open mind. As we explore our humanity, let us begin the journey free of judgment. My Dear Old Friend, join me as we briefly walk the path together.

As earlier remembered, we are all the recipients of free will and now each of you can choose to explore more deeply the ways in which you have been affected by the disease and how it continues to impede your evolution. Also, with gentle care you may choose to study how you afflict others with the disease.

Through this self-examination, each will grow in awareness of the negative influences of the disease and the increased awareness will enhance one's ability to determine a treatment uniquely designed by the true self for the recovery of the human self."

*

As I rested in the silence, my heart was full. I felt accompanied. The feeling was real, yet inexplicable. I simply knew I was not alone. It was comforting and reassuring to be in this place of safety. Curiosity made an appearance, but it didn't stay long, for it seemed to understand that it was not needed. The mind that has a mind of its own also made a brief visit, but it too quickly recognized its presence was not required. As the silence deepened, I became less aware of my surroundings. Part of me seemed rooted in my Sacred Space. I could feel the favorite chair beneath me, and yet, another part of me seemed to be elsewhere. I was acutely aware of this sense of bi-location. I was in my home and I was somewhere else in a place that seemed familiar, yet unidentifiable. And I felt completely at ease with this unusual experience because I knew I was not alone and that my companions, whoever they were, were watching over me. The sensation was fascinating. I wondered if I should be afraid, but fear was nowhere to be found. I wondered if I should be cautious, but no signs of disruption warranted such a reaction. I simply was at ease with myself, with my surroundings and with my companions. It was a remarkable state of serenity. I was at peace.

"Welcome home, Dear Friend! We are most grateful to be in your presence once again. Your transition incurred no difficulties. For this, we are pleased, because we have much to discuss before you make your transition back to the Sacred Space of your current realm of existence. Old Friend, many have gathered on your behalf. A celebration has been prepared."

Unrest filled my being. "Celebration? What on Earth is going on here? And where is here?"

"Be at peace, Dear Friend. There is nothing to fear. As you have already intuited, your embodied self still remains safely within the confines of your lovely Sacred Space while Friends of Old carefully watch over you at that location. And at the same time, your true self is currently here in this location where many more of your Old Friends have gathered."

"But where is here?" My response was insistent. Perhaps, an apology was in order, but the inclination did not rise to a state of action. My impetuous self wanted an answer immediately.

"Old Friend, a deep breath might be beneficial. Your confusion is understandable. Join me, my Friend, for a short walk. There is something I wish you to see." His gentle manner was so hospitable that I could not resist his invitation. After taking the deep breath as suggested, we began to stroll down a path that seemed to be glowing from beneath the ground. It was beautiful, but confusing. The path was sparkling with golden light and my Companion was also aglow, but beyond that I could not discern any other features off the path. There was dimness about us, not darkness, but certainly a dim quality that was of a curious nature. *"Just be with me, my Friend! You are in no jeopardy. We have only a few more steps to take before we reach our destination."* The Companion's

words spoke the truth. Only a few more steps were taken before we came to a stop. The glowing Being, my Companion, turned to me and advised me to taken another deep breath. *"The next step, my Friend, we will take together. I am so honored to be at your side for this important moment of your journey. Let us both take another deep breath."* This was done in unison as invited and then he said, *"Welcome Home, Dear Friend, your Family awaits you!"* And with that said, we took the next step together.

Words will never adequately describe what unfolded with that memorable step. The view was forever...in every direction, indescribable beauty extended on and on and on. "Where am I?" This time the question was barely a whisper.

"You are Home, my friend! Breathe the beauty in, and feel it within you, and know that this is what you seek. When you wonder what is next to come, remember this is the place from which you came and this is the place to which you will return. This, my Dear Friend, is Home!"

"Is this Heaven?" My whisper was a bit stronger this time, but not much.

"Many refer to this as Heaven," the Companion responded, *"but most residents simply refer to this as Home."*

"Have I died? Surely not!" came my reply to my own question. "I have too much to do. Death simply cannot interfere with the assignment that was just presented to me. Surely this is a mistake!" My Companion's laughter echoed throughout the expansive celestial views that rested before us. I hoped this was a good sign.

"Your strong will and dedication to service precede you, my Friend. Allow me to clarify your position. You have misinterpreted your situation. You are not dead! You are simply visiting your Home because you have been invited here. As you accurately stated, your assignment is too important for you to depart your present situation, and it is because of this assignment that you have been called here to review your responsibilities. The time is now, Old Friend! The task that has been presented to you and your friends is indeed one of extreme importance. Not only is the Earth in great jeopardy, humankind is also. Because of this existential crisis, you have been asked to meet with those who originated the assignment.

It is my privilege to escort you to their chambers. I suggest we go there by way of the Path of Remembrance."

My mind was whirling, desperately trying to process all this information. *Heaven. Home. The time is now. The Path of Remembrance. Existential crisis. Breathe. Breathe. Breathe. Give me peace of mind, please.* And it returned. Peace returned to my mind and body. "I don't know who to thank for that quick response to my request, but please hear me. I am grateful. And I'm ready to meet those who invited me here."

"You are most welcome, my Friend. Let's move along the Path of Remembrance now. It will quickly take us to the Hall of Chambers. My Friend, your request for assistance was efficient! Please remember this for future reference. Whenever you are in need, we are but a breath away."

My amiable Companion seemed to be a Being of many talents. I hoped that sometime during this unusual experience he or she would tell me more about him or herself. It was odd that I just realized that the Companion seemed genderless. *I wonder why I immediately responded to this Being as if he were male. Isn't that fascinating. More questions to ask him...or her!* I finally noticed my mind had enjoyed a bit of distraction. *How like it! Excuse me, dear mind of mine, I need to take charge again. Oh, and thank you for the insight regarding our Companion.*

"Before we begin our walk, may I ask what your name is? What am I to call you?"

"You have called me many names before, Old Friend, and more names will come in the future; however, at this point in time, may we just honor our ages and ages of Friendship. I call you Old Friend, because you are, and I will be most pleased if you call me the same. My anonymity is useful at this time, but do not fear, our memories are forever, and the good times we have shared will be remembered again." The gentle wisdom of this magnificent Being appealed to me.

"Old Friend, will you please take the lead? I believe it is time for us to go." And this we did. We ambled down the path, which was an extraordinary experience. One friend after another welcomed me along the path, and with each exchange, a memory of sweet kindness returned to heart and mind. Visions from the past came and went with such rapidity that I could not appreciate the significance of each encounter. And yet, each face seen resonated deeply within me and each individual was remembered with gratitude. Regardless of the lifetime or the experience shared, the profound sense of love and connection could not be denied. All was well! No resentments were held. No malice existed. Only wholehearted acceptance and joy were shared. It truly was a heavenly experience. As we reached what was apparently the end of the path, I turned around for one more look. The smiling faces showered me with love and each and every one who embraced me on the path now wished me well on the journey ahead. Peace filled my heart. Sadness did not enter the picture, because there was no place for it. Farewells were unnecessary. Eternal life really exists. Our friends will always be forever.

Eventually, I turned to my Companion and announced, "It is time for us to continue."

"Yes, it is time for you to meet with those who requested your presence." I wondered if I should be nervous about the next part of this remarkable experience. A reply to my thoughts was quickly offered. *"Indeed not, my Friend, there is no cause for unrest. Dear Old Friends await you. This will be another experience of camaraderie and mutual respect. Please allow the love and joy that fills you to continue as you enter into the Hall of Chambers."* The Companion gestured the direction to proceed and with one step taken, we had arrived at a pair of massive doors that undoubtedly held the Chambers to which we were bound. My Companion chuckled. *"The doors are indeed exceptionally large. Do not be intimidated by them. When you see the other side, you will understand the practicality of these ancient monuments."* I pretended to understand what he was insinuating and waited for him to open the doors, but the Companion took no action. *"This is the end of our time together, Old Friend. It has been a pleasure to be with you again. And most certainly, we will meet again. What lies beyond these doors is of goodness. That is why you have been invited. I must take my leave of you now, Old Friend. Safe travels!"*

"Wait!" My reaction shocked my Companion. "My Friend, please allow me to say goodbye." The Companion paused. "I know that goodbyes are unnecessary here, but you have been so kind to me. I am deeply grateful. Thank you for escorting me through the maze of memories. This has been a stellar experience and your assistance has been memorable." We bowed to each other, paused, and then he or she was gone. The Old Friends who had lined the path were gone as well and the dimness along the path had returned. The path itself remained lit from below as before, but I knew that path was not mine to follow. The massive doors were mine to pursue. I took a deep breath and turned around to face the obstacles that awaited me. To my surprise, the doors were ajar. Anticipating that a shoulder would be necessary to move the door forward, I prepared myself for the task, but once again, this magnificent structure surprised me. The door opened as if it were light as a feather. I barely touched it and the door slowly and smoothly swung open. What was revealed was beyond imagination! The chamber was an outdoor room that extended forever, equally as beautiful as the first vista my Companion had introduced me to upon my arrival. *Maybe this really is Heaven!* My thoughts turned to my friend, Barbara, and I wondered how I would describe this experience to her. How can you describe the indescribable? My thoughts undoubtedly were overheard, because those who were nearby all turned in my direction. Again, the reception was unbelievable.

"Welcome Home, Old Friend!" The greeting was repeated over and over again, and each time it was spoken with the same sincerity as the first who greeted me. It was humbling to be treated with such warmth and compassion. Each individual who approached me clearly regarded me as an Old Friend. I wondered who they were, and how it was that they knew me, and once again I just accepted that it simply didn't matter. Obviously, these wonderful Beings held memories that I no longer remembered, but the fact that they held our relationship in their hearts was all the evidence that I needed to believe in what was transpiring. We were Old Friends and this incredible experience was real.

After the greetings subsided, I was invited to a circle of chairs. Clearly, this was where the meeting was to be held. I was directed to a chair and graciously accepted the invitation to sit down. Once I was seated, the other chairs were occupied one by one. And beyond the circle were those who held the space for the meeting. Their numbers were endless. I wondered if this was the moment that fear would rise within me. Never had I seen so many people before in my life. The circles of followers continued beyond my range of sight. I was stunned by their presence...and by their energies. The love that existed within these Friends was unbelievable. There was no reason for me to be afraid. The positive energy generated by this extensive Family was immeasurable. *Were these the Companions of whom our visiting Companion spoke? Were these the ones who came before? Were these the ones who were devoted to saving the planet Earth?*

"Yes! Yes! Yes! Yes!" The replies continued into the distance until I could no longer hear them, but I knew that the end of those declaring their participation was not done. They were the legions of the Earth. My heart raced with joy and gratitude. Surely with this many participants, we can save the Earth!

"Dear Friend, we are most grateful that you responded to our call. As you can see, many have travelled far to be here on this occasion.

Although you do not know all of these Family members by name, you are their descendant and they remember you and have come to express their gratitude to you." Applause echoed throughout the Universe. Even my overactive doubting mind was in awe. One could not deny the love that reverberated within and throughout this mass of people. These were Those Who Came Before! Tears streamed down my face. Of course, bewilderment fleeted through my mind. *Why me?* But that was a question to ponder at another time. This moment in time was the time of relevance and it demanded my full attention.

Eventually, the applause subsided. The masses in unison appeared to enter into a state of meditation, as the participants in the inner circle prepared for what was to come next. Not knowing what to expect, I took a very deep breath. My Companions did the same.

"Welcome, Old Friend! Be at peace!" I looked about the circle but was unable to discern who was taking the lead. Embarrassment washed over me. *To whom do I reply?* These gentle Beings had shown me great respect and I wanted to respond in like manner, but my senses were betraying me. *Who was the one who had just welcomed me? It appeared that no one had spoken, yet they all looked at me as if they each had done so. How do I handle this?"*

"Dear Friends, I am overwhelmed by your hospitality and delighted to be in your company. No words can adequately express my gratitude for this opportunity to connect with all of you. This is a humbling experience and I am deeply touched by your kindness. I had no idea that my extended Family was so large." My naiveté did not shock them. Undoubtedly, others had experienced similar reactions to this newfound information. "I am honored to be here, but please forgive me. It seems that I am not familiar with your ways. I definitely heard your opening welcome and your invitation to be at peace, but for some reason, my senses failed me. I seem unable to distinguish which one of you is speaking. Please excuse me for not being able to answer you properly." Tender smiles crossed the faces of those in the circle and I instantaneously felt engulfed by a sense of gentle warmhearted affection. I truly was being wrapped in a blanket of loving-kindness. Resistance was not an option.

"Dear Old Friend, we feel your tender heart and are grateful for your desire to honor us. We speak truthfully when we say that you already have. We are grateful for your acceptance of us and hope that

you feel our love and acceptance of you." The tears that trickled down my cheeks confirmed their aspirations. *"Your senses, Dear One, are not malfunctioning, but are actually incredibly fine tuned. Your confusion is related to our state of Oneness. Because of your exceptional skills you not only hear the individual, but you also hear the Voice of Oneness. You have often experienced this from your plane, but it appears differently to you now for you see the faces and hear the voice simultaneously. We hope our way is not problematic for you."*

"Not at all!" my reply came quickly. "Your explanation has clarified the situation for me. Please continue." The Companions seemed pleased with my response. They appeared to have an agenda. They were here for a reason. And it was obvious that I was as well.

"Indeed, dear Friend! We have gathered for a reason! Your willingness to proceed is a relief to all, for there is no time to discuss minute details. Old Friend, as you well know, the planet Earth is in great distress. The situation worsens as we speak. Those who deny this are causing great concern for those who observe from outer regions of the Earth's orbit. Her protectors are stunned by the lack of regard demonstrated by residents of the planet. We exist in disbelief and yet, the truth is undeniable. The Earth is retreating into dormancy. This is a fact that cannot be denied. And still, the deniers continue to deny the truth! This too is a fact that cannot be denied.

Action must be taken immediately. Although the valiant efforts being initiated by loving caring individuals are noteworthy, these sustainability actions are not enough to alter the course of destruction that the peoples of Earth are facing. They refuse to accept the catastrophe that is in progress. Old Friend, we apologize for speaking so truthfully, but we must do so. This places a huge burden upon you, but the truth must be heard and it must be delivered to the peoples of the Earth. The people must be informed. Governments and selfish industries are too self-serving to become leaders in this terrible situation. They foolishly believe they can withstand the circumstances that are unfolding and somehow profit from the ramifications of the aftermath of her decline. Their ambitions, founded in greed and arrogance, will not serve them.

The peoples of Earth do not need the leadership of the foolish. Within each person lies the ability to assist the Earth. Compound this by more than seven billion people and you begin to understand the power that is available to restore the Earth to full health. What we speak is the truth, Dear Friend. The essential life force that exists within every one of you is an energy so powerful that healing the Earth is within your means. She need not fall into dormancy. You, the residents of Earth, can save her. There remains time for this necessary action, but the efforts must begin immediately.

As you have heard so many times before, Dear Friend, you are not alone. Perhaps, today you have experienced this reality in such a way that you understand the fullness of this expression. You are not alone! What you have seen is a truth limited only by your human vision. Please trust that the legions ready to assist the Earth are far more expansive than you witnessed.

We are here and we are ready to assist; however, our assistance can only be utilized if the people of Earth choose to help themselves. They must choose to change their disrespectful ways. They must choose to accept everyone rather than promoting the needs of a few. Existence does not tolerate the order of judgment and exclusion. Existence does not affirm actions of meanness and cruelty. These are traits unbecoming to the highest good of everyone in existence.

The peoples of Earth face a situation that demands change. If they wish to continue, they must change their ways. If they wish to continue their selfish ways, they must accept the fate that lies ahead. The choice is theirs, but Those Who Came Before beseech their descendants to open their hearts to change. Please, for the sake of humanity, love your neighbors as you love yourselves. No other choice is available. Those who foolishly think they can escape this catastrophe will not find answers in the stars. The behaviors of greed and selfishness are not cherished in other areas of space. Change is the only route to safety and to continuance." The voice spoke a truth that everyone must hear. I wondered how one would gain the attention of humankind long enough so that the citizens of Earth would actually hear this message of urgency. One would think a species on the verge of extinction would listen carefully, and one would hope that these listeners would be eager to find out more about their abilities to save the Earth. *How will humankind respond to the truth of these circumstances?*

"Old Friend, have faith in humankind. Believe in these Children, as do we, and hold their fear in your heart at all times. Fear is the factor that disables them. The peoples of Earth are founded in goodness and they are more than they appear to be. Beneath the dimness of their fears shines the truth of who they really are. We stand beside them because we know their

truths. We accept them now even during this time of disillusionment and disappointment. Fear is a challenging obstacle for every individual, but when this debilitating energy consumes a civilization, it is an impediment of immeasurable force.

Stand with us, Old Friend, as we stand with the peoples of Earth. We have not lost faith in those who are our Family. Our love for them remains strong and our commitment to the Earth and to our children remains resolute. There is reason for hope and You are the reason we have hope. You and all your fellow humans can save the Earth. The energy of which you are comprised is the healing energy that the Beloved Earth needs to regain her full health once again. No more than this is required."

*

A passage from
Beyond The Day of Tomorrow
A Seeker's Guide
(Chapter Thirty-One)

"Our examination begins with the acceptance that one suffers from the disease of judgment. Are you willing, Old Friend, to honestly and openly accept that you suffer from the disease called judgment? Are you willing, Old Friend, to accept you are a carrier of this disease? Are you willing to accept your disease without judgment?

Are you willing to accept responsibility for your wellness? Are you willing to accept the responsibility for discovering a cure for your disease? Are you willing to pursue treatment through self-exploration and examination? Are you willing to truthfully answer these questions without judgment of self or others?

Please spend time with these questions and examine each one fully, for each builds upon the other. Study your own process as you derive your answers, and carefully examine how this insidious disease impacts this phase of your self-discovery process."

*

"Your commitment renders me speechless. Every cell in my body feels the love that you have for Mother Earth and for humankind. I am stunned by your generosity and your resolve."

"We can react in no other way, my Friend. The Earth accepted our seedlings without hesitation. We requested her assistance and her response was immediate. Because of her kindness and generous nature, Our Kind has existed and evolved upon her for millennia. She has nurtured our youth and provided sanctuary and sustenance to all who have followed us. Without her openheartedness, Our Kind would be no more. For all that she has done for Our Kind, we are eternally grateful. She is a Friend to whom we owe our existence. Our commitment to her is everlasting."

*

A passage from
Beyond The Day of Tomorrow
A Seeker's Guide
(Chapter Thirty-Two)

"Now that you have given yourself time to ponder these questions, are you ready to proceed? Be certain of this...trust your self! If your true self is ready for this phase of the journey, your human self will experience awareness of this readiness. Old Friend, this is not a test and this is not a value judgment.

You are the only one privileged to make this decision. While many may wish you to choose their preferred choice, none can choose for you, and whatever you choose is the right choice for you at this particular time. Know this as your Truth, my Friend, and honor your Truth.

This step of the process, which we will call our first step, must be made from deep within, and it must be made without judgment. You cannot take this step to please another, nor can you expect another to step with you, for along this path each step chosen is uniquely individual. While many travel the path, and paths cross along the way, each is done separately, and each is done in conjunction with guidance from the true self, which resides within.

So, Dear Friend, know you will have companions along the way, and you will experience the camaraderie of friends and loved ones at various times, but also know that within this connection of cherished closeness, you will experience the aloneness of the seeking seeker.

Do not be frightened by this aloneness, for it is purposeful. Discern the difference between loneliness and aloneness, for one is a signal of imbalance while the other is a state conducive to learning from within.

If you are in loneliness, simply choose to connect with someone in a manner most suited to you to alleviate the lonely experience, but if you are in aloneness, choose to embrace the opportunity and await the unfolding lesson.

Along the path you will often experience aloneness, for this is the opportunity given to acquire awareness and knowingness from presented unfolding lessons. Old Friend, learn quickly to embrace aloneness, and to attend loneliness. Both are necessary, for one addresses the true self and the other attends the human self.

Proceed now, Old Friend, if you so desire. Your path awaits you."

*

"My friends, you have summoned me here for a reason. Please tell me how I can be of assistance." Empowered by my ancestors' courage and commitment, I felt inspired to take the next step. How I could help remained unknown to me, but I was certain that my presence mattered. Looking beyond my immediate circle, the legions of assistants stood in waiting and their presence mattered. Each of them, at some point in time, must have wondered just as I have, about the act of assistance they would participate in, and here they were now, standing up and holding the space for this meeting, which would undoubtedly lead to more interactions. The point is: one step forward leads to another and another until the tasks required are fulfilled. If these millions and millions of individuals made themselves available for this occasion, so could I.

"I stand ready, my Friends. How may I be of assistance?"

"All are grateful for your readiness to serve, Old Friend. You confirm

what is already known about the Children of Earth. We know they will rise to the occasion, as you have just done."

*

A passage from
Beyond The Day of Tomorrow
A Seeker's Guide
(Chapter Thirty-Three)

"As we proceed with this phase of the journey, let us begin by again remembering that we are the recipients of free will. Why, you may ask, is this message repeatedly reminding us of this concept? Enough already, you may be saying! And you're right...enough already!

We are all granted free will, and by now, one would hope that we all understand this. But do we? Do you really accept the idea that you indeed possess free will and do you really understand what that means?

Lesson One

Free will is free will for all to access for all times forever by all who choose to choose free will.

So, Dear Friend, now do you truly grasp this concept? The Gift of Free Will is yours to choose to access, but you must choose to do so."

*

"Old Friend, the message has been given. The truth has been spoken. Please take this message to those with whom you associate. They too must know the truth regarding the crisis that besets the Earth and her residents. Explain to them what you had learned from this experience. Speak truthfully about your time here, so that others will comprehend the legions of ancestors who stand by to be of assistance. Also, speak truthfully of the Others in existence who will assist as well.

The Earth is a Beloved Life Being and those of ancient beginnings are deeply saddened by the circumstances contributing to her poor health.

Changes must be made. Please emphasize this to your Friends and spread this information to all who will listen. Concentrate your efforts on those who are of positive mind and heart. This is the energy that must be harnessed, activated, and focused on behalf of the planet. Every contribution of healing energy matters! But the Earth is a very large Life Being and she will require many infusions to regain stability. And then, more will be needed to revitalize her to a point that she is self-sustaining, once again. This is not wishful thinking, my Friend. What we propose is founded in truth. We apprise you of your healing powers so that you will access them wisely. For the sake of your species, action must be immediate and consistent. She will not recover from one infusion, but she will be grateful for the kindness and the act of generosity will raise her spirits. Please understand the benefits of this as well. Health is revitalized by love and support. This is why everyone must understand that every act of kindness on her behalf matters.

People must change their ways. She must become the object of humankind's affection, just as they were to her. Every day, she must be attended, as is any human who is terminally ill. She requires infusions of healing energy daily and frequently, and every minute of every day, she must also be shown respect and adoration for her goodness, her generosity, and for her presence. Without her immediate acceptance of Our Kind, so many years ago, none of us would be here today. This is the truth about the planet Earth. This is who she is and this is what she has contributed to our existence.

Share this with your Friends, Old Friend, and make them understand. Please assist us in this way." A loud sigh reverberated throughout existence accompanied by a sense of relief. A task was completed; the message was delivered. A moment of rest was taken, but only a moment. So little time; so much to do! Our ancestors were ready to attend the next step of their mission to save the Earth.

Tender wishes were exchanged, loving-kindness was shared, and the event of connection and remembrance came to an end.

11

A passage from
Beyond The Day of Tomorrow
A Seeker's Guide
(Chapter Thirty-Four)

"Perhaps another reminder is unnecessary, but just in case you haven't quite accepted the Gift yet, let me remind you again, you have free will. Just accept it as given so your journey can continue."

*

"**G**reetings Everyone! Please come in and make yourselves at home." My friends were prompt as usual. Our gathering, scheduled for seven o'clock, was duly noted when Mark's cellphone delivered a pleasant melody by Mozart. Not only did the tune bring notice to the punctual nature of our group, but it also reminded all of us to switch our phones to silent mode.

"How wonderful it is to be together again!" declared Faye. "I for one am eager to hear about everyone's encounter with the assignment. I found it very fascinating and heart-rending at times. Actually, I believe it is an exceptional assignment." Faye's eyes turned downward and I took advantage of the moment to extend a more gracious welcome to my guests. This was easily achieved because our relationships were of long standing. Everyone seemed happy and eager to get started.

"Well then, how would we like to proceed with this exercise tonight? Any suggestions?" My questions were selfishly based. Because my energy was low, I was hoping someone else would take the lead. Friend Barbara quickly came to my aid, which made me wonder if she was listening to my thoughts.

"You know, I actually gave this some thought earlier today so if I may, let me share with you what came up for me. I'll begin by acknowledging that the advice we were given about reviewing our positive attributes first was great guidance. Whew! I briefly stepped down the wrong path and learned quickly that the suggestion was founded in wisdom. So, based upon my brief encounter with misfortune, I think we should follow the same guidance as we share our stories tonight." That idea gained approval very quickly and inspired Barb to continue. "And, I think each of us should take a moment to assess our present circumstances. If someone is really feeling energized about sharing the positive experiences that came up for you, then take the lead. Trust yourselves, and take the lead. But if anyone is feeling hesitant, please trust that emotion as well."

"Well said," interjected Mark. "I have to admit that this self-exploration assignment was more complicated than I expected. Truthfully, it was a challenge, and I have mixed feelings about sharing my experiences. And all of you know, my reluctance has nothing to do with you." Glancing about the room, Mark shared a smile within his friends. "I totally trust all of you. And still, I'm going to sit back and let someone else go first." His friends supported his choice and expressed admiration for his willingness to take this action of self-care. I watched Mark's courageous step and realized it was time for me to fess up. Glancing towards Barbara, I saw an eyebrow move slightly upward. She was tracking my energy level.

"Mark, thank you for being such a wonderful role model. You and Barb have both assisted me this evening and I suspect both of you are acutely aware of doing so, but some of you may have missed what just transpired, so I need to come clean." Faye looked as if she was tuned in to the situation, but others looked surprised.

"I'm not aware of anything, dear! How like me!" laughed Annie. "Can you clue me in to what's happening?" Shaking my head in embarrassment and frustration, I attempted to clarify for my friends what was going on with me. My initial start got me nowhere. I tried again, but found it equally difficult to say anything." Barb's antennae were on alert.

"Sister, are you okay?" The sound of her voice startled everyone else in our group to attention. The focus was totally on me. My head was whirling about and for a brief moment I was concerned that I might faint, and then my friends were encouraging me to take a deep breath. "Just relax, Sister! And take a few more breaths." Jim, returning from the kitchen, placed a glass of water next to me. I hadn't even noticed him leaving the room. *What is going on with me?* "Sister, you are white as a sheet! Have you eaten today?" Her question seemed absurd, until I realized she was right. Jim immediately returned to the kitchen and grabbed the snack tray containing several options of protein.

"No wonder your energy is so low," affirmed Faye.

"Exactly!" added Barbara. A few bites of cheese and a couple of almonds made a huge difference, but it clearly wasn't enough. Both Faye and Barb urged me to have a few more slices of cheese. My friends were wonderful. Dave humorously teased me about eating all the treats as he reached over and grabbed a piece of cheddar for himself. And then Annie grabbed the tray and passed it around to everyone. It was a sweet way to take the focus off of me while giving me a few minutes to recover from my dizziness.

"Oh, goodness! Aren't you the best?" My attempt at sounding chipper fell flat when my weakened voice revealed that I was still not myself.

"Well, of course, we are!" Barb answered shortly. "And so are you, Sister! But something is up with you. Your energy level is all out of whack. I knew it the minute we entered the door. Do you have any idea what's going on?"

"Your Friend has experienced a most unusual encounter," came a familiar voice from outside the circle of Friends. The visitor attracted everyone's attention. Although this was not his intention, his invisibility often caused such a reaction. The furniture was quickly rearranged and another chair was moved into place. Before their guest sat down, he materialized before his companions. It is accurate to say, Dear Reader, that bearing witness to such an event is a sight to behold. Giggles, mumbles, and gasps were heard about the room.

The Old Friend, found anew, moved closer to the one known as Sister and quietly stood before her. *"You are drained of your energy, Old Friend. May I be of assistance?"* The question snapped everyone to attention. The Sister of Choice indicated that she would appreciate his help. *"And may I employ the assistance of your friends in this exercise of rejuvenation?"* Again, the answer was yes.

Turning to face his companions, the Old Friend requested their assistance. *"Our dear Friend has suffered a severe energy loss because of an encounter that she recently had. She is not in jeopardy; however, we are capable of restoring her back to full health. Will you please assist me in this healing experience?"* Naturally, everyone agreed.

"Close your eyes, dear Friends, on behalf of this fine servant, and prepare to offer her an energy infusion. Similar to our previous session, I ask you to blend with the breath that sustains you. Slip deeper and deeper into the silence that you all know so well. Allow your breaths to refresh your own energies.

One of your own has inadvertently depleted her energy and she is in need of assistance. How grateful we are to be of assistance for one that we hold so dear. What a privilege it is to be of service. She has offered her permission to allow us to proceed. Let us prepare to do so now. Strengthen your own energy with several more deep breaths. And now, let us each access one particle of our essential life energy and move that sacred particle to the center of our circle. Envision the particle exiting through your shell and spanning the space to the center of the circle. There, our energies merge together and become even more powerful and we celebrate this union knowing that our energies will enable our dear Friend to enjoy complete stability and wellness once again. Now, my dear Friends, let us complete the transmission of energy by envisioning the source energy moving from the center of our circle to the recipient of our intentions. Allow the energy to gently engulf our Friend. As she absorbs this infusion of energy, we trust that our energies will serve her as needed and we express our gratitude for the opportunity to participate in this energy exchange.

Rest now, Beloved Sister! We are grateful that you allowed us to be of assistance. As you rest, so shall we. And when the moment is right, we will all return to face the tasks that lie ahead.

In peace be, my Friends."

Time passed as is its way, and those in attendance held the space for those who had participated in the energy transfusion. One friend to another, the sacred energy of life enriched the life of the One in need, as well as the Ones who willingly offered themselves for another.

Mark Goodman was the first to return from the mission of good will. As he waited for his friends to join the present with him, he noticed a similar sense of peacefulness that also occurred when the group of friends shared energy with the Earth. He wondered if this was normal. Questions were surfacing, as was his curiosity. He quickly glanced at his watch to see how much time had elapsed. It was less than ten minutes since the visitor has arrived. *How can that be? The energy transfer must have taken at minimum thirty-five to forty-five minutes.* As he pondered the mystifying aspects of time, his companions one by one returned from their inward travels. Typical of these kinds of situations, movements were heard, sighs were quietly expressed, and bewilderment spread across the room as the participants realized they had no idea what had just transpired.

"Welcome home, dear Friends! Your efforts were successful. Please focus your attention to your Friend. She is radiant!" The difference was astonishing. Questions began to fly, but the visitor gestured that they remain silent. *"And now look at each of you. Notice that you have changed as well."* Again, the change was profoundly noticeable. Dave Moore carefully observed the receiver of the group's energy and could not deny that a change was evident. Then he turned to his Beloved Sally and saw that she looked healthier and more energized as well.

"Obviously, you're trying to make a point here, but I want to be sure that we're all on the same page, so will you explain yourself?" The Old Friend laughed and applauded his friend's approach.

"You are correct, Old Friend. I am attempting to make a point through this demonstration of good will. By freely giving, you also receive. And by willingly receiving, you also give. Through this charitable experience of assisting a Friend in need, we all benefitted. Is that not a miracle of Divine Making?" Silence befell the group for what appeared to be a lengthy amount of time, which of course, was not the case.

"You are a Being of great wisdom," whispered Faye.

"As are you, Dear Friend," the visitor responded. A smile came to Faye's face followed by the trail of doubts. She attempted to toss them aside. Committed to freely receiving his compliment, she indulged in a long deep breath and embraced the satisfaction of her effort.

Turning his attention to the recipient of the energy infusion, he stated, *"Old Friend, you are at your best again. Thank you for receiving the gift of rejuvenation."*

"Thank you for assisting me. I can attest that this was an incredible experience. Thank you all for helping me. I am ready to continue, if the rest of you are!"

"Sister, please tell us what happened to you?" Barb's curiosity reached a tipping point. She had seen her friend's energy level turn about in a matter of minutes, which was sensational, but what caused the energy depletion to begin with? She wanted answers. "Our Friend here said that you had an experience that depleted your energy. Tell us everything, please!" My heart felt for her. She was someone who wanted to know everything immediately and she was a joyful friend. *A gift that will always be cherished*! But the request she made was one that could not be accommodated in that moment.

"I can't wait to tell you everything!" My reply was as enthusiastic as Barb's curiosity. "But I must wait, dear friend. For reasons, which will become evident shortly, I must decline your request. I am so grateful to you for watching over me this evening when you arrived. I knew you were aware that something was wrong. Your presence mattered!" I looked about the room and made eye contact with every friend. "Words of appreciation simply are not enough for what you did for me this evening, but it is all I can do. So, thank you for restoring my energy!" Then I took a huge deep breath and my friends joined in and I took the lead.

"Dear Ones, we are here for a reason. The assignment we were given is the priority of this evening's gathering. I apologize for delaying our meeting, but the lesson learned was one of importance for the work that lies ahead. Barb laid a wise path for us to follow at the beginning of our meeting. I believe that we should follow through with her suggestion. So, the floor is open. Who would like to take the next step?"

*

A passage from
Beyond The Day of Tomorrow
A Seeker's Guide
(Chapter Thirty-Five)

"*Now, perhaps you are wondering about this Gift, and particularly, you may desire to know if there are strings attached to this Gift. You may be asking: are there rules, regulations, or restrictions that are attached to the Gift?*

Lesson Two

There are no rules, no regulations, no restrictions attached to the Gift; however, there is one exception to honor. The exception concerns the concept of caring for others' free will. Never must one interfere with another's free will. In honoring the free will of all others, likewise one's own must be honored. Free will is a Gift given equally to all and must be honored equally by all. Hold no Gift in higher regard than another, for all Gifts are equal. As do you hold your Gift dearly, so too hold another's with equal regard. As do you hold your Gift as uniquely yours, so too honor this in another. As do you accept the Gift of Free Will, so too foster such in others. As do you practice free will, so too accept others' practice of their free will.

Old Friend, study this well and find comfort in the lesson. Know from deep within that the Gift of Free Will is purposeful and meaningful. How purposeful and how meaningful you experience the Gift is of your free will to choose."

*

"My friends, perhaps, it may be assisting if I share my reflections first." Our invisible friend's offer came as a surprise. "Ah, I see that you did not expect me to participate in this activity. You presume that one who is unseen is beyond such need of self-assessment. Rest assured, my friends, all in existence must face their evolutionary developments." This disclosure also surprised his companions. "I am here, my Friends, to be of assistance. This is my reason for being at this particular moment in time. Long ago agreements were made and now the agreements must be enacted and fulfilled. The sense of responsibility that I feel is my driving force. I believe my previous experiences have prepared me for this moment in time, and I humbly acknowledge that there is evidence to substantiate this. Within me, there is awareness that I have served well in various and numerous situations. I know this is my truth, and I cling to this evidence of my merit. It is necessary for me to do so, because I also have other remembrances of times when my service was lacking. My behavior was not, shall we say, noteworthy. While I would prefer to forget such memories from the past, they are a part of my historical development that has strengthened my resolve to improve myself. My challenge is to remember to view these times as the assets that they were, rather than interpreting those unfortunate moments as everlasting condemnations.*

Like you, my friends, it is easier for me to have compassion for another than it is for me to have compassion for myself. So, I say to you, with my heart fully open, that I am one who is committed to service, and in my experiences of service, I have served well at times and other times, I have fallen short. My greatest hope is that I will be of service to all of you during this time of great need when we gather to serve on behalf of the Earth. For her sake, may we all serve to our full potential.

I thank you for accepting me into your Circle of Friends, and I am grateful for this opportunity to share my heart with you." Our new Old Friend fell into silence. By going first he demonstrated to all of us his commitment to the Earth and to us. He bore his heart to us, even though he was as nervous and as reluctant as were we.

"Thank you for taking the next step," Annie softly spoke. "You served well, just now. By going first, and sharing your soul with us, you have shown us the way. Please hear me when I say, you have served well. Thank you."

"Thank you! Your words of kindness warm my heart. And will you now take the next step, dear Friend?" Annie indicated that she would and led the way with the usual deep breath. As she inhaled several times in a row, so too did her friends. It was an act so subtle that it was barely noticeable and yet the power behind this action of kindness was immeasurably significant. With each deep breath taken, the union of Oneness strengthened.

Anne Anderson, Annie to her dearest friends, was a woman who sparkled. Her eyes sparkled with delight. Her aura, for those lucky enough to see it, sparkled so brightly one would think they were looking at a Christmas tree adorned with hundreds of lights. She was one who entered a room and immediately filled it with joy. Annie amazed me. I loved her presence, I loved her manner, and I loved her joyfulness. Even when circumstances were not at their best for her, she managed to be the one who remained steadfast and hopeful. She was one to emulate. And I'm sure that her husband Jim knew this as well. His adoration of her was blatantly obvious. Their playful interactions bespoke a very happy marriage. I was excited to hear about Annie's self-discoveries. "Isn't this an interesting assignment? When our wonderful invisible Friend suggested that we do this life review, I was excited about the opportunity and foolishly thought it would be an easy adventure. Needless to say, it was more demanding than I thought it would be.

And of course, I delved into my bag of never to be discussed memories first. Hopefully, all of you are wiser and healthier than me and do not maintain such an unsightly bag. I wish I didn't but honestly, it has come in so handy throughout my life. Things that happened which were troubling to me were neatly and cleverly stored away, never to be dealt with again. When I peeked into the bag, it was shocking. Fortunately, the guidance received from previous conversations resounded loudly in my mind and I quickly tightened the string on my bag of unacceptable misbehaviors. By the way, Friends, that was very good advice.

Well, after that glancing blow with reality, I realized it was time to center myself. So, I began a meditation with intentions of opening my heart to positive aspects of myself. It took a while! That brief moment of looking back at my past indiscretions jarred me. I had stored those acts of unkindness, of thoughtlessness, of meanness so far away in the confines of my mind that I had actually forgotten my insensitivities. It was an eye opening experience.

Now, I can honestly say that I am grateful for this renewed awareness of those past events. I made mistakes that were so shameful to me that I tried to hide them away so no one would know about that part of me. But in so doing, I also forgot about that part of me, which is still there waiting to be acknowledged. Actually, that part of me is waiting to be healed. I made mistakes for which I am deeply sorry, and I want to apologize for those acts of ill will so that I can truly improve myself. I cannot take back the hurt that I've caused, but I can change my future behavior. And I am committed to doing that.

Because of this assignment, I am now better equipped to make the necessary changes. I know, and am very grateful for, the good parts of me. Generally speaking I am a good person. Thank goodness for those who nurtured me and pushed me in the right direction. They served me well. And the errors that I've made are my responsibility to own and to clean up. I intend to address the pain that I caused, and then I'm going to put a big bow on my bag of sorrows and give it a new purpose in life. From now on I'm keeping a bag of positive memories to remember for all the days ahead." Annie paused, took in a deep breath, and sighed in relief.

"Thank you my friends, for standing by me. My heart is feeling much lighter now. I'm so grateful for all of you. Each one of you is a blessing to me!" Jim reached over and hugged his beloved. He was very proud of her. He knew there would be many more discussions about the revelations gained from this assignment. And he was looking forward to them. The ramifications of holding onto painful memories are as damaging as the initial events. He was glad that Annie had shared her pain with their friends. She was already a wonderful woman and now she was free to blossom even more.

*

A passage from
Beyond The Day of Tomorrow
A Seeker's Guide
(Chapter Thirty-Six)

"Now, as you review and study the message of Lesson Two, ask yourself, what am I to learn from this? If I am truly to rid myself of this insidious disease then I must be open to learn all there is to learn from each lesson. Perhaps preparing oneself to accept free will first entails understanding the concept of free will. What does free will mean?

This may give you pause, but do not be concerned, for the pause provides a moment of aloneness to seek within for the answer to this question. At this point you may be thinking to yourself, doesn't this book have a glossary? Can't we just look it up and be done with it? Oh, but if it were that easy, life would be boring!

Well, let us ponder this together. According to the lesson, the Gift of Free Will is mutually shared by all, and we are to honor each other's gift as we do our own, and we are not to interfere with another's gift. About now you may be saying to yourself that this Gift, which has no rules, regulations, or restrictions attached to it certainly appears to have some particulars clinging to the conceptual present. These particulars sound like rules, look like regulations, and feel like restrictions. Well, this doesn't feel comfortable at all. So, how can we accept this Gift, if we're feeling so uncomfortable with it?

And now each of you must ask yourself, 'Why am I feeling uncomfortable with the idea of honoring myself, and others, in this endeavor of accepting the Gift of Free Will?'"

*

"Well, this lovely lady is a hard act to follow, but I'm going to give it a try." Jim Anderson, as is often the case in his relationship, was inspired by his wife's courage and dignity. He often referred to her as grace personified. So confident is he in Annie's goodness that he often loses sight of his own. Nevertheless, Jim's friends have no doubt about his goodness. They've witnessed his subtle acts of kindness and his generous nature for decades. Like Annie, Jim is a stable force: one who can always be relied upon and one who is always available when a need arises. He began his story with a muffled chuckle. "As you probably already know, my mind also went directly to the side of me that is least favorable. Perhaps it is human nature to do so, but one wouldn't think so. After all, we spend so much time trying to hide our negative qualities that one must wonder why the mind is responding in this way. Is it trying to force us to face our ugliness so that we will finally accept our issues and change our ways? That's an interesting thought," Jim mused. "Maybe our inner self wants us to release the pain and the negativity so we can be free to live without the burden of our real and presumed failures." Jim's ideas were fascinating and as he spoke he seemed to realize that the part of him that he had hidden for years was begging him to be set free.

"My friends, it seems that I have lived two different lives. One brings me satisfaction and pleasure and I am humbly proud to acknowledge it as a good life. This life is one that has been lived well and gives me the sense of being a good person. And then there's another life that most of you probably know only a smidgen about, but it's real. This life is the Jim that I'm not proud of, and in truth, I'm darned disappointed in this guy. He's been a rascal at times and I'm not inclined to accept him as part of me. But I must! This guy who has made a ton of mistakes and who has repeatedly behaved foolishly is part of me. I have to own up to this and I have to accept this part of me as part of me. I'm sorry for the tactless, thoughtless times when I bulldozed my way through life and I apologize to all those folks who were wounded by reckless behavior. I was arrogant, rude, and irresponsible. And I am so sorry." Tears welled up in his eyes and his friends held the space for his emotions. Even though they thought he was being too hard on himself, they did not interfere in this delicate moment in time. Jim was cleansing his heart and soul of old, old pain. His description of his actions was his to choose. They trusted his process. After a few moments of silence, Jim reengaged. He faced his friends, making eye contact with everyone. "I'm better than this. I'm a much better man than these old behaviors indicate, but I cannot deny that those old acts are mine to own. So, my friends, I'm doing that now.

I have made mistakes, but I am more than my mistakes. I am a good person who is in need of fine-tuning. And I am committed to improving my ways. I do this for my beloved wife, for my friends, and for the sake of the Earth. I am a good person, but I intend to be better. That's my promise to all of you." Jim emulated his wife by taking a deep breath and sighing in relief. And of course, his friends joined him in this exercise. Our group needed a break.

Barb and Sally stepped out of the circle at the same time. Within minutes they returned with more goodies and glasses of water for everyone. The timing was perfect, as evidenced by the quick consumption of the refreshments.

*

A passage from
Beyond The Day of Tomorrow
A Seeker's Guide
(Chapter Thirty-Six)

"What does this arouse in you? What are you feeling? How are you feeling? Where are you feeling this in your body? Perhaps an example may assist you. When contemplating this for myself, the feelings stirred included suspicion, doubt, fear, anxiety, and anger. (Just to name a few!) I became suspicious that others might not honor my Gift. I doubted that others would be as honoring of my Gift as I would be of theirs. I feared my Gift would be different or less than others. I became anxious about the fairness of this and suspiciously doubted and feared others' participation. I became angry anticipating the lack of involvement and participation by others.

Whew! No judgment involved here! My Friends, it is embarrassing to own these reactions, but unfortunately, each response existed and one built upon another, and it happened quickly...so quickly, it is unimaginable. From the thought of accepting the Gift of Free Will spawned the judging nature, resulting in the creation of judgment. The birthing receptacle for this creation was the mind.

How does this affect me now as I read my words to you? I feel sadness...and it is heartfelt. This sadness, coming from the heart, embraces my concerns for others and for myself, creating a connection with others and a sense of responsibility for others and a commitment to honor others. This feeling, spawned in the heart, practices the message regarding free will without thinking about the message. It simply exemplifies what free will purports.

Old Friend, to practice free will, one must live it from the heart, for there within lies the true self, which holds your answers.

Listen carefully to the heart. It speaks in a whisper, but in moments of quiet aloneness it is easily discerned. Choose, Old Friend, to practice free will at a heart level and you will feel no rules, regulations, or restrictions binding you. Instead you will experience the expansive freedom contained in this incredible Gift.

Know it as freeing and it will be so, or choose it to be restrictive and this will be your Truth.

Choose wisely, Old Friend."

*

"My dear friends, you honor us. By bearing your souls and sharing your insights we have all grown, and still there is more to come. Let me check in with everyone, for the evening has been both rewarding and intense. I'm assuming that we all want to continue, but that is presumptuous of me, so please let me know where you stand." The reaction was immediate and affirmed my presumptuous assumption. "Great, then let's continue. Who would like to go next?" My friends respectfully checked in with one another and the Goodmans offered to take the step. Then the couple checked in with each other and agreed that Faye would go first.

"My friends, it is a privilege to be in your company. I am enriched by your stories and inspired to reach for the clouds." She paused reflectively. "Reach for the clouds," she repeated again. "Isn't that an interesting thought?" Faye was a person of many interests. Blessed with artistic creativity, she often dreamed about what might transpire if she could actually use the clouds as a canvas. She imagined herself not on scaffolding, but walking from one cloud to the next as if she required no assistance whatsoever. And there amongst the clouds, she would create masterpiece after masterpiece. Her dreams, ever present and always powerful in their intention, sustained her lust for knowing everything that could be known within the Grand Existence, as she referred to it. In private moments, she would admit to her greatest dream. *Someday, she would say, someday, I will be with the Grand Ones of the Universe and they will tell me everything. We will travel across the great expanses together and they will show me everything there is to see, and all that is to be known, I instantly will know. Oh what a wonderful day that will be,* she would say. And then she would laugh and change the subject to some other marvelous topic. A woman of many gifts and accomplishments, Faye was one who was capable of anything!

"My friends, the assignment forced me to face my vulnerabilities. Because I am so passionate about so many facets of existence, I have a tendency to believe that I am more than I appear to be. Please excuse me for sounding so egotistical. The truth is I believe that we are all more than we appear to be, and when I am deeply, deeply in touch with this belief, there are times when I actually think that I can reach the clouds and beyond without anyone's assistance. My dreams are so vivid that sometimes I wonder if they are only dreams, or if in fact, they are my truth. I admit there are times when I truly believe I have travelled to places far beyond the scope of human technology. But that is another story for another gathering.

My dear friends, I love each of you dearly. You all mean so much to me, each in your own unique way. So now, I am going to impose upon our relationships by sharing with you where my experience with the assignment led me. This is difficult for me to acknowledge, but I must. I am a person of judgment. It saddens me to think this, but it is my truth and I can no longer pretend that it isn't. Although I do not have a bag like Annie so successfully used, I do have a hole hidden deep within me. This hole is like a black hole, where I quickly deposit everything about myself that I find loathsome. So quick am I to judge others for the most ridiculous reasons, and then in the wake of my disapproving behavior, I discard my unkindness, my meanness into the abyss so I do not have to face my humiliating behavior. So, I do not have to face my conscience. I know this behavior is wrong. It isn't just wrong, it is unacceptable, and still it flows from me and through me as if I am entitled to behave in this way.

I am not entitled to do so, nor is anyone else, but it is not my charge to command others. I can bear witness to the judgment in others, but I do not have the right to judge their judging ways. When doing that, I am not managing my own judgmental nature. And it is my judging ways, my actions of unkindness for which I am responsible. I would like to say that this is a new awareness that just came to my attention, but it is not. I've known this about myself for a very long time, and now is the time to address this behavior fully.

My friends, I know that there is also goodness within me, and for this I am so grateful. Sometimes I wonder how my goodness can tolerate this other side of me. How can they mutually co-exist within the same body? I don't know the answer to that...yet! But my commitment to myself, and to all of you, is this. I am going to change my judging ways. And I'm going to better myself. No longer will I tolerate this meanness within me. No one deserves my judgment. No one deserves to be judged, period. I promise to address this compromising issue everyday as long as it takes."

Then the traditional long breath was taken followed by the sigh of relief. "Thank you, my dear friends for listening and supporting me."

*

A passage from
Beyond The Day of Tomorrow
A Seeker's Guide
(Chapter Thirty-Seven)

"Now, here we are again, beginning another chapter, and still we do not really understand the concept of free will. Has she given us the definition yet? Will she ever do so? Old Friend, the answer to both these questions is No.

I cannot give you the definition of free will, for it is yours to define. If I give you my definition of the Gift of Free Will, then I am imposing my free will upon you. This would be a violation of your free will, if you chose to be impacted by my imposition. But remember, you have free will, so you could choose not to be impacted by my definition. Instead you could accept my definition as a gift from which you could choose to study and learn all you can learn as it relates to your definition of free will. In that way, the sharing of gifts enhances self-study, resulting in increased awareness of self and others.

Now, perhaps this sounds familiar to you. Isn't this how we typically learn through the mutual exchange of ideas? But there's a catch to this exchange. Through this mutual sharing of gifts, we must do so by practicing the arts of acceptance and free will and we must do it without harboring judgment. If we are to pursue this course of study together, then I offer this to you: I commit to strive with heartfelt intensity to honor you and your free will, and I promise to be actively involved and fully participatory, and I accept my responsibility for the caring of your free will.

And you, Dear Friend, are you able to choose this course of study for yourself? Will you offer to another your proclamation of commitment to honor the other's free will? Will you promise active involvement and full participation in the endeavor? And will you accept responsibility for the caring of the other's free will?

While you ponder these questions, do it from the heart, for the mind can and will attempt to distract you from this path. For each heartfelt 'yes,' the mind will pose numerous logical, illogical 'nos.' As your heart gains clarity, the mind will assert itself with greater fervor and provide compelling distractions, but know from your heart that the heart is your guide. The inner debate waged between the heart and the mind is conceived in the mind and is not a function of the heart.

What is experienced as heartfelt comes from deep within and moves quietly and passionately as the warmth of your existence. Know this experience, my Dear Friend, and know it clearly, for once experienced, it is the guiding light for all other such experiences.

Once this experience is known, you will never doubt again your inner wisdom, for it is the warmth of awareness that awakens the glow of knowingness, and it is your knowingness that is your true self providing you guidance.

This experience of receiving guidance from deep within is experienced very differently than the directions given by the mind. One is experienced as a tender, gentle embrace while the other is most often experienced as harsh, controlling intentions.

Discernment between the two dueling factions, the mind and the heart, is quickly gained through commitment and practice."

*

"I guess it's my turn to fess up," declared Faye's husband. He clearly wasn't ready to open up. Faye reached over and tenderly placed her hand on his. It was a sweet gesture, one that was far more influential than the Circle of Friends realized. The energy generated by an act of love empowers all in existence. Although this may seem to be a statement of exaggeration, it is not. Love begets love begets love begets love. The energy of love quietly, gently resonates from one existence to another to another throughout all existence for all existence. If only humankind could understand the power that exists within them. One small act of love selflessly offered empowers goodness for all eternity.

Faye's simple gesture strengthened Mark's courage. He began his story with the same deep breath as those who preceded him. "Why is it so difficult to face our failings?" He bowed his head and took another deep breath. "The truth is my friends, I know with all my heart that each one of you will listen to my story and when all is said and done, you will continue to hold me in your hearts and you will continue to call me friend. I know this, and still, it is difficult to do this. Part of me just wants the rubbish to remain in the pit where it belongs." Mark shook his head in disgust. "Like the rest of you, my baggage came to the surface very quickly. Before I even had a chance to think about the quote-quote good guy image that I have of myself, the past surfaced with its ugly truth. Needless to say, the good guy image turned sour very quickly." Mark realized his friends would be thinking that he was being too hard on himself, so he responded to their unspoken thoughts.

"Now, friends, I know you want to protect me and to take care of me, but what's happening here is necessary. I have a past! And this assignment is making me look at it. It's okay. This is way overdue." His friends looked on sympathetically. They knew he could handle this time of reflection and they admired his tenacity.

"Since this beautiful free spirit came into my life, I've tried really hard to grow up. And let me tell you, it hasn't been easy. I was a spoiled brat, and an entitled one. Looking back is not a pleasant thing for me. I was a belligerent teenager who took advantage of every situation. Selfishness was my mainstay. My behavior was misguided and unacceptable. I'm surprised someone didn't take me down, but I think my actions were so frightful that people were too afraid to try. And they had good reason to be afraid, because I truly was a terror." Mark closed his eyes as if to hide from the behavior that he so regretted. His friends breathed in unison with him, hoping to stabilize his own breath.

"Thank you, friends. That helps. So here's my truth, as I now know it. Because of Faye's help, I am a better man. I have changed my ways and I have grown up, but I've never apologized for my youthful transgressions. A lot of people felt my anger and my dissatisfaction with life. And I am so sorry. I hope by apologizing here to all of you that somehow those who experienced my meanness will at last be released from it. I pray for that.

And I promise all of you that I will continue to review my past and make amends for what I've done. I don't ever want to hurt anyone again, and I certainly don't want the Earth taking on anymore of my garbage. I've done enough harm to her...no more!

Thank you for listening. Thank you for being my friends. You know all of you are role models for me. I'm very blessed." Mark reached a place of completion and his friends just sat with him for a while. His work had touched everyone and made us all realize we had more to do.

"Mark, I am so grateful to you. Actually, I'm grateful to everyone for embracing this exercise in self-discovery. We are getting to know each other at a much deeper level than before. After all these years, we are sharing and bearing witness to the secrets that we all have.

It's interesting for me to experience this new aspect of our relationships, because I've always been so grateful for what we have together that it never occurred to be that it could get any better. For me our friendships simply are the best part of my life. But now, the depth of connection I feel is even stronger than before. Love really is an endless source of energy. I'm so grateful for your company this evening." Turning to Dave and Sally, I assumed one of them might be ready to share their insights, but instead, Barbara offered to take the next step. The Moores graciously encouraged her to do so.

*

A passage from
Beyond The Day of Tomorrow
A Seeker's Guide
(Chapter Thirty-Eight)

*"If you are reading this, then I assume you have chosen to continue your path with **A Seeker's Guide** a while longer. So, let us continue with our next lesson.*

Lesson Three

Communication with your true self requires commitment. Communication with your true self requires commitment to practice. Communication with your true self requires commitment to practice with discipline. Communication with your true self requires commitment to practice with discipline and with devotion. Communication with your true self requires commitment to practice with discipline and with devotion through preparation. Communication with your true self requires commitment to practice with discipline and with devotion through preparation and willingness. Communication with your true self requires commitment to practice with discipline and with devotion through preparation and willingness to persevere.

When you are willing to digest this and commit to Lesson Three, you will have chosen to move forward."

*

"Well, my friends, I must repeat what my Sister of Choice just expressed. It is such a privilege to be here and to have all of you as friends. I don't know why I am so lucky to be part of this crowd but I'm living in gratitude." Barb's enthusiasm always sparked the group. Even though the work thus far had already enlivened all of us, it was also very intense, and Barb's joyfulness was uplifting.

"What is happening here, my friends, gives me incredible hope for the future. I believe it is fair to say that our experiences here this evening are enriching our lives." Remarks of affirmation traveled around the group. "Well, if we can do this, so can others. And this will create change! I have a better appreciation for what our Old Friend is attempting to do. This exercise is creating change and it's creating a level of camaraderie that has also expanded our relationships; and as we all know, we began this experiment with healthy friendships. So, as I look around and see the courage and determination that is being demonstrated in our small group, I just feel giddy about the ramifications that are yet to come.

I'm hopeful, and I'm realistic. As I watched you open your hearts, I was reminded of the huge amount of suffering and pain that folks carry every day of their lives. Such immense heartache! No wonder there is so much disruption around the globe. When I think how fortunate we are to have one another and then I imagine what it must be like to live without this support, I have greater understanding of why our people are in such disarray. We are like wounded children who do not know where to turn for help."

Barb's imagery was extremely helpful. My heart ached. *Children in fear and pain and they do not know where to turn for help. This described most of humankind. We must change for everyone's sake!*

"Yes, exactly," responded Barb to my unspoken thoughts. "We must change for the sake of humankind. And what we are witnessing tonight shows willingness and determination to do so.

When I attempted to reflect upon the positive aspects of myself, I found myself reflecting upon all the positive things that have happened to me lately, and I realized how excited I am about life currently. Don't get me wrong, I'm aware of the frightening circumstances that our civilization is facing at this time, but I'm also stunned by all the unusual coincidences that are happening that seem to be leading us in the right direction. Now, I know none of us believe in coincidences, and that's my point. So many different opportunities are falling into place, all leading us in the direction of saving the Earth and ourselves. This assignment is one of the opportunities I am referring to!

Folks, let's be honest here. An invisible guy from out of nowhere just happens to show up and gives us this heart opening assignment that is creating change right now as we speak. This is happening for a reason, and we are reacting positively.

My greatest challenge in this assignment is to resist my fears. Part of me is a force of nature." Barb chuckled at herself. "I think you can all attest to that. But there's another part of me that can crash because of a doubt that metastasizes into a full fledge fear. Just like a cancer, the fear spreads throughout my body and distorts my perception of the world.

Well, I am more than my doubts and more than my fears and I am not going to allow this nonsense to derail me from this mission that we all know we've been called to participate in. I'm going to fight this disease that plagues me. I will no longer allow fear to be my guide. I will not allow fear to turn me into someone that is not the Barbara that I want to be!

So, my commitment to all of you is to change my fearful personage into a fearless one. I will of course need your help at times, but I promise to practice and to persevere." And with that announcement, Barb took her deep breath and so did the rest of us.

"Goodness!" exclaimed Annie. "You really are a firecracker. Thank you for that boost of inspiration."

"Amen to that!" added Jim. "You keep that fire burning, because we all need you to keep us moving in the right direction."

*

A passage from
Beyond The Day of Tomorrow
A Seeker's Guide
(Chapter Thirty-Nine)

"It is time now, if you are willing, to accept who you really are. This does not mean you must have awareness of all you have been or all you are to be, but it does mean you must be open to discovering who you really are, how you really are, and why you really are.

Choose not to be intimidated by this task, for it is the task of a lifetime. If you expect to find the answer in one sitting or one lesson, perhaps your expectations are just a bit high. Our answers and our life experiences unfold before us, but we must be awake to recognize the unfolding process as an answer or the experience happens without our awareness.

It is unfortunate that long before we awaken many unfoldings have already transpired and often are lost to our conscious awareness. However, it is possible to recapture those aha moments by making your history a component of your self-study.

The process of discovering messages from the past can be an adventure approached with eyes of curiosity or it can be viewed as a tedious task. Perhaps it is a little of both, but if one focuses on the complexities rather than the mystery then one creates a tedious experience.

Choose your approach, as you will, for this too is part of our unfolding, but be awake, Old Friend, as you make your decision. The discovery process requires your attention and to achieve this, you must practice. The ability to be watchful, alert, and attentive is a learned skill and one easily gained by all, but you must appreciate the need for this skill before you will commit to acquiring the skill."

*

"Oh, dear! Dave, we should have insisted on going before that ball of fire. Girl friend, you are a hard act to follow." The Moores both laughed at themselves and openly admitted that they were still reluctant to speak up, but Sally decided to go first for reasons that she was still not clear about. "Don't worry, Dave. I'm ready for this. I think!" Her reticence still showed, but her friends were there ready to support her.

"Not to worry Sal. We're here if you need us," Annie's tone was kind and reassuring. Sally knew there was no reason to hold back.

"Well," she began, and then paused to take the necessary deep breath. "Don't want to start without that," she playfully scolded herself. "The truth is my friends, I don't really understand why this is so difficult for me, but my suspicion is this: I'm probably afraid of a surprise lurking about in my past, of which I am totally unaware, that will surface and really ruin my day.

I guess that's the point of this self-exploration process, but I really don't want to deal with any more stuff from the past. Frankly, I've been doing that most of my life, and I'm just tired of it. Having said all that, I know my rationale is totally illogical. If something is still lingering that needs to be addressed, I certainly have the skillsets to do that, and I do not want to be the cause or the victim of any more misunderstandings that might harm anyone, including the Earth.

The truth is, I feel good about myself. I've done a lot of inner work already, which is not to say that more isn't necessary, but I've really been enjoying a respite from introspective work. I hope this makes sense. You all know that I've worked through a lot of my issues, and there were many, but right now, I'm at a good place. That doesn't mean that I don't want to continue growing, it just means that at this point in time, I feel good about my life.

The purpose of this assignment speaks to me and I will definitely look more carefully at my present and past behaviors. I know this is an ongoing process that we all must invest in, and I will. That's a promise to all of you. I'm onboard with this self-exploration task. I see it as my life's work. And I will definitely continue to work towards improving myself."

"Well done!" declared Faye. "I am so glad that you honored your present circumstances. You have been working on yourself for a long time. It's been part of your journey! And by the way, it shows. Truth is, you're ahead of us and that's great, because you give us something to aspire towards. I'm proud of you, Sal!" Faye's affirmation of Sally's growth was very comforting. She was in a good place, but Sally was embarrassed to acknowledge it. She was afraid that she might come across as if she were boasting or acting as if she were more advanced than the others, which was not at all how she felt.

"Thank you for supporting my position, and as I think about this, it is becoming clear to me that I was truly feeling awkward about my present sense of wellness. We need to keep this in mind as we become more actively involved with others. We are going to encounter people who really are more advanced in a variety of ways than we are. These folks will be role models for us and we must remember to celebrate their gifts while we also invite them to continue the path of self-exploration. You know, I wasn't certain why I was so reluctant to talk about this, but now I realize it was related to my embarrassment about feeling good about myself. Thank you for listening my dear friends. It's helped me to understand how I may be of assistance in this process of continuing to invest in one's own self-improvement as we move forward with helping the Earth."

"That was great, dear!" Dave was grateful for the insights that Sally had just gained. She was one that was happiest when she was learning more about herself, whether it was a positive experience or not. She just accepted what came as a gift. Her ability to accept the negative as graciously as she accepted the positive had been a benchmark for him. It never occurred to him that one might accept a negative aspect about oneself. Sally had always been one of Dave's most important teachers. Listening to her now, he realized what a valuable asset she would be in the collaborative work that was ahead of them.

*

A passage from
Beyond The Day of Tomorrow
A Seeker's Guide
(Chapter Thirty-Nine)

"From personal experience and experiences shared with me by others, it appears that the discovery process typically begins with many interruptions. Our excitement fluctuates with perceived successes and failures and our level of participation ebbs and flows in conjunction with our perceptions.

Now it is time to remember an earlier reminder. Failure does not exist. Please, Old Friend, accept this, for belief in failure debilitates your energy and saddens your spirit. In an instant, joy can turn to pain when one chooses to believe in failure.

In a world filled with competition and obsession about winning, perhaps this concept is difficult to accept, but open your heart to this and you will gain understanding. I repeat: open your heart. If you attempt to think your way through this, you will most likely be consumed by the mind's rationale for the existence of failure. The mind thrives on this belief...delights in it!

Endless time can be and is occupied by living and reliving experiences of disappointment or difficulty. What is achieved by this exercise? Rarely does one feel better after such an effort. More likely, one feels fatigued, deflated, and defeated. You choose the adjectives that reflect your personal experience and be with that for a moment.

How does it feel to relive (in the mind) a failure experience? Where do you feel it in your body? What is your mind telling you about the experience? What is your mind telling you about what others are saying about the experience? Now, is any part of you feeling uplifted by this reenactment the mind just provided for you?

When you begin to understand with more clarity the way the mind works, you will find yourself choosing to think with your heart rather than the mind. Realize my Friends, this is not a proposal encouraging you to reject your fine mind. On the contrary use that fine mind to discern when it is functioning in your best interest, as opposed to malfunctioning due to misunderstandings and misguided beliefs.

Discernment functions from the heart and will assist you with this task of reeducating the mind. For some, this idea will be most unsettling, and many will resist the idea that it is the heart, not the mind, which is the leader of our purpose.

I invite you to open your heart to this idea. Know your mind will resist this concept in its usual logical, illogical ways, but you must persevere. The heart knows the answer, for the heart is the keeper of all your knowingness. The mind is merely a tool of the heart. When you gain appreciation and understanding of this concept, the journey becomes less tedious and so much more pleasant."

*

"Well, I wish my reluctance to approach this subject was the same as Sally's, but unfortunately, it is not. My past still haunts me. Of course, I prefer to think that it doesn't matter anymore. But it does, and I am all too frequently reminded of this when from out of nowhere comes a comment or a retort that is totally out of character for the person I am today. Why this continues to happen is befuddling, but it is what it is. Every time one of these incidents occurs, I feel foolish and I assume everyone within listening range also witnessed my foolish behavior, which makes the event even more embarrassing. I suspect few people actually notice my unsightly moments, and those who do probably forget about it very quickly because they don't think my emotional hiccups are a big deal.

What is amazing to me is the power of the mind. It grabs onto something, exaggerates the situation, and then tenaciously repeats the situation over and over again until you start believing the nonsense that the mind is asserting. You know, if you listen to the same lie repeatedly, it eventually becomes an accepted untruth. Think about that for a moment. The lie is still a lie, but you've heard the mind repeat it so often that you come to accept the lie as if it were a truth. Folks, that's scary! A lie is a lie. And an untruth remains an untruth no matter how many times it is repeated. But the mind, over time, convinces you that the untruth is a truth.

So, this is where I stand with my self-discovery process. I'm a work in progress, friends. It's true that I'm a pretty decent guy, but there's always work to do when it comes to my developmental process. And I'm willing to speed up the process for the sake of Earth. She doesn't need to be waiting on me. She's been good to me for a very long time and I owe her. So, I'm here to assist this process of improving humankind. We all need to do our share. We all need to own our flaws and we need to accept responsibility for becoming better people. I'm in!"

"Old Friends, well done! You have faced yourselves and made good progress. As Dave just stated, we are all a work in progress. Now that we have faced this information, both individually and collectively, you can review the similarities revealed, as well as the issues that remain an obstacle to our progress.

Your progress this evening surpasses our hopes and dreams. The foundation has been laid for future self-assessments. By doing this regularly, everyone benefits. My friends, I am deeply grateful for your dedication to this project."

"Excuse me, Old Friend, but it appears that you are calling this meeting to an end, but we are not finished. My Sister of Choice has not had an opportunity to share her encounter with the assignment, nor has she explained what caused the severe depletion of energy that she suffered at the beginning of our meeting." Barb addressed her thoughts to the Old Friend, and then, turned to her dear friend. "Sister, don't you wish to participate before the meeting closes?"

*

A passage from
Beyond The Day of Tomorrow
A Seeker's Guide
(Chapter Forty)

"Now let us again discuss more thoroughly this idea that the heart serves as the leader of your purpose, not the mind. We are a people who pride ourselves on intellectual

achievements, and in many various ways, we reward, honor, and celebrate intellectual accomplishments. Our appreciation of the intellectual mind is warranted and expressions of gratitude and praise are beneficial to the achievers, demonstrating potential for others to so aspire.

Recognition of a good day's work and achievement of any nature are noteworthy. Our process of honoring the mind, while initiated with good intentions, unfortunately misled the mind into believing it was more significant than was intended, and in this state of misguidedness, the mind began to believe it was the leader of the individual's fate.

Through generations of operating from this misunderstanding, individuals came to accept the mind's insistent, pervasive role of authority. Concurrently, as the mind grew more controlling, the heart became increasingly less acknowledged and recognized as the source of leadership. Subtly, yet quickly, this malfunction occurred, leaving a populace's evolutionary development to unfold under the guidance of a leader operating from misunderstanding."

*

The Old Friend turned to the one called Sister and she turned to him. Neither spoke aloud, yet communication did transpire. "My friends, it seems that I have more to say than anticipated, so I must check in with you regarding your own energy levels because of the time that might be needed to complete my story. If you still have reserves to continue, then we shall, but if even one of you has reached the point of depletion then we must honor this." Group members turned to one another in curiosity. Before anyone answered, Barb intervened.

"Sister, is this another lesson?" This comment caught the attention of everyone, who immediately turned to the Old Friend rather than the Sister.

"Friends, I will address that question." Attention turned back to the other local member of the Circle of Friends. "Your question is founded in wisdom, Barb. This is indeed an opportunity for us to learn to assess the wellness of our bodies, as well as our energy reserves at any given time. Because our conversations have been so intense and riveting, we have expended a great deal of energy; however, each of us must assess our own circumstances.

My question was not intended to be a test; however, it has brought a situation before us that will enable us to be more highly functional in the future. So, let's evaluate ourselves and see what we can learn from this." Each individual determined that they were still energized and they also agreed that the meeting needed to conclude within the hour. When everyone had spoken, I turned to our guest. "And what of you, Old Friend? How are you feeling at this time? You have been visible for a lengthy amount of time. Are you waning?" Our guest paused, closed his eyes, and then revealed his own discernment.

"Yes, my Friends, I am indeed waning, so with your permission I will release this form. Then I will be easily able to continue. Shall we begin?"

I took the necessary deep breath, glanced at the clock on the mantle, and launched into my story. My friends were captivated by my experience. Many questions arose, but the one that was most significant came from the invisible Old Friend. *"Old Friend, what do you believe was the primary purpose of your experience with the beyond?"* His question gave me pause, but it was also very helpful for it assisted me in focusing my intentions upon the truth of this experience.

"Thank you, Dear Friend! I must apologize to all of you because there was so much to share that I got lost in my story. The experience itself was multi-purposeful. My friends, there is more! Life truly is eternal and those who came before really do continue. And guess what? Where our ancestors reside, there is peace. The hostilities that we experience here on Earth do not exist there. Peace reigns in that realm of existence. It was remarkable to behold the beauty and the serenity. I truly wish that I could make a video of my experience so that each of you could experience it as I did. My friends, there really is more!

Obviously, everything I've already shared was extremely important to me; however, I believe the primary reason for this experience was related to the Earth. It was sobering, my friends."

*

A passage from
Beyond The Day of Tomorrow
A Seeker's Guide
(Chapter Forty-One)

"As a result of this evolutionary development based in malfunction, the mind, believing it was the leader, gained

control over the masses, persuading the innocent peoples of ideas and creating beliefs from those ideas, which have caused endless misunderstandings and wrongdoings.

From this unfortunate circumstance we must now review our situation and form new understandings and correct old wrongdoings and this must be done in union. For reparation to occur at a planetary level, all must join together in this global project. For one person to change is a beginning, but all must change to correct the malfunction. Each person must participate, for each mind will resist, and each mind will continue to spread the disease if it is allowed.

To cure a populace of a disease that spawns in judgment is extremely complex, for the mind suffering from the disease will reject the idea that it is in illness, and in its rejecting efforts, it will afflict others with the disease.

Now, Old Friend, ponder this. Do you wish to be a carrier of this disease or do you wish to be a participant in the cure of the disease? The choice is yours. You have free will. In making your decision, you must be certain that you are making the choice rather than your mind, for your mind does not believe it is unwell. For this decision, you must search deep within and listen carefully to the wisdom of the heart, the true self, for your guidance. From this source of guidance, you must make your choice."

*

"The Earth is falling into dormancy. There is no other way for her to manage her decline than this. Unless we, meaning all of us, decide to change our ways and eliminate the mean, cruel, atrocious behaviors that we perpetrate every day, she will not be able to recover from the damage that has already been incurred. For her, the only means to survive our potent negative energy is to retreat into a state of dormancy. For us, the only means we have to survive is to alter our negative behavior by changing our destructive ways.

Within us, we have the means to bring her back to full health. Just as you helped me earlier this evening, so too, can we save her. But we have to get this information out to all the peoples of Earth. Our energy can restore her health, but if we don't change our behaviors of ill will, she will continue to be contaminated by our negative energy. So we must confront this issue from both perspectives. We must stop our perpetration of ill will at the same time that we assist her with the powerful energy that lies within us. The other factor that we witnessed this evening is the benefit of participating in energy exchanges. As we share our energy with another, we also benefit from the experience. So in essence this is a win /win scenario.

Our ancestors want to help us and this is why they are reaching out in the many ways that are happening across the globe, but we must do our part. Again, it really doesn't matter how many legions of individuals are ready to assist us, if we don't eradicate ill will from our daily lives, then the efforts of others will not be enough. Somehow, we humans have to realize that we are the problem. Our negative attitude is literally killing the Earth, and no one can correct this situation but us. So, the bottom line is this: if we want to survive Earth's crisis, we must change our ways.

My friends, I am sorry to bring this sobering news to you, but it must be done." The room fell silent. Time passed. Eventually, the visitor took charge.

"Beloved Friends, be at rest. The news is shocking and there is reason for hope! It is difficult to face such discouraging possibilities, but we must, for there remains time to correct this dreadful situation. Have faith, my Dear Friends! This evening, you witnessed and participated in many positive experiences. You facilitated an energy transfusion that restored your Friend to full energy and each of you witnessed the mutual benefits of that transaction. You also shared commitments among you to effectively alter your behaviors so that the negativity that still remains in you will be stilled. And you heard from your Dear Friend that there is more in existence than you ever imagined. Your Family of Old exists. You are not alone in existence. And you have found ways in which you can save the planet that originally hosted your species on her surface. Much you have learned about who you are and you have also learned that much is required of you in the days ahead. This has been a remarkable evening and now you must return to your homes and indulge in a good night's sleep. Know that you will all sleep well this evening, for Those Who Came Before will facilitate this for you.

As always, I am most grateful to be in your company. In peace be, my Friends. I bid you goodnight!"

"Well, my Friends, this has been a memorable evening." Perhaps that was the biggest understatement ever, but it certainly spoke an undeniable truth.

"Any assignment for us?" posed Faye to the speaker of the understated remark. Her question brought silence to the room again. "Oh dear!" she declared. "So sorry to have asked that question. Just forget what I just said, please!" Her response set off a round of laughter that was well needed.

"Oh, goodness!" giggled Annie. "I'm so glad for this release. We cannot lose our humor, friends. We must remember this. And by the way, Sister, thank you for hosting this gathering. This is such a loving setting. Do you mind if we continue meeting here?"

"Not at all! You are an easy crowd! I'm glad you are comfortable here!" The space really was a good fit for these meetings, the right size and atmosphere for contemplative and expansive work. "My friends, I am so grateful for each and every one of you. Thank you so much for being in my life." A group hug was shared, followed by individual embraces on the way out the door. The other factor about this setting was its convenience. Everyone was in walking distance.

I stood at the door until everyone was out of sight, and then inhaled the last deep breath of the evening before letting out a sigh of relief and contentment.

All was well!

12

*

A passage from
Beyond The Day of Tomorrow
A Seeker's Guide
(Chapter Forty-Two)

"As each of you ponders this for yourself, know it is time to take action. Our planet grows weak from this disease; and the plague, spawned in judgment, contaminates the people of every land. Political unrest, racial prejudice, and religious misunderstandings all serve to worsen the situation. As we infect one another through our own personal flavor of judgment, new flavors of maltreatment surface daily. This plague, which has polluted the Earth for millennia, is not waning. It grows stronger and more destructive as each innocent is infected and then innocently carries it to another.

Our participation in this communicable disease must be understood and accepted, and all must accept responsibility for its treatment and its cure. As a people, we must join together and recognize all are needed for this task. No one can be excluded. Individuals must come together for the common cause.

As we endeavor to overcome this affliction, that which drove us apart will have to be discarded so that we can unite as One. It is time to lay down the weapons of anger, hatred, and violence and choose to exist as One. Lay down your armor of pride, for it does not serve you. As individuals craving to be special, we lost our awareness that all are special; for the mind in its illness believed that to be special meant to be more than another. Through this myth of the mind grew a greediness to have more than another and in this greed, we lost sight of the abundance that is available for all. Blinded by our unawareness, we became fearful in the darkness, and out *of fear we innocently created a need to protect ourselves from the unknown. In this fearful state, protection from the unknown grew to be a conviction that any unknown was to be feared and thus judgment was created.*

My Dear Old Friends, we must join together now. We must choose now. No longer can we wait."

*

"**F**aye, are you awake?" Her husband's question was barely audible, but she responded immediately.

"If you just asked me if I'm awake, the answer is yes." She rolled over to face Mark, hoping that he was in a mood to discuss the assignments that were lurking in the back of her mind. She definitely had more to mull over, and wondered where he was after opening his heart so fully the night before. Dawn was just peeking into their bedroom windows and highlighted the tears twinkling on Mark's cheeks. "Dear One, please tell me what's going on." Faye assumed his tears were related to the conversations from the previous evening. More tears began to flow. "Mark, please let me help. I want to know what's happening. Don't struggle with this by yourself."

"Faye, I am so sorry. The things I said last night were so lacking in what should have been said. You're the one who felt the brunt of my negativity. And I'm so sorry. I've never apologized to you for my moodiness, my outbursts, and my arrogant smugness. I just tried to put things behind me and prayed that part of me would never sneak out again. And I guess I hoped that you would forget, but how could you? How could you forget about those times?" His tears overwhelmed him. "Why didn't you leave me, Faye? Why did you stay?" Faye waited for Mark's emotions to calm before she answered those important questions. She knew he had been holding all this burdensome shame and fear inside for decades. And she knew that some day it would have to be discussed. Today appeared to be the day.

"Sweetie, I stayed because my love for you was greater than the fear I sometimes felt when you were angry. And I think, at some level, I understood that the anger wasn't about me. When your anger came out, it wasn't you standing in front of me. It was another person who was damaged by life and was screaming for help."

*

A passage from
Beyond The Day of Tomorrow
A Seeker's Guide
(Chapter Forty-Three)

"As you now grow in awareness of the task that lies ahead, I invite you to consider your choices. As a carrier of the disease called judgment, you can choose to remain in denial and simply proceed as you have done thus far. This is your privilege, for you do possess free will and free will allows freedom to choose. Perhaps, however, another option for you to review is the opportunity to choose freedom from the disease. For just a moment, imagine what it would be like to live in a world free from judgment. No critical voices, no shaming looks, no actions based in anger, hatred or violence. Imagine such a world and choose, Dear Friend, to make it REAL.

Choose it now, for now is the time. If you choose to change your world and I choose to change my world, then we are working together to change our world. Your decision, and your commitment to your decision, will spread to others and each person you touch will touch another. In this way, you and I working together will touch others who will touch others, and soon the cure for this illness will spread throughout the people of all lands. But it begins with you and with me. Together, with discipline and devotion, we can willingly choose to commit to persevere.

Old Friend, in union, let us proceed."

*

"I'm so sorry, Faye. And so grateful that you stayed with me. I would be lost without you." Mark's tears continued to flow.

"I'm grateful too, dear. It was the right decision for both of us. Mark, I'm so glad you are finally releasing all of this pain. Now, I need you to listen to me, okay?" Her husband wiped his tears and adjusted his position. He sat up straight as if he if were preparing for a scolding. Faye noticed this posture immediately and asked him to relax.

"Mark, I want your full attention because I really want you to hear how grateful I am that you worked on your issues. You may have thought no one was noticing, but I did. I knew you were battling with your past every time you went for one of those long walks. And I always hoped you would talk with me. I knew you couldn't do it then, but I'm glad you're doing it now, and I want you to know that I'm grateful. We were both very young and emotionally naïve when we got married. I'm so glad we survived the rough times, and I am grateful we made it. You're a good man and a good husband and I am very, very happy. Your judgment of yourself is far worse than your behavior actually was. And I'm not saying that you were a saint, because you weren't, but never once did it occur to me to leave the relationship. I loved you too much. Still do!

I've watched you make the necessary changes to become the person you wanted to be, and it was inspiring Mark. I hope you will help me to do the same now in this phase of our life. We both have to make decisions about improving ourselves for each other and also for the sake of the Earth. Fortunately, this time we have more maturity in making these decisions and we have each other. I can't do this without you, Mark. I don't want to! We're in this together." Faye and Mark curled up together, embracing every moment of their connection. Eventually, they both dozed off, each recovering from the expense of old negative energy.

*

A passage from
Beyond The Day of Tomorrow
A Seeker's Guide
(Chapter Forty-Four)

"*Yes, take a deep breath. You deserve it, for you have chosen to participate in changing the mood of our planet. Know that it is a task most difficult, and at times you will wonder why you chose to participate. You will wonder how you are to participate, and also, at times you will wonder who you are that you chose this path of participation.*

*And as with all times since the beginning, you will be
seeking answers to the ageless questions. Who am I? How
am I? Why am I?"*

*

The Goodmans both jumped when the alarm went off at 9 o'clock.
They were not people who slept late, and rarely was an alarm necessary
to awaken either one of them. Embarrassed by their tardiness, they both
expressed surprise at their behavior, and then, they remembered their
earlier experience. "Mark, dear, how are you feeling now?"

"Good," he said hesitantly. "Yes, I'm feeling much better. Thank
you so much, Faye. Your loving support got me through that purge of
darkness." He paused for a moment, while remembering the conversation.
"I heard everything you said, Faye. And I'm very grateful. Grateful for the
conversation and grateful for all the years we've shared."

"Oh good!" she replied. "I'm so glad we're on the same page. We've
got a lot of work ahead of us."

"So it seems! But how are you dear? You listened to me this morning
and assisted me greatly, but what about you? How are you doing after
last night's gathering?" Faye took a deep breath and tried to remember
what she was thinking about when the sun just started to peek into
their eastern facing windows. "Hmm! You know there was something I
wanted to discuss with you, but what was it?" The topic seemed to escape
her, and then Mark made a suggestion.

"I was wondering how you felt about sharing some of your secrets
last night. I know in the past, you've leaned towards being somewhat
closed mouth about your thoughts and dreams, and I was wondering
how it felt to be more open about it. Any regrets, dear?"

"You're right! That's exactly what I wanted to talk about. Did you
read my mind, Mark?" The couple chuckled about the possibility, which
was becoming more and more prevalent in their lives. "If you did, I'm
ever so glad, because my mind momentarily lost sight of that topic.

So, let's do discuss it for a moment if you don't mind." Her husband
urged her to do so.

"I don't regret talking about my hopes and dreams, but doubts did
arise as the evening wore on. You know how it is, in the moment you
feel good about yourself, and then a doubt slips in and causes you to

second-guess yourself. So, I would like some feedback. Did I come across as a kook? Or worse, did I come across as an arrogant kook?" Although Faye's voices was strong and solid, a bit of moisture did well up in her eyes. Mark recognized this response. His wife was a strong woman, but at times her passion about the unusual things that she believes in overwhelmed her. The point being, Faye believed her passions were real, but also realized that many people would judge her beliefs as irrational. Normally, this didn't bother her, but on the days that it did, it bothered her deeply. After bearing her soul the evening before, she was feeling vulnerable and needed reassurance.

"Faye, I don't think anyone perceived you as a kook, and they certainly do not regard you as an arrogant person. Your friends love and respect you and I don't think anyone of them has ever doubted what you believe. I think they believe every story you've ever shared with them and want to hear more. They trust you, and even though they haven't had the same experiences as you have, they believe you. More importantly, I think each one of them would love to have your experiences." A deep breath was heard, and then of course, the sigh of relief.

"You were great last night, Faye! I admired your courage to speak out about your dreams and hopes and I also thought you did a wonderful job assisting the facilitation of the discussions. You're a leader, Faye, and you manage that skill really well. You know when to help and when to allow someone else to do so. I was very proud of you, Faye."

"What a lovely thing to say, dear. I was very proud of you as well."

"Maybe," Mark said reluctantly, "we should think about getting out of this bed. It's a beautiful day and a long walk would do us both good!" The suggestion was well received and the couple was dressed and out the door in less than twenty minutes.

13

"**J**im, wait for me, please! In case you haven't noticed, I'm not at your side." Annie's sense of humor was ever present. Even when Jim became lost in his fascination with nature, she managed to keep a happy face. *His passion for the Earth overwhelms him at times and he seems to forget everything else, even me! Oh well!* She forced herself to walk faster and realized that she also needed to speak louder, which was not easy for her. Instead, she reached deeply into her hiking trousers and pulled out her trusty whistle. This was not just any old whistle. It was in fact, her father's whistle from the days when he was a beat cop. As a little girl, she lusted after his whistle and was often caught trying to abscond with it. He would tell her that stealing a policeman's whistle was a serious offense that could get her into a great deal of trouble. She believed this story for a long time until she once saw her Dad winking at her Mother. Then she realized her father's story was actually a tall tale, and from that point on, her mischievous tactics became more calculating.

Annie's high-pitched whistle echoed throughout the forest. She successfully aroused Jim's attention! He quickly turned around and was surprised that she was so far behind. He waved and immediately headed in her direction. "So sorry, dear! I cannot believe I've done this again. Are you okay, Annie?" His apology was accepted and the walk began again.

"Maybe, I should put a halter on you like they do with children nowadays." They both laughed at the idea and Jim admitted it might be a good idea. He apologized numerous more times in between brief commentaries about this plant and that plant. Of course, the fern colony demanded a rather lengthy discussion because it was, after all, the most spectacular undergrowth of the forest, according to the world-renowned naturalist, Jim Anderson. Truth is, Jim loved ferns. In fact, if it were up to him, their back yard would be nothing but ferns.

"Now, Jim, I know this is a difficult thing for you to do when we are enjoying a nature walk, but dear, we do need to talk about last night." Her husband surprised her when he came to an abrupt stop on the trail.

He turned, looked her in the eye, and said he was ready to pursue the conversation.

"You're right, Annie. Do you want to continue walking or shall we find a nice place to sit?" He knew what the answer would be, but it seemed polite to ask.

"You are always polite, dear, and yes, I do prefer to keep walking." He chuckled under his breath, and quietly acknowledged that she had just done it again. "It is happening more and more often, isn't it?" Jim nodded and suggested that she begin the discussion. The now expected deep breath was taken. "Thank you, dear, I am ready to talk about this, so yes, I will go first." She glanced upward to see the sun peeking through the tall pines trees. The rays reflected beautifully through trees, bouncing from one limb to another.

"It was a spectacular evening, wasn't it? Such heartfelt intimacy! Goodness, it was an evening to remember. There are many aspects of the event that I would like to discuss, but I believe it is wise if we focus on our own issues, Jim. We must face this complex issue of rescuing the Earth. The idea that humankind's negative energy is the primary issue of her decline is astonishing. And I believe it. I am just so glad that we now have a platform for discussing this. Trying to address climate change without changes from the instigators of the problem never made sense to me. This scenario makes sense to me and it is more possible for everyone to deal with. We are destroying ourselves, and the planet, with our outrageous inhumane behaviors. How can we possibly help her if we don't stop our destructive behavior towards one another? I've often wondered about the pain she must suffer every time a bomb is tested or when warring actions are undertaken. How could we possibly think that this would not hurt her? Jim, please forgive me for saying this, but we are not the smartest species on this planet. We like to think we are, but we are not. So, now that I've ranted, let me rein myself in. My question is this. How am I going to behave from now on so that I am an asset to the Earth, not an encumbrance?" Her question gave both of them pause. Jim realized that his dear wife had given this a great deal of consideration and wondered what her answer to the question would be.

"Jim, I don't have an answer. That's why I'm bringing this up, dear." They walked in silence for a few more feet and then Jim took the lead.

"Actually, I think the answer is that we must choose to be proactive." Jim's initial response stirred Annie's curiosity. "We've already agreed to address our personal negativity. I want us to be more specific about that. We need a plan, even if it is as simple as committing to a certain amount of time for reviewing our behavior and strategizing how to improve it. Frankly, I don't see why we can't do this every day. Perhaps, at day's end, we discuss what went well during the day, and what didn't go well. If we do this daily, our progress will be more rapid and consistent, because we will be paying attention to our behavior on a regular basis. I'm afraid if we do it only once a week, too much will slide, and eventually we will forget the commitment." Annie agreed and encouraged Jim to continue.

"And, I think we should take the idea of proactivity to mean that we should take our thoughts and plans out into the public. I don't exactly know what that will look like but we can start working on that and get a sense of what we can do individually and collectively. What we've learned about the Earth is important and we can't just sit back and do nothing. If this information doesn't spread, then we will fail her. We must change ourselves and we must reach out to others."

"Jim, that was spectacular. You answered my question beautifully." The two old friends exchanged a youthful high five and then shared a huge hug. "I feel really good about this, Jim. Are you ready to head home? I want to get all this down on paper. I'm going to call our work the To Do List For Saving The Earth!" With that said, the couple turned around and headed out of the forest.

*

A passage from
Beyond The Day of Tomorrow
A Seeker's Guide
(Chapter Forty-Five)

"My Friend, I am so grateful you chose to proceed."

*

14

"**D**ave, are you available?" Sally called out to her husband who was up in his so-called office. It was actually his hideaway, the place where he went to think big thoughts, as he referred to it! She noticed when he left the bedroom before sunrise, but chose not to interfere with his alone time. This was not uncommon behavior for Dave. He was a quiet man, who required a lot of solitude. Fortunately, she is one who also requires a lot of 'me time,' as she calls it. The Moores are what many people would identify as a match made in heaven.

*

A passage from
Beyond The Day of Tomorrow
A Seeker's Guide
(Chapter Forty-Six)

"As by now you have surely gathered, this decision to change the mood of the planet begins here, with you. Within you is the knowingness of who you really are, how you really are and why you really are, but how do you access this knowingness which hides somewhere deep within. Why is it hiding anyway? Why doesn't it just surface and show itself? Sound familiar or at least similar to the thoughts you are probably experiencing?

Well, actually, your knowingness is not hiding from you at all. In truth, it is constantly trying to gain your attention so you will notice what is usually directly in front of you.

Is there someone in your life who seems to be on another plane spiritually? Someone who is always having insights and who appears to be at peace with the journey? Does this person excite you or deflate you? It probably depends on the day or the minute that you encounter that person, right?

On any given day, engaging with such a person might pump you up and make you want to jump headfirst into this self-discovery project, but another day, a similar encounter might bring dissatisfaction. In any number of ways you might incur disappointment, envy, deprivation, shame or embarrassment, to name just a few possibilities.

Ask your self why?

Lesson Four

Why am I feeling uplifted in response to this interaction? Why am I feeling dissatisfied in response to this interaction? If I were to choose how I wanted to respond to this interaction, how would it be? Why would I choose to respond in that way? Who would I be if I chose to respond in that way?

Please allow yourself to practice this lesson, and practice equally with each option, for this will provide you with more self-awareness. And remember the catch to pursuing self-discovery: you must refrain from judgment. Obviously, it is much easier to think positively of the uplifting experiences, but the responses of dissatisfaction are equally informative. Both bring valuable awareness to the individual even though experienced differently. The task of accepting all equally is tantamount to the lesson. So let us expand on the lesson.

How am I reacting to my response? Why am I reacting this way to my response? Who have I become by reacting in this way to my response?

Again, practice carefully and gently. No judgment, please. As you commit to diligently persevere through this lesson, notice how frequently you move into judgment. It happens quickly, doesn't it? Recognize it, but do not judge it. Each recognition is a new awareness, and each new awareness is movement towards wellness. With this said, accept that you are on the road to recovery."

*

"Yes, I am! Are you coming up or am I coming down?" Dave's response, from past experience, implied that the view from above was awesome, so Sally headed up the stairs. She gently knocked on the door before entering; it was just common courtesy. She heard the invitation to come in, but hesitated briefly, wondering what she might find. Before she reached for the doorknob, Dave opened the door for her. "What are you waiting on girlfriend?" The good morning embrace ensued.

"Good morning, dear heart! Thank you for that wonderful big hug!"

"Thank you! It is so wonderful to see you. Come look at the view. They stood together hand in hand looking out over the backyard and beyond. The morning light was so strikingly beautiful. Rainbows of color! This was such a wonderful time of year.

"So what's been going on up here this morning?" Sally asked the creative genius. "Are you creating some wonderful new art piece?" Sally never knew what was up in her husband's marvelous mind. He was always working on some project or planning the next one. Entering his private space was always an entertaining experience. She was curious to see what he was up to this morning.

"I am creating something new," he said somewhat shyly. "Sit down, dear, I want to show you my new creation." Sally did as she was asked and closed her eyes in anticipation of the new piece that was about to be debuted.

"Okay, Sal. Open your eyes!" There, Dave stood empty handed, in front of her. She was surprised.

"What's this?" she asked looking confused. Her husband just stood there smiling at her. "What am I looking at, Dave? Explain this to me, please."

"You're looking at me, Sal. I'm the new piece of work! I've been working on me, and if you're up to it, I would like to share the new me with you."

"My goodness, this is very exciting, and yes," she responding eagerly, "I am definitely up for hearing about the new you. I suspect this may be the most important piece of work you ever created." Dave's shyness came into play, leaving him unable to reply to his wife's comment. Instead, he welcomed her to join him in front of the bay window that was the distinctive feature of his private space. Sally seated herself opposite his favorite chair and noticed that numerous slips of papers lay about his workspace. Clearly, he had made progress delving deeply into his self-discovery project. "I see you have been very busy this morning, dear! Tell me everything, please."

Dave took the now anticipated deep, prolonged breath, and Sally joined him. She placed her hands to her heart to show support of his work.

"Sally dear, you are the best thing that has happened in my life. For years, I've watched you do exactly what we are all being asked to do now. You reached down into the core of your soul to try to find the secrets of who you really are, and you maintained a sense of grace and hopefulness during the entire process. Even in the darkest times, you always believed that your efforts were worth it and that you were benefitting from the process. You've truly been a role model for me, Sal, and because of you, because of what I've observed from your hard work, I was able to tackle this work today.

I remembered the pick me up phrases you quietly said to yourself over and over again: I can do this. I can be a better person. And you did it! You did the work and you kept on improving yourself. I'm so grateful to you, Sally." Dave turned his head to quickly wipe a tear away. A private man, his emotions were carefully guarded. Then he turned back to her and boldly spoke a truth she had never heard before.

"This is one of the things I'm going to change about myself. I'm not going to hide my emotions anymore. My gratitude is huge and it's because of you! I love you more than life itself, and I know you know this, but it's time you hear it! It's time that you hear this from me on a daily basis. You deserve to know how special you are to me, and I need to have the courage to articulate my love for you." Sally started to interrupt him, but he stopped her. "Sal, I know you appreciate the ways that I've attempted to express my love to you, and thank goodness you were able to be satisfied with my limited efforts, but you deserve more. That's my point! You deserve more from me, as do other folks as well. And Earth definitely deserves more from me than I've offered in the past.

So, one of the ways I want to improve myself is by speaking my truth. I want to be better at demonstrating and articulating my love for those who are important to me. That's the first step in this process. The next is to be more forthright in speaking my truth about other topics as well. I want to stand up for goodness, which includes speaking kindly about issues that are difficult. For some reason, social graces seem to have been lost. Where have our good manners gone? We seem to celebrate profanity and outrageous demonstrations of indignity rather than appreciating the art of quiet discussion and compromise. There are no middle of the road conversations anymore. Everything is black or white and there is no openness to hear the other side of a topic. When did we lose our skills of peaceful interactions? I just don't understand what has happened to us, Sal, and I'm tired of feeling helpless and hopeless about what seems to be a major component of our declining ability to work collaboratively." A deep breath was necessary and the couple both participated in the act of self-care.

"Sally, as you well know, these are not my skill sets, but I'm committed to working on this. People like us have to speak up. We have to help bring sanity back to our world. I'm going to need a lot of help with this, so I hope you are willing to assist me in being a better person. I want to do the right thing! And I want to change for the sake of the future." Dave settled back into his chair and stared out the window, taking in the beautiful views. "She needs our help, Sal! We've got to do our part." Sally reached over and gently placed her hand on her husband's arm.

"You're a remarkable man, my dear friend, and I love you dearly. Let's walk this path together, okay? Hand-in-hand, side-by-side, let us stand up for Mother Earth and for humankind."

*

A passage from
Beyond The Day of Tomorrow
A Seeker's Guide
(Chapter Forty-Seven)

"You are now actively participating in the healing process of the disease called judgment. Perhaps we might call this disease judgmentitis or judgmentopathy. But if either of these descriptors or any others that might be concocted were chosen, they unfortunately would become another way of judging others and creating yet another misunderstanding which would require more healing. So let's refrain from developing a new label and continue to focus our energy on the healing process. But first, let us discuss the use of the term disease in understanding the impact of judgment.

It was a conscious choice to describe the impact of this behavior in medical terminology. Review the properties of judgment. It is infectious and virulently contagious, spreading rapidly from one to another through direct or indirect contact. It flares as a fever, as do many other illnesses, and once infected, it functions in an addictive manner making it very difficult to treat. In its worst-case scenario, it can be terminal.

The intention in delivering this discourse about judgment is not to judgingly describe it as an illness, but instead to hopefully educate everyone to its disease like qualities so that an increased awareness of this unidentified plague will develop.

None of us wishes to accept the idea that we are ill, and certainly we do not want to believe that the entire planet is suffering from a plague. But Old Friends, look at what is happening here, there and everywhere. If you have the courage, look at the news or read the newspaper. What you will find is far more frightening than any scary movie or spine-chilling novel.

Our actions are harming others. Our words of unkindness are provoking others, and our intentions are causing others to have doubts and suspicions about us. This is easily seen on a global level, but I encourage you to look directly in front of you. What are you doing in your life space at this particular time that is contributing to the problem? We must first clean up our own space before expecting others to attend theirs and, if everyone across the globe would simultaneously accept responsibility for cleaning up their own circumstances, then the potential for major planetary changes would be a plausible possibility.

This planet-wide restoration begins at home: your home, and my home! The work required for this clean up project must be done by each individual individually. We cannot hire someone else to do this work for us. That someone else has his or her own work to do.

No, my Friends, each of you will be responsible for your own space and your own clean up. Would you really want to delegate this extremely personal job to another? Hopefully not!

Let's just take a deep breath and get the job done!"

*

"Well, Sal, what do you think? Am I heading in the right direction?"

His wife's opinion mattered to Dave. He wanted her approval even though it made him feel a bit childlike.

"David, this is a marvelous piece of self-exploration." The use of his proper name caught Dave by surprise. Sally only called him David when she was really trying to make a point. His attention span skyrocketed. "I'm very impressed and envious," she proceeded. "You just sneaked out of the room this morning, came up here into your escape station, and created a masterpiece. This is really hopeful and ambitious work, and you're capable of making these changes. In fact, from my point of view, you're already the man you want to become. You're kind, gentle, loving, and considerate of others. Those are stellar traits, Dave, and they've always been there inside of you. Now your task is to own them. I am so happy for you. And so very grateful that you're my dearest friend." Her husband took in every word. Sally's positive opinions emboldened him.

"Thanks, Sal! I appreciate your perspective and can honestly say that you're right. I am the man I want to be, but I need to feel comfortable in that man's shoes. I'll be a better person when those shoes really fit these feet of mine." They sat quietly for a while taking in the views. The Earth truly was a beautiful Life Being. *How gracious she is!* The thought, so sincerely believed, was silently expressed simultaneously by the Moores.

*

A passage from
Beyond The Day of Tomorrow
A Seeker's Guide
(Chapter Forty-Eight)

"*With your permission, I will continue to use the term disease as we move forward with our discussion of judgment. At this time I would like to assist you in discovering the severity level of your disease. Now,*

*remember to leave judgment out of this lesson and simply
approach this with curiosity and with interest.*

Lesson Five

Please answer True or False to the following statements.

*Sports are a favorite passtime for me.
I prefer driving big cars (vehicles).
My career is the most important part of my life.
Men should earn more money than women since they
are the primary breadwinners.
I attend services regularly in accordance with the
doctrines of my particular religion.
I enjoy a fine wine with my evening meal.
Election time...I'm voting for the (Democratic)/
(Republican) ticket.
I often wish that there were more to life than what I am
presently experiencing.
I believe in the idea that we are all here for a reason.
I am certain life is eternal.*

Now, how did you respond to these statements? Why
do you suppose that you responded as you did and what
ideas were stirred for you by these statements?

Did you notice any judgment flaring? Those of you
who drive small cars, did you have a flash of big car
judgment? And you, the one who lives with a sports
enthusiast! Did any words of judgment enter into your
mind? And what about you, the one basking in the belief
of eternal life? Are you concerned about your friend who
doesn't share your belief? And by the way, do you honor
his or her beliefs?

Remember, dear reader, judgment is often disguised
as concern or worry. Better to check your concern for
a trace of judgment before passing it on to another. By
now, I'm sure you realize there are no correct responses
to these statements. This lesson was presented simply to
demonstrate how innocently judgment develops and how
quickly. It is pervasive and insidious, and once activated,
difficult to extinguish.

The birth of one judgment creates another, which spawns another and soon the exchange from one to another breeds more judgment, all based in experiencing experiences differently.

Now that you have distanced yourself from these innocent statements, it might be interesting to engage with them again. Take another peek and see how you react this time around."

*

"Dear One, may I ask a very big favor of you?" Sally's question surprised Dave. She was a remarkably self-reliant individual, who rarely asked for his assistance.

"Anything, Sal! You're always helping me out with various tasks, but you are not one to ask for help. You tend to manage things on your own. So yes! Please ask away." Sally wondered how to broach this topic. She really needed her husband's assistance and she also believed that the collaboration would be beneficial for both of them.

"As I said last night at the meeting, I have worked on myself most of my life. Certainly all of my adult life! And I'm tired of it. Please don't misunderstand, I know the work is never done and I'm not naïve about my own process. I am a work in progress and always will be one, but for the moment I feel stalled. I certainly know there is more to be done, but embracing this task is proving difficult for me. I'm just not jumping up and down with joy about leaping into muddy waters again. Dear one, this puzzles me. It's not my usual way. Can you help me sort this out? I need your insight, Dave. You know me better than anyone. Do you have any ideas about what's happening here? I'm just not myself."

*

A passage from
Beyond The Day of Tomorrow
A Seeker's Guide
(Chapter Forty-Nine)

"If we are to conquer this illness, most deliberate we will need to be. Each time we notice the disease within us, we must quietly effect change and each time we see

it in others, we must choose not to participate by either accepting the disease or by spreading it on to another.

A difficult task, yes, but only in the beginning. As with all challenges, once accepted, practice conquers the task. With each new training session, another judgment experience, your recognition of the judging event and your awareness of its impact increases and your ability to reframe the situation also improves.

Rather than judging the appearance of another judgmental experience, instead embrace the opportunity for more training and self-study. We learn and we grow through such opportunities. Experience it as an invitation for growth and it will be so, or view it as a burden and this will be your Truth."

*

Dave carefully thought about Sally's request and he realized that this was an opportunity for him to practice being the person he wanted to be. This was a time to give Sally's needs great consideration, and it was also a time to articulate his thoughts in a manner that she would be most likely to hear and understand his intentions. He knew he needed to speak from a place of loving-kindness.

"Sally, in all the years that we've been together, I've never known you to be reluctant to participate in any activity. So, I agree with you, this is unusual behavior for you, and it gives me pause. The same way that it's giving you pause. And it makes me wonder about the purpose of this unusual reaction. Sally, this is happening for a reason. There's a lesson in this puzzle that's escaping both of us at the moment, but I'm optimistic. In fact, one of the best pieces of advice you ever gave comes to mind. Goodness, it's been years since this happened so you may not remember it, but you shared a belief with me that still remains in my mind.

You said, when all else fails, and you simply cannot resolve a puzzle that's standing right in front of you, then you must stop what you're doing and ask yourself a question. 'What am I afraid of?' was the question, Sally. You said that from all the inner work you had done, you found that fear was always the underlying manipulator of your issues. If memory serves me, you said that fear could take on many different identities, but underneath the disguise, fear lay orchestrating the chaos of the moment.

You also compared fear to an imposter, trying to trick you into believing something that was not your truth.

I may be totally off base here, but I'm going to go with this for a minute." Dave changed his position so he could look directly into his beloved's eyes. " Sally, what are you afraid of? And how can I help? I want to walk this path with you." The question took Sally to another time and place, a time when she promised herself that she would never be afraid again. It was a turning point in her very young life, when she resolved that she would survive the circumstances of her home life. She made a commitment that day that she would never allow anyone to hurt her again, and at that very young age of eleven years old, she took control of her own life. Tears began to stream down her face.

"What am I afraid of?" she mulled over and over again. Sally turned to Dave and asked if he had any idea what the answer might me. He reached over, held both her hands in his, and whispered. "You used to tell me to seek within." She sighed in relief, but did not let go of her husband's hands.

"Do you really want to walk this path with me?" she whispered back to Dave.

"Yes! Yes, I do. Just tell me what I can do to assist you." Sally took a deep breath and seemed ready to take action.

"I don't know if this will help, but I'm going for it," she announced. "Dave, help me position our chairs side-by-side facing the windows, please." They both rose out of the chairs and Dave moved the furniture closer to the windows and arranged them as instructed. "I'm going to try an old exercise I used to do when I was trying to recover old memories. Haven't needed to do this in a long time, but maybe this will help me understand myself. I need you to sit beside me, Dave, and please hold my hand. And please, don't close your eyes. I need to know that you will be watching over me."

"I promise!" he vowed and reassured Sally that he would be vigilant in protecting her.

"Okay! Wish me luck!" and with that said, she closed her eyes, stabilized her breath, and sank into a very deep meditative state. Sally anticipated a journey into her past, but found that she had been looking in the wrong direction. The past was not seeking her company, but the future was. There above the Earth, she found herself observing the beautiful blue planet below. She automatically reached into her pocket to grab her phone, thinking that it was an exceptional moment to take photos. Alas! The flowing gown that she was in had no pockets and no phone to be found. *This is weird. I must be having an out of body experience.*

"Yes, that is an accurate description of the experience you are presently participating in. Rest assured that your embodied self remains comfortably beside your husband and he is still holding your hand and vigilantly protecting you. He is unaware of your present circumstances."

"And what exactly are my present circumstances? Have I passed on? Dave will be very unhappy if I have departed without him. We have an agreement about that and I want to uphold the agreement we made."

"Old friend, you have not departed your current life experience. We are aware of the agreement made and will strive to honor your wishes. At this particular point in time you are sitting in the chair by your beloved, and you are also here enjoying a view that few of your fellow Earth residents have experienced. You are here and you are there and in both places you are safe and need not fear what is transpiring.

My friend, the question that you were introduced to decades ago was one intended to keep you on your path until the time when the question would arise and awaken you to the reason for which you volunteered a very long time ago. You are indeed here for a reason and the time has come for you to remember why you are here and who you really are. The question that awakened you at this particular time is the reminder that was necessary for you to continue the mission that you are intended to participate in for the sake of the Earth and all her residents.

From this view, you can fully see the magnificence of this incredible Life Being. This is why you are here, Old Friend. Her situation has not been rectified. Her health continues to fail and that which was most feared is unfortunately coming to pass."

"That which is most feared is coming to pass," repeated the one called Sally. "No! This cannot be true. You must be mistaken. This cannot be happening!" Her heartache resonated throughout all existence, and as she wept, so too did the residents of the Universe.

"Old friend, our hearts share your sorrow. We are so sorry to awaken you to this dreadful reality. The Beloved Life Being Earth is nearing a point of no return. She strives to continue, but her residents do not comprehend the severity of her circumstances. If the situation does not change quickly, she will have no other alternative but to retreat to a state

of dormancy. The life force within her now is very weak. You must enter into the race to save her life. The time for action is now, Old Friend. You must return to your present life experience and you must take charge. Your leadership is necessary. You are prepared for this. Fear not your fears, for you are not alone. Remember you are one of legions who are here to assist the Beloved Life Being.

Old Friend, hear me, please. You are not alone! Many are here to assist and you are one who chose to assist from the Earth's surface. We stand beside you on the planet and we surround the Earth from afar. We are here and we are ready to serve. So, too, must you be!

Be not afraid, my Friend. There is reason for hope!"

Sally gasped for air and Dave drew closer. "You're okay, Sal! Just take a few deep breaths. You're okay!" Sally did as he said and then slowly sat erect in her chair.

"How long was I gone?" she asked. Dave looked a bit confused but explained that she had been quiet only for a few minutes.

"I expected your meditation to take longer than just a few minutes, but I guess insights can transpire quickly. So how are you doing, Sal? Did you learn anything about your fears? Did you find the answers you were seeking?" Sally remained silent. She was still recovering from her recent trip into the beyond. She wondered how she was going to explain this.

"Sweetie, why don't I go downstairs and get us a few snacks and some coffee? Looks to me like you could do with some nourishment?" Sally agreed, but suggested that they both go downstairs. "I need to take a few notes before I attempt to share this. Give me fifteen minutes and then I'll meet you in the kitchen."

*

A passage from
Beyond The Day of Tomorrow
A Seeker's Guide
(Chapter Fifty)

"As we grow in our desire and our willingness to understand the properties of judgment, our attitude towards this approach changes. No longer will you be inclined to participate in an activity that is so clearly recognized as destructive. When the impact of your

participation is seen and understood, you will choose to influence in other ways.

How, you may ask, am I to recognize the signs and how am I to reframe the situation?

Lesson Six

At all times, when you are engaged with self or someone other than self, you must be consciously present. Perhaps you may be thinking 'Well, of course, I must be present, isn't that a rather inane statement?'

Actually, it is a skill many of us do not possess, and those of us who do practice the skill inconsistently. Our task is to master the skill and be consistent in practicing this necessary means of connection. To create mastery of the act of being consciously present, one must practice with devotion and diligence, willingly and committedly.

- *Practice being consciously aware.*
- *Practice being consciously aware consciously.*
- *Practice being consciously aware consciously noting your presence.*
- *Practice being consciously aware consciously noting your presence in the environment.*
- *Practice being consciously aware consciously noting your presence in the environment conjointly with others.*
- *Practice being consciously aware consciously noting your presence in the environment conjointly with others in the environment.*
- *Practice being consciously aware consciously noting your presence in the environment conjointly with others in the environment and consciously notice your impact on the others.*
- *Practice being consciously aware consciously noting your presence in the environment conjointly with others in the environment and consciously notice your impact on the others and the others' impact on you.*

- *Practice being consciously aware consciously noting your presence in the environment conjointly with others in the environment and consciously notice your impact on the others and the others' impact on you and consciously assess without judgment.*
- *Practice being consciously aware consciously noting your presence in the environment conjointly with others in the environment and consciously notice your impact on the others and the others' impact on you and consciously assess without judgment the wellness exchanged.*
- *Practice being consciously aware consciously noting your presence in the environment conjointly with others in the environment and consciously notice your impact on the others and the others' impact on you and consciously assess without judgment the wellness exchanged and consciously choose.*
- *Practice being consciously aware consciously noting your presence in the environment conjointly with others in the environment and consciously notice your impact on the others and the others' impact on you and consciously assess without judgment the wellness exchanged and consciously choose to enhance the wellness.*

As you can see, we have our work to do, and it must be done consciously!"

*

"Dave, what a lovely table you've put together. Thank you so much!" The couple took a moment for another good morning kiss and hug.

"Hope you're hungry, dear. I'm starving and couldn't decide upon one item, so this is the result. Just pick and choose and we can have the leftovers later." Sally indicated that she too was very hungry and immediate reached for a piece of cranberry sourdough bread.

"Oh, this is my favorite! Thank you so much for presenting this wonderful array of goodies. I suspect we may be naughty. I can see us nibbling our way until all is gone." They both giggled about the possibility as they continued selecting various treats for the first round of their breakfast conversation.

"So, tell me Sal. What did you learn during your brief meditation?" Curiosity and concern led Dave to push their discussion forward. "Don't mean to rush you, dear, but I really am interested."

"I know Dave. And I'm not feeling rushed. To be perfectly honest, dear, I don't really know how to share what happened, but it has to be done. What I realized, while taking a few notes, was that this is an opportunity to practice what we were discussing before. We need to learn how to speak the truth comfortably, gently, and kindly. And at all times, we need to hold the listener in love and compassion. This is easier said than done, but it is not an impossible task. We just need practice."

"Sounds like you have some grim news to share. Naturally, I'm having some reactions to this thought, but that's okay. I will monitor myself as the listener, as you monitor yourself as the presenter of the message, whatever that message may be. In this way, we can study our approaches and make improvements along the way. Am I sounding overly methodical?" Dave's question was actually a demonstration of the consideration he was giving to this learning experience. Sally reassured him that there was a reason for his method and agreed that it would be beneficial for both of them.

"We both need to acquire better communication skills, dear, and I think this is a wonderful time to practice. So, let's go for it." Dave sat attentively while Sally contemplated her recent experience. The information was indeed grim. *How does one deliver such unpleasant news? What is the best way to introduce such sadness?* Her thoughts made her realize how difficult it must have been for the one who accompanied her during the out of body experience. "Oh, my!" she spoke aloud. Turning towards Dave she explained her awareness.

"Here I am trying to determine how to discuss my experience with you and I now finally realize the burden that lies upon the bearer of the news. Dave, it seems during by brief meditation, I actually experienced an out of body sensation and in that moment of being elsewhere, I was accompanied by a loving, caring being who kindly reminded me of my reason for being here at this particular time and place. Now, I truly appreciate the burden of his mission, for I too now understand how cumbersome this task feels. I am so grateful to him for taking the task on. And I must do the same. Wow!" The simple three-letter word described the importance of her new awareness. "What we learn, we must pass on," she mused. "For the sake of the Earth, we must spread the news to all who will listen."

*

A passage from
Beyond The Day of Tomorrow
A Seeker's Guide
(Chapter Fifty-One)

"How, might you ask, are you living your life unconsciously? Well, let's consciously think through this together and discover just a few examples from which you can expand, based upon your own personal habits.

One example, which most of us can identify with, is driving in the car. You leave one destination and arrive at another and have no conscious memory of how you got from one place to the other. This is a prime example of how we zone out. I'm sure you can identify other activities as well (television, computers, chores, etc.) in which this occurs, but what was really occurring during that period? Rarely are we able to quiet the mind to a state of inactivity without extensive training in some meditative discipline. It is a very strong possibility that in your zoned out state, your mind was actively processing, as it is so inclined to do. Whether it is focused on a past event, a future happening or some other idea of interest is not the issue, but the point is the mind is working and whatever it is working on has impact, and if you're not consciously aware of the mind's project, you are still impacted, even though you are not consciously aware of the impact.

The mind is a powerful tool and as with all tools, one must be consciously present when operating the tool."

*

"During my experience, Dave, I was viewing the Earth from above, from outer space. It was a spectacular! She is so beautiful! I wish everyone could experience this. Then perhaps, we might have a better understanding of the magnificence of this incredible Being. As I was witnessing her beauty, I became aware that I was not alone. My Companion reassured me that I was indeed experiencing an out of body event at the same time that my embodied self was here with you. He affirmed that you were still holding my hand and watching over me. Thank you, dear, for keeping your vow to me. The Companion also assured me there was nothing to fear because I was safe in both places.

And then, Dave, he spoke the truth about the Earth. Basically, it was the same information that our guest shared with us the other evening. The situation really is grim and time is running out. He told me that I was here to help spread the message about her circumstances, and the reason I was reluctant to participate in our visitor's assignment was because I was afraid to hear this terrible news and also afraid to bring the news forward. When he told me this, it really made sense to me. He said his task was to remind me of my task as we had agreed a long time ago. Of course, I have no memory of making such an agreement, but I recognized he spoke the truth. I could feel it in every cell of my body. I knew that we were old friends and that he was present to remind me of my reason for being in this particular life experience and particularly at this point in time. I have no doubt that he spoke the truth to me.

So, my task is to speak the truth to others. I am so sorry to confirm this news, Dave. It is difficult to hear that our beloved Mother Earth is in failing health. I am so sorry." Deep breaths were taken by both, as were a few moments of silence.

Dave eventually released a very loud sigh. "This is sobering, and because you are telling me this, I am feeling the reality of her situation more strongly. This is very interesting, Sal. When our visitor brought up this topic, I listened and I heard what was said, but the information was surreal and I am just now realizing how limitedly I digested the truth. Because you are giving me this information, I am truly internalizing this dreadful news.

This is important, Sal! I am fully grasping the situation now, which obviously is no fun, but this is important information about how we distance ourselves from the complexity of a situation. I have truly felt completely involved in this tragic news since our guest informed us of the truth about the Earth, but now, I realize the truth at a completely different level. The news has truly sunk in." He took another long deep breath while he sat with the information. Tears trickled down his cheeks.

Dave made no attempt to cast them aside. *The Earth deserves to see my concern. She needs to know that someone cares.* His unspoken words were heard...and appreciated.

Eventually, Sally and Dave were present to one another again. Their time in respite in the confines of their respective minds was necessary. One can only bear unbearable news for brief amounts of time and then one must get grounded again. This is not a sign of disrespect, but is a necessary act of self-care.

"Do you have any idea how you are to proceed?" her husband asked.

"Not exactly," she replied. "But it's obvious to me that the reminder I received is in alignment with the work you've committed to. We are together for a reason, David. We've always known that, and now, we have another project. I'm so glad we are in this together.

Tell me, dear, is there anything I could or should have done differently just now when I shared the story to you. Did I present the message appropriately? I really want feedback, dear." Her best friend of decades took this question very seriously. He appreciated the significance of the work that lay ahead, and he understood that every step taken was one that needed to be done with careful consideration.

"Sally, I thought you handled the situation really well. The news was powerfully felt, which is good. As I said earlier, the reality of Earth's condition really sank in this time. I think it is extremely important for us to understand that there is a delayed reaction to hearing such news. We cannot expect people to fully grasp the extensive nature of this truth instantly. If we talk about this dynamic with folks, they will know what to expect. Like I said before, I foolishly believed that I had digested everything our visiting companion had shared with us. Well, now I know differently. By talking about this with others, we can prepare them for what is coming. Maybe by incorporating this step into your presentation, people's process of accepting the truth might be expedited and their ability to take action on the Earth's behalf may actualize more quickly.

Your presentation was well done. You spoke softly with no sensationalism, which to me is critically important. The information is bad enough. We don't need to make it worse by focusing upon doom and gloom. As our friend said, there is reason for hope, and that must be enunciated repeatedly. There is reason for hope, which means to me that actions must be taken immediately so that our hopes are actualized. Sally, you spoke the truth beautifully, and I know how you are," he said with a big grin on his face. "Your delivery will improve each time you take this task on and people will get through their grief and be able to move forward just the way our group has. I am so glad we're a part of this." She placed her hand on his and squeezed tightly.

"So am I, dear. So am I!"

15

A passage from
Beyond The Day of Tomorrow
A Seeker's Guide
(Chapter Fifty-Two)

"This wonderful tool, the mind, comes with no operating manual, yet it functions continuously, non-stop, every minute of every day. Doesn't it make sense that the mind could use some assistance? From whom, you ask? From You, she replies!

After all, it's your tool...your responsibility. So how are you going to assist this tool, your mind? Old Friend, you will assist your mind by being consciously present and consciously aware, and from this state of focused intentions, you will bring order to the wandering mind."

*

$\mathbf{T}$he one called Sister rose early the morning after the eventful evening. She was well rested, but restless. *What am I to do?* The inquiring thought repeated through her mind. As she showered, the thought surfaced from within her. When she lingered over her breakfast, the words kept repeating themselves. "Well, this is interesting!" Her announcement to the empty kitchen brought no response. "It's obvious to me that this question is happening for a reason. What am I to do with it?" She chuckled at herself. The same question was now questioning the question.

"Me thinks you are whining, my friend! Might it be a better idea to seek within?" Although her preferred cultural accent of the moment fell short of her expectation, the advice was noteworthy nonetheless. She returned to her Sacred Space and settled into the favorite chair.

"My Friend, may I be of assistance?" The arrival of the formless voice was now a matter of familiarity. She was excited by the visit.

"Thank you for coming!" Pointing to the empty chair, I invited my guest to make himself comfortable. "Are you really here to assist me or are you here with another message?" The answer was immediate.

"*Both!*" he acknowledged. "*The question repeatedly interrupting your consciousness is indeed happening for a reason. My Friend, be at peace. Because you have not defined for yourself exactly how you will proceed with your mission of assisting the Earth, the void of not knowing is causing you discomfort. I come to assist you with this misunderstanding that is developing within you.*" I thanked my companion for his intentions. It was reassuring that he was here to help, but I was unaware of the misunderstanding to which he was referring.

"*Yes, your unawareness of the developing misunderstanding is the problem that must be addressed. I have no doubts about your ability to address the misunderstanding once you are aware of it, but in the meantime, the problem brews and gains more authority over you without your awareness that a problem is even occurring.*"

"Obviously, this is an important lesson to learn. Will you teach me everything I need to understand about this peculiar misunderstanding that is developing without my knowledge?"

"*Your openness to this situation will make it easy to rectify. My Friend, you feel the burden of your mission, and because you are one who prefers to take action when you feel responsible for a particular task or project, your current lack of direction disrupts you. Even though you are not cognizant of this internal disruption, it is happening nonetheless.*

While your unconscious self attempts to manage this issue, your conscious self has no clue that a problem is arising. Thus, the first critical factor in this scenario is that you must be consciously aware of what is happening within and about you. Old Friend, you have been reminded of a task for which you volunteered a very long time ago. This was and remains an unexpected responsibility that you must adjust to. It is a responsibility of extreme importance that in some ways is flattering and in others ways is frightening. Part of you feels a sense of specialness to be involved in such an important mission, and another part of you does not! This other part is wondering what am I to do? Old Friend, your response is normal. The anxiety related to such a task is real and you are feeling the brunt of this reality. Fear is an obvious response to such responsibility." A deep breath was taken as the truth of his message sunk in.

"You're right! I am feeling the burden of this task, which does not mean that I am rejecting it, because I'm not. That isn't even a consideration.

But I do feel a sense of urgency about moving forward. What am I to do? That is the question that needs an answer."

"So shall it reveal itself! My Friend, please remember you are not alone. Many are here to be of assistance. The image you have of the legions of helpers remains the truth. Do not allow fear to override that image of truth. My Old Friend, what you are experiencing is normal for this situation. I am here to remind you that fear is insidious when it is not recognized as such, but once known for what it is, fear is easily managed.

You worry about how to proceed. Rest assured, guidance will be provided. You question whether you are capable of such a task. Your assistants do not share your doubts. You are already prepared, and you will continue to be assisted. Conscious awareness of this truth will assist you in diminishing moments of doubts and worriment.

You fear you will fail your responsibility and you cannot face this possibility. Old Friend, we all share this concern. We all fear we will fail the Earth and that we will fail humankind, and we cannot imagine living with that failure. You are not alone with this fear. But we continue because we must! We are able to do this because we have faith. We trust one another to take the next step, and we avow each day our own commitment to do so. We have hope, Old Friend, and this sustains us and gives us reason to continue."

A deep breath was heard and I joined the gesture. My heart was full with the resolve of this individual. *Please help me to do my part.* The unspoken words did not go unnoticed.

"I am here to do so, my Old Friend." Another deep breath was necessary.

*

A passage from
Beyond The Day of Tomorrow
A Seeker's Guide
(Chapter Fifty-Three)

"Have you noticed through this process how the mind seems to have a mind of its own? Amazing, isn't it? No matter how hard you try to guide your mind in a particular direction, it appears to choose its own direction unbeknownst to you and suddenly you find yourself thinking about something, which was not your intention. Let me reassure you, you are not alone. The

habitual meandering of thoughts is not person specific. It is widespread among all peoples in all lands.

This process of wandering through acres of stimulating ideas is complemented by another equally distracting habit of obsessively thinking about a particular idea at any given time. Each approach distracts the self from its inner mission, but combine the two approaches and it makes for a sizeable problem to correct.

But not to worry! We have fine minds, right? We'll just use our fine minds to handle this pesky problem. And how will we do that, you ask? Well, put your mind to it and see what happens.

Lesson Seven

Our task is to focus on a solution to the distracting effects created by the meandering mind and its particular style of functioning. Begin now by focusing on quieting your fine mind. Shh-h. Be quiet! Shh-h-h-h. Be quiet, please!

What happened? Were you able to hush the mind just for a moment? If you managed to quiet your fine mind for a moment, applaud yourself. Pat yourself on the back. Celebrate! You have done a good day's work. Old Friend, I am not making light of you. I am sending you light, but I am not making light of you.

This task is difficult and at times it can be very discouraging, but do not be dismayed. Take solace knowing you are not alone in this struggle, for it is a struggle mutually shared by all.

When I first attempted to quiet my mind, it was an exercise in futility. I would create the perfect environment with candles, gentle music, etc. I tried sitting with crossed legs as I had heard others discuss and all I managed to accomplish was frustration and hopelessness. The more I tried, the more persistent my mind became in its meandering ways. I was astounded by how many thoughts could be had while practicing quieting my mind. What I learned from these many varied efforts was the tenacity of the mind and its determination to continue in its preferred way.

Then in a moment of fleeting insight, I decided to combine this exercise of quieting the mind with my favorite exercise, walking. For years, I had used walking for health, relaxation, and processing my daily concerns. It was already an established regimen that I practiced with discipline and commitment. So, by combining my exercise of choice with my newly proclaimed exercise of quieting the mind, I would accomplish two chores at once and eliminate the need for finding time for this additional project. I thought myself very clever.

If I told you it happened easily and quickly, you would know I was pulling a fast one on you. It was not easy. It was not quick. Fortunately, I lived in a community with a beautiful walking/running trail that encircles a river as it meanders through our city. As the river meandered, so too did my mind. Each day I would struggle to gain control over the impetuous mind and each day I would shed tears. I just couldn't do it.

After a while, a long while, I developed a strategy. The mind loves to strategize! As per plan, I would choose a tree, usually only fifteen to twenty feet ahead of me and during that very brief distance I would desperately try to quiet my mind. By the time I reached the tree, my fine mind had already engaged in numerous tantalizing distractions. I'm certain this tale is similar to experiences you may have encountered. But I persevered and eventually over time, I could reach the tree in silence, and then the next tree, and the next. And my life changed.

For more moments than not, I was able to practice stilling the mind and with practice, the skill became more refined and the task became easier. It still remains a task, but it is no longer insurmountable and the benefits gained from practicing provide you with inspiration to continue.

The quieted mind, once experienced, propels you to strive for the experience again, which creates more desire for the quieting experience; for when the quiet experience is known, you know more than was known before."

*

"Your words of wisdom inspire me, my Friend. I am grateful that you shared both your faith and your vulnerabilities with me. They both exist! To deny this reality would be unhelpful and foolish. Old Friend, what is the next step to take? What am I to do?"

"Schedule the next meeting, please? Invite your friends to be prepared to participate in another energy infusion on behalf of the Earth. She is in great need. We must be available for her. In peace be, Old Friend!"

"In peace be, my Friend!"

∽ 16 ∾

Barbara's phone startled her. She was certain that she had turned the ringer off before settling into a moment of silence, but undoubtedly she was wrong. The caller ID indicated that the call was coming from her hometown even though she did not recognize the number. She was perplexed. Although she didn't want to distract from her quiet time, she felt compelled to answer the phone. So she did. "Hello!" No one responded to her greeting, so she tried again. "Hello, anyone there?" Barb waited a moment longer, certain that she was not alone on this call. "Hello, who is this please?" Still no response came. Barb ended the connection and tried to quiet her mind. She reseated herself, trying to find a more comfortable position to relax into.

The phone rang again. The call originated from the same location as before. Assuming it was an unwanted solicitation call, she reached over to end the call, but stopped herself from doing so. Again, she felt compelled to answer the phone. "Hello!" Barb tried to restrain the frustration she was feeling.

"Barbara, is that you?" The voice sounded a million miles away.

"Yes, it is," she replied while attempting to increase the volume level of the phone. "Who is this, please? I can barely hear you."

"It's me, dear. It's your Mother." Barb immediately sat up straight and gruffly replied.

"Who is this? What kind of prank is this?" Her tone was far beyond frustration. Barb was angry and couldn't believe that anyone she knew would play such an insensitive joke.

"Sweetie, it's me! I know this is hard to understand, but it really is me, Barbara. Please don't hang up." Barb was in shock. Her Mom had died years ago, but the heartache was as severe today as it was when she received the news over the phone that terrible wintry day. She couldn't believe that her mother was dead then, and she couldn't believe that this phone call, presumably from her dead mother, was real now. *"I know this must seem very weird to you, dear, but it's really me and this is really happening. I need to talk with you, Buttercup! Please don't disconnect the phone."* Her mother

hadn't called her Buttercup since she was a child. None of her adult friends knew that this was a pet name for her. This couldn't be a joke.

"Mom, this is really you!"

"Yes, dear, it is and I need to take advantage of this connection. I don't know how long it will last but I have a message to give to you and you must listen carefully. This is important. I'm so sorry to have to do this, Barbara, but I have to tell you that the Earth is very ill. This isn't a joke, she's really struggling and no one seems to be listening. Most of the news that you are receiving about the Earth is incorrect. She's very sick and the situation is getting worse by the minute. The disasters that are already happening are just the beginning. Sweetie, it's going to get much worse unless people start changing their ways. The negative energy that people themselves generate is making her so sick. Every time someone behaves in a mean way, the Earth feels that unkindness. She is literally dying from the negative behaviors carried out by humankind. People have to change Barb, or she will not make it. Now, listen to me, okay? You've got to help her. You have to take part in saving her. You have all the skills and positive energy to help her. You can help her by giving her some of your positive energy. You can do this, Sweetie! Trust me, please. This will help! And get others to do the same as well. She needs a lot of healthy energy to be able to rejuvenate.

Barbara, our connection is starting to fade out. Please believe me. This call is real. I love you, Buttercup!" And with that expression of love completed, the phone went dead. Barb sat rigidly still, and then jumped up and ran to her computer. She began recording everything as quickly as she could. It only took minutes to capture the essence of her conversation with her mother.

*

A passage from
Beyond The Day of Tomorrow
A Seeker's Guide
(Chapter Fifty-Four)

"Your process in managing your meandering thoughts will be of your own choosing. There is no right way to do this, but there are many alternatives for you to pursue. Your journey of self-discovery may include exploration of various mind-quieting techniques while you develop a style, which complements your wellness. Your process will

be unique to you as mine is to me, for while many may choose similar techniques, the individual mind demands its own unique attention. As individuals, we are uniquely defined by our experiences and our mind's interpretation of the experiences; thus no one individual truly knows what another individual knows. While we may think we know what another knows, in actuality that is impossible.

Often the mind endeavoring to determine a solution will repeatedly focus upon a topic to the point of obsession. While in such a frame of mind, the mind can also capably and excessively scan numerous other options for possible solutions. The mind is capable of managing these operations for extended periods of time. Functioning in tandem or separately, these two methods of operating distract us from our self-discovery process and prevent us from connecting with our inner wisdom. Perhaps an exercise exploring repetitive thinking is in order. Please give each suggestion careful consideration. It may be helpful if you record your findings.

Lesson Eight

Think for a moment of a recent dissatisfying interaction with someone you know, possibly a loved one, a friend, or a co-worker. Focus on the dissatisfying interaction. Remember what the other person said or did and how it was said or done. Remember how it made you feel. Remember how you responded and how your response affected you.

Now try to remember how you felt an hour or so later. What were you thinking at that point? Try to remember what you were thinking and feeling twenty-four hours later. How long did the repetitive reliving of the event continue? How did the event change as you repetitively relived it over and over again? How was your wellness during this recycling of the event? What have you learned about yourself and your repetitive mind?

How did you fare with this exercise? How much do you suffer from repetitive thinking and how much is it interfering with your life? This process of reliving events offers few benefits. Certainly we can gain awareness and knowledge by reviewing a situation for the sake of learning from the experience, but how many times must you review it to acquire the information? Are you repeatedly reviewing to gather more information or are you reliving the experience for another purpose?

This takes us down another path of self-study. Why are you repeatedly reliving a dissatisfying event if not for knowledge's sake? Now is the time to be very honest with your Self, my Friend. Perhaps you believe reliving the event might change the results. Not likely...the event has already occurred, remember? Reliving the event in your mind changes nothing, except your state of well being.

Perhaps, you believe that reliving the event prepares you for the next encounter so that you will be ready. Ready to do what? Perhaps, you want to tell the person off, or make the other person feel guilty, or manipulate the situation in some way so you feel better about it? Do any of these suggestions ring true for you?

The task here is discernment. When a situation occurs that creates dissatisfaction, we must practice previously learned lessons. We must choose not to accept the impact of the other's disease. We must choose not to think the worst of the other and we must choose not to participate in spreading the illness.

Now, I am not suggesting that you do nothing, although at times doing nothing indicates discernment. With each incident, one must learn when one is to take action, what action is appropriate, and what impact the chosen action most likely will create.

All these points must be considered and they must be processed by the mind, but the decision must be made from the heart, not the mind. The heart discerns appropriate action based in kindness and wisdom. Before discerning appropriate action, the heart must discern between repetitive thinking used to enhance a learning opportunity versus excessive thinking based in a state of unwellness. What particular vein of unwellness you lean towards is for you to discover, but know that excessive thinking rarely benefits one positively.

Discernment is gained when you recognize the futility of excessively reliving an event. Study the lesson most definitely and more than once if necessary, but know in your heart when the lesson is over and the unwellness begins."

*

"Mom, thank you for connecting," whispered Barb. "I know it wasn't easy to deliver that message, but thank you. Your information validates what I've just recently heard, but hearing it from you makes me more accepting of this terrible truth. And I've learned how to give the Earth energy infusions, so I will definitely continue doing that. I hope you also can do it from wherever you are. She needs all the help that we can give her." A deep breath was taken while another was done from afar. "I love you, Mom!"

17

"**W**elcome, everyone! Please come in and make yourselves comfortable." The chairs were already arranged, and in anticipation of a visitor, an additional chair was also placed in the circle.

"Are we expecting company tonight?" Annie's hopefulness was evident by the tone of her voice and the sparkle in her eyes. "Hope springs eternal!" Her joyfulness set the stage for the meeting.

"I believe we will have the privilege of another's presence this evening, so I just thought it would be prudent to have the chair ready."

"Good planning," praised Jim who was as excited as his lovely wife.

"Is it my imagination or is there an abundance of excitable energy here tonight?" Barb's question preceded my own, and she received the response that I was anticipating. We exchanged smiles. It was good to see Barb looking so radiant. Something definitely was up with her.

"I'm pumped," responded Dave. He caused a round of laughter as he flexed his biceps like a teenager. "I'm ready to send energy to the Earth. I'm prepared as instructed." His friends applauded his enthusiasm.

"Well, do we start now?" Faye asked, "Or do we wait for our guest?" Her question gave the friends a bit of a pause. Everyone looked around the room hoping for a clue and then I posed an option.

"You know, Friends, we need to learn how to do this on our own, so why don't we practice. We all seem to be exuding extremely high energy right now, so let's take advantage of the moment. I'll take the lead if that suits everyone." My suggestion received approval so I began with the expected deep breath. And everyone joined me.

"My dear friends, I am so grateful to be in your presence. The opportunity to assist the Earth has come before us, so let us begin by centering ourselves. Each of you know how to do this, so please do what you do so well and follow your breath to that special place of serenity.

As we prepare ourselves in this way, let us also ask permission from Mother Earth to facilitate an energy infusion on her behalf." The room was silent except for the rhythmic breathing of the friends readying themselves for the transfusion.

"My sense is that the Earth is grateful for our offer. Unless someone else senses otherwise, we will continue." No one indicated a negative response.

"Beloved Friends, we come on behalf of the Life Being Earth, who has provided us residence for longer than any of us can remember. So much she has done for us. We are honored to assist her in this remarkable yet natural way. Please take another deep breath, my friends, and heighten your energies even more. Visualize your energy exiting through your heart space and moving towards the center of our circle. And allow our energies to merge, increasing the power of these united energies. Envision this powerful energy rising above this house and moving towards the canyon to the west of us. And see yourselves standing at the edge of the canyon at the Old Overlook, as the essential source energy moves over our heads out into the middle of the canyon. There we offer this powerful mass of energy to the Earth. Like a grand display of fireworks, let the energy sprinkle its gifts all over the canyon floor, each sparkling particle seeping into the Life Being and filling her with healing energy. We trust that our efforts are successful and we restate our vows of commitment to assisting the Earth. We are here, Old Friend, and we remain ready to assist you again. In peace be, Dear Mother. We are most grateful for everything you have done for us.

And now, my friends, return from the canyon's edge and settle yourselves back into your bodies. Return to your center and express gratitude for this incredible opportunity to be of service." Silence prevailed as the group of old friends savored the moment.

*

A passage from
Beyond The Day of Tomorrow
A Seeker's Guide
(Chapter Fifty-Five)

"In our endeavor to learn discernment, we must go deep within to seek our answers. As always, when answers are desired, our first inclination moves outward to gain the desired knowledge. We seek guidance from others, or we consume self-help books, or we obsessively think about whatever our latest concern happens to be.

This process is long standing and as earlier discussed, our old methods of study have been encouraged, taught, and rewarded for many ages. There is merit to this when knowledge is being sought; however, when seeking discernment, knowledge is not the objective. Knowingness is the seeker's purpose.

The gathering of information refers to the acquisition of knowledge and indeed knowledge expands our knowingness, but knowingness is not gained by gathering information. Knowingness simply is. It is the collective awareness of all that is known and all that has been experienced by all. Deep within at our very core of existence is the memory of all that has been. Here lies our knowingness. It is our core, our heart, which is the receptacle of our knowingness, and it is through our heart that our answers must be sought.

The wisdom of all through all ages resides within you and is yours to access. This concept is indeed large in scope and leaves us grasping for understanding, which of course, activates the mind into its old pattern of gathering knowledge. Perhaps, Old Friend, one might choose to rest with the idea that this large concept requires time to consume."

*

"*Good evening, my Dear Friends. You served the Earth well! Many from afar who observe your act of kindness are most grateful for your efforts.*" The familiar voice welcomed the energy team back into the comfort of the Sister's home. Everyone was pleased to be in his company once again. Not knowing if he would be visible or not, each friend opened his or her eyes in the direction of the available chair in hopeful anticipation. Disappointment was evident when the chair appeared to be empty.

"*My Friends, I apologize for the inconvenience of my present form. While invisibility can be most beneficial at times, it can also be very confusing for those who are not yet partnered in the experience.*" His comment piqued the curiosity of several in the group, but no one spoke out. "*May I join your circle, Dear Friends?*" His question demonstrated the awkwardness of not being seen. The seated friends just assumed he was also seated as well. Apologies were quickly made when they realized this was not the case. *"Please do not worry about this. It is one of the inconveniences associated with invisibility. My Friends, your energy transfusion was successful. I hope that you are pleased with this experience, because it was indeed beautifully achieved and with the desired goal. You demonstrated good teamwork. Please take pride in this task and accept the feedback that is given. Your next step as related to these energy infusions is two-fold. On a daily basis, it is essential that you each individually provide the Earth with energy. Your individual contributions are significant and the simple act of attention means more than you can imagine. For so long has she been neglected that she is starved for acknowledgment. As all Beings require kindness and attention, so too does she. So please attend her regularly because it matters. A thought of kindness, a glance of admiration, or an expression of gratitude can raise her spirits and boost her resilience.*

The second part of your assignment is to continuing practicing your group activities. Each one must practice facilitating the exercise and gain comfort in doing so, because you will soon be teaching others how to do this as well. As you now realize, this truly is a simple act of faith in which everyone can successfully participate. But with all new endeavors, a period of practice is extremely helpful. My friends, you are already capable of doing this, but for your own comfort, I advise you to practice with one another, so that you feel no anxiety when sharing this activity with others. A few words of advice regarding the presence of anxiety: if you recognize that you are nervous before such an experience, realize this is a natural response from someone who is not accustomed to presenting in front of other people. This will pass with practice. However, simply acknowledging your momentary discomfort to your fellow participants will facilitate the release of your anxiety very quickly. They will understand your discomfort and hold you with tender care during your brief moment of uneasiness.

My Friends, before we move on to another topic, do you have any questions about your recent participation?" Faye immediately raised her hand. Her avid desire to know everything was evident once again; however, on this occasion, her curiosity was focused on the possibility that the group's participation had been assisted.

"While we were looking over the canyon," she began and abruptly stopped. "I realize the way I just described that sounds as if we were actually at the canyon's edge, and honestly, it did feel that way for me. And perhaps, that is why I feel so curious about what I witnessed or what I think was witnessed. As our energy burst into its fabulous array of sparkling colors, I think there was more energy involved in the experience than ours alone. It seemed as if another distribution of energy particles was coming from far above our own and merged with ours as they drifted down into the canyon. So, my question is this: were we being assisted by others during this exercise?"

"Yes, you were being assisted!" The answer was gratifying. Faye and her friends waited for a more expansive explanation but none was forthcoming. Her patience was not to be found.

"Fine Sir! Can you please tell me more? For instance, who was assisting us? From where did they come? Are they always available to us? Can we personally request their assistance?" Her questions exited her mouth so quickly that everyone including the invisible guest chuckled in response. Mark sat up as if to intervene, but before he could speak, the visitor replied.

"Ah, the inquisitive mind has a voice of its own. Your lust for understanding pleases all who watch over you, Dear Friend. Indeed, you were assisted during your efforts to aid the Earth. This is more common than you know. Whenever one is within listening distance to someone who is attempting to assist the Earth, those who are available will join in the activity. The fact that you witnessed this assistance is remarkable. Your skill must be nurtured Old Friend, but we will talk more of that at another time. You wish to know if you can request assistance when participating in these events, and the answer is yes. Those who are residing in other areas are eager to be of assistance, so please reach out to them at any time. The more who participate in these energy infusions, the more rapid progress will be made. Have I sufficiently answered your questions?"

Faye acknowledged that she had much to think about and thanked him for his assistance.

"Are there any other questions, my Friends?"

*

A passage from
Beyond The Day of Tomorrow
A Seeker's Guide
(Chapter Fifty-Six)

"How well are you faring with just resting in unknowingness? It's unsettling, isn't it? We are not a patient people and we quickly grow uncomfortable with situations unknown to us. Magnify that discomfort to a Universal degree and perhaps the uncomfortableness experienced is a little more understood, but still not accepted. To the inquiring mind, dissonance does not adequately equate knowledge. For in its logical illogical way, the mind has determined peace of mind as the factor that satisfies the answers sought.

Here again, the mind functions from its own myth. This tool, which thrives on stimuli and dissonance, accepts neither as a plausible solution to a given situation. The mind's misunderstanding of pertinent information leads it astray from the desired truth.

Our discomfort with the unknown is our propelling force for seeking. It is our signal to proceed with the journey. Each time we gain awareness, there is a delightful pause as the knowingness washes over us, and as we bask in this brief encounter with the warm recognition of memory, we are at peace.

Unfortunately, the mind interprets this pause as peace of mind when, in truth, it is peace of heart. Just as quickly as the knowingness comes, the awareness of unknowingness returns and the mind misinterprets this as a dissonant event rather than the signal it is meant to be.

The need to seek is our purpose for being—uniquely different in each seeker, but also purposeful in each seeker! To assume we will learn all there is to know limits our scope and our possibilities, for all there is to know is ongoing, never-ending. Always we will seek, always we will find, always we will experience the warmth of knowingness, and always we will seek again."

*

"My Friends, there is more for us to discuss this evening. I begin with a

phrase that many of you have heard throughout your life at various times in various places. Be in peace! These three words are more important and more powerful than any of you realize. Make these three words your mantra, if you will. Keep them near to your heart and share them with all you encounter.

For millennia, these words have been shared with humankind, and still, the significance of these words remains a mystery to those who hear them. Some become fascinated with this powerful phrase, but not many, and this is so unfortunate. These words are the instructions needed to save the Earth. Be in peace! This day, and tomorrow, and all days to come, be in peace!

So simple the instructions were that no one paid attention. Perhaps if the instructions had been made complicated and confusing, then the peoples of Earth might have given them notice. We will never know that because there is no time for such frivolous experimentation.

My Friends, the planet is in grave danger, and because of this, so too is humankind! This is the truth! No matter how much one wishes this not to be, the truth is truth nonetheless and the peoples of Earth must face this terrible truth before it is too late. No one takes pleasure in bringing this truth to the forefront. No one wishes to deliver this message that no one wishes to hear. And yet it must be done.

Old Friends, there remains time to correct this dreadful catastrophic event. The answer is simple. Be in peace! Your violent ways must come to an end immediately. Your unkindness and disrespect of others you perceive as different must come to an end immediately. Your maltreatment of the Life Being Earth must come to an end immediately. These words are spoken bluntly because they must be. Those of you who feel these words do not apply to you best look in the mirror and face your truth. Those of you who feel these words are apocalyptic, and thereby judge them as unworthy of your consideration, best read these words again. Those of you who read these words and pause in wonderment are beginning to understand the truth of your circumstances.

Be in peace is the answer to humankind's ill health."

*

A passage from
Beyond The Day of Tomorrow
A Seeker's Guide
(Chapter Fifty-Seven)

"In our desire to seek more knowingness, we must also gain acceptance of the times in which knowingness escapes us. These times, while not as satisfying, are of equal significance. These are periods of unrest in which our discomfort with the unknowingness stirs us into action again. During this uncomfortable unrest, the ache for more knowingness permeates from our inner core, for it is through this ache that we are reminded that there is more. And then the reality that something is missing is comprehended.

This ache, so misunderstood by the seeking seeker, is actually the seeker's signal to again move forward with the journey. The ache, so deeply felt, is the longing for connection; and the warmth experienced when knowingness occurs is the connection for which the ache longs.

Once found, through the instantaneous moment of knowingness, the seeker at last feels the connection for which all long and in this instant of knowingness, the seeker knows more than known before."

*

Silence befell the meeting. Eyes closed to avoid contact with one another, even though the others were dearest friends. Sadness filled the room. Without anyone's notice, the invisible guest materialized. He waited for his Dear Old Friends to recover from the bitter news. His breath was shallow as he tried to quiet his emotions. *Such great pain have I caused. Please forgive me. And please assist these Children of Earth!* His plea was heard by many, both far and near. The pain he incurred delivering the message brought his companions out of their stuporous state.

"Old Friend, please be in peace! Do not blame yourself for our sorrow.

The news you delivered confirmed what was already known. We are grateful for your kindness and for the message you brought to us. It is true none of us want to hear this dreadful news, but we must. Living in blissful ignorance will accomplish nothing." Other friends from our circle offered similar statements of reassurance. One by one, the visitor's friends urged him to be in peace. The words were healing.

"My Friend, it takes great courage to do what you just did, and the effort made has taken a toll on you. Once again, you are the consummate teacher. In fulfilling your commitment to assist the Earth, you demonstrated for us what we will be doing in the near future, and we witnessed the consequences of this difficult task. You have thoroughly prepared us, Old Friend. Your commitment to assist us is humbling. Please do not now worry about our sorrow, for we must feel pain to fully accept what is happening. You have served us well. You are truly a messenger of peace. And now, I ask you to do as you have told us. Be in peace, Dear Friend."

⚏ **18** ⚏

*

A passage from
Beyond The Day of Tomorrow
A Seeker's Guide
(Chapter Fifty-Eight)

"When it is time for you to remember more of who you really are, you will receive this through the heart, not the mind. As the heart brings vibrancy to the shell, so too does the true self bring memories through the heart. Enriched by the new awakenings received from the true self, one gains more awareness of the true self, thus gaining more awareness of who one really is.

This collaborative effort between the present self and the true self brings more understanding and comfort with the one whom you are discovering. With each new awakening, your journey moves forward down the path of self-exploration in discovering who you really are."

*

The evening was very emotional for everyone. The meeting ended earlier than usual because we were exhausted. For a brief moment, a very brief moment, I wondered if we should attempt to reenergize ourselves, but that notion went by the wayside when I realized fatigue had gripped my body. As my friends helped me get the furniture back in order, their exhaustion was obvious as well. They departed quickly, each wishing one another to be in peace. It was a lovely gesture! As always my eyes followed my friends until they were out of sight. I waved to the last one and then quietly sent an internal message to them all. *Be in peace, dear friends.*

The few dishes remaining in the kitchen did not call to me and I chose to let them rest for the evening. My drowsiness took me straight to the bedroom. Tonight was not a night to stay up late processing what had transpired in the meeting. What was intended to be remembered would be. I trusted that and in minutes, I was undressed and in bed. Sleep came easily and quickly. My dreams took me to places not seen before. From one beautiful setting to another, I witnessed the grandeur of Mother Earth. I viewed the gracious scenes not knowing if this was really a dream or if I was having another unusual experience. Then it occurred to me that it really didn't matter. I was consciously aware that something was transpiring about me and whether this was happening through a dream or via an unusual experience, I was having an experience of some sort.

I waited for more information to follow, but none seemed to come. The wonderful landscape and waterscape scenes continued to flow through my internal screen and with each scene viewed, I felt better. My fatigue was diminishing, the sorrow was as well, and my sense of hopefulness was returning. Eventually, the encounter with Mother Earth faded, and I rested peacefully through the night.

Little did I know at the time that each of my dear friends also enjoyed this panoramic engagement with the Earth during the night.

My phone, situated under the pillow, came to life before five o'clock the next morning. Disoriented and confused, I couldn't believe anyone would call at this ridiculous hour. Not even Barb would call this early. The scenario finally sank into my poorly responsive mind. No one would call at this hour unless it was important. *Answer the phone!* The task seemed beyond my capability until fear rose up within me. *Something is wrong! Where is that rascal?* By the next ring, I was on my knees searching under the pillow for the missing device. Finally the screen activated illuminating the entire room. I grabbed the phone and huffed into the speaker. "Hello, who is this?"

"It's me, of course! Are you up for a walk?" Barb's voice was its usual chipper self.

"At this hour?" came a gruff response as I tried to make sense about what was happening. Why would Barb call at this hour after such an intense evening?"

"Sister, are you okay?" Her demeanor was as pleasant as always. *Apparently, she is not aware of the hour.*

"Yes, I am," she replied to my unspoken assumption. "Sister, are you still in bed?" My silence said it all. "Oh my goodness! I am so sorry. It never occurred to me that you wouldn't be up at this hour. Sister, I've never known you to sleep in. Are you okay?" Her reaction surprised me, and obviously, mine surprised her.

"Barb, I'm fine, but I was sound asleep. According to my clock it's not even five o'clock. Am I mistaken?" My dear friend explained to me that it was almost nine.

"You're kidding!" Looking about the room, I realized the curtains were drawn tight. No wonderful morning sunlight announced the day and undoubtedly my electricity had gone off during the night. I glanced at the clock again and noticed that the cord had been pulled out of the socket. "Goodness, how did that happen?" I shared that bit of information with Barb who was also befuddled by it.

"Well, that doesn't make sense. Maybe one of your guardian angels unplugged the clock so that you would actually get the rest you needed." The image of an angel assisting me in that way made me smile. "Clearly, you needed extra sleep last night, Sister, and it doesn't sound as if you are ready for a walk at this point. So, let's get off the phone and maybe you should take time for some gentle self-care." Her advice made good sense to me, so we scheduled a time later in the day to catch up. Barb reassured me that she was doing fine, but just wanted to check in.

Self care? Hmm! "I don't think hanging out in bed is particularly what I need at this point, so what might be helpful?" My question was meant for no one but myself, but another was listening. "First, I'll make this bed. No!" I responded to myself. " First, I will open those curtains and greet the day properly." Still in my bedclothes I stumbled towards the windows and addressed the task. With the curtains pulled, the day burst forth into the bedroom. "Ah! Good morning, Sweet Beauty!" The view before me brought back the memories of the panoramic adventures that were seen during the night. I pondered about the experience. *What was that about and what was the purpose of that adventure? It certainly happened for a reason.*

"Indeed, Old Friend, the viewing of Earth's glory did happen for a reason."

"Goodness, my Friend, you've caught me in my pajamas!" Embarrassment washed over me as I stood there appearing very unkempt. *"I apologize for this intrusion my Friend. I have arrived at an awkward time, but time is of the essence. May we speak briefly?"* My response was welcoming even though I admitted my discomfort with my present appearance. *"My Friend, you are a vision of Divine Beauty. I see only the energy of one of God's Children."* His compliment floored me. Numerous quips raced through my mind, but fortunately, I managed to refrain from following the distractions. I invited my invisible friend to have a seat in front of the window and joined him in the opposite chair.

"Did you unplug my clock last night, my Friend?"

"Yes, I am responsible for that," he replied. *"I took the liberty of facilitating an extended rest. It was a decision made with your best interest in mind. I hope that my actions have not offended you."*

"I am not offended, but how did you discern that more rest was needed. Obviously, you were aware of something that was not known to me. I am grateful for your assistance last night, but it would also be helpful for me to assess my own wellness."

"Because of my present state of existence, I am able to view the energy that surrounds those who are in embodied forms. You expended a great deal of energy during the meeting last night, which you were aware of when you readied yourself for bed. Perhaps you have forgotten that, but you were cognizant of your extreme fatigue. I simply enhanced your ability to recover from the depletion of energy that you experienced."

"Yes, I do remember now feeling very exhausted after the gathering, but I thought a good night's rest would be enough. Were you also responsible for the panoramic viewing of the Earth that occurred during the night?" The answer seemed apparent to me, but my presumptions are often wrong, so it seemed appropriate to ask.

"No, I was not!" His response surprised me! If he wasn't responsible for the incredible scenic adventure, who was? My confusion consumed me for a moment while my Friend listened to the ramblings of my mind.

"So quickly your mind takes command of the puzzle! It is amazing to witness the speed with which the human mind can operate. Your assumptions thus far are incorrect. May I be of assistance?" Through my unspoken thoughts I invited him to do so.

"Dear One, your facilitation of the energy infusion last night was well done. And the participation of your friends was also well done. You have all learned rapidly and the transfusion of energy from the group to the Earth was extremely meaningful for all involved. The Earth was deeply moved by your loving assistance. And she expressed her gratitude by showing you various aspects of her beauty. These wonderful images are areas that are still vibrant and she wanted to remind you that she still lives. She wanted you to know how grateful she is for your assistance.

The review that you experienced was her way of expressing her heartfelt gratitude.

She is a marvelous Life Being whose generosity is worthy of notice."

My heart filled with appreciation and concern. The effort made by the Earth was stellar, but I could not help but wonder how much energy she expended by doing so. *Oh please take care of you, Dear Friend. And please know that we will continue sending you energy, and we will find others who are willing to do this as well.* I hoped she could hear me! I hoped she could feel the gratitude in my heart.

"Indeed, she does! The connection between you is strong. My Friend, it will be no surprise to you that I come on behalf of the Earth. Another meeting is necessary. Please schedule it at your earliest convenience. Thank you for hosting these events. Your setting is conducive to these gatherings. We are most grateful Old Friend, for you and for your Friends. I will explain more when we all meet together." I nodded in agreement. Goodbyes were quickly said and then the day began. Fortunately, our friends were all available for another gathering this evening.

⊱ 19 ⊰

*

A passage from
Beyond The Day of Tomorrow
A Seeker's Guide
(Chapter Fifty-Nine)

"This concept of the true self, working collaboratively with the present self, may be for some of you somewhat difficult to grasp. It certainly was for me, and still remains a challenge at times. And what about all this talk of the heart being the receptacle for all our knowingness? Weird? You and I both know the heart is an organ, a vitally important organ, but nowhere is it referred to as a keeper of all memories. At least, I have no memory of learning that in my classes. Unless I skipped that lecture, I am almost certain that the heart was never identified as the receptacle for all that is known.

So what does this mean, when it said that the heart is our pathway to our inner wisdom? Followed by the supposed clarification of 'suffice it to say,' it simply is! Well, that isn't going to satisfy the curious nature of the seeking seeker, is it? We are a people who want clarity and find little satisfaction in mysterious concepts that seem to lead nowhere. Our tolerance for such ambiguity is quite low.

Well, Old Friends, our journey of self-discovery also includes lessons of patience and tolerance, as unfoldings unfold, revealing sought after information. In the moment, rarely does unfolding information feel sudden, but in retrospect, it is sometimes amazing how quickly our journeys propel us forward. Likewise, there are times when expansion is so rapid that it is beyond comprehension, but in the moment, it sometimes feels as if movement is at a snail's pace. During these times of perceived diminished progress, perhaps what is actually unfolding is an opportunity to pause and assimilate what has been recently learned followed by a period of rest before new unfoldings bring more information to be processed.

If, indeed, the pauses are perceived from this perspective, the value of these pauses is more evident and the benefits more appreciated. Also, when awareness of the pauses becomes more apparent, the meaningfulness of these intermissions is better understood. With each new awareness gained, time is required to assimilate the new information. Thus, a pause is necessary to provide more time to comfortably digest the new knowingness.

What often have been misperceived as diminished progress are actually those times, which were purposefully provided to facilitate recovering from the previously acquired knowingness while also preparing us for the next knowingness to be received.

All is needed. The times of rapid growth must be followed by pauses for recuperation and the cyclical nature provides necessary balance for the whole during the journey process. This ongoing, ever moving process gains momentum, flourishes, requires rest, and then moves again. In this way the seeker seeks, the seeker finds, the seeker assimilates the newly found discovery, and the seeker seeks again.

As this cyclical pattern of seeking proceeds through time, it encompasses many life experiences. We transition from one experience to another, to another, and always our lessons learned from an experience transitions with us. Our knowingness gained from all the lessons of a particular life experience is not lost. Death, as we refer to the transitioning, is not the end. It is the beginning of yet another experience. As the shell fades in its existence, the essence of that shell carries onward. The transition from one experience to the next is not the same for everyone, for as with all other aspects of existence, the transition is unique to the one transitioning.

Wherever the individual journey transitions next is, of course, the chooser's choice, but no matter where is chosen, the knowingness of the transitioning individual resides within the essence of the transitioning seeker. At the very core of the seeker's essence lies the knowingness of all experiences for all times, and it is this core, which has come to be known as the heart of the seeker. Unfortunate it is for the seeker that through the transitioning process, the essence of the seeker is lost to the seeker's memory. For it is the essence, the true self that remembers and carries all known memories. The lost memories are not lost forever. The transitional process reduces the seeker's ability to remember all that has been experienced, so that the new experience is not impacted by previous experiences. This temporary pause from knowingness allows each seeker to begin anew in the upcoming experience.

Without the memories of earlier experiences available at initiation, the seeker enters the new life experience as if life has never been experienced before. Each new occurrence of a new life experience is begun from this state of innocent unknowingness and as each new innocent proceeds with his or her experience, an awareness grows from deep within that there is more than appears to be. From this, the curiosity of the innocent seeker is stirred to know all there is to know about all that is, and from some source yet unknown to the seeker, the seeker knows there is a reason for existence and there is a purpose to existing. From this awareness, the seeker's quest to answer the ageless questions of who am I, how am I, why am I, begins."

*

As agreed, Barb arrived early to help me set up the table and to arrange the chairs in the living room. Her assistance really did make the task more fun and less taxing on the body.

"So, dear, what was on your mind this morning when you called at the ghastly hour of nine o'clock?" My question ignited my friend who was already high energy.

"Oh my gosh! Thanks for reminding me. We still haven't had a chance to talk about what happened the other day." Barb proceeded to tell me about her remarkable phone call with her mother. It was a very exciting story. She asked if it was appropriate to share the story with the group and I encouraged her to do so.

"Yes, indeed! Barbara, this is a sweet story that your friends will appreciate hearing for many different reasons. These encounters with deceased loved ones are so affirming. I think it is really important to share them, because it gives people hope, and at the same time, it diminishes our fears about death. Please do share this experience with our friends. It will mean a lot to them, Barb, and it is so relevant to our gatherings. For that reason alone, you must share your story."

With that said, the doorbell rang and our friends arrived. Living in close proximity was such a blessing. The conveniences of a small community were many. Being able to walk everywhere, including taking care of errands, was a delight. Barb did a wonderful job of warmly welcoming everyone into the living room. "Grab your favorite chairs and make yourself at home. You all know the routine." Hugs and laughter were exchanged as this group of old friends settled down for another conversation about topics that were not discussed until very recently. Annie Anderson delightfully expressed her joy and anticipation as she positioned herself in her chosen chair.

"I am so excited about being here. Even though I have no idea what will happen tonight, I'm just so glad to be part of this unfolding adventure." She giggled freely and then added another thought. "We are on an adventure!" Annie turned to her husband of several decades and repeated, "We're on an adventure! Who would have thought, at our age, that we would be having an adventure? Yay!!!" Her excitement tickled her friends, who were actually having similar feelings.

"I agree with you, Annie!" reacted Sally. "These meetings are exhilarating and powerful. It's wonderful being involved in a project that is meaningful. And I realize that talking about saving the Earth as a project doesn't quite exemplify the importance of our task, but frankly, no words can adequately describe what we are now facing. I'm just so grateful to be part of this process." Her comment aroused similar thoughts. Everyone in the circle of friends had their own personal involvement in this so-called project and the feelings ran deep.

"Dear Ones, we haven't even begun our meeting and already our connection to the Earth and to one another is heartfelt. This project has brought our long-standing relationships to another phase of intimacy. We are so blessed to have one another and to share this experience. Shall we hold a moment of silence for the Earth and let her know how much she is loved?" The friends immediately fell into silence and each individual communicated their affection to the planet. And the renowned deep breath concluded the brief moment of heartfelt connection.

"Let me continue for just a moment, if I may." Not knowing when our invisible friend would arrive, I decided to invite everyone to check in. "Friends, as you know, our Old Friend, requested this meeting, and as usual, it is difficult to know when he will arrive, so perhaps, we might update one another on our happenings. Of course, it's only been twenty-four hours since we last met, but I suspect we all have thoughts to share." I glanced toward Barbara to encourage her to share her story. She eagerly accepted the opportunity. Waving her hand, she asked to take the lead and was welcomed to do so.

"Well, I'm actually very eager to share what happened a couple of days ago. I meant to tell you about it last night, but obviously there was no time to do so." Barb paused and took the necessary deep breath in preparation to share her news. "I've had the most delightful, unusual experience." Her smile brightened the room. "My mother, as you all know, died some years ago. Well, the other morning as I was preparing myself for meditation, the phone interrupted my process. I was taken aback because my practice is to turn the phone to silence mode before beginning the meditation. Anyway, when I reached over to end the call, I noticed the area code was from my hometown. This surprised me, so I took the call, but no one responded, even though I felt certain that someone was on the line. After several attempts to get a response, I just tapped the magic button and returned to my meditation. Well, before I could even take a deep breath the phone rang again from the same number, so I answered it. This time there was the most amazing surprise awaiting me. It was my mother. Needless to say, I was startled and confused, but the voice kept insisting that she was really my Mom. As you might imagine, I so wanted to believe it was. When she called me Buttercup, I knew the experience was real. It was so wonderful to hear her voice. Even now, it makes me smile and also brings forward a few tears, but oh my goodness, it was a wonderful experience. Needless to say, it was an inexplicable event that will never be forgotten.

And as you might also imagine, there was a reason for her call. She wanted to talk about the Earth and she confirmed everything that our new Old Friend has shared with us. She emphasized how serious the situation is and that we must help. She talked about the negative energy that humankind produces and how we must change if the Earth is to survive, and she also reiterated what our Friend has said about the energy infusions. Mom said that these transfusions really do assist her and that we should not doubt this. She was adamant that we needed to continue doing this energy work and that we should also apprise everyone who will listen that they need to participate in these activities as well." Barb ended with another deep breath and thanked everyone for listening. Her friends were as excited about her experience as was she.

"How wonderful for you, Barb!" expressed Faye. "If she connects with you again, please give her our love. She was such a loving woman. We miss her so." Mark nodded in agreement as his wife spoke of their fondness of Barbara's mother.

"Barb, that was an amazing story!" noted Dave who was incredibly curious about the process of such a connection. "Did she say anything about how this connection actually occurred?"

"No she didn't Dave, but she was trying to convey her message very quickly, because she didn't know how long the reception would maintain. It was obvious that she was somehow utilizing technology to facilitate the connection. I don't understand it Dave, but I have heard similar stories about this type of connection." He nodded and acknowledged that he also recalled stories of this nature.

I turned to Barbara to be sure she was finished. Before I could say anything, she confirmed that she was done and invited me to give us an update. I accepted the opportunity.

"Well, I too have had a delightful experience, and I'm curious to know if the rest of you have also shared this experience. After last night's experience, I was really exhausted and went straight to bed after all of you left. I remember setting an alarm before settling in because I wanted to rise early and take care of a few tasks on my To Do List.

So, there are actually two parts to this story. First, I fell asleep very quickly and was blessed with this remarkable panoramic experience of witnessing various scenes from all around the globe. It was a lovely experience." I knew without asking that my friends had shared the experience. "Wasn't that incredible?" Everyone agreed of course. "Well, the second part of the experience occurred this morning after I was rudely awakened by this Friend who called me at the horrendous hour of nine o'clock." Barb and I both laughed, as we shared the funny experience. Our friends agreed that they could not believe that I actually slept in until that late hour.

"Anyway," I continued, "shortly after we had our weird encounter, I open the curtains to find this beautiful day that was well on its way to being spectacular, and while I stood there in my pajamas, our invisible Friend announced his arrival. Turns out he was responsible for the clock being unplugged. He believed I needed a long rest! Obviously, he was correct. So, I asked him if he was also responsible for the beautiful scenic views during the night and he said that he was not." This caused a reaction from my friends, who also presumed that he had somehow orchestrated the event.

"Well, he then proceeded to tell me the most remarkable thing." Tears welled up in my eyes. "I'm still reeling from this because it is so tender. Our Friend said the scenes were provided by Mother Earth. It was her way of saying thank you for the energy infusion. He said she was deeply touched by our efforts and wanted to express her gratitude by sharing the parts of her that are still vibrant. She wants us to know that she is still alive. Isn't that incredible." I had to stop. The sense of heartfelt connection silenced me. I was not the only one in the room who was in tears.

"Wow!" whispered Jim. "That is a story that must be shared with everyone. She's reaching out to us in such a gracious way. And she is letting us know that our efforts are really helping her.

Who would have imagined that such a simple task could be so effective. This really encourages me to continue with these exercises. I was hopeful before, but now I'm certain that this process really helps her. My goodness, Friends! We really can help the Earth, by just sitting here in our comfortable chairs and sending her healthy energy. This is too simple to be true, and yet, it is.

Wow!" he said again. "We have to get this information out to everyone."

"Yes, we do!" Faye announced adamantly. "I've been thinking a lot about this: we need to expand this group. Let's think about other folks who might be interested in this and bring them into our group. The more people who know about this the better, and then these folks can take what they've learned and start other groups. We can't keep this important information to ourselves."

"I agree," declared Mark. "The eight of us may need to split up and start other groups. That might be a way to gain more momentum quickly."

"Yikes, Mark!" reacted Sally. "That's a great idea, but the thought of splitting up our group saddens me. We're just getting started and it is so delightful being together. I don't want to lose this connection that we've been sharing." Similar comments were shared. But the reality of Mark's suggestion could not be ignored.

"Okay, everyone, I have a thought. We're all in agreement that we do not want to let go of our group gatherings, and we also know that Mark's suggestion is an excellent idea. So, let's do both!" My idea spread around the circle of friends instantly and a sigh of relief was heard.

"This is an idea of great merit, my Friends. So quickly are you responding to the needs of the planet! Everyone is most grateful." The arrival of their guest was timely for many questions were racing about in the minds of the group. He was appropriately welcomed and invited into the circle. *I apologize for interrupting your check in, but your discussion is the reason for this meeting. May I take the lead for a moment?"* His request of course, met with everyone's approval.

"As you all know, the Earth's situation demands immediate attention. And your efforts last night demonstrated that you are already prepared to take action on your own. Because of your initiative and because of the Earth's response to your assistance, it is evident that you are ready to be assistants to the Earth's needs. We are so grateful for your quick response to her ill health.

I have a question for all of you. Please give it careful consideration. Right now, in your current life situation, are you able to think of a few people whom you might invite to one of your meetings?" The circle of friends did as he asked. They deliberated over the question and couples spoke softly to each other as they puzzled over a list. They were actually surprised by what was discovered.

"Have you discerned the possibilities of expanding your numbers? Please discuss this now, so that we are all aware of what is transpiring. Sally, would you like to accept the leadership role for a while?" His question pleased her, and she immediately stepped up.

"Well, Dave and I surprised ourselves. We actually think we can create a short list of about thirty people, and our long list may double that amount. This is not a definite, but since we are talking about possibilities, we think this is feasible. And we are very excited about this. I'm glad you posed this question. It's comforting to know that we can spread this information more rapidly than we imagined. How about the rest of you? What have you discovered?"

Jim spoke out on behalf of the Anderson clan. "We were surprised as well. At first, we didn't think we knew more than a handful of folks who might be interested. But then we realized that we were making judgments about these people without even checking in with them. Isn't that ridiculous? I'm glad we noticed what we were doing, because the truth is, we don't know how people will respond. Let's check our silly misconceptions at the door, and open our hearts to optimism.

Anyway, we know that there will be some duplication going on here because we do have mutual friends, but so what? The more invitations that are given; the better our chances are at increasing our numbers. These invitations are our opportunity to spread the word. It's a means of announcing what's going on locally that they can get involved in. Annie, do you have anything to add to this?" She shook her head no and gave him the thumb's up sign.

Attention went to the Goodmans, who chose Mark to be the speaker for them. "We are excited as well. I am truthfully stunned by the finger list that we came up with. It's very reassuring. And we are eager to talk some more about how to take the next step forward."

Barbara and I collaborated with one another and also discovered that our list of hopeful possibilities was far more than we anticipated. We too wanted to move ahead on taking action to expand our numbers. I turned to our invisible Friend and asked for his guidance. "Now, that you have heard about our group's potential for growth, what is your advice, Old Friend?"

*

A passage from
Beyond The Day of Tomorrow
A Seeker's Guide
(Chapter Sixty)

"As we continue to explore our reason for being, more clearly we become aware of the purpose of eternal life. This process of learning all there is to know is simply too large a project for one life experience. How then, you ask, did this all begin? And why? And who decided this was necessary?

Did you notice the questions of how, why, and who, again? These questions are our activators. Always, when faced with a curious situation, these are the questions that spark our imagination. This was true in the beginning and it has remained true throughout all time. Perhaps these questions are as much answers as they are questions.

Who is responsible for the beginning presumes there was a who, and excites the curiosity of someone to begin seeking for said who, which then leads the someone to curiously wonder why and how the who did whatever is being sought.

This process is no different now than in the beginning. When consciousness was sparked so long ago by the first whisper, the ageless questions began. What was that sound never heard before? Who made the curious sound? How was the curious sound made? Why was the sound made? And at that point, so very, very long ago, the journey to know all there is to know began.

What began in mystery remains a mystery, inspiring curiosity to unravel the mystery. This need to solve the mystery excites and energizes the curious seeker, and from this need to know comes the burning desire to know, which catapults the seeker into journey after journey after journey.

Each time we start anew, we are void of our memories from previous experiences so that the new experience is as never done before. From this place of innocent unknowing, we view the new experience with eyes of wonder, and curiosity is again stirred. Thus, a new journey is embarked upon and new discoveries of oneself are found in the pursuit to learn all there is to know.

What remains a mystery is why someone would choose to return repeatedly to learn more lessons when, as we know through our own experiences, life can be very difficult. Some of you may be experiencing circumstances now that demand understanding of the whys, hows, and whos. Often we have heard others, and at times ourselves, proclaim how difficult life is and that there is no way we would have chosen such a situation. Why, you may ask, would anyone choose a life filled with discomfort, illness, and unspeakable hardships?

Old Friend, why indeed?"

*

"*My Dear Friends, your willingness to proceed pleases all who watch over these proceedings. How very grateful we are for your commitments to assist the Earth.*"

"And we are grateful for yours, Old Friend, and for those who watch over us!" Faye intervened. "Will we ever be so fortunate to meet these other Beings that you so often refer to?" Her question revealed the curiosity of all in attendance and amused those who listened from afar. "*My Companions are amused because they wonder how I will respond to your question. And so do I!*" To our surprise and delight, our invisible Friend materialized in his designated chair. "*Oh how dear it is to see you from this plane of existence. You are all bright lights of energy composed of an array of colors that far surpass your present color charts. Suffice it to say that you are beautiful Beings!*" His sincerity could not be denied. His joy of seeing us from his present perspective was so tenderly expressed. "*My Old Friends, how dear you are to me. I am most pleased to be here with you in this way. So often have we done this before, at other times in different places, and always the questions are the same. Who am I? How am I? Why am I?*

The questions of the ages are always asked, no matter where one is at any given time or regardless of the location. The questions are always present. My Friends, the Companions who watch over you are as are you, and as am I. We are all One, regardless of our present location or our present form. We all live eternally, we all seek answers to age old questions, and we all desire to know everything there is to know about All That Is." Our Friend paused, took a deep breath, and faded into the chair once again. "*Please excuse my invisible form, but my energy must be conserved. It was a selfish act to materialize, but I so wanted to see you as you truly are. So grateful I am.*

My friends, no greater gift can I offer you than to speak this truth. Those who watch over you, you have seen many times before, and you will see them again. These are Friends of Old with whom you have lived many lives before and who will continue be a part of your lives for all time to come. This is the way of eternal existence. I hope this truth provides you with a sense of deep and satisfying comfort. You are never alone, my Dear

Friends." A sigh was audible as the invisible friend fell quiet. His respite was brief before he began again.

"*With your permission, my Friends, I would like to return to your request for guidance. You have already devised a fine plan on your own. My suggestions are few and based upon information gained by other assistants across the globe. We have found that it is wise to invite individuals into your own group for a short period so that they have the experience of sharing stories, as you have done. This introduction to the importance of story-telling aids them in understanding their own stories before they begin leading their own groups.*

As have all of you learned from one another; so too will the people on your list. I urge you to create your list and strategize how you will proceed. I believe your lives will become very busy in the days ahead. There will need to be many meetings to accommodate the numbers that you have derived. Large groups do not make good first impressions; therefore, it is wise to invite only a few at a time. If you can group people who are well acquainted, this facilitates a positive response as well. The advantage of participating in numerous groups is that your facilitation skills grow rapidly, as does your ability to assist the Earth. Please remember to practice self-care and to emphasize this with your participants.

My friends, it is time for me to leave you with the task of overseeing your guest list. May we meet again soon to review your progress?" The group immediately huddled together for a brief moment and then announced that they would be prepared for another meeting the following evening. Their Friend from unknown parts agreed that he would make an appearance. His comment caused a round of chuckles.

"*A delightful way to end a meeting! Be in peace, my Friends!*" announced their friend. He bid them goodbye and departed without a sound.

"Well," announced Mark, as if he was about to say something very important, and in fact, he did. "I'm starving. Can we have some of those goodies hanging out in the dining room?" Everyone rose at the same time. Nourishment was definitely needed. The circle of friends circled the table for a while, nibbling and chatting about the possibilities for the upcoming meetings. Then Jim grabbed a plate and loaded it up with treats.

"I suggest you all fill up a plate, because we need to get back to work!"

Everyone agreed his plan was a good one and followed suit. Back in the living room the discussion about the guest list continued.

By the end of the evening, a plan was made and the guest list was organized so that four to six guests would be invited at a time. If adjustments needed to be made they would do so, but for now they were comfortable with the option chosen.

"We've done it," declared Annie. "We've had another adventure!" Her joyfulness was contagious.

"My friends, before we close for the evening, let me address one more item with all of you. We didn't finish checking in earlier. The meeting morphed into another form very quickly, and that task went unfinished. So let's check in now. Is anything pending that needs to be brought up?" It appeared that everyone was in peace and ready to call the meeting to a close.

I waved goodbye to everyone as they made the turn towards their respective homes, turned off the porch light, and headed for the bedroom, turning off lights along the way. It was another special evening. My heart was full. And then I remembered that our group had been remiss! So focused were we on the future meetings that we forgot to acknowledge the Earth during the meeting. *How easy it is for us to forget this task!* I immediately texted everyone and reminded them to do an energy infusion on their own when they got home. Everyone responded with red hearts, appropriate for our love for the Earth. *Hopefully, we will be more diligent during our future meetings and in our daily practices.*

Once in the bedroom, I parked myself in the chair by the window. "Dear Mother Earth, I come to offer you a particle of my essential source energy. If you are agreeable, I would love to send it to you now." With the question posed, I awaited for an answer. Although I do not know how to explain what was sensed, I am certain that a positive response was given.

"Thank you, my Friend! So, now I will invite anyone within listening range to join me in this moment dedicated to the Life Being Earth. Even though I do not know your location, or who you really are, your assistance is deeply appreciated. She needs our help, and your gracious gift will be well received.

So now, my new Friends, please take a deep breath and enhance the strength of your already powerful energy. Envision it growing within you and when you are ready, allow the energy to flow from you towards this beautiful Life Being. Wherever you choose to send the energy is yours to discern. She is a very large Being and she requires many doses of energy, so you choose the place you wish to release your energy. Wellness to the Earth! May our energy serve you well!

Old Friend, we are so grateful for all that you have done on our behalf and we will continue to share energy with you as long as it is necessary. Please allow us to help you as you have done for us. In peace be, Dear Friend.

And to all those who assisted this evening, be in peace! And thank you!"

As I readied myself for bed the phrase 'Wellness to the Earth' kept running through my mind. *What a lovely thought! I must remember to share this with my friends."*

20

*

A passage from
Beyond The Day of Tomorrow
A Seeker's Guide
(Chapter Sixty-One)

"The time has come to know more about who you really are. You are not who you appear to be my Dear Old Friend, you are much more. We think only of the present image we see reflecting in our mirrors and we believe this is who we really are. This could not be further from the Truth. You are so much more! And at some level you know this.

In your present life experience, how often have you felt misjudged or misunderstood by someone and how frequently have you done the same to others based solely upon appearance?

Perhaps they or we are too fat or too thin, too short or too tall, too dark or too light, too this or too that, etc. In essence, judgments are being made without evidence, based upon appearance and our own prejudices regarding anyone who is different from our perceived self. Differences, the source of endless learning opportunities and enrichment, erroneously grew to a circumstance of suspicious fear of anyone different from ourselves.

From this fearful state, judgment flourished creating beliefs founded in misunderstanding. What was meant to be avenues for exploration through the exchange of differing ideas came to be the roadblocks to connection and mutual growth. This planet, so rich in diversity, populated with such immense variety, offered opportunities for self, other, and mutual exploration for endless time: a cornucopia of experiences, within an experience, available for all to discover and to enjoy.

So what went awry? When all this abundance was available to everyone, what occurred to create such suspicion and doubt towards one another? What grew from remarkably indescribable beauty and vast variety evolved to be a space filled with fear, doubt, suspicion, and grave dissatisfaction. How could one derive from the other? Ponder this, Old Friend, and wonder in astonishment. But as you ponder, take care to wonder about this happening without judgment, for it was the judging nature that evolved on this beautiful planet, which created its deterioration.

Wonder about this from a state of compassion and experience the sadness of this evolutionary mishap. Wonder about this from a place of determination, for what has transpired is not what must be. All are gifted with free will and all are capable of changing this unfortunate circumstance.

The mood, which resides in the essence of all, is not of a judging kind and it is this mood of ancient unity that we all seek. From deep within, the need to connect with that unity permeates throughout our very existence. We know from a place of deep awareness that we are One with all others; yet unknown to us in human form is who the others are.

Old Friend, everyone knows this at some time, in his or her own unique way. All is inclusive of all! You, me, and everyone, no one is excluded! So, if no one is excluded, then those we have doubts and suspicions about are also included. This is an idea worthy of consideration."

*

Morning arrived early, it seemed. I awoke before sunrise, filled with energy and readiness to begin the day. Within minutes the bed was made, casual wear replaced my PJs, the curtains were drawn, and my chair was positioned so that I could greet the morning sun. *What a delight this is!* My mind told me that a walk would be good for me, which of course is a suggestion of merit, but I wanted to wait here in my quiet space to see the sun rise over the hills. My walk would come later.

"A decision based in wisdom my friend. May I join you?" My invisible

friend's unscheduled arrivals no longer surprised me. His presence was always welcome.

"Please do!" I rose to rearrange his chair for the morning unveiling, but he surprised me by moving it himself. "Geez, wish I had that on film! You do realize that from my perspective the chair just lifted into the air by itself and turned to face the window. Ha!" she giggled to herself. "That was so cool! So you do have the ability to move physical things about in your present form."

"*Yes! I am capable of this and much more,*" he said in a playful way. "*There are advantages to being in my present form, just as there are advantages of being in your present form. Life is filled with potential, regardless of the form that is chosen in any given life experience. Just as you wish to take advantage of being in the right place at the right time this morning, so too do I.*"

"Ah, so you are here for a reason. Imagine my surprise!" For some reason the two of us were very lighthearted this morning, which was delightful, and a nice change from the heavy-hearted topics that were typically discussed. "Fess up, my Friend. What is the reason for this early morning visit?"

"*My Old Friend, once again, you know me well. This has been true in many lifetimes. So, as you say, I will fess up. I am here for two reasons. As always there is a mission of purpose that must be addressed, for time is of the essence. The work that was achieved last night after my departure does not require another review. What you accomplished is what is needed to take the next step, so let us do this. Please connect with your friends if possible and choose four to six friends to join us this evening. Does this meeting with your approval, Old Friend.*"

"Yes, of course. I don't see any problems with this, other than availability of our new participants, but we can certainly hasten our timeline. It makes sense to do so. Now, tell me what your other reason for coming is." My visitor inhaled deeply, which was another unusual event to experience. Hearing a deep breath taken from a space that is empty is eerie. *How grateful I am to have these unusual experiences happening around me. Thank you!* Of course, my unspoken expression of gratitude was heard.

"*Thank you for being receptive to what appears to be unusual while in your present form. We are grateful that you so quickly adapted to the presence of those who are always around you. Now, my friend, I will fess up to the second reason for my visit. Selfishness brings me here, my*

Friend. So often have we seen the grand ascension of the morning sunrise together that I wanted to experience this with you once again. I hope that my company pleases you as much as yours pleases me." My Friend's sincerity filled me with joy. I assured him that his company was most welcomed and satisfying. We sat quietly, awaiting the arrival of another Dear Old Friend. The Sun did not disappoint! Tears streamed from my eyes. *What a peaceful moment this is! Everyone should take time every day to experience this. I am so grateful for this blissful experience.*

"*As am I,*" replied my known, yet unknown, Companion. The sun met its early morning task in its usual spectacular fashion, leaving my Friend and me both filled with energy to meet our own tasks. We parted company knowing that we would connect at the evening gathering.

Phones calls were quickly made to the Circle of Eight apprising them of the Old Friend's wishes for the evening. Everyone was in agreement with his decision and action was readily taken. Within the hour, four positive responses to our invitations were received.

*

"Well, that's good news!" Mark responded to his wife's update regarding the change of plans for the evening meeting. "I guess this means that our visitor thinks we're ready to take on a greater leadership role." Faye agreed and added her concern that it also reflected the urgency of Earth's crisis.

"Mark, dear, do you feel we are ready for this? I mean it's all happening so rapidly. And I am not complaining, it's just that this is so important and I want to do our best. Guess, I'm feeling a bit antsy." Faye's wonderful husband addressed her worriment in the most delightful way.

"Let's remember what was said last night, dear. Be in peace! Let's both just take a deep breath and remember to be in peace. We can do this, Faye!" The couple held each other as they practiced what was learned the evening before and each experienced the benefit of the exercise.

"Thank you, Mark! Wow! That was effective! How can such a simple technique be so powerful?"

"It is amazing, isn't it? What we have to remember about this technique is to *remember* it! When your anxiety came up, I experienced what is probably referred to as a flashback. All of a sudden the conversation from our meeting flashed in front of me, and I knew we needed to practice what our Friend had told us. Be in peace! Sweetie, we must remember this! When one of us has a sinking spell, the other one has to rally. I promise to play my role in this important partnership." Mark's comments were uplifting and Faye particularly appreciated the idea of referring to this process as a partnership.

"You're being exceptionally brilliant this morning, dear! Your reference to this scenario as a partnership is truly a stroke of wisdom. We must bring this up to the group. By committing to this partnership, we are moving the process forward. Well done, dear!"

*

"Hey You! How did you know I was just thinking about you? Were you intercepting my inner communications again?" We both laughed at our goofiness. "So, why are you calling on me, my friend?"

"Well, actually I came by because it occurred to me that you might have something you want to tell me." Barbara's intuition was truly off the charts.

"How do you know this?" My question obviously answered her assumption. "Of course, I have something to share with you, but how do you do this?"

"Sister, it just comes to me. Is it an insight or an intuition or a message that I'm supposed to follow up on? I truly don't know. It just comes to me. And as you well know, there are times when I overhear your inner ramblings, but I promise that I'm not snooping about in your head. It just happens."

"Barb, it's getting stronger! You do know that, don't you?" She looked mystified, but nodded her headed in agreement. "Is this happening with other people as well, Barb? Obviously, I've seen it happen in the group, but I'm just curious about the frequency of this gift."

"Certainly, it happens more frequently with you, and I assume it's because of our deep connection; but yes, it is happening more with other people as well now. It surprises me at times, because one never knows what to do with the information. You and I have fun with these experiences, but that may not be the case with other folks. So, I'm just trying to take everything in at this point without immediately smarting off as I do with you. Actually, I'm trying to breathe into the experience and discern what I'm supposed to do with the information. Hmm!" she mused. "Now that I think about it, I'm doing what you told me to do, Sister! So thank you for the advice."

"Well, it's a joy to see you growing so rapidly. You have a gift, Barb, and it's been given to you for a reason." She smiled and acknowledged that she was aware it was a gift and that she was taking it very seriously.

"Except with you!" she laughed. "I feel like we can have fun with this mysterious gift while also holding it high regard. So now, let's get back to the reason for my unexpected visit. What's going on?"

"Well," I started and then paused. "Isn't that interesting?" Turning to Barb, I just stared at her in amazement. "I can't believe this. Now, I have two things to tell you. Goodness, the coincidences are working overtime. Okay, so let me tell you this latest story.

Once upon a time, there was a meeting at this very house that was focused on saving the Earth. When the gathering ended and everyone had gone home for the evening, I paused briefly to review the meeting in my mind. And I realized that the group had forgotten to address their primary goal for the Earth. We forgot to send energy to the Earth!" The reality of the story washed over Barb's face. "So, it occurred to me to take action, which I did. And I must humbly acknowledge that a good energy transfusion took place. But, what was so fascinating was the ending of the session. As you well know from your own experiences of guided meditation, sometimes the words just flow through you and you're not even sure where they're coming from." Her friend nodded in agreement. "Well, this phrase just naturally came through. I heard myself saying 'Wellness to the Earth!' And it seemed the right thing to be saying. Afterwards, the phrase kept repeating itself and I realized it was important to share with the group tonight. And then, just now, as I started to tell you about this, the first word that came out of my mouth was that tiresome four-letter word 'well.' This reminded me of a book that a client told me about recently. It's actually a trilogy that talks about saving the Earth. That phrase, 'Wellness to the Earth,' becomes both a greeting and an expression of action on behalf of the planet. When I heard it flow through me last night, it sounded familiar, but I didn't make the connection until just a few minutes ago. Undoubtedly, the characters in these books made a commitment to speak the phrase every time they started a sentence with the word well, and then incorporated it into their energy sessions for the Earth."

"Sister, that means other people are already becoming aware of energy transfusions for the Earth!" The possibility of others participating on behalf of Earth was very exciting. "We really are not alone in this endeavor. Yay!" We both cheered at the same time.

"Hey, what's the name of that trilogy?" Barb inquired.

"Hmm! The first book is called *The Answer* followed by *The Answer Illuminated* and *The Answer in Action*. My client spoke highly of the series. Said it was a transformative approach to saving the Earth.

*

Annie's excitement about expanding the group was growing. "We really have an opportunity here, Jim, to do some meaningful work; and the folks who responded to our invitations are good people who have different connections in the community than our group has, so they will be able help spread the word to more people." Jim agreed, but showed a slight reservation. His wife encouraged him to speak about it.

"Annie, this is moving so rapidly, and of course, it has to. We can't sit around talking about this forever; we have to take action. I just wonder if we're moving too fast."

"We can change our approach if we need to, dear. This is just another step in our commitment to help the Earth. If it doesn't turn out the way we hoped, then we will regroup and make some adjustments. Just take a deep breath, dear." They both participated in the simple action of self-care.

"You're right, of course, and we just need to have hope and to practice what our Friend commended last night. Be in peace! My goodness, that was a memorable discussion, and as important as it was, it escaped my thoughts until now. Let's work on this Annie. Be in peace! These are words that we must never forget!" The both paused and took another deep breath before Annie took the next step.

"Let's get ready for the gathering, dear."

*

"Three nights in a row. What happened to our quiet evenings at home?" Dave's question caught the attention of his wife, who was hurriedly getting ready for the gathering. She responded in a very matter of fact manner.

"This is important, David. Once we get to the meeting, we will be

277

happy to be there. This is just a moment of fatigue interrupting our commitment to the Earth. And we can't let that happen."

"No, we can't. Thanks for clarifying this lull as fatigue. That helps! I was misinterpreting it as disillusionment, which I do not have. I'm definitely onboard with this project and I can deal with a little fatigue."

"Of course, we can. I'm really looking forward to our guests this evening. Hopefully, they will be as excited about this project as we are. I suspect the meeting tonight will energize us both. By the way, speaking of energy, we didn't do an energy session on behalf of the Earth last night. We got so involved in other topics that it slipped by us. I'm so embarrassed. We must speak of this tonight. It demonstrates how easily our attention is distracted even when the overriding topic is about the Earth. Let's have a session for her now, dear!" And this they did.

~ 21 ~

*

A passage from
Beyond The Day of Tomorrow
A Seeker's Guide
(Chapter Sixty-Two)

"My Dear Old Friend, your participation is this experience, your life, is of your own choosing, and your reason for being is of your own choosing. What if, perhaps long ago, you and I and many, many others all agreed that we would enter into this life experience and assist the innocent people of Earth with their struggle against the disease of judgment? And what if, in so doing, we all agreed that we would participate in attempting to change the mood of the planet by living life in a judgment free way? If all these what ifs are too much for you and the idea of ancient agreements is more than you can bear, then let me bring this into the present for you.

Are you willing to participate in changing the mood of the planet? Are you willing to learn about your judgmental nature and are you willing to effect changes to eliminate this judging behavior? Are you willing to practice with conscious awareness recognizing, acknowledging, and accepting your own judgmental ways?

Are you willing to recognize judgment in others without participating in their process and without accepting it as yours? Are you willing to accept that you suffer from this illness and accept that it is your responsibility to treat the illness? Are you willing to participate in this project to rescue humanity for the sake of the future of humanity?

My Dear Old Friend, the task is large and will at times be most tedious, but humanity requires our assistance. We must persevere and we must do so from the heart. Our contributions must be heartfelt, compassionate, and free of judgment. If we wish others to change, we will first be required to change ourselves and through example, we can offer an alternative to this judging existence.

As we practice and share our newly gained skills with others, they too will be inspired to teach others, and in this way of living a judgment free life, we will provide examples for others to study and include in their own life circumstances.

To effect global change, we must begin in our own homes. From these centers, new ways of being can develop, flourish, and spread. This is not fantasy. Judgment spread rampantly across this planet and it happened by example, one touching another, until the impact was of plague proportion. The cure can spread with equal impact, but we must choose to participate and we must persist with conscious awareness.

Old Friend, awaken. Remember who you are and assist with this Mission of Rescue."

*

The Circle of Friends all arrived fifteen minutes early, as agreed. The fellows carefully arranged the living room chairs, under Barb's guidance, to allow for four more participants, and of course, the empty chair for our guest of unusual form. While they attended to that task, the rest of us placed the goodies and two pitchers of water on the dining room table. We debated briefly if the extension should be used to provide more space and then decided against it. "We need more room for people than we do for the refreshments," declared Annie.

Just as we were proudly approving our achievements, the doorbell rang. As is often the case for small events, everyone arrived at the same time. Introductions went smoothly and soon we were all gathered into the living area. As everyone found a chair that best suited them, I wondered if another space would be necessary if our numbers continued to grow. When everyone was finally situated, Barbara cheered, "Yay! We made it!" Her good humor set the stage for the evening.

"Welcome, everyone! We are so happy that you have joined us and grateful that you were available on such short notice. We aren't typically so impulsive, but by the end of our meeting I think you will understand our motivation. I hope all of you are comfortable, and if not, please let us know, so we can play musical chairs." No one voiced any complaints, so the meeting continued. "I just realized that we should have created name tags for this first engagement. I apologize for not thinking about that."

"Not to worry," announced Barb. "I'm on it!" She jumped up, left the room, and returned briefly with a stack of paper and a large magic marker. Her energy tickled the group, who applauded her ingenuity. "Please continue, Sister. I'll take care of the name tags while you're getting us started."

"As you can see, Barbara is one who has enough energy for all of us. Actually, she also has a wonderful way of telling a tale that I'm going to copy in my attempt to tell you about how our group got its start. So here goes!

Once upon a time, there were eight friends who had been friends for a very long time. These friends always kept in touch with one another over the years, but in this last week, they've spent a great deal of time together. And I think it is fair to say that the time has been rich!"

"That's the understatement of the year," joked Annie, which amused her friends and guests as well.

"You can say that again!" chuckled Jim, and so she did. Humor was taking an active role in our meeting and I was very pleased about that.

"Ah! You now begin to see that this story is based in truth and you're beginning to realize that your invitation happened for a reason. And it did!" My smile reached out to everyone and was returned in like manner. "You will understand shortly what I'm talking about. So, you see, this group of friends gathered together just a few days ago for the first time in a long while and we shared some stories that we had recently experienced. Well, it turned out that all of us became very curious about these stories.

And then," I said taking a deep breath of air, "we all shared an unusual experience together here in this living room." Before continuing, Annie broke the brief moment of silence with one of her announcements.

"Well, go on dear! Tell them what happened!" My mind was racing with numerous ideas. *How does one tell newcomers to a group that we were recently called upon by an invisible visitor?*

"Please excuse me, I'm struggling with words at the moment. You see, we had a very unusual encounter recently and this event needs to be revealed appropriately. I do not wish to cause anyone alarm or discomfort because the experience does not warrant that type of reaction."

The newcomer to my right placed her hand upon mind. "I can see this is very difficult for you and I want you to know that I appreciate how considerate you are trying to be on our behalf. To refresh your memory, my name is Carolyn and this is my husband Ron. We are the Barkleys and we just live a few blocks away towards the shopping district. We are both very curious about your group and we're eager to hear what's been going on with you. So please, just take your time, dear, and also remember, we are here because we choose to be." Her warm response was persuasive.

"Thank you, Carolyn, your kindness gives me strength to speak the truth. Carolyn, Ron, Jill, and Stephen, we are so grateful that you joined us tonight. We've had several meetings this week that involved the crisis situation of our planet. In conjunction with this serious topic, we have had the pleasure to meet with someone who knows a great deal more about the topic than we do. Our Friend is a story in itself, but it's a long story that can be told at another time. I will simply say that our Friend comes from unknown parts. As you can see we keep an extra chair in our circle just in case he chooses to accompany us, which so far he has done at each meeting. My friends, to state this forthrightly, our Friend is invisible most of the time. He can and has materialized in our presence, but it requires a great deal of energy to maintain a visible form, so he needs to conserve his energy. We assume he will join us this evening."

"Can we meet him now?" asked Carolyn in a very unfazed manner. "Are you able to reach out to him or does he come and go as is necessitated?"

Mark immediately responded to their guest's questions. "Carolyn, you seem very comfortable with this news and it makes me wonder if you have had similar experiences." Her husband Ron interjected a comment.

"Friends, let just say that Carolyn has a bucket list, and you just tapped into one of the top five. And I will also say that we are very open-minded about many topics, so I think it's fair to say for both of us that we would like to hear more." Sighs of relief were heard about the room.

"May I have a word, please?" Another of the newcomers spoke out. "I just want to let all of you know that Stephen and I are very interested in helping the Earth and we want to hear more about what you folks are doing. We've never encountered an invisible being before, but it sounds like a remarkable experience. So, please speak freely. Your gentle way of making us welcome is well received and now we hope you will all just relax." Another round of sighs were released.

"Goodness!" comment Sally. "How gracious you are and what a gift to us. We truly have had a remarkable few days and the information is so profoundly important we felt compelled to reach out to others even though it is happening at such a fast pace that we feel a bit clumsy in our efforts. I cannot tell you how happy we are that the four of you are accepting of our circumstances."

"We are accepting, Sally," added Stephen Carson. We've wanted to get to know you and Dave for quite some time, and now it seems, we have an opportunity to meet some of your dearest friends as well. This is good for us in many ways. We wanted to expand our relationships with other people in the community and we are ardent about working on Earth's behalf. So, I would say that your group has chosen wisely."

Our meeting had barely started and already the new and old group members were bonding. I sat quietly by watching the beauty of what was transpiring. *How fortunate we all are!* I could not help but wonder if our selection of new members had been assisted. *I feel as if we are all Old Friends gathering for the purpose of saving the Earth. Could that be possible? Were we all pulled together to this small community for a reason? If so, this orchestration had been going on for a very long time.*

"Sister, it seems our group has melded nicely!" proclaimed Barbara happily. "May I take the lead for a moment?" I urged her to do so.

"Well, new friends, thank you for coming. As you've heard from several of us, we've gathered frequently this week, and each time we joined together we shared our stories. We believe that by sharing our stories, we learn more about one another more quickly and because the Earth's situation is in a state of urgency, we feel we must push forward. We are also learning through our story telling that we are not alone in our unusual experiences. And even though each experience is unique, it is also similar to other stories being told. Truthfully, there's a lot going on around us that we are oblivious to, including the Earth. So, we would like to bring you up to date with our happenings by summarizing some of stories for you. And of course, we want to hear your experiences. Please feel free to participate. You've already demonstrated that you are capable of doing that, so please jump in at anytime!"

Barbara asked permission to share her most recent story regarding her mother and her old friends encouraged her to do so. And she did.

Her emotions were free when she spoke of hearing her Mom's voice on the phone. She told the newcomers about the message that her mother presented and how it validated everything else that she had heard from the visitor from unknown origins. "Truth is, I totally trust our invisible friend. I do not doubt anything that he's shared with us, but hearing similar information coming from my mother was significant for me. So my encounters with both my mother and the invisible Friend have changed my life, and I am committed to helping the Earth.

By the way, the last time we met with him, he emphasized the importance of this phrase. *Be in peace!* He repeated it numerous times and said that this small phrase was the instruction for curing the Earth. I share that with you because it certainly had a profound effect upon all of us. So I will end now and encourage all of you to be in peace tonight, tomorrow, and all days to come."

"Yay!" applauded Annie. "Nicely done, Barbara!"

"That's a remarkable story about your Mom. How fortunate you are. Bet you will never forget that experience." Jill's response was indicative of one who has also lost her mother. She confirmed it as she shared a story.

"Well, I have an experience that nicely tags onto yours Barb, if I may?" Everyone graciously welcomed her story. "This occurred about five years ago when I was walking along a beach that was one of my Mom's favorite places to walk. It was a beautiful, bright sunny day and I was oblivious to everything except the ramblings in my mind. Some issue was doing a number on me and I did what my mind so loves to do. We, my mind and I, assessed the issue over and over again trying to come up with a better result than the result that had already played itself out. There was no way of changing what had already happened, but the mind continued to cogitate over it, as if doing so could effect a different outcome. I'm sure some of you are acquainted with these efforts in futility. Well, for some unknown reason, my mind continues to avoid the truth about this malfunctioning practice. Anyway, I was strolling up and down the beach in a daze, unaware of anyone else around me. And then from out of nowhere, I heard this soft, gentle voice.

Be careful, dear! The voice articulated the words clearly. I stopped, turned around, looked in all directions, but no one was close by. The nearest person was at half a mile down the beach.

Well, as you might imagine, I was confused, but there didn't seem to be anything I could do, so I took another step in the same direction and the voice repeated the message again with a greater sense of urgency. *'Jill, dear, you must be careful!'* I asked the voice to explain, but there was no reply, until I initiated another step.

'Jill, dear, please look down! You are in a precarious situation.' I did as told and sure enough, I was in a predicament. Numerous bottles were broken at water's edge and I was planted in the middle of all the broken glass. I carefully put my flip-flops on and easily maneuvered myself out of the situation. Standing away from the site, I thanked the voice for helping me, and much to my surprise, my mother replied to me." *'Now Jill,'* she said, *'You must be more careful when you come out here. You could have really hurt yourself, dear, and you are parked miles away from here. My goodness Girl, it is good to see you. I do miss you so!'* I asked her if she was well and she said that she was well and happy. *'I can walk the beach anytime I want to now. I'm in perfect health, and of youthful appearance, Jill. So don't you worry about me, I'm doing just fine'.* I asked her if she was there everyday and she said yes. But she also said that it was very difficult for her to reach out to me, so she didn't want me to expect it to happen again. Then she told me to just know that she was always with me. At the beach, at home, at work, everywhere! She said I was never alone, and that many were watching over me every minute of the day."

Tears streamed down Jill's face. "That was five years ago and I will never forget that experience."

Various members of the group reached out to Jill, thanking her for the story she shared. Barb in particular was deeply moved by her experience. "It is so comforting to know they are near us and watching over us. I am so grateful that you shared your story, Jill, and I'm really glad you've come tonight. I hope you will come again."

Faye looked about the room and shook her ahead in awe. "Isn't this amazing? Here we are only minutes into our meeting with new people and we've already reached a level of endearing intimacy. Wow! Thank you, Jill! You've honored us with your story."

"It feels good to be able to share it," replied Jill. "I've only told a few very close friends about this because I've been afraid of people's reactions. I cannot tell you how refreshing this has been for me to freely express myself about the encounter." She took a deep breath. "This is good! I feel relieved and energized at the same time. Thank you all for listening to my story."

"Thank you, Jill! Not only are we delighted to hear your story, but also, we are pleased to hear that sharing your story was a positive experience for you. That has been the case for us as well. Perhaps, someday we will encounter a situation when the impact is not positive, and if that happens, we will simply honor that reaction as well. We recognize that negativity is unfortunately a part of life that must be lovingly dealt with."

Carolyn raised her hand and attention immediately turned in her direction. "Excuse me. I do not mean to interrupt, but I feel a need to acknowledge the manners of this group. You are such amiable people. You treat each other so respectfully that it is noticeable. Isn't it sad, when you are stunned by decent behavior? I must admit this is a very nice atmosphere to be in. Your home is serene, the company is friendly and good-natured, and," she paused obviously trying to find the perfect word. "There's really good energy here! Yes, that's what I'm sensing. You folks are filled with good, positive energy. Wow! How sweet this is!" Her compliments were happily received. Annie was the first to react.

"Thank you so much for noticing, Carolyn. You have no idea how important your feedback is to us. It's true that we are good friends and we are very close, but we are also working on ourselves. We've each made a commitment to improve ourselves for the sake of the Earth. We are in the beginning process of this Self-Improvement Project, but we are determined to become peaceable beings. We will tell you more about that shortly." I quickly intervened and looked to our established group.

"Well Friends, Annie just opened the door for us to shift to the primary topic for our meeting. Shall we just go for it?" Everyone, including the newcomers, was in agreement.

"Oh yes!" encouraged Carolyn, "please tell us everything." This made Barbara chuckle. She wondered if Carolyn and her Sister of Choice were sisters, which made her chuckle some more.

"Don't mind her," I teased. "Barb's just enjoying an inside joke that she will no doubt articulate at another time. In the meantime, who would like to tell our new friends everything?" Eyes turned one to another to another until all fell upon me. "Ah! I get it! Okay then! Will everyone join with me in taking a long deep breath? I ask you to do this for yourself and for me, because I need your support as we delve more deeply into this story." Another deep breath was necessary to calm myself, so I indulged.

"As was earlier stated, we have recently encountered a most interesting fellow who we simply refer to as Old Friend. We know nothing about his origins or his identity, but we have come to trust him as much as we trust each other. He approached Barb first and then visited me, and then he joined us for our first meeting so that our good friends could have the pleasure of meeting him as well. He has continued to attend every meeting thus far. Our Old Friend has become an Honored Teacher and Guide for lack of a better title. Certainly he has taught us much about the Earth's precarious situation and also guided us in ways that have been life changing.

His message to us has been startling and awakening. He claims that the Earth's condition is far worse than the populace really comprehends. He also insists that humankind's negative energy is a primary reason for the Earth's declining health. Our other behaviors of maltreatment, and blatant neglect and disregard are outrageous and extremely harmful to her, but they pale in comparison to the negative ramifications of the ill will that humans generate and perpetrate continuously.

While he sincerely praises the efforts being made on her behalf, he persistently declares that humankind's ill will is the cause of the Earth's crisis. Our Friend also adamantly asserts that we must become beings of peace if she is to survive. Every time we act inappropriately towards self, another, or the planet herself, the Earth feels the injury incurred. Compound this by the acts of unkindness of over seven billion people on a regular basis and you begin to realize the magnitude of pain and suffering that she is enduring. Personally, when I allow myself to imagine all the wounds of ill will that she encounters every day, I am in awe that she can still hold on. Obviously our actions for sustainability do not address such offenses. Even though these actions are necessary and must be continued, they will not save the planet as she now is.

Only the people of this planet have the power to restore her to good health and that demands that we change our ways. Our behaviors of ill will cannot continue. We must change or she will fall into a state of dormancy." I had to pause. The serious nature of this reality was exhausting. A deep breath was taken and my friends joined me. A quick glance around the room was informative. All eyes were closed as they absorbed the truth. I knew there was more to be said. *Tell them there is reason for hope. Do not end on this heavy note.* My breath hastened. There was more that must be said.

"My friends, I am so sorry to be the bearer of such bad news, but it is the truth, and we have been asked to speak the truth truthfully. Please forgive me." Now I fully understood how our Old Friend felt when he informed us of this agonizing situation. I ached with him and wished that he were here now to reassure all of us, and particularly, for those who were hearing this information for the first time.

"My Dear Friends, may I join your company please?" The new voice immediately drew attention. All heads turned to the empty chair. Silence ensued until Sally realized he was waiting for a response to his question.

"Old Friend, we are most grateful you have joined us. Please make yourself comfortable." The newcomers were wide eyed, which is appropriate for this occasion. Truth be known, the old timers are also wide eyed every time our invisible friend arrives.

"I am very comfortable, my Friends, and I am most eager to meet our new Old Friends. Welcome to you all. We are most grateful for your presence this evening." With that said, our invisible Friend materialized in front of us. There were many oohs and aahs as always, but Barb surprised everyone when she burst into laughter.

"I just love this," she exclaimed joyfully. "I'm never ever going to get used to this! What a hoot!" Her laughter spread to others and soon the room was reenergized by the gift of Barbara's good will.

"My Friends, please notice how the energy of this group has shifted. One so small, and yet, so powerful was able to quickly restore joy back into the circle. Make note of this, dear Friends. Even after spirits diminished because of the despairing news that was delivered, Friend Barbara and her excitement for life reenergized the group." Our Old Friend truly was an excellent teacher. Using Barb's reaction as an example for changing the energy of a group was stellar.

"New Old Friends, you have just heard the most difficult news and unfortunately, everything that was spoken is the truth. Humankind is in a perilous situation because the Earth can no longer continue to sustain herself. Her natural resources and her vital fluids have been depleted and poisoned to a state that she cannot heal her own illness. The situation of our Beloved Life Being Earth saddens All in Existence. Never was this intended to happen. The Universe weeps at the prospect of her falling into dormancy. The losses that will be incurred are unthinkable. Therefore, we focus instead on saving the Earth and all who inhabit her. Our Old Friends have already been apprised of this possibility and now it is time for you to hear this message as well. There is reason for hope!

Within each of you is the power to heal! I speak the truth and ask you to accept this truth, because we do not have time for resistance. My

Friends, I wish there remained time for conversations and debates, but there is not. That time has passed and action must be taken. The Earth must be healed now.

Again, I speak the truth. Each of you possesses the ability to heal self and others. This is a natural ability within all life beings that awaits activation by the possessor of the ability. The process is so simple that you may not be inclined to give it credence, but I beg you to open your hearts to this possibility. Already, those who welcomed you tonight have participated in numerous healing sessions for the Earth. They will reveal their stories to you and hopefully this will enhance your acceptance of this truth.

Our major concern is that the people of Earth will reject this solution to their problem. So sad this will be, for it is the only solution available to you at this time. The Earth is an extremely large Life Being and she will will require many healing sessions to regain a sustainable life force, and it will take many, many more to bring her back to full vibrancy. Having said this, the peoples of Earth are capable of doing this. One individual cannot do this alone, but seven billion people can most certainly accomplish this feat.

The energy within you is the same life essence within the planet. She is as are you. If you share a particle of your life essence with her, she will regain strength. If you do this multiple times a day, she will recover more rapidly. Compound this by billions of people participating in this act of generosity and the Earth will be able to avoid an extensive period of dormancy.

Dear Friends, the act of kindness that is required simply takes a moment of your time, which is discerned by you. Many enjoy offering the Earth a particle of their pure life essence at day's end, when they are comfortably resting in bed. Others enjoy participating in this generous act while they are meditating. Others incorporate this ritual into their favorite exercise. The point is, my Friends, the time that you allot to the Earth is yours to schedule. Even one who is extremely busy can find a moment to share with someone who is very ill. Fortunately, one does not need to travel to a hospital to assist this Beloved Patient. Wherever you are, she is! And she desperately needs your assistance." Our Old Friend paused and allowed for a moment of respite. I sat quietly, assuming that he would continue his discourse when he believed it was wise to do so. At the precise moment, he did just that.

"My Friends, before we continue with further discussion, I would like you to join me in a healing session on behalf of our Mother Earth." The newcomers appeared to be excited and antsy at the same time, while the old timers simply went about making themselves more comfortable for the session. *"Please make yourselves ready for this experience. My new Old Friends, please be in peace. What we are about to do is easy. I ask you to play with the rest of us. We are all learning how to finesse this ancient ability and we will proceed in a lighthearted manner, for the Earth is in need of humankind's good nature.*

So, position yourselves comfortably in your chairs and relax into the moment. Our journey together is multi-faceted. We will enjoy each other's company, we will practice a new technique, and we will learn how to facilitate an energy exchange from our own body to the body of the Beloved Life Being Earth. Take that in, please, with a long deep breath. And as you find a pace of breathing that is comfortable for you, I will continue providing guidance that hopefully will be of assistance. If, along this journey, you find another path of achieving the goal of assisting the Earth, please follow what calls to you. Many paths are available. What we do together is just one method.

My Friends, our first intention for this journey is to seek permission from the Earth to facilitate an energy transfer to her. So now, as you continue to quiet your mind and open your heart to this journey, we ask boldly. Dear Old Friend, Mother Earth, we come on your behalf, and we wish to offer you an energy infusion. Old Friend, does this suit you at this time?" Silence prevailed throughout the room. Breathing was light and rhythmic. The setting was conducive to this act of generosity. *"My Dear Friends, unless someone senses a negative response, we will continue."* No one indicated such a response so our Old Friend continued.

"Now, my Friends, we begin the work of engaging the energy within us. I ask that you simply play with this activity and also take it seriously at the same time. Within you lies your pure life energy. This is the energy that exists in all existence. This is the energy that empowers you and all others. This is the energy that unites us as One. Breathe this reality into your hearts and your souls." Again, a moment of silence was provided for the circle of Friends.

"And now, Dear Friends, imagine the life energy within you strengthening. You may envision this energy anywhere in your body. You may picture it in your heart space or your abdomen or anywhere

else. Simply see and feel the energy growing stronger and stronger. And with each deep breath that you inhale, feel your energy becoming more powerful.

Now, my Friends, choose one tiny particle of your energy source and move it from your body out into the center of this room. Only one particle is necessary, Dear Ones! So project that particle from you to the center of the room and allow it to merge with the other energy particles. Envision this, my Friends, and witness the union of your energies. There, in the center of this space, the combined energies become even stronger. And now, allow this energy to rise through the ceiling, hover over the house, and then move it to the north where the large pond is located. See this energy move through the sky over to the pond and then let it rest above the pond for a moment. Take another deep breath, and when we are ready, let us all release our energy contribution to the Earth into the pond. There, the energy submerges with the natural resources of the Earth. Feel the Earth receiving your gift, and feel the appreciation that she sends to you.

Be with this experience, my Friends. Feel the depth of participation that you shared with your companions. Feel the gift of giving to the Life Being Earth. And feel the gratitude that she now feels for all of you. No greater gift can you give to her. Breathe this in, Dear Friends, and trust that your actions were effective." Another deep breath reverberated throughout the room, and then the silence returned. Time passed.

"Precious Friends, when you are ready, please return to the present." As is always the case after one of these sacred experiences, gentle movements begin to be heard, soft sighs are released, and the closed eyes open to the setting that was momentarily escaped. All returned home safely.

"Welcome home, Dear Friends! Rest assured, your energy is assisting the Earth as we speak. I am so grateful to you for your participation in this act of generosity. Breathe deeply, dear Friends, as you center into your bodies once again."

Faye was the first to speak. "Thank you, Dear Friend, that was an incredible experience. I really believe that our efforts are making a difference. And I know we are just beginning this process, but it feels powerful already. I'm sure the more we practice the more effective we will be, but this really seems worthwhile to me. At least, I hope it is. You are sure that our efforts are assisting her, aren't you?"

"Yes, I am certain of this, because I am gifted with the ability to see

the energy merging with the Earth and also witnessing the effect upon her. She responded openly to our gifts of energy. Then I noticed a shift in her coloration around the point of entry. That is evidence that the transfusion was a success. Her vibrant colors have diminished with her illness; however, after the infusion, her colors were more lively and spectacular. My Friend, you are indeed serving well. Trust this process and continue to offer her assistance every day." Faye was beaming with delight, as were those who were enjoying her sense of being helpful. Our desire to be of assistance to the Earth was sincere, and Faye's reaction to hearing our Old Friend's praise made us all feel good about the experience.

"My new Old Friends, do you have any questions or thoughts that you wish to share regarding this experience." Carolyn attempted to restrain herself, but was unable to manage the feat. She immediately raised her hand and waved. Then, struck by embarrassment, she pulled her hand down to her side.

"Old Friend, you heart desires to speak, but your mind has scolded you for having no restraint." His comment stunned everyone. Obviously, he is one who can hear the inner voice very easily. *"Dear One, I desire to hear the questions of the heart. Please feel free to speak in this loving and accepting community of friends."*

Before she spoke, everyone heard the ever-present long deep breath. "Thank you for inviting me to talk. You are one who has remarkable skills. I hope some day there will be time to talk more about that, but for now, it is prudent that we stay focused. First of all, I want to tell you that this may have been one of the most profound experiences I've ever had. And I want to thank everyone here for inviting us over tonight and I especially want to thank you for facilitating that healing session.

I have many questions. That's just the kind of person I am, so I will try to be selective. You were very adamant about us only accessing one particle of our energy. That is perplexing. It seems that we should send as much energy as possible so that the Earth can heal more rapidly. Can you explain this please?"

"A question of merit! The reason is two-fold: first, the giver of energy is not intended to deplete his or her energy for another. Although it is instinctual for one who is a giving individual to desire to give more, it is not wise to do so. The Earth's health will demand infusions for a long time in order to regain her full vibrancy. This demands that the caregivers of healthy energy must maintain their own wellness or they will not be able

to continue assisting her. Wisdom tells us that the caregiver must take care of self in order to be a good caregiver.

Now, the other factor that is also essential to her recovery process is that she is not overdosed by too much energy at any given time. This may sound odd to you, but you must realize that many are participating in this healing process. Hopefully, the numbers of human participants will grow rapidly because their participation is necessary. However, there are many other Beings who are also committed to assisting the Earth. You are not alone, Dear Friends. The Life Being Earth is carefully watched over and protected so that well-intended individuals do not unintentionally cause her more harm. She is in a very fragile moment and I ask you to honor my request on behalf of her and also you."

"Thank you for explaining that. It's very helpful and I will definitely honor your request. I think my other questions can wait, but I do want to acknowledge something that transpired during the experience. When we were envisioning the release of the energy into the pond, I saw the energy around the area change colors. It was amazing! But I want you to know I've never experienced something like that before, so it may have just been my imagination. Anyway, the whole experience was wonderful and I'm really grateful to have had the opportunity to participate in this. Thank you all!"

"Carolyn, thank you for being here and for sharing your experience with us. We are so happy that your experience was positive. And by the way, I am glad that you asked that question because I wanted clarification about it as well." At that point, I realized my response might have interrupted our Old Friend, so I quickly turned the lead back to him.

"You did not interrupt, Dear Friend. I am most happy and pleased with the interaction that is transpiring. Does anyone else wish to contribute to the discussion?

"Yes, I would like to share my thoughts about the experience," stated Jill. "As I said earlier, Stephen and I are very involved in environmental issues. We have attended many lectures and workshops in recent years trying to educate ourselves about being good stewards of the Earth.

We were truly embarrassed in the beginning because we were so oblivious to all the ways in which we were unwittingly harming her. Geez! We were so unconscious of her needs. Truthfully, we just took her for granted. This is actually very hard to admit, but it is speaking the truth truthfully.

I'm happy to say that we've incorporated what we've learned into our daily practices and we feel good about the changes we've made, but we both know this isn't enough. So, we've been searching for ways to expand our efforts. And I must say, what you have introduced to us this evening speaks to me. I appreciate you reaching out to expand this work to others, and I also want to commend your courage. This is certainly an alternative way of thinking about helping the Earth, and unfortunately, it may receive a great deal of criticism." Jill made eye contact with her new friends and immediately expressed what they needed to hear. "Thank goodness, you have the courage to do this. What you are pursuing gives me hope! Like you, I understand the risks you are taking, but I'm so grateful you're doing it. This work is important! I believe it with all my heart. And I want to be part of this project. So, if you are accepting new members, count me in!"

Sighs of relief led the way for cheers. Faces were bright with smiles and a few tears were making their presence known. The old friends, the original members of the group, were delighted by Jill's acclaim of their work.

"You have made our evening," proclaimed Barbara. "Thank you so much, Jill, and yes, we are accepting new members. So, welcome!" Before any more expressions of appreciation could be articulated, Jill's husband entered the conversation.

"Okay, new friends, let me tag onto my wife's comments, if I may. First, let me also thank you for your invitation tonight and also for this truly remarkable experience. I must admit to all of you that I typically have a difficult time with meditation, because my mind is highly active, and its preferred modus operandi is to avoid silence at all cost. This is not something I'm proud of, but it is my truth. So, when the meditation began, my resistant mind attempted to interfere with the process. It did not succeed, which is incredible! I was able to join with your process and found it deeply moving. I cannot say to you that I understand what just happened here, but I'm okay with the mystery. I believe we were actually of assistance to the Earth and that awareness is still within me, and I am enjoying it.

I agree with Jill's comments about your courage in promoting this process. There will be some who will discount your work. So be it! People have been discrediting the power of prayer for ages, and still, it remains a viable resource for millions of people on our planet. This healing session tonight reminded me of being in prayer. I found it comforting and it made me feel as if I was contributing. I want to join your group as well!" The circle of friends was delighted. More tears and good cheer were shared, as Stephen was also welcomed into the group.

"My, oh my!" mused Sally. "Isn't this marvelous?" She turned to Ron, wondering if he had any feedback for the group. Their eyes met and exchanged smiles.

"Yes, Sally! I do have feedback that I would like to share." His response to her unspoken thoughts tickled her. She laughed and shook her head in wonderment.

"Another Friend, who has exceptional hearing! Please share your thoughts with us, Ron." He repositioned himself in his chair, leaning forward so as to be more engaged with everyone.

"I found this experience fascinating and I want to be a part of your group! And I'm sure Carolyn does as well." Turning to his beloved for confirmation, he apologized for speaking on her behalf.

"No problem, dear! I definitely want to be part of this project as well. This feels like home to me!" The visitor from parts unknown observed quietly. *That which was desired has transpired. The movement rapidly spreads. My Friends, there is reason for hope!* I turned to our Old Friend, as did Barbara. We silently acknowledged his internal conversation.

More good spirits were shared before attention returned to Ron. Sally graciously veered the conversation back to him with a small, but common statement among this group of friends. "So Ron, tell us everything!" This brought more smiles to the circle.

"Well, *everything* might take days, so I will try to be concise. Like Stephen, I am very curious about this process, but I am also very tolerant of its mysterious ways. Because I believe there is much more going on around us than is evident to the physical eye, I am extremely interested in knowing more about all aspects of this healing project. It's intriguing and in alignment with some of my own beliefs. I find this opportunity very exciting!

I too appreciate this invitation. Frankly, your courage stuns me and I hope the reception you're getting tonight encourages you to take more risks. This information needs to be shared now, and I would like to help with that process. I'm in!"

"Yahoo!" announced Barbara. "Can you believe this?" Her enthusiasm was a delight to watch and equally shared by all involved. I observed the gathering with a full heart and inquisitive mind. *How could we be so blessed! The meeting was unfolding beautifully. It was a gift from heaven!* As I enjoyed my companions sharing their happiness, the presence of another washed over me. I turned to our Old Friend and he acknowledged my look with a barely noticeable nod.

"My Dear Friends, you bring hope to the hearts of all who are observing this meeting. Many from far and near look upon this joyous occasion and are astounded by the beauty of connection. So long have we waited to see our Old Friends united again. It is indeed a blessing to witness this event. We are honored to bear witness to this time of reunion.

Each of you, in your own way, recognizes that you are here for a reason. Each has experienced his or her own journey on the way to this present location and now, the journeys of the twelve seekers have purposefully crossed paths at this particular time in this particular place. Ironically, none of you believes in the concept of coincidences. This belief has served you wisely throughout this lifetime and many others. And it does once again now as the twelve of you come together this evening. Perhaps it is appropriate to say Welcome Home Dear Friends. You have arrived at precisely the right time and the right place to fulfill your mission of purpose. We are most grateful for your return and for your commitment to the Life Being Earth."

More To Come

A FINAL PLEA FROM THOSE
WHO CAME BEFORE

Dear Readers,

For some of you, this book will sound like a fairy tale, and if you view it as such, that is your choice; however, other readers will understand the point that is being represented. Within each of you there is a reason for being and there are others of similar kind and nature who also share a similar reason for being. Through this story, we witnessed twelve uniquely different individuals who came together as One as if they were intended to do so.

This is also your truth, Dear Readers, Old Friends. You were intended to come together and you are intended to work together on behalf of the Life Being Earth. We are so grateful that you have awakened to your reason for being and that you have so promptly and diligently responded to the call to reunite, as you have so many times before.

My Friends, we must speak of the future and we must do so with open minds and tender hearts. The Earth is in crisis, and so too is humankind. So many times have we brought this news forward that we have lost count, and still, the peoples of this planet refuse to accept the truth. Time is of the essence! Unless immediate action is taken on her behalf, she will have no option but to retreat into a dormant state. For those of you who do not comprehend the meaning of this, the truth will be spoken truthfully. If this situation transpires, the Earth will be unable to provide assistance to any of her residents. What you have taken for granted for millennia will no longer be available to you. As she retreats further into her dormancy, there will be increasingly less opportunity for survival by any life beings remaining upon her surface. The thought of this tragedy is unbearable, and yet we cannot deny the evidence, which points in this direction.

Old Friends, there remains time for the people of Earth to save the planet. This story is presented to offer you the means and the opportunity to save the Earth and to save your own species. What is presented is the truth, even though it is offered in the form of a fictional story. Please take this story seriously and please take action now. Practice the healing techniques presented throughout this story and create your own group with whom to work.

There is reason for hope. If you choose to participate in saving the Earth and then another does the same and another and another, the movement to save the Earth will grow into a reality. As you now know, the primary reason for the Earth's decline is the negative energy that is being created by humankind. Acts of unkindness, disrespect, meanness, and cruelty can no longer be the norm for this civilization. Humankind was never intended to be so thoughtless towards one another. Differences and preferences were never intended to be reasons for discontent and hatred. The diversity that you were granted was an immeasurable gift for your evolutionary expansion. So sad it is to see what has happened.

There is time to change, Dear Reader. You can improve your own manner of being by choosing to be a person of peace. You can live the mantra of 'be in peace' every day and you can share this mantra with others. In so doing, your energy will return to a positive state and you will no longer be causing the Earth harm. This will help her recovery process. This is so little to do for one who has taken care of a civilization forever.

Please give this careful consideration, Dear Reader. Such a small act is required and you will benefit from this act of generosity as much as the Earth will. Be in peace, Dear Friend. Do this for yourself and do this for the Earth!

Old Friend, please take action. Look for a group to join or create your own. You just read this book and you can see how easy it is to practice offering energy infusions to the Earth. Just as the characters resonated to the healing sessions, so too can you. Please take action for your sake and for the sake of the Earth.

Old Friend, one last request must be made. Please delve into this series of books. Two more books in the 'Seeking Our Humanity' series will follow and each will continue to provide you with helpful demonstrations so that you can incorporate the examples into your daily lives. Also, the preceding series known as The Answer Trilogy will be a very good resource for your own expansion. These books provide guidance and answers for those of you who want to help the Earth. My Friends, this is not a ruse to sell books. This is a plea and a plan to *help the Life Being Earth. I hope you will choose to take action. You are needed!*

Be in peace,
Those Who Came Before

Wellness to the Earth!

...WHAT IS NEXT TO COME...

Dear Reader,

I want to apprise you that another information guide is already in progress. Just as *Seeking Our Humanity* was intended to provide ideas and examples for you to use in assisting the Earth, so too will the upcoming sequel. The next endeavor is to expand peoples' awareness of their ability to heal the Earth. As you well know by now, healing energy resides within all of us, and you also know that this important information must be made known across the planet or our efforts to save the Earth will be profoundly limited. This is not the time for humankind to think limitedly.

There is no need to repeat the messages regarding the Earth's critical situation. The point has been clearly made; however, as a gentle reminder, the urgency of this situation will be repeated. There is no time for delay. Therefore, the upcoming book called *Seeking Our Humanity, Part Two* will take the next step by speaking the truth truthfully about our responsibilities to save the Earth. As a Reader of *Seeking Our Humanity*, you have learned that the primary reason for the Earth's declining health is humankind's negative energy. We, all of us, must change our ways, so that she can regain her health.

The information provided in this present book is the foundation for creating change. The truth is, we can all use some fine-tuning and the Earth will truly benefit from our efforts. If we alter our negative ways, the Earth's health will improve. So, please continue with your personal project of improving your present way of being, and also continue participating in energy transfusions to the Earth on a daily basis. Your acts of generosity are essential, Dear Friend. Each healing session matters! Each act of kindness matters! She needs us and we need her!

Dear Reader, dear Friend, please practice the simple healing techniques demonstrated in this book. Do it for your Self, do it for Others, and do it for Mother Earth. And in the meantime, another project on behalf of the Earth will continue moving forward. *Seeking Our Humanity, Part Two* will be completed SOON!

In peace be,
Claudia

Printed in the United States
By Bookmasters